# HATE *to* LOVE YOU

NYT BESTSELLING AUTHOR

TIJAN

ISBN 978-1-951771-38-6



Edited and proofread by: Paige Smith, AW Editing,
Allusion Graphics, LLC, Chris O'Neil Parece,
Amy English, and Kara Hildebrand
Formatting by Allusion Graphics, LLC, www.allusiongraphics.com

To everyone who helped me get this beast together!
To my own time at college, to those in college now, and to those who love a trip down memory lane. College was some of the most dramatic years of my life, but also some of the best adventures and it's a place where hopefully you'll make some of your lifelong friends.

# CHAPTER ONE

Shay Coleman tanked my dream of going pre-law.

Okay, not really. That was an exaggeration, but it had been my dream to be a lawyer. I joined mock trial. I was a witness the first year. The head defense lawyer my second year.

I knew my shit.

I knew the loopholes. I knew all the motions, what I could object to, what I couldn't, and what I still wanted the imaginary jury to hear. I went the whole nine yards.

I was *going* to become a lawyer.

Until I marched into my first political science class and everything went downhill from there.

I learned four things right away over the first couple of weeks:

1. Memorizing laws was boring. No, really. It was *really* boring. Too boring for me. I knew I'd have to cut my losses here.
2. While I didn't need to study in high school, I sure as hell did in college.
3. I needed to learn *how* to study.
4. Arrogant pricks could be real assholes in college, too.

Shay Coleman taught me that last one.

"Break into groups of four or five." The professor raised the worksheet in the air. "Go over these discussion questions, and one person will share with the class. Go."

I glanced around from my spot in the second-to-last row. This was where I cursed myself for not forcing Kristina to take the course with me. I was a freshman and this class was mostly upperclassmen.

Gripping my seat, I was ready to turn it in one way or another, but nope. Blondie on my right was in a group. Her back was facing me. The same thing straight ahead.

I knew *who* sat on my left and I didn't want to look that way.

They sat there the first day of class. I was in the second-to-last row on that day and had watched them, one by one, as they trailed in.

They were big.

They were muscular.

They were gorgeous.

All six of them.

One was tall with broad shoulders, dark blond hair, blue eyes lined with ice, trim waist, and the kind of cheekbones girls would melt into their seats and sigh about. He was model material, and it was so cliché, but of course, he was the school's quarterback.

Shay Fucking Coleman.

The others were a starting defensive lineman, a wide receiver, a tailback, an offensive lineman, and the lankiest one was the team's kicker. I knew this because my brother, Gage, made me go to not one, not two, not five, but seven of the games last year when he was a freshman. Then, as if that weren't enough, he'd quiz me on their stats when we walked back to his dorm.

It was the best part of my visits.

Note the sarcasm.

But back to that first day of class—his five friends had taken the entire last row, and the only chair left open had been the one right behind me.

Shay paused, bringing up the rear. He looked at the chair and then at me.

Here was the thing.

I was young, but I knew I had that Nina Dobrev look. Slim body, long brown hair, and long legs. I was a couple inches taller than normal girls so I didn't understand the appeal, but guys liked how I looked, or they did until they found out Gage and Blake Clarke were my brothers. Opinions changed after that, though I had hoped that would change in college. Dulane was big. It was a private university, but it was still big enough that I could go four years and never see my brother on campus.

Over fourteen thousand students attended Dulane.

I rarely got hit on in high school, but people used me to get to *both* my brothers, Gage and Blake. Girls loved me, and guys either respected me or hated me. It depended on how they viewed my brothers, but there'd really only been one of those two reactions. The guys mostly showed me respect. That lasted until Gage graduated. Blake was years older, so he was out of the house long ago, but Gage was the hold-out. Once he went to Dulane last year, everything changed.

Guys in my grade remembered how I looked, and respect went out the window. I was hit on enough that the girls began to hate me. Add that year to an event that already happened when I was a freshman . . . well, let's just say it all came together and made me instantly hate the guy standing behind me.

His top lip curved up, as if he were holding back a laugh. His eyes were mocking me.

I gritted my teeth.

I would've been sitting right in front of him. He would've been staring at my neck. He could've reached forward, pretended something was in my hair just so he could touch me. He could've checked my ass out the whole time since our backrests only covered the top half of our backs.

Shay Coleman wasn't just the big guy on campus. He was a *big* fucking deal. He was loved beyond being loved. I heard enough about him from Gage, from Gage's friends, from even the rumors in my dorm when I would walk down the hallway that I didn't have to know him personally to know just how adored he was. It was an odd reality, but it was what it was.

There were people openly watching him, and there were others who were more discreet, but they were still watching. What happened here could set the gossip mills spinning.

I knew that was a drawback, and he could set the tone for my entire year. If the high school harassment was going to start here, it could come from him.

Flashbacks from last year flooded my mind, and I couldn't take it.

Feeling a chill down my spine, I grabbed my bag and tossed it to the empty seat two down in my row.

His eyebrows rose.

Then everyone who was just watching him was watching me.

A sudden hush came over the people closest to us.

I grabbed my books and phone and then I stood. I moved right in front of him, and he stood there, holding his own books in front of him. Dumping the bag onto the floor, I plopped back down. Then I sat, and I stared straight ahead.

He didn't move. I knew he was looking at me.

My eyes flickered to the right, and I saw confusion written all over a girl's face. She bit her lip, her eyes skirting from me to Shay until I felt him move past me.

My shoulders dropped and I relaxed until I heard him say, "Linde, switch seats with me."

I closed my eyes.

The offensive lineman didn't argue. He grabbed his things and moved, sitting behind where I had been.

Shay Coleman sat behind me, and I sucked in my breath.

*This guy shouldn't bother me,* I tried telling myself. I knew *of* him, but I didn't actually know him. I had never talked to him. He had never hit on me or called me a bitch after I turned him down. He hadn't dated me and then slept with one of my best friends behind my back.

There was no reason for this instant loathing, but it was there.

I tried to force a calming breath out. Maybe there was no reason for my alarms to be going off. Maybe no one noticed? They just thought I was weird, which I was, but maybe it wasn't as noticeable as I thought—but nope.

He leaned forward and whispered, his breath teasing my neck, "Checkmate." I heard his soft and low laughter.

I would sit in the front the next time. I made my mind up. He'd stay in the back with his friends. I could move. It wouldn't be a big deal.

Our professor announced, "I hope you enjoy where you sat today, because these are your permanent seating arrangements."

I expelled a sudden and not-so-quiet groan. That had been a bad joke.

Just like this freaking group project now.

The only place I could turn was where *he* was.

I had an irrational hope that he had pulled into the group on my right. That would make sense, but no. When I remained there, the only one not in a group and still sitting forward in my seat, I heard him say, "You can join us, Clarke."

Clarke.

He said my last name as if we were friends.

But I was the friendless loser in that classroom.

Resigned, I grabbed the edge of my chair and began moving it around. The other four guys were in a separate group. Shay was pulled in as well, along with Linde, a girl who sat across from me, and another girl, too. Both of the girls started at the mention of my name, and I felt their curiosity right away.

One was dressed in a tan sweater and skinny jeans. Her hair was piled high in a messy bun, and if she had told me she was a sorority girl, I wouldn't have been surprised.

I was stereotyping, and I felt bad for that, but I swear that she had *the look.*

The other girl was less flashy but dressed similar to the first girl. Skinny jeans and a white sweater instead of tan. Her dark hair hung loose. Both wore natural-looking makeup, light pink lipstick, and eye shadow. The first was beautiful, but the second girl's eyes were a little too wide for her face to put her in the same category.

I skimmed a look over at Linde. He had a round face with laugh lines creased by his mouth and eyes. I'd heard him laugh enough over the past two weeks to know they were there for a reason. He was large, built like an ox, and whenever I looked at him, I was hit with the urge to hug him like a teddy bear.

"How'd you know my last name?" I refused to look at Shay Coleman. Did he know my first name, too?

"Gage told me to look out for his little sister, Kennedy Clarke."

I looked over and tried not to feel the punch to my chest. God. He was gorgeous. Those eyes were focused right on me. They weren't looking away. All of his concentration was there. My mouth was dry.

"You're friends with my brother?"

When did that happen? I doubted that was true. Gage would've been preening like a peacock about it.

Those eyes were still laughing at me. He lifted his lips up in a slight smirk, slight grin. "He was at a party. We got to talking about classes. Told me to look out for you." Those lips lifted the rest of the way into a full smirk. "He said his sister would have a chip on her shoulder. Knew right away who he was talking about."

Air escaped me. Gage was a shithead.

I struggled to keep a mask on my face. "That's hilarious."

The twinkle in Shay's eyes told me he thought it was, and I got it. I did. I came off as a bitch, but trust me. There was a reason. I'd learned it was better to start swinging first than to get hit by someone else, metaphorically speaking.

Linde lifted up the worksheet. "We're supposed to talk about abortion." He pointed at the other two girls. "Guessing you two chicks are pro-choice?"

The prettier one rolled her eyes. "Shut up, Ray. Just because we have vaginas doesn't mean we're about abortions."

"Yeah, but don't you want to have the right to choose?"

Shay moved his seat closer toward them, which brought him also closer to me. His large knees brushed against mine, then they moved as he leaned forward and rested his arms on his desk.

The prettier one didn't say anything. Her lips pressed together, and her eyes shifted to her friend.

"Uh." The friend coughed and jerked forward in her seat. Her elbows rested on her desk. "What's the worksheet asking us to discuss? Our individual opinions?"

Linde's finger smacked at his sheet. "Number one." He angled his head to read from it. "Discuss the abortion law."

"That doesn't mean we have to talk about our personal opinions." The prettier one ripped the sheet from his hands. She hunched over it, her finger moving as she read more of the question. "To further develop your own position on abortion, review the following points raised by a pro-life and a pro-choice view. Your group must present your discussion to the class." She snorted and pushed the worksheet back to Linde. "Fuck that. I'm not presenting anything."

Linde looked warily at the paper.

"I'll present it for us." Shay leaned forward, his knee resting against mine again as he reached for the worksheet. "What about you, Clarke? What's your opinion on abortion?"

I shrugged. I had no opinion.

*Why was his knee touching me?*

"Come on." The prettier girl raised her eyebrows in encouragement. "You have to have an opinion."

"What's yours?"

A low chuckle came from Shay, and the girl's eyes snapped to him. He ignored the look, picking up a pen to write whatever she said. His leg could've moved from mine again, but it didn't. He kept it there, pressing right against me.

He raised his eyebrows, too. "Hmmm, Becs? I'm ready to write."

"Fuck you, Coleman." She flushed. Her neck grew red, but his eyes were holding steady on her, and a little grin appeared on her face. "I don't know. What do you want me to say?"

"Say what you think and why," Shay drawled. That smirk was still there, along with another twinkle in his eye.

Her cheeks were full-on pink as she looked down at the desk, shrugging her slender shoulders. She clasped her hands together, resting her arms fully on her desk so they fell off, as if she were reaching toward him. "I don't know. I mean, my family's religious."

"You're pro-life, then?" Linde asked.

"Yeah. What about you?" But she wasn't asking him. Her eyes were on Shay. It was obvious whom her question was directed toward.

He lifted up his pen and grinned. "I'm just the reporter for the group. You guys tell me what to write."

Linde swore, grinning and shaking his head.

"Come on." Becs' smile spread. "You have to tell us."

He grunted. "What about you, Amy?"

The plainer friend coughed. "It's Aby, and I don't know." The two girls shared a look. "I guess I feel the same. My dad's a pastor. I kind of have to be pro-life, you know?"

Linde's eyes widened. "Your dad's a pastor?"

Becs laughed, gesturing her hands in a lowering motion. "Settle down. She's got a boyfriend."

Linde frowned at her. "It isn't like that. I'm just surprised—"

Aby cut in, "He doesn't go here."

Becs's head went back to her friend. "Why would you say that?"

Aby shrugged again, tucking some hair behind her ear. "What? I mean, he doesn't. He goes to Methal. It's four hours away."

"Isn't Methal a Christian college?"

I glanced sideways to Shay. He had a serious look on his face, but not in his eyes. It's the same look he gave me the first day of class. He'd been laughing at me then, and he was laughing at these people now.

"Yeah." Both girls turned to him. Aby pulled on one of her sleeves, smoothing it down. "I'm sure he's pro-life, too."

This was grating on my nerves.

I must've made a noise, because all eyes turned to me.

I could feel Shay's smirk growing even as he asked, "Yes? You got a different opinion?"

I straightened in my seat, shrugging. "I don't have an opinion, but it isn't because of who my dad is or if my boyfriend goes to a Christian college. I don't have an opinion, *because* it hasn't happened to me yet. When it does, *if* it does, I'll figure it out then. It'll be my opinion, though. It won't be because someone close to me told me how to think."

Linde's lips puckered together, and he leaned back. I thought I heard a, "Well, damn" from him.

Becs inclined her head toward me. "Are you saying I don't have a real opinion?"

"I'm not saying it to be mean, but that's what you said. And that's my opinion on what you said."

"Excuse me?" Her lips thinned.

"You're pro-life because your family's religious." I held my hands out toward her. "You said it yourself." I looked at Aby, but she already knew what was coming. She started to shift back in her seat. "You said the same thing. Your dad is a pastor, and you can't think a different way. I'm not sure about the whole boyfriend thing, but you still used your dad as your defining point." I leaned back in my seat.

See. I still had some of the lawyer spark in me. Not enough to keep going with these classes, but it was there.

Linde started laughing.

I turned to him. "How about you? What's your opinion since Mr. Reporter is pleading the fifth?"

"Uh." His laughter dried up, and his eyes shifted among all of us. "I guess," he tugged at his shirt's collar, "I'm pro-choice." His head dipped just slightly to the right, as if to say, "There, I said it." Then he turned to the other girls. "My sister was raped. She didn't want to have his kid when she was fourteen. So, yeah"—his eyes flicked to mine again—"I'm pro-choice, because there's no way I'm going against my little sister and the guilt and torment she feels every day because some dick decided to force *his* inside her."

I didn't spare a look at Becs or Aby. I felt a flash of remorse for forcing the matter, but the professor called time. We had to go around and present our discussion. When it came to us, Shay stood. "We came to a deadlock."

The professor folded his arms over his stomach. "You have five members. How could there be a deadlock?"

Shay glanced to me before saying, "Two for life. Two for choice. And one person who doesn't have an opinion yet."

I felt surprise from the two girls, but for some reason, I wasn't surprised he was pro-choice. I glanced at Linde. I never would've imagined what his opinion had been just by looking at him.

As if feeling my attention, he looked over and dipped his head in a nod.

There it was.

I got what so many guys coveted from a starting football player at Dulane University. The nod of respect.

I grinned back, and he matched it.

My chin lifted an inch higher.

I just made my first friend in poli-sci, but my enjoyment was short-lived.

The professor announced, “Okay. Good discussion. Now exchange numbers and information with your group members. This is the group you’re going to be doing your final presentation with at the end of the semester. It’s one-third of your grade.”

I groaned and let my head fall to my desk.

Shay’s laughter fell down on me. He leaned close to my ear, whispering, “Look at that. More to look forward to.” He patted my back. “Thanks, Clarke. I knew this class wasn’t going to be boring.”

I suddenly had a bad taste in my mouth.

# CHAPTER TWO

My reservations were up the day I met my roommate. Again—bad memories from high school, but the initial meeting went fine.

Her name was Missy.

She had a round, pimply face with a large forehead. Almost coarse-like black hair hung down past her shoulders. She was a couple inches shorter than me and quiet. Good gracious, she was quiet, but she laughed when she found out I had never watched *Titanic*.

She could quote the entire thing. And shocker, her bin of movies were chick flicks.

We looked at mine: all action-adventure.

She turned her nose up at *Gladiator*.

Really?

The similarities ended there—the fact that we both liked *some* (I'm being generous with that word) movies.

Her best friend and the best friend's cousin also lived in our dorm. I went once to an ice cream shop with them and saw the pity in their eyes when Missy relayed the lack of *Titanic* in my life. I was put in the help category. Meaning, they thought I needed help and I was no longer in their group because it's *obvy* I'm weird.

*Dirty Dancing*, *A Walk to Remember*, *Hope Floats*, and so many other movies were the repertoire of *their* conversation. I wasn't allowed in. There were inside jokes, inside quotes, even a weird inside-type of laugh.

The one friend I did have was Kristina. She was a gift from above, though she lived two floors below, and I always jumped at *her* movie night invite.

Sometimes, I was tempted to ask how high, but I refrained. She wouldn't have gotten the joke.

See, I could have my own inside jokes. Take that, snotty roommate and two friends.

Insert karate chop here.

Kristina had a heart-shaped face and short, auburn hair. She was nice, really and truly nice, and she was gorgeous. A small chin under plush lips and hazel eyes, mixed with an infectious laugh, and if she hadn't come to college with a steady boyfriend, she would've been "wifed up" real quick.

Even now, after leaving poli-sci and seeing her standing by the post before the food court, there was a handful of guys giving her the double look. They looked, turned away, and had to look back. A couple narrowed their eyes, saw the ring on her finger, and turned back to their friends.

I shook my head as I drew abreast. "That promise ring Abram gave you was a stroke of genius."

She lifted her head from her book and frowned. "What?"

Reaching into my backpack for my ID, I gestured to her finger. "You would've got hit up if it wasn't on."

"Oh." She rolled her eyes before ducking her head down. "I'm sure it didn't. And it isn't a promise ring. It's just—" Her finger fiddled with it. "I don't know. It was an 'I love you' gift."

I nodded. "And it works. Everyone knows someone loves you." I coughed into my fist. "I.e., you're taken."

She laughed. "Stop, Kennedy."

Then her eyes trailed behind me and rounded. She sucked in a breath.

It was like I knew.

The hairs on the back of my neck stood, though not from fear. From a different emotion, and I ignored it. I ignored the delicious shiver that wound down my spine because that didn't make sense, but I knew who had come up behind me. I felt him, and because of that, I was on edge right away.

"Clarke."

*Damn him.*

A low and smooth chuckle. That voice was a caress in and of itself. I was sure a few panties were melting in our close proximity.

I rotated around. Instead of the smirk I assumed would be tugging at his lips, he wore a serious expression. It made his eyes even more smoldering, if that were possible.

He held out a hand.

I looked at it, saw it was empty, and brought my eyes back to his. "Yes?"

"Give me your phone." His hand didn't move. "You didn't exchange numbers with anyone."

I moved back a step. "Why?"

"I live off-campus. You're not going to be able to look me up in the school directory."

He had a point.

"I'll look you up on Facebook or Snapchat."

"No, you won't. Give me your phone."

I felt it being pulled out of my pocket, and I was too late. Kristina wore a smug grin as she quickly coded in my password and then handed it over. "Here. It's all ready for you."

"Hey!" I tried to grab it, but Shay moved in, blocking me with his back. I ended up pressed against him and bit back a growl. It was as if he was an athlete or something in how quickly he moved. My hands rested against his back, and I felt his muscles tense there, shifting under his shirt. He typed in his information, but paused to grin over his shoulder. "Feel free to explore more. I won't turn down a quick grope."

I pulled my hands back as if I'd been burned. I shifted to the right, but he moved with me. He continued to block me as he finished and then handed the phone back to Kristina. "Thank you for the assist."

"You're welcome." She held her hand out. "Kristina Collins."

He shook it, starting, "Shay Co—"

"—Coleman." She laughed. "Trust me. My roommate and friends are fully aware of who you are." She looked at me. "I wasn't aware you were friends with Kennedy, though." She made it sound like I'd been holding back tickets for the Super Bowl.

"Oh." Shay shifted back, coming aside me again, and threw his arm around my shoulder. A girl gasped a few feet away. He pulled me against his side. "We're good friends. You'll be seeing more of me. Trust me." He released me, but not before his hand skimmed down my back and rested on my ass. He patted me, leaning in and whispering, "A grope for a grope, right?" He swatted me there and headed off, chuckling under his breath.

I ignored the attention we had garnered.

Kristina hit me on the shoulder. "Kennedy! You know Shay Coleman?"

I grimaced, turning for the food court. "No. I technically don't."

"That didn't look like you were strangers to me. He touched your ass."

I repressed a shudder. "Don't remind me." A line had formed for the cafeteria, and we stood at the end. "And I meant it. Today's the first day I've ever talked to him. We got put in a group for discussion."

"Why'd he give you his number?"

"Because we have to do a final presentation at the end of the semester." I saw the excitement forming. "The whole group, not just us two."

"But still." She reached for my arm. "Sarah, Laura, and Casey are going to go nuts over this. Casey, especially. She's been fawning over him since the first football game."

I didn't need to be reminded about that, either.

Casey was Kristina's roommate, and the other two were friends from Kristina's school. Where Kristina was more reserved, she didn't drink (that much) and had a steady boyfriend—the others were not. Casey was another "it" girl. And she was single. After the first day of orientation, she had guys calling at all hours of the day. She, Laura, and Sarah divided their time between their own dorm and the guys'.

We had a no-boys-sleeping-over policy in our dorm, but Sarah and Laura had already broken that four times that I knew of. Casey stayed with them those nights. And I only knew of those four times because I'd been watching a movie with Kristina when Casey came in for booze reinforcements. She always smiled and offered an invite to party with them, but I was too chicken shit to risk being caught.

We hadn't even gotten to homecoming yet.

The four formed a clique, and while I wasn't really in the clique, I hung out with them on occasion. I was Kristina's friend, but she was the type who was friendly with everyone. If this had been high school, I would've given up because Kristina would've had thirty other friends. I was lucky. I got her the first week of college when she didn't have umpteen friends already. Besides the other three, I knew Kristina considered me one of her closest gal pals at college.

I needed it. I needed her. My other option was my stuffy roommate and her friends.

I frowned. Maybe I was the problem?

Nah.

I shook my head and moved forward with the line. That couldn't be the case. I oozed warmth. I drew people to me like sap to bears. Come and eat me, animals.

My lip twitched.

Even my own jokes were pathetic.

"Wait a minute." Kristina had been watching me. Her eyes narrowed. "You're not going to tell them, are you?"

I glanced back, the same incredulous look on my face that she'd given me when Shay first walked away. "You're kidding, right? There's no way I'm telling them."

They'd want his number. They'd want me to call him. They'd want me to talk to him.

They'd want to use me. This was not going to be high school all over again.

I had rules: no hot boys and no drama. This was a new year, new school, and a new me.

I was going to study my ass off and not get swept up in everything extracurricular.

I clipped my head side to side. "I'm not using his number, and he's right. I'm not answering if he calls." That made me look like a brat, but I had alarms going off. Big, huge, red alarms and there's a reason I instantly didn't like Shay. I was listening to those alarms. The last time I hadn't, well, it hadn't been pretty. It'd been a disaster.

"How are you going to get in contact about meeting for your project?"

"Linde." I'd already formed my plan as I was walking out of the classroom.

"Who's Linde?"

"Raymond Linde. He's an offensive lineman." Thank you to my brother for that random fact. "And he's also in the group. We're pals." He nodded at me. Same thing. "I'll train Shay so that if he wants to talk to me, he'll have to go through Linde to do it."

Her eyes narrowed, and she stepped behind me as we entered the cafeteria. "Shay Coleman doesn't strike me as the type to be trained. He's the type who would *do* the training."

I handed my card to the clerk, and as it was swiped, I said to Kristina, "Well"—I took my card back—"he's never met me before."

Then I stepped forward.

My stomach growled at the first smell of that ice cream bar, and I headed right for it.

My priorities were in place.

# CHAPTER THREE

I had to see Shay twice more during the week since our classes fell on a MondayWednesday-Friday schedule, but both of us escaped alive. We weren't forced into group discussions, and the one time we had to pair up with someone, Linde signaled for me right away.

See, we were friends.

It was around three that Friday afternoon when I was heading back to my dorm. I was passing along behind the art building, going down the sidewalk where it curved to the right and would pass through a bunch of trees, and then into my dorm. The whole campus was set up like that. There were trees everywhere. They hid most of the buildings, so you constantly felt like you were walking in a forest until your sidewalk dipped into whatever building was your stop.

I was six feet from my clearing when I heard my name being called.

I tensed, but no. That wasn't Shay. That wasn't his voice, and an instant scowl formed because I *did* recognize that voice.

My brother was standing behind some trees, waving at me.

I hurried my pace. "Gage. What are you doing here?" I pushed him deeper into the trees and looked over my shoulder. The walkway was clear. My shoulders sagged in relief. I gave his chest a good whack. "First rule of Clarke Club. We don't know each other."

He rolled his eyes, running a hand through dark brown hair, which was the same shade as mine. We had the same dark eyes, too. He was a year older, but people thought we were fraternal twins. Gage liked to joke he was the smart one, and I was the dumb one who got held back a year. I smacked him in the back of the head whenever he said that, and I was considering doing the same thing here. He knew not to come to my dorm. I'd been adamant about that.

Being used in high school was out of my control. I did ask my mom when I was in eighth grade if I could switch my high school, but the only other one within driving distance was a private one, which got a big, firm nope. Her lips popped saying that word. We didn't have the money for even a semester, much less the uniforms and all the other expenses that would've come with it.

But I had control now, and the first rule of being Gage and Kennedy Clarke: we pretended we didn't know each other.

It was a subset of rule number two: no drama.

Clarke wasn't a common name? What? I had no idea. It was just a huge coincidence.

That was my planned argument if anyone tried to press the matter.

"Ow." He rubbed his chest, giving me a pained puppy-dog look. "Why do you always have to hit me? Contrary to what chicks think, guys don't appreciate it. Our instincts are to hit back, and we always have to curb those primal instincts."

He flexed as he said primal.

I rolled my eyes.

"Make it quick." Someone was bound to come down the sidewalk. "What do you want?"

His hand dropped down. He was all business now. "I'm going to a fraternity party tonight."

"Okay?"

"I heard some girls from your dorm are going, too."

I narrowed my eyes. Two other subsets of rule two were that he couldn't admit to knowing me, much less being related to me, and he couldn't sleep with any of my friends. That'd been awkward in high school, and it was still awkward in college.

"Okay?" I asked again.

"They're the chicks who you've been hanging out with. You know"—he tugged on his shirtsleeve—"the slutty ones."

"Oh!" Laura, Casey, and Sarah. "Yeah. You can't sleep with them."

"Come on." His tone turned pleading. "That Casey girl is hot." He groaned the last word. "Seriously hot. What if she hits on me? Huh? I'd hurt her feelings. She might turn around and become a clinger? You know, those kind that if they're rejected, they become instantly besotted." He shook his head, whistling in sympathy. "You wouldn't want that, would you?"

"Casey can have any guy she wants. I'll risk the odds it'll be you whom she falls in love with."

He frowned. "What are you talking about? Chances are high. If you haven't noticed, we're good-looking. Both of us."

I groaned. "Stop talking."

"I'm a catch. I don't make girls do the walk of shame. I give them a ride home."

I raised an eyebrow.

He added, glancing away, "Or call a car for them." His eyes flashed at me. "See. Thoughtful. That's me." His hands formed fists and his thumbs pointed to himself. He winked at me. "And I would be really thoughtful to Casey. I could go over the top, make her think I'm in love with her. That'll send her running. Hot girls like that don't like clingy guys. I'd do it for you."

"You'd do *it* for you." My hand rested on my hip. "And, still no. Stay away from those girls."

"Okay, okay. What about that Kristina girl?" He whistled. "She's smoking, too. I don't know why she hides those puppies. A lot of guys already know her as Tits Girl."

I shoved him back. "She has a boyfriend, and she's my only friend. You shut that shit down real quick, you hear me? Real fucking quick."

"Okay, okay." His eyes turned sober, and his grin finally fell away. "But guys are going to want to know why I'm defending this girl. It'd be easier if I made it known that it was because she's friends with my sister. And speaking of you, I don't want you hooking up with any of my friends."

"Not going to be a problem."

No hot guys—rule number one.

"Hey." I remembered the bone I needed to pick with him. "You told Shay Coleman I'm your sister."

His eyes lit up. "Yeah, I did. That guy's awesome."

"Why did you do that?"

He snorted, rocking back on his heels and putting his hands in his pockets. "Are you kidding me? You were my golden ticket to introduce myself to him. I heard him and a bunch of other players took political science this semester. I asked if a chick who looked like my female twin was in his class." He smirked. "He knew right away who you were."

"You told him I had a chip on my shoulder."

"You do."

"You don't have to *tell* people that."

His mouth curved up into a wicked grin. "Are you joking? That's the quickest way to explain who you are to guys. Girls don't get it, but guys do."

I hit him in the shoulder. He was part of the reason that chip was there.

"Don't talk about me anymore."

"Why? If anything, I'm doing you a favor. Coleman seemed interested in who you were."

I suppressed another shiver, but this one was from disgust. "You're not doing me any favors. I don't want to know Shay Coleman like that."

"Did I say I was doing *you* a favor?" His grin went up a notch. "I meant I was doing myself a favor. You hate guys like that."

Yeah. I did.

I shook my head.

Shay Coleman was another Parker Stanson, my ex. That angry thought chased another one—fuck Parker and fuck Shay Coleman.

"Whatever." I shoved Gage back, gently this time, and forced a lightness in my voice. "Go to your fraternity party and stay away from my friends."

He was going to argue. I saw the words forming and shook my head again. "I mean it. And stop talking about me to football players. Got it?"

He looked at me for a second, his head tilting to the side in thought. "You okay?"

I heard the kindness and my throat swelled up a bit. "I'm fine." I would be. Studying. That was my goal right now. Guys like Parker couldn't hurt me anymore. I wouldn't let them. "Now, go. Before someone sees you."

He chuckled, and a couple of seconds later when I'd gotten my emotions in check, I looked back up to find him gone. No brother anywhere.

I was passing by the front desk when the girl looked up. "Kennedy Clarke?"

"Yeah?"

She was an upperclassman and had been the front desk attendant since the first week of classes, and I waited for her to say whatever she called me over for.

"Shay said to say hi to you."

I instantly groaned.

Of course, Shay would know this girl. She was too pretty to be ignored. I half-joked, "Let me guess. You're his girlfriend?"

She laughed, sounding actually nice. "We're friends. He said to say hi to you, that you're pretty cool."

I glanced around. There were a few girls in the lobby, so I stepped closer to the desk. "Can we keep that on the down-low?"

"What?" Another genuine laugh. It was almost making me like her, sort of. She added, "That you're cool?"

"That I know Shay, and I only know him from class. We're not friends or anything." I had to stress the last part. "And if you were dating him, my condolences."

"Shay isn't that bad of a guy, but yeah, I'll keep it quiet."

She frowned a bit as I held my hand up in a farewell wave, heading for the stairs and toward my room. Having a front desk attendant who was nice to you? That was gold. There could be drunk times ahead, and you never know when you needed someone to look the other way.

I had an extra bounce in my step when I let myself into the room, but it careened to a stop.

Missy was at her desk, wearing a big scowl.

"What's up?" I shut the door and tossed my backpack onto my bed behind her.

"Holly wants to go to the library tonight." She was stabbing at her keyboard.

Holly was her best friend from high school, the girl who lived a floor above us with her cousin. "What's wrong with the library?" My desk was across the room, and I sat down on my chair before spinning so I was facing her.

"Nothing, if it were Sunday or any other day of the week. But it's Friday. She has a crush on one of the workers there."

Holly developed a new crush twice a week. "Not many people are going to be there. Makes sense she'd want to go tonight. Prime time for flirting."

"I don't want to go to the stupid library."

"What else are you going to do?" Where Holly and her cousin went, Missy went, and vice versa. The three didn't stray far from each other's sides.

She shrugged, glancing at our television. "We could watch movies in here?"

I almost recoiled. I was movie buddies with Kristina, not Missy, not the roommate who laughed in my face because I didn't like the same chick flicks she did. Plus, I knew she talked shit about me. I walked in once when Holly and the cousin were there. The room got completely silent. I had no clue what they could've even been saying about me, but I had no doubt it'd been happening.

"I was planning to go to the library tonight, too."

"You were?"

Her disbelief was almost complementary. She *did* think I had a life.

I shrugged, spun back around, and booted my computer. "Why not? I need to study. And besides, the library closes early, doesn't it?"

"So?"

"Maybe Holly's crush will have a party to invite you guys to. The best plans are usually not having any plans."

"Yeah?"

Someone knocked on the door just as I was pulling up my email. I stood and nodded to her. "Yeah. I'd go with the plan of hoping to find some action afterward. No one goes to a party before ten anyway."

I opened the door as I was finishing that sentence.

Casey Winchem stood there, the same Casey who Gage had been begging me to let him sleep with and the same Casey who intimidated me because she was so confident.

"Hey." I blinked a couple of times. I was on friendly terms with Casey, Laura, and Sarah, but none of them ever came to my room. A part of me wasn't even sure they knew my name. They always referred to me as "Hey, You."

"Hey."

"What's up?" I opened the door wider.

She looked past me and waved. "Hi."

Missy didn't wave back. I think she was in shock I knew someone else.

Casey frowned slightly but then looked back to me. "Uh, we're going to a fraternity party tonight. Did you want to come with us?"

"Uh . . ."

"You have a car, don't you? Sarah and Kristina had to go home for the weekend. It's just Laura and me."

*Now* it made sense.

Sarah had the only car they used. No one else brought one since parking was a challenge around freshman dorms. I had a car. Everyone in my family had one. It was the one big gift our mom splurged for when we graduated. We weren't wealthy so it was the last big gift I'd be getting until I got married.

When I was in my thirties.

If ever.

I shook my head. Back to the conversation. "You need a ride to the party?"

"Well." She bit her lip. "Kind of. I mean, we can get a ride with Adams or Kreigerson." Names I didn't know. "It's the getting home part we're worried about. The guys will get drunk and take off on their own, if you know what I mean. If Laura or I end up hooking up with someone, that's another thing, but yeah. I'd like to have a backup plan if anything happens."

Backup.

That was me.

I was plan B.

And I wasn't a pushover, either. "No, thank you. I'll see you later. Have fun tonight."

I shut the door.

I knew I was coming off like a bitch, but I ignored my roommate's still gaping mouth. She didn't understand. No one used me anymore. I wasn't going to let it happen, not again.

And with that in mind, I eyed my computer.

I really *did* need to learn how to study. This weekend was just put into that slot.

# CHAPTER FOUR

I was going to be a psychologist . . . maybe?

I had it narrowed down. I got sick at the sight of blood, and being a lawyer was out, so that really only left being a psychologist. Not a psychiatrist—again, sick at the sight of blood. I'd had to endure that before I got to see the people in the padded cells. The other option was going for my MBA, but that meant business classes, lots of them. I wasn't sure. Gage was going for business, and he complained about his classes. Not often, but enough that it left a bad taste in my mouth.

Still, I had to keep my options open.

Depending on my job experiences, I would have a better idea which to choose. That meant getting a job at a psychiatric hospital, or becoming a research assistant for a Ph.D. student. I could do that during the school year, and when I went home for the summer, I'd figure something else out.

All in all, I was content when Sunday night came around.

I was back on my course for college. No drama, and I'd studied, studied, studied.

My studies were done. All the chapters were read and highlighted. I went the extra mile and created a second set of notes. I was getting this studying thing down pat, and I was sure by the time the first exams rolled around that I'd get all A's.

My four-year plan was done, too. I created an extensive class schedule over the weekend that spanned the rest of my college years. If everything went accordingly, I could receive a major in either of the two degrees with a minor in the one I didn't choose. A psychology major combined with a business minor, or the other way around, equaled my being prepared for life.

It never hurt to be too prepared. There was no such thing.

I had it all figured out.

Type-A, that was my new personality. I was acing it.

I was in my dorm room, printing off my weekly planner for the next five days when Kristina knocked on the door. She poked her head around. "Hey-a."

I waved her in. "Missy's in Holly's room."

She shut the door and dropped into Missy's desk chair. "Does she ever leave there?"

"She was here Friday afternoon." And again that evening. The party happened, but not for her or Holly's cousin. Holly got an invite from the library front desk clerk and ditched both of them. I'd been hoping they would head to Holly's room to watch movies, but no dice. They stayed, and Missy enjoyed retelling the story of how I told Casey to "sod off." Those were Missy's words, not mine.

"And speaking of Friday . . ." Kristina hugged the back of Missy's desk chair, letting one of her arms hang loose. "Did you ditch Casey and Laura?"

I frowned. "Is that what she's saying?"

"She's saying she asked you to go out, and you shut the door in her face."

"That's half-truth, half-exaggeration."

Kristina's mouth dropped open. "You shut the door in Casey's face? I thought she was joking."

"She wanted me to be their backup in case they needed a ride." I snorted, taking the pages from my printer. "I might keep to myself, and I might be focused on my studies, but I'm not a loser. And I'm not anyone's option B for the night. I said no thank you, wished her a good night, and told her I'd see her later. *Then* I shut the door." I paused a second. "I might not have said all that in that order, but yes, she was technically still standing there when I shut the door."

"She's pissed."

I didn't care, but I kept that tidbit to myself. I didn't think it'd make the situation better.

No, that wasn't true. I did care, but then I thought about how the night would've gone. I'd take them there. They'd probably ditch me. Then I'd be expected to be around in case they needed a ride home.

If I had to come off as a bitch, then so be it. It was better than getting walked all over. No one was there for you when that happened.

"Did you finish all your studies this weekend?"

"No. We're going to the library. I was going to ask if you wanted to come."

I didn't say anything, waiting for her to explain who else was going.

She chuckled, shaking her head. "Casey's going to be there, and she's probably going to have a few words to say to you."

I was going to decline, but then I heard someone coming to the door. Both Kristina and I turned, waiting for the door to open. It didn't. Instead, my roommate's muffled voice said to someone else, "I don't know. I think she's in the computer lab downstairs." She laughed as the doorknob started to twist. "It isn't like she has a life."

She opened the door and took one step inside.

Her eyes went to Kristina first, and then her head rotated like a robot's to me.

I narrowed my eyes. It wasn't as if I hadn't heard that before.

Holly stepped behind Missy, and my roommate's face drained of color. "Uh . . ."

I stood and spoke stiffly, "I'm going to the library."

She seemed to be holding her breath. The air was strained and awkward. Kristina moved around them as if she were tiptoeing past a mouse, one that scared the crap out of her. Holly's hands rested on my roommate's shoulders, and I could feel both of them share a look as I stuffed my backpack with my laptop and books.

"Um." Holly coughed, an uneasy laugh stuck in her throat. "Kenz, hey—"

I pulled on the bag's zipper harder than I needed, cutting her off. Slinging it on my shoulder, I turned back around and narrowed my eyes. I ignored Holly, only having words for my roommate. "I don't have to explain myself to you or why I'm alone at times, but if you think you can laugh at me, you're delusional. Tell me one thing. How'd you be if you didn't come to the same college as your best friend and her cousin? My guess is that either you'd scurry back home or you'd find someone else to latch on to. Now, excuse me. I have to go to the library because I don't have a life."

I swung past, purposely clipping Holly in the shoulder with my bag. Missy was too short.

Kristina was waiting in the hallway, and we started down the back stairs, which were the closest exit. I could feel the weight of the atmosphere around us, her sympathy piling on top of it. After going through the door to her floor, she gave me one of those pitying looks.

"I'm sorry—"

I shook my head. "She just proved what my gut has been saying the whole time." I gave her a tired grin. "She's a weak bitch."

She laughed, opening her door.

Casey, Laura, and Sarah were inside, and they stopped laughing as we walked in.

"I have a bone to—"

I cut her off, too. I was on a roll. "Would you have asked me to go with you if Sarah had been here?"

She stopped, and her face twisted up.

The answer was her silence. "That's why I didn't go with you." I dropped my bag onto the floor and slumped down on the edge of Kristina's bed. "I'm not a backup."

Her mouth shut with an audible clicking sound, and she hung her head. "I see." She swallowed, glancing to her friends, neither of which seemed to know what to say.

Just like upstairs and just like walking back with Kristina, the air was heavy. Too heavy. I grabbed my bag and stood. "Maybe I'll just see you guys there?" But it wasn't really a question as I breezed past Kristina.

"Wai—"

She started to follow me down the hallway, and I turned around. I held my hand up. "I'm worked up, and I might say something I don't want to regret later. It's better if I go now. Trust me. I'll be on the second floor if you want to come find me. If you don't"—I lifted my shoulders—"that's fine, too."

The front desk attendant, Shay's friend, was there, but I didn't feel like talking. Thankfully, three girls were talking to her, so she was busy, and I slipped past them.

The library was busy.

That was normal for a Sunday evening. Friday and Saturday were for fun. Sunday was for last-minute studying. After going through the main door, I went through another small hallway that housed a small coffee cart, and then through another set of doors. Four detectors were set up for everyone to walk through. The large front desk was immediately to my left. There was a large computer lab across the main floor with glass doors that separated it from the rest of the library. People could be louder in there, and it was where a lot of people met to work in group projects. The rest of the library was a mishmash of computers, individual studying nooks and crannies, and bookshelves everywhere. There were a bunch of tables set up on the main floors, and each floor held study rooms lined against the walls with similar glass doors separating them from the rest of the library.

When Casey, Laura, and Sarah came to the library, they picked a table in the large computer lab or a table out in the middle of the main floor. It was still the rule to be quiet, but there was leeway given to those tables, and that was why they only sat there. They came to the library to somewhat study, but mainly to socialize or see if they could get answers from any of their party friends.

Kristina was prone to seek out a quiet place for studying, so thirty minutes later when she found me at my own table on the second floor, I wasn't too surprised.

"Let me guess." I grunted, grinning with a pen between my teeth. I took it out. "They're talking more than studying?"

She sighed, sliding into a seat across from me. "They're still at the dorm."

"What?"

She rolled her eyes. "Casey felt bad. They were going to stop and get food to bring to you as a peace offering, but some guys showed up, and they went downstairs to study instead."

My grin was back. "And they wouldn't shut up so you decided to come without them?"

"I was coming anyway. It isn't your fault Casey was insensitive, and she does feel bad." She leaned closer. "I know my friends come off a certain way, but they can be really sweet sometimes. They don't mean to be mean." She waited a beat. "Most of the time."

I laughed, was hushed by someone we couldn't see, and clamped my mouth shut. "Thank you for coming," I whispered before picking my pen back up and returning to my notes.

Kristina and I fell into an easy routine.

I was caught up for the week, but that didn't mean I couldn't get ahead, and poli-sci was a class I really needed the help. The boringness of it wasn't exaggerated. Even my eye sockets wanted to be ripped out if I had to go over any more laws.

We studied for an hour before Kristina got up for a bathroom break and to get coffee. When she returned, I went for a walkabout. That was what I called it when I just needed to get up and stretch my legs. I was doing my walkabout past the front entryway, considering if I wanted to get some soda or just go straight for the coffee cart. It was around nine at night, but I had a feeling I'd be up late anyway. My mind made up, I stepped through the detectors when I noticed someone standing just beyond the outside doors. There was a girl there, reading a book. No, wait. She was pretending to read a book. Her eyes were on someone else near her, but when she saw I noticed her, her head lowered back to her book. I looked at whomever she'd been watching. They were on the other side of the library doors, their back to me as they talked to someone else.

Shit.

I averted my eyes instantly. I knew who the girl had been watching, and I started counting down the seconds while I had to wait for my coffee.

I wanted to get it, pay for it, and be gone before Shay came past me.

There were other students behind me in line, so if anything, I hoped to blend in with the crowd, and he'd walk right past.

He was still outside talking when my coffee was handed over to me. I took it, having already paid, and was about to head back into the library when a hand grabbed my free wrist.

"Hey!"

Shay ignored me, dragging me outside at a clipped pace.

"What are you doing?" I asked once we were out there and looked around for whomever he'd been talking to. I was surprised to see no one. "Whom were you talking to?"

He ignored that question and pointed into the library. "You have your books and stuff close by?"

"No. Why?"

"We have a pop quiz tomorrow."

He wasn't joking. His face was dead serious, and that smoldering effect was back in place. I ignored the twisting of my stomach. "How do you know?"

"Because the girl I was just talking to saw the quizzes. She was in Professor Muller's office just now."

"But that doesn't mean it's tomorrow."

He held his hands out. "Who the fuck cares? Let's study, just in case."

"Let's? As in you and me?" Uh-uh. No way. I turned to go back inside.

"Yes. You and me." He grabbed me and hauled me back. "And Linde and some of the other guys. We're all doing a round robin study thing at the house."

"What house?"

My stomach dropped to my feet. He couldn't be talking about the football house, not where he and some of the players lived. Where I knew Casey wanted to party because she wanted to seduce Shay. Where I knew she'd keel over in jealousy if she found out I was going there to study, because that was quality time. That wasn't drunk time. That wasn't party and less-than-meaningful time.

I swallowed. Oh, Lord.

I wasn't normally nervous about being around guys, and I was nervous now.

"I'm here with a friend."

"That girl from the food court?"

I nodded.

"Ask her to come with."

My neck was so stiff. Why was I doing this? But on wooden legs, I went back inside. I ignored the curious looks of those still waiting at the coffee cart and made the trek to our table. Kristina looked up, saw my near-state of panic, and asked, "What's wrong?"

I began packing my stuff. "Um." The computer had to be turned off first. "I ran into Shay."

"What?"

It was stuffed into the bag. My books were next. I reached for my notebook last. "Yeah. He said we have a surprise pop quiz tomorrow."

"Surprise?"

"I guess."

She cocked her head to the side. "Why are you sweating?"

"Shay wants me to go to his place and study with him and the guys." My throat was parched, too. "Would you come with me?"

Her eyes rounded to ovals, and she laughed to herself as she began to pack her own things. "You're inviting me to a place that my roommate is almost stalking because she wants to be invited to one of their parties, and you're acting like I'm doing you a favor?"

"You can't tell her you went."

She finished and stood, pulling her backpack on. "If I did, she'd be up my ass asking how I got an invite. I don't even know if she'd believe me."

I gave her a grateful smile. "Thank you."

She shook her head, laughing wryly. "You really don't have to thank me. For real."

Shay was lounging against a bike lock post when we came out. The girl who'd been watching him was gone, too. His legs were stretched out and his hands were in his pockets. He straightened and gave Kristina a nod. "Thanks for coming." He gestured to me with his head. "I don't think she would've come, otherwise."

That same laugh slipped from her, softer. "You're both thanking me. This is classic, just . . . classic."

His eyes found me, growing wary again. "My car is parked around the corner in the library parking lot. Do you trust me enough for a ride? Or are you going to follow me to the house?"

I glanced to Kristina, but she shook her head. It was my decision to make.

If we took my car, I'd have to go back to my dorm room. Kristina would go with me. We could run into Casey or the others, and they'd want to know where we were going. Not to mention that I'd have to see my roommate if she was in the room.

For once, Shay was the easier choice.

I motioned ahead. "Lead the way."

Shay drove a black Jeep Wrangler. I didn't know what I was expecting him to drive, but I stopped short when he unlocked the doors and the lights flashed. It was a two-seater so Kristina was able to climb into the back seat. I had an irrational urge to pull her back and slip back there myself.

I did not want to go to Shay's house, but he said Linde was there. And it was a smart idea to study with others. I did need all the help I could get. There wasn't a case where someone could get too much help.

Shay opened his door, but when I didn't move to follow Kristina inside, he paused, irritation flashing for a brief second in his smoldering eyes. "What's the verdict, Clarke? Having second thoughts? Thinking maybe this is all a ruse to kill you?"

I gulped. "I didn't till now." My mind was going to race with that thought. I groaned, tipping my head back and marching past him to the passenger door. "If you try to kill me, I will gut you and rip your balls off, Coleman."

His low and smooth chuckle followed me as I passed him, and I swear that it got inside me. I could feel it under my skin. I climbed in, gritting my teeth, and shut the door closed with a little more oomph than was needed.

He got in and watched me from the corner of his eye as he started the engine.

As he drove out of the parking lot, I looked out the window, but only one thought kept racing through my mind.

Why did I feel this guy inside me so much?

# CHAPTER FIVE

I didn't know what to expect from the football house.

It was an older house, three stories tall, and Shay parked in the front. We walked around to the back, and we went in through the back door, Linde raised an arm. A loud cheer filled the room.

"Clarke's in the house!" He came over, bent down, and hoisted me over his shoulder. "Now we can really study!"

I lifted my head and saw Kristina. She had a dazed expression on her face.

Shay moved around us, rolling his eyes before slapping me on the ass. "Okay. Put her down. We know you're ripped up and ready to memorize. We don't want to scare off the girls."

"Oh." Linde was breathing heavily as he set me back down. His eyes were glazed as he smiled at me. "Sorry about that. Just excited to have my pal here." He blinked a few times, and then realized I wasn't the only girl present. He stuck his hand out. "I'm Raymond Linde. Who are you?"

"Uh." Kristina was slower to shake his hand, but she did. "Kristina Collins."

He turned to look at me and then back to her. "You're friends with Clarke here?"

She nodded, some nervous laughter slipping from her.

I scoffed, going to the end of the table where there were open chairs. "Why do you sound surprised?"

Shay snorted, going by me to the kitchen.

"Uh." Linde scooped up his books and joined us at the end. He plopped down across from me, pulling out the empty chair by him and patting its seat for Kristina. She sat, moving slowly, as he said to me, "You're not the friendliest, Clarke."

I couldn't—no, no, I could. I shrugged, giving that to him. "Yes, I've been told."

Linde added, "We know better. We can tell you're a chill chick, but other idiots won't see through your whole charade." He waved his hand in the air, motioning toward me. "They'll actually think you're a bitch, but we know better. You're all soft inside, aren't you? You gush over puppies and bake cookies for your friends, don't you?"

I just gazed at him a moment, startled for a minute.

Then, I grinned. "Linde, look at you. Are you projecting on me? Tell me the truth. You were baking cookies for me today, weren't you?" I said it like a proud mother, and the rest of the table choked up with laughter.

One of them pounded Linde on the back. "Okay. I see now what you were saying." He nodded his approval toward me. "She is chill. You guys were right."

Drinks were dispensed, then Shay took the other seat beside me. I skimmed over the rest of the table. It was a long table, stretching enough to seat sixteen people or so. Most were football players, but there were a few others I didn't recognize.

Linde waved a hand, answering my teases, "That's the persona I give off. Fucks with my enemies. They get all confused. Think I'm this nice guy and then bam!" He pounded a fist on the table. "That's when I take 'em out."

One of the guys leaned forward. "And by enemies, he's talking about the other teams on the football field."

Kristina nodded, her head bobbing up and down. "Totally."

She had a wide-eyed or starry-eyed sort of expression on her face. It took me aback. I'd been nervous when Shay pulled me aside and invited—rather, demanded—I come study at his place, but I figured that was because this was unknown to me. And because of him. He was just a lot. His presence overwhelmed me. He could be standing a few feet from me, and I felt like he was in me. But when Kristina snuck a look at him, I knew it wasn't just me. It was him. He had this effect on everyone.

I started to relax after a bit.

Linde was over the top. Guys were like that, especially if they were jacked up on something, and speaking of, I glanced at his own glass in front of him. Beads of sweat lined his forehead, and a vein was popping out from his neck. Noting his tank and how tight it was against his bulging muscles—they seemed to be bigger than what I noticed from class—I glanced over my shoulder to the kitchen.

A big, white plastic container was pushed up against the corner, a measuring cup beside it with a dust layer on the inside of it.

Protein shakes, or something more serious.

Shay cleared his throat, pulling my gaze to his. I saw the reproach in them, and he shook his head silently.

He didn't want me poking my nose where it didn't belong. I got his message and settled on my political science textbook. Apparently, geopolitics needed to be my business, not whatever Linde was on.

Still.

My eyes went back to him, and then Shay kicked my chair. My head snapped back to his, and he widened his eyes again. A second warning.

I frowned, scrunched my nose, and turned back to my book. Whatever. Fine. Geopolitics, my ass, though.

"Okay." Linde waved a sheet that we were given earlier in the week. "Clarke, tell me similarities and differences between political institutions and behaviors from state to state." My mouth dropped open, but he held his hand up and continued, "*And* between communities. Go." He sat back, folding his arms over his chest.

A soft gurgle rippled up from my throat. "You're serious?"

"You're Ms. Planned, Perfected, and Prepared. You should be able to rattle this off with no problem at all."

I opened my mouth again, flashing back to some notes I'd written earlier today, but one of the other football players spoke up, "This is the shit you're learning in that class? Damn. I'm glad I kept to my gym major."

A few others laughed, joining in with their own comments, and soon the four of us at the end of the table were no longer the center of attention. I had a feeling this was how it'd been before we showed up.

Linde pointed at me. "I'm waiting. Go."

And I did, doing exactly what he challenged me to do. The answers fell from my tongue, and once I was done, his eyebrows were arched up to his forehead. He nodded, slowly, and whistled. "Boom. You nailed it. You get an A, as far as I'm concerned." Grabbing his glass, he shoved back his chair and rounded the table for the kitchen.

I wanted to look.

I fought it.

I tried.

I failed. I snuck a peek over my shoulder.

My chair got another swift kick. Shay leaned forward and hissed under his breath, "Stop."

Kristina, who had been reading her book, paused. Her eyes looked up to watch us.

I ignored her, leaning forward and whispering back, "My older brother had a problem. Sue me for caring."

She leaned forward. "What are you guys talking about?"

"Nothing." He spoke to her, but his eyes never left mine. He added to me, "I mean it. Stop. You've known him four minutes. You don't get a say."

"Then why'd you bring me here if you expect me to be oblivious to shit?" I hissed back.

"Because Linde asked." His eyes darkened in anger. "Not me. Okay?"

Well.

Fuck.

Now I was even more concerned. I checked. Linde was still mixing the drink together. I lowered my head even closer to Shay's. "Tough shit. You opened the door. Don't expect me *not* to walk through it."

His eyes narrowed. "What the hell does that even mean?"

I sat back, and letting my voice back to its normal level, I said, "If you wanted a dumb chick to study with, you fucked up. Becs and Aby have no problem being told what to think. Remember?"

Linde was coming back but paused behind us. "What's going on?"

The rest of the table quieted, too. All eyes were on us.

I felt the heat of their attention and stood. "I'm feeling the need for some fresh air." The path was blocked from my side, so I went around Linde, behind Shay, Kristina, and their side of the table. "Be right back."

I wanted to let the door slam behind me but I caught it and closed it with a soft click, instead. A picnic table was on their back patio, and I slumped down on the far side of it, brought my elbows to the table, and I buried my head in my arms.

Why was I reacting so much? Even for me, this was more than normal.

The screen door opened and shut, but not before Shay pulled the inside door closed, too. He rounded the table to the opposite side where I was, but instead of sitting down, he leaned back against the post. Using his hands for balance, he kicked up and sat toward me, his long legs dangling. He hooked one foot around the picnic table, jerked it over, and rested his feet there.

This made him even more opposing in my mind, and as he crossed his arms over his chest, I averted my eyes.

Why did he bother me so much?

I didn't speak.

He didn't speak.

A full minute passed before he groaned. "Are you serious?" He let his arms fall back to his lap. "Are you this stubborn with everyone?"

"Are you?" I shot back, not hiding my own anger. "You came out here to apologize. What handbook says that I have to start that conversation?"

He snorted. "Who said I came out to apologize?"

I shut my mouth. *Asshole.*

He laughed quietly. "Relax. I did come out to apologize, but not really at the same time. You're not dumb. It's partly why Linde thinks you're cool. You're not like other girls."

I motioned for him to go on. "I know the anticipation to tell me to mind my business is just burning inside you. Let it out. Let's get on with this."

Another half-laugh, half in surprise and half in amusement. He grabbed the back of his neck. "Fuck, you're feisty."

"Two brothers. One who got really messed up on that stuff, or stuff like what Linde is taking."

"It isn't steroids." He grew somber, folding his arms back up again. "It's to help him bulk up. A lot of the guys take it, and it *is* legal for them to do that."

"It's legal because some company paid some lobbyist to convince a Congress person to allow it. That's why it's legal, but it shouldn't be. It can really mess with the body. He's going to have problems long after his football career is done."

His eyes darted to the house behind me, and he then held his hand up. "Chill, please. It really isn't a problem for him. Some guys, yes. Not Linde. He's going to stop taking it after football. I'll make him, and besides, he'll get upset if he knows that's why you're out here."

I frowned. "Why does he think I'm out here?"

He shrugged, his lip lifting in a crooked grin. "That I might've touched your leg in a place you weren't having it. Your friend knows I was lying, but the guys don't. They think I came out to hit on you again."

Hitting on me. I scoffed, but my body warmed at the same time, which pissed me off even more. This guy had power over me that I didn't like, power over me that no other guy had had before. It was because he was Mr. Superstar at this college. That was all.

He affected other girls the same way. It wasn't just me.

"What are you thinking?" He was watching me, wary again.

I shook my head, closing those thoughts down. "Nothing."

"You have nothing to say about the guys thinking I'm hitting on you?"

"Nope."

He whistled under his breath. "Thought that'd get some sort of reaction from you."

"No." My throat burned. I let out a breath and tugged at my shirt's collar before casually smoothing down my sleeves. "We came to study, right? Maybe we should do that." I stood. My legs felt like they were filled with lead.

His eyes narrowed, and he cocked his head to the side. "You're lying to me right now."

My eyes went to his.

He nodded to himself, the smolder melting into a smug expression, but it did nothing to lessen the impact he was having on me. If anything, it increased it.

I was really starting to hate this guy.

I scowled. "Whatever. Let's go in. We have that quiz."

I brushed past him, going inside, but my mind was racing. Did I really have to be there? I already studied for the week. I could leave. Though, when I glanced to Kristina and realized she seemed to be enjoying herself, I couldn't. I knew she was getting a kick out of studying and hanging out with these guys.

I looked at Linde and saw his forehead scrunched as he was trying to memorize something in the textbook. He still had sweat beaded on his temples and definitely looked tense, so I kept my mouth shut.

Shay slipped into his old seat, and his eyes met mine.

He told me Linde asked for me to be there. Linde was my friend. I felt a tug in my chest—Linde was whom I cared about.

I picked my pen back up and began underlining.

Linde was whom I would stay for.

# CHAPTER SIX

Kristina was all giggles on the ride home.

After studying for two hours, most of the guys had gone to bed or left for wherever they lived. The only ones up were the four of us and one other football player from class. Shay and that guy moved farther down the table and were quizzing each other. I moved so I was in the middle of the table, and Linde and Kristina were at the end where we'd originally been sitting.

Then Linde declared he needed a drink.

I declined. So did Shay and the other guy, but Kristina was persuaded to have one with him. It was a strong one. A really strong one.

"One drink." She dissolved in more soft laughter, holding her hands together over her mouth. "One drink, and I'm like this."

When we went to Shay's Jeep, I scooted into the back. I was tired, and I didn't want to feel the stress of sitting next to him. Kristina twisted around, pressing her nose to the back of her seat. She gazed at me, her eyes wide. "What am I going to say to the others? To Casey? She's going to know."

I glanced to the clock on the dashboard. It was after three in the morning. A normal roommate would be asleep by now, but this was Casey. I shrugged. "If they didn't end up partying tonight," because you never knew, "you can sleep in my room."

"Missy won't care?"

"Missy starts snoring at ten on the dot every Sunday through Thursday night. You'll be fine." We had a loveseat that could get pulled out into a third bed for the room. If Missy said something in the morning, I'd be surprised. After her comment this afternoon, I figured she'd avoid me for at least a week. Plus, to her, Kristina was one of those popular girls who should be treated like a unicorn—mystical, beautiful, and only found in fairy tales.

"Okay." She hiccupped, turned around, and slumped down in her seat.

I glanced to the rearview mirror, saw Shay watching me, and felt another bolt of energy in my chest. This was how it was going to be. I had to get used to it. He just affected me. He didn't really do anything to cause it, but it was there. It wasn't going away. There was no judgment, sympathy, or amusement in those blue eyes as he watched me. He was literally just looking at me, and I let out a sigh.

This semester could be the longest four months of my life.

When he pulled into our dorm's parking lot, I leaned forward. "You can pull up to the back door there."

Kristina was swaying on her feet as we got out.

I was crawling from the back, when he quietly asked, "Do you need help with her?"

I looked back at him. "I'm sure we're fine."

"Sabrina's at the front desk. Let her know if you need help."

Sabrina.

I paused, my fingers sinking down into the seat. Of course, she'd have an equally beautiful name.

I dipped my head down, murmuring, "Thank you. And thank you for the ride."

I didn't say anything about Linde, because he was right. If Linde became a close enough friend where I could voice my opinion, and if he asked, I would say it then. It would've been me passing judgment on him, otherwise. I was prickly enough with people judging me. Hello, pot meet kettle.

I climbed out the rest of the way, shut his door, and held a hand up in a farewell wave as he wheeled the Jeep around deftly and pulled away. Holding my ID to the back door scanner, it opened for us, and I made Kristina wait in the stairwell so I could scope out her room situation.

The hallway's low lights were on. Light shone from underneath a few of the doors, but they were quiet. I got to Kristina's and used the key she gave me to open the door an inch. No light was on inside, and I waited—I didn't hear anything. No deep breathing. No light snoring. I opened the door wider, then stepped inside and waited again.

No reaction.

No one moved in their bed.

I hit the switch, and the room flooded in light. Casey's bed was empty. That answered Kristina's dilemma, and I relayed the information. She sagged against the wall, her hand to her chest. "Thank goodness." Her smile was a little messy, and her pupils dilated. "Thank you. It was a fun night. Those guys are nice."

I nodded, and said another good night.

Moments later, I was in bed, and Missy's snoring shook the post. I was used to the noise and vibrations and closed my eyes. The sound almost lulled me to sleep now.

The alarms started too early, way too early. Missy's started at six, and went off every ten minutes until seven o'clock, which was when she finally shut the damn thing off. The bed shook again as she climbed from the top bunk, and I drifted back to sleep.

She woke me again thirty minutes later when she returned from the shower. I listened without opening my eyes as she moved around getting ready for the day and groaned when my own alarm woke me at eight.

It felt like an elephant was sitting on my shoulders when I got up, but I had to hurry it up.

Bathroom took five minutes.

Brushing teeth was two.

Face was cleaned. Another minute.

Dressed.

Brushed the hair.

No. That looked bad.

Hair was pulled into a ponytail.

I cringed. Horrible.

Hair ended up in a messy bun. Nod of approval.

Bag was already packed from the night before—and after a light coating of lip-gloss and swipe of eyeliner, I was out the door.

So was everyone else. I got behind a group of five girls leaving the dorm. There was no time for breakfast, but I veered by the library. Everyone grabbed their coffee from the coffee shop on campus, or a few in the food court. Everyone forgot about the library, because who was really there so early in the morning?

Coffee ordered, paid for, then picked up, and I was back outside. All the sidewalks were full now. It was nine-fifteen when I spotted my poli-sci building. I reached for the door handle, opened it, and it was caught by a hand above mine.

I looked—I shouldn't have.

Shay Coleman smirked down at me, his body close enough that I felt a draft of warmth from his heat. He curved his lips up, pleased to have caught me off guard. "Morning."

I grunted and was acutely aware of how he was right behind me up the two flights of stairs to our class.

A line of students stopped at the top, waiting to enter the room. I waited at the end, needing to cover the last two steps. Shay was right behind me. His one arm was on the handrail as he moved his foot to my same step.

He was leaning right over me.

Tension filled me.

I could lean my head back against his chest. He wouldn't move away. I didn't think he'd move at all, and considering it, some of the tension faded, but that effect he had on me was still there. I bit down on my lip. I couldn't move away from him. The group of students moved forward. One more step. One to go.

I moved up.

So did Shay.

He resumed his same stance.

His breath coated the back of my neck, and I almost groaned. Almost. I held it in.

Pop quiz. Those words surged in my mind. I needed to remember what we were doing, where we were going.

The last step was cleared, and then we were through the doorway. Shay walked behind me, his arm lifted and rested on my shoulder.

I could feel Becs's and Aby's attention sharpen, so did so many other girls in the room. If I shrugged him off, that'd produce more attention. We all knew how much I loved attention.

Shay's soft chuckle grazed my ear. We moved farther down the middle aisle until we got to my desk. His arm fell away, he swung into his seat, and like one being, we both sat at the same time.

The back of my neck grew hot.

Something was thrown at me. I turned and Linde mouthed, "WTF?"

Shay chuckled again—so sure of himself, so arrogant, so cocky.

Linde lifted his hands up, still waiting for my response.

What could I say?

I rolled my shoulders before turning back around. The professor arrived, and it was like how Shay called it.

"Close your books. Clear your desks. Take out your pens. Pop quiz, everyone."

"Girl."

That was Linde's greeting to me once class was done. Shay got up and left, not looking back. Becs, Aby, and two other friends picked up their pace. I had no idea if they were going after him or just excited to leave class.

I knew what Linde was asking with that one word. "I felt like I would've caused a scene if I pushed his arm off."

"What is going on with you and Shay?" He waited in front of me as I grabbed my bag. We walked together out of the classroom and building. "Is he messing with you?"

"Does he do that with girls?"

He opened the door, holding it for me, and I glanced over for his response.

He let the door go, falling in line again beside me. "I've never seen it, but that's weird. You want me to say something to him?"

Say something? After Shay told me not to poke my nose in Linde's business, and Linde was offering to poke his in this business. Ironic. My mouth dried up. If he did, Shay could tell him about my concerns. Linde could be pissed at me.

I shook my head. "Nah. It'll sort out. I'm sure."

Some guys called Linde's name as we neared the food court. He pointed a fist toward them, then broke away from me. He started walking backwards. "I'll say something if you want me to."

I just gave him a grin. I didn't want that. Linde was my second friend here. "If I do, I'll say the word."

He stretched his arm out toward me, a cocky grin on his face. "Word. Just say it."

"Say what word?" Kristina asked from behind me. I turned, watching her sort through a stack of mail as she looked between Linde and me.

"Nothing." I fixed her with a smile. Shay was gone. I wouldn't see him for another forty-eight hours. Already things were feeling better. "How are you feeling?"

She groaned. "Embarrassed. I never drink. Now you know why."

We laughed, heading through the line into the cafeteria. I grabbed a salad and water first. Linde didn't just pour drinks last night. He ordered a pizza, so today was healthy me. Today was my fight against the freshman fifteen. No to pizza, yes to leafy greens.

My stomach was frowning all on its own as I sat down. Kristina was still in line. She was grabbing a bowl of soup.

Then I saw her roommate and other two friends, as well. They were heading toward the table with bags in hand. Casey tossed her bag onto the table across from me. "Hey, Kennedy."

I picked up my glass of water, holding it to my lips. "So, you *do* know my name."

Her grin faltered. Laura and Sarah dropped their bags in their own seats and turned for the food, but Casey paused. "Did you think I really didn't know?"

"There was suspicion."

Kristina came back, bypassing Casey and setting her tray down. "Where'd you stay last night? I didn't see you this morning before class."

"I—" She scratched behind her ear. "I stayed in Laura and Sarah's room."

"No, you didn't." Kristina rounded the table to sit next to me. "I knocked on their door. They didn't answer either."

"Because . . ." Her eyes darted around as if she were stalling before she continued, "Because we all slept in. We were all late for our classes today." Her hand pointed behind her. "I'm going to grab some food. I'm starving."

"That's odd." Kristina watched her go.

I stabbed my lettuce.

"What's odd?" Sarah was the first back, only an orange and water bottle in her hands.

"You were late for class today?"

Her forehead wrinkled, and her eyebrows pinched together. "No, we weren't. We didn't go. This is us finally getting up."

Casey had lied.

Kristina glanced to me but asked Sarah, "What'd you guys end up doing last night?"

"Studied downstairs with Kreigerson and Boots until they asked if we wanted to head to a party. We all slept at their house."

I still didn't know who these people were.

"Casey told me she stayed in your room and you guys were late for class this morning."

Sarah laughed, finishing unpeeling her orange. "I don't know why she did that, but we didn't and she didn't. We finally got our asses up an hour ago and had to beg Kreigerson to give us a ride to the dorm. I already skipped one class, no way am I missing the rest of them today."

Casey and Laura came back, but Kristina didn't mention anything. They talked about classes. There was more Kreigerson talk, among other guys' names.

I watched how Kristina's shoulders slumped farther and farther through lunch. Casey's lies were hurting her. I held my tongue. Like Linde's protein/or-whatever-else-it-was shake wasn't mine, neither was this. And with that final decision, I pushed it out of my mind.

We finished lunch, and I went with the other three to check our mailboxes. After that, we parted ways. I checked my phone. I had enough time to look up local psychology jobs that might be open.

Pop quiz was aced, and I was back to my regular schedule of being a loner.

# CHAPTER SEVEN

Missy was studying in Holly's room. Not surprising.

I was in mine, busy looking for a job. It was the beginning of my search. I'd have to narrow everything down before I even got to the part where I started filling out the applications.

I was going over one more search on the Internet when my phone rang.

I picked it up. "Hello?"

"Don't you answer your cell phone? Ever?"

It was my brother. I frowned. "No one calls me. Why would I?"

He groaned from frustration. "I did. I have been all day."

It was Thursday. The rest of Monday through Wednesday had been uneventful, which was glorious in my mind. I was purposely avoiding leaving my room that night because Thursday night was also the beginning of the weekend for the partiers. I still had two classes tomorrow. It wasn't the beginning of my weekend.

I replied, "Do you need something?"

"Do you know what happened to your friend?"

"Kristina?"

"No, the queen of the slutty ones."

"Huh?"

"The girl I asked if I could sleep with."

A light bulb turned on. "Casey?"

"Yeah. Do you know what happened to her? Or what the rumor is?"

Gage always laughed and joked. It was his personality. His humor was missing now, which made me grip the phone tighter to my ear. I felt a tightness forming in my throat, right at the base of it. "What are you talking about?"

But she had lied to Kristina.

I didn't know what happened after that. I hadn't seen or gone down to hang out with them. It wasn't an everyday thing for me. "The last time I saw them was at lunch on Monday. Why?"

"She was raped."

I hadn't heard that right. "No. No way."

He let out a deep breath. "Yes. Yes way. Listen to me." His voice sounded closer to the phone. "She has to report it. You have to talk to her about it."

This wasn't—I was breaking out. I was sweating, even my armpits were feeling it. This was not something I did. "How do you know this? Are you sure? Most rumors aren't true. We both know this."

"Listen."

God, he was so serious. It was freaking me out. Ice settled in the pit of my stomach.

"I'm telling you she was raped. I heard enough to believe it. You have to talk to her."

This was not my area of expertise. Being alone. Not being included, not getting involved, those were my areas. Hanging out with guys and not flirting or dating them, too. But this—I looked down. My shirt was soaked under both arms.

"I'll talk to Kristina."

"Who's that?"

"My friend! The non-slutty one." And fuck. We should stop referring to them that way. I amended, "I mean, she doesn't go out with them that much."

"I know what you meant."

"Yeah."

He was silent a moment, then gave me a quiet, "Yeah."

I scooted back and pulled my feet up to rest on my desk. My legs were pressed against my chest, and I rested my head against them, the phone still to my ear. "She was raped. Are you sure? Who was it?"

A lone tear slid down my cheek. I didn't know it was there until it made its trek down.

"She was, and I don't know for sure. I heard enough to know it was a football player, but that's it. Be safe, okay? If you go out with them, tell me or tell someone. Just be safe."

"I will."

I didn't say how I wouldn't go out with them, or how they wouldn't go out after this, because the truth was that they would. If Casey was raped, and I only kept the 'if' there because she hadn't said the words herself, she was acting as if she hadn't been.

"Call me if you need anything."

My fingers felt numb. My lips, too. "I will." The words tumbled from me.

I felt removed from my body as I hung up, and I sat there. I didn't know what to do or what the best plan of action even was. Casey wasn't my friend, not really. I picked up the phone and then put it back down. Should I tell Kristina? Should she handle this?

That was an easy opt-out. It was more right for her to handle this, but Gage called me. He told me.

Shit.

I didn't want to be the one to say something. Who would? Casey could hate me. She could yell at me, or hurl things at me. I didn't know what she would do. This was like telling a friend her boyfriend had cheated on her, but a hundred times worse. Or maybe not. Maybe she'd dissolve into tears, happy that someone else knew and someone else understood.

I sucked in a ragged breath.

I didn't plan on it, but I watched as I reached for my cell phone. My finger pulled up Shay's number and pressed the call button.

I was so glad Missy wasn't in the room. That was an afterthought as I heard it ring.

A second later, he answered, "Yeah?"

I didn't reply. My throat wasn't working.

"Clarke?" he barked into the phone.

I still didn't say anything, but I sniffled. Another tear slid free, and I flicked it away.

"Kennedy?" He softened his tone.

Why did I call him? I hated him.

Then I asked, my voice making myself grimace, I sounded so raw, "You were pro-choice."

"Huh?" There was loud music in the background, and he added, "Hold on." A moment later, the music faded. His voice was louder. "You're asking about the abortion issues? Do we need to know about it for tomorrow?"

"Linde said his sister was raped. I was wondering why you were pro-choice."

He was silent.

Then, "Are you pregnant?"

My throat hurt so much. My fingers curled into my jeans by my knees. "Why were you pro-choice? Can you tell me? Please."

Another beat where he didn't answer.

His voice dropped. "Why are you asking? Kennedy, were you . . . "

Oh, my goodness. He was going to ask me.

"No! Just tell me why you were pro-choice."

"Look." He cleared his throat, sounding so kind, so considerate. So gentle. "Why are you asking me this stuff? Kennedy, did someone hurt you?"

"I just want to know."

"I won't tell you until you tell me."

He was so stubborn. I groaned, pressing my knees to my chest. "Why do you have to be so difficult?"

He laughed quietly. "Uh, we're kind of a match there." He prodded again, "Tell me why, Kennedy. Did someone hurt you?"

"No." I lifted my head back up. My voice grew hoarse. "But a friend of mine might've been. My brother called and told me he heard someone I knew was raped. And I have no clue what to do."

"Oh."

I waited, bated breath. My heart even paused.

Nothing.

I cried out, "Are you going to say anything?"

"I don't know what to say. I was worried about you. You're not hurt? Are you sure?"

"Yes, I'm not hurt. Why were you pro-choice?"

He cursed under his breath. "You're pushing this on me now? Fucking A. Okay, I didn't share because I didn't want you to look at me how you looked at those girls. I'm pro-choice because Linde is, because he's my buddy, and I'm going to back him up. That's why."

"For real?" I didn't know if I was relieved or even more frustrated. "I was hoping you could tell me what to do. I have no fucking clue." I chewed on the inside of my cheek. "What would you do?"

"Talk to the girl."

"I'm not really friends with her."

"Are you friends with someone who is friends with her?"

"Yeah, but if it were me, I wouldn't want anyone to know. Not until I chose to tell them."

He was quiet for another moment. Then, so damned softly that the kindness I heard from him dislodged more tears, he said, "Then you have to go to her. I'm guessing she hasn't said anything."

"Yeah."

"I'm sorry."

"Yeah." I had to go. I didn't want to. My fingers had formed knots around my pants. They didn't want to let go either.

"Look, do you want to talk to Linde about it?"

I should, but I heard myself saying, "No." Linde was easy. He was a surface friend. Things were good with him. Things weren't with Shay, but he was someone I'd already gone deep with. That made sense. That was why I called him and not Linde.

I had to go.

"I'm going to go talk to her."

"You want me to come, just be there for you?"

I barked out a quiet laugh. "That'd be weird."

"I know, but you seem like you could use some support."

I could have him come. I could tell Kristina. I could put this on either of their shoulders, but that wasn't the right thing to do. His presence would put the whole dorm in upheaval. If he visited any girl there, everyone would know. If I told Kristina, I'd be breaking Casey's confidence, even though she hadn't chosen to give it to me.

Both were easy-outs, and I couldn't indulge in either.

"I'm going to hang up and go talk to her."

"Okay. I'll have my phone on all night. Call if you need anything."

That felt nice, but I frowned. "I still hate you."

He laughed. "I know. I hate you, too."

We hated each other again. Everything was right again.

Kristina was in their room, but Casey wasn't. Their door was open, but I still knocked, rapping my knuckles against the wood. "Hey, uh, where's your roommate?"

She was sitting in a similar position I just stood from, and putting her feet back on the floor, she motioned for me to come inside. "You can shut the door. I think they're downstairs baking." She laughed under her breath. "Sarah wanted to send cookies to some guy—" *Cookies again!* "—and they decided it was the greatest idea in the world. The last plan I heard was that they were going to do a bunch of cookies, put them on plates, and give them away as gifts."

I joked, "Linde might like to be their friend."

God.

Worst timing ever.

I was horrible at this stuff.

I lingered in the doorway. I didn't come inside, and I hadn't closed the door.

Her slight grin lessened. "Haven't seen you all week."

"Yeah." I lifted up a shoulder, holding it because that was the most awkward thing to do, right? I had to remember to let it drop. "Just been busy with stuff." A girl came up through the back door, and I could hear laughter coming from in there. I looked over, thinking it may have been Casey.

"You okay?"

"Yeah." My attention went back to Kristina, but she had returned to her book. Her highlighter was in the air. "Anything happen with you guys this week? You okay? Casey . . ." I looked back to that door to the stairway.

"Yeah. Why?" She ran the neon yellow marker over some words.

"No reason." I edged back. I got my answer. "I'll—uh—I'll talk to you later?"

"Sure." I heard her response but was heading for the door. "Wait. What—" That came as I opened the door.

Heading down the last two sets of stairs to the kitchen in the basement, I could hear them laughing down there.

Sarah was saying something.

Laura shrieked.

I waited, but no Casey. I pushed open the door and rounded the corner. Aromas of baked cookies filled my nostrils. I could identify the chocolate chip right away.

Casey was sitting on the counter, fiddling with a fork.

Laura was mixing the dough. Sarah was rolling the dough into a large spoon and putting them on the pan. The two were talking to each other, but not Casey. She seemed zoned out.

"Hey!" Laura noticed me. She held up a different mixer covered in dough. "Want some? We'll get you your own spoon."

Sarah turned my way, too, but not Casey. She continued looking down, still holding that fork.

I gestured to her. "Actually, Casey."

She looked.

"Could I talk to you for a second?"

"Me?"

Even Sarah and Laura were surprised, sharing a look.

I nodded, feeling my neck and legs still filled with lead. "Yeah." Holy shit, I didn't want to do this. My insides were screaming for me to turn around, but there was something in the middle of my chest not letting me. If I did, I'd regret it. I didn't know why, or when, but I knew I would. Alarms, and gut instincts. This was the year I was listening to mine.

I motioned for the hallway. "Maybe in the chapel or something?" That'd be empty, for certain.

All three exchanged looks, but Casey shrugged and jumped off the counter. "Sure." She followed me inside.

I stopped, surprised by how quaint and cozy it was. There was red carpet, a small altar, two sitting chairs, and a wood counter with a Bible on top. It was also creepy. I sat on one of the chairs, folding my knees against my chest and wrapping my arms around them.

Casey frowned, sitting on the bottom step of the altar. She threaded her hands together, letting them fall onto her lap. Her legs stretched out before her. "What's up?"

*Um. I heard you were raped. Were you?*

Was that a decent start for this conversation? No. That didn't seem right. "Uh . . ." Kristina was going for social work. She was nice and sensitive. I should've dropped this on her lap to deal with. It was too late for that. "Okay. This is—weird for me, but I have a brother who goes here. I don't know if you knew that."

Her eyebrows smoothed out, arching slightly. "No. I didn't know that. Wait." They pulled back together. "Not Gage Clarke?"

Fuck. She knew my last name. I nodded. "Yeah. Gage."

"We partied with him Sunday night. I had no idea he was your brother, but"—her eyes narrowed and she nodded to herself—"yeah, I can totally see it now. You guys look just like each other."

And speaking of Sunday . . .

I coughed. A lot of phlegm was in my throat. "Um, okay." I put my legs down, rubbing my palms over them. They were suddenly sweaty. "What do you remember from that night?" Wait. Did she not even know herself? Was I going to be the one to tell her?

Maybe I shouldn't do it then. If that were the case, maybe I should make a pathetic excuse and talk more to Gage, get more facts before I said anything. Yeah. That felt more right. I was more comfortable with that.

Then she murmured, her eyes flooding with tears, "You know, don't you."

My throat stopped working. That hadn't been a question.

Her head hung down, and her hands reached for the bottom of her shirt. She balled it into her fists. "I can't believe you know."

My voice was just as soft as hers. "So, it's true."

Her head lifted, just a little bit. "Yeah."

She was raped. Gage told me, but a part of me hoped it wasn't true.

I had no clue what to do now.

I scooted off the chair. I didn't want to assail her, but getting closer, a little below her felt like the right thing to do. I looped my hands together, pulling my feet together with my legs flat against the carpet. "Uh . . . What happened?"

"You don't know?" She glanced up, wiping at a tear.

I shook my head. "I was just told there's a rumor."

"There's a rumor?" A sob left her, a slight note of hysteria blending with it. She began rocking herself back and forth. "I can't believe this is happening."

"Hey!" Laura knocked abruptly on the door. "Can I come in? What's going on?"

Panic flitted over Casey's face. "No. They can't come in. They don't know."

I rose and locked the door swiftly. "Um, just give us a second. We . . . uh . . . " I looked back to Casey. She was watching me with pleading eyes. My heart broke. If it'd been me—my resolve hardened. "I'm, um, I'm thinking about losing my virginity." I backed away from the door. "It's extremely private and personal, and embarrassing, and I'd really like as much privacy as possible. Thank you."

Would that work?

I added, biting my bottom lip, "And don't tell anyone about this. Oh, and Casey might have to talk to me about this at times. Just so you know. I am going to do it, so, yeah . . ." I raised a finger to the door, trying to sound convincing. "Don't try to change my mind."

"Um. Okay. We're heading up. Casey, can you hear me?"

Casey cleared her throat, too. "Yeah. I'll be up later."

Once Laura left, Casey snorted into quiet laughter. She shook her head, wiping at some of her tears. "You're the worst liar in the world."

She'd be surprised.

I shrugged, taking my seat again, but an inch closer. "They'll bug you later. You can tell them anything you want. I'm sure they bought it."

"Thank you."

My gaze met hers. I found myself nodding again. "Yeah." My heart plunged once more. Back to the real topic. "I'm sorry about what happened to you."

She picked at the bottom of her jeans. "Yeah. Well. What can you do about it?"

Everything.

That word stuck in my throat.

I reached forward and touched her hand, stopping her from pulling a whole thread from her pants. She didn't look up. "You can say something."

She didn't move.

I licked my lips. They were so dry they almost hurt. "I don't know the details. I don't know what happened, or who it was, but my brother called me and told me he heard a rumor you were raped." I paused. My heart was beating so hard. "The rumor wasn't saying that a guy slept with you. It wasn't saying you were a whore, a slut, or an easy lay. He didn't say that someone scored with you. Whatever he heard was enough for him to call me because he was worried it would happen to me, too."

She pulled her hand away, but not far.

"I talked to someone about someone I knew who was raped, but I didn't say it was you."

Her head lifted, and her eyes were full of alarm.

I repeated, "I didn't say it was you. And this person doesn't know we're friends. He won't figure it out."

"He?"

"It wasn't my brother."

"Oh." She went back to picking at her jeans.

She was so silent.

Was this how it was supposed to be? Was I supposed to do something else? Were there fucking cue cards for this?

"I haven't told anyone else."

She looked back up again.

"I'm here. If you want to talk, whatever. Hug. Cry. Scream. I'd rob an ice cream shop with you if you wanted."

She started to laugh.

"No, really. I would. That should have its own square in the food pyramid as far as I'm concerned. They lump it in with dairy, but it should be on its own. It's the best food invention of all time."

Her laughter rose, and she flicked away a couple tears. "Thank you for that."

"For what?"

A third bout of laughter. I frowned. She thought I was joking. This was a problem.

"Thank you." She reached forward. Her hand covered mine. "I mean it. Thank you."

"Okay." I was still frowning. "I'm not joking about the ice cream. I'm really not."

"I know." The laughter subsided, but a few chuckles escaped. "And that means a lot—that you'd break in somewhere for me."

"Burglary. Breaking in is just that, breaking in. Burglary is breaking in with the intent to steal, and my intent would be to steal ice cream. By the gallons, if I could." Fuck. "Do you want to do that right now? I could figure out a way to break into the cafeteria. That wouldn't be burglary because we already have a right to that ice cream. We'd just be breaking in."

"No." She shook her head. "But thank you. It does mean a lot."

"Okay." Just as long as she knew. "Do you . . . are you okay?" I was an idiot. "No. That's the wrong question. I'm not good with this stuff."

"No. You're actually being fantastic." Her head hung low again.

"Okay."

Kristina would know what to say if she were here. Or Shay. Linde, for sure. What would Gage say? He'd know. He was someone I could channel. I ran through all the jokes he might say, but he wouldn't. He'd be nice. He'd be kind. He'd say the perfect thing.

I should've had him come.

"I don't know what to say. I'm sorry for that, but I'm here."

I let out another deep breath and just sat there. What else could I do? Then, after a few minutes of silence, she reached out. She didn't look at me. She didn't get up and leave. She just sat there and she cried and she held my hand.

I would've sat forever if she wanted me to.

# CHAPTER EIGHT

"Clarke."

I was walking to class the next morning when Shay hurried his pace to catch up. He gestured to an empty sidewalk around the side of the building, and I went with him. We moved farther away to an abandoned set of stairs that led off the left side of the building. It was rarely used because there was nothing it led to, just a patch of grass and trees all around. I had a guess what Shay was going to talk about, and for that, it was perfect.

He lounged against one of the two pillars by the stairs. "Is your friend okay after last night?"

I nodded, sitting down on one of the steps. I gathered my bag on my lap, hugging it to me. "Yeah. She knows I'm there for her. That's all I can do."

"She say who raped her?"

I shook my head. "I didn't ask. If she wants to tell me, I think she will."

"Was she raped at a party?"

I looked up. There was a reason he was asking. "You heard?"

"Was it Sunday night's party?"

He did know. "You heard."

His jaw clenched. "Yeah. I heard. That shit pisses me off."

"Me, too."

"Look." He sat next to me, turning his head my way. "I heard the rumor. I know who did it. I know who it was done to. I just needed to know if the girl from Sunday's party was your friend or not."

I frowned. "What are you hearing?"

He paused a second, like he was deciding if he should tell me or not. His jaw clenched once more. "You heard it was a football player?"

I nodded. My stomach twisted in a knot.

He said, "I know the guy. Casey Winchem. That's your friend, isn't it?"

He knew the guy. Of course, he would know him. He was on his team.

I said faintly, "Yeah. She's my friend."

He swore, turning away. "He has a type. Long legs. Brown hair. Dark eyes. He likes pretty faces." He glanced back, his eyes lidded. "You fit that type."

Wha—

"Are you saying . . ." No. What was he saying?

"If you'd gone to that party, it could've been you."

Gage's phone call made so much more sense. He'd been worried about me. My friend. Similar type.

*It could've been me.*

Shay's words echoed in my head. I felt the first slice of fear. I'd never been legit scared of men before. There were other feelings about guys. How I hated them at times, how they were annoying, how they wanted to screw me, or use me... But I'd never been scared like this. This was . . . I wanted to bury my head on my lap. This was new. This was alien. This was not what I wanted to feel.

"Oh."

He frowned at me. "Oh?"

I swallowed a knot. It could've been me. "I never thought of that. She asked me to go to a party Friday night." I might've gone. If I had, maybe I would've had fun. I might've gone a second time. I might've gone instead of going to his house and studying. "We were at your place that night."

"I know." He cursed again before standing. He pulled out his phone to check the time. "We gotta go. Look, this could be a problem for the team. Is she going to report it?"

"Why?"

Did he want her not to? Did he want me to encourage her to stay silent? I was getting pissed just thinking about that. It was a violation of her body, and he was going to suggest—

"She should. This asshole's done this to other girls. He needs to get locked up."

Oh. My whole argument deflated.

"You *want* her to report it?"

"Fuck yeah." He narrowed his eyes. "Wait. You thought I wouldn't want that to happen?"

I used his words. "This could be a problem for the team."

He rolled his eyes, cringing at the same time. "Bad choice of words. Yes, I want her to report it. This school handles sexual assaults in a good way. They take it seriously and the girl's not blamed. They have policies about it. Every now and then, we hear about a rape and the team gets a whole lecture, in case one of the guys decides to do something stupid. It's a whole preventative strategy, or that's what Coach told me one time.

From what I heard, he drugged her, took her to his bedroom, and raped her. She tried to get away, but the fucker had her so doped up that she could barely lift her arms. Her friends thought she hooked up with someone and stayed, too."

I gazed down at the cement. I hadn't asked Casey for details because a part of me didn't want to know.

I wished I didn't.

She couldn't fight him. She couldn't lift her arms.

He cursed. "I thought you knew."

I shook my head. "I just knew it happened, not the details."

He raised his hand and then held it in the air. He didn't know what to do with it. He finally patted my knee. "I'm sorry, Clarke."

My last name felt right. That put space between us again. I could muster my composure again.

I nodded a couple of times, wiping my palm over my eyes. "I'm fine." Class was probably starting. "Go to class."

He didn't leave. He stayed. "Are you coming?"

I shook my head. "No." My heart hurt too much.

"I'll take notes for you. I'll stop by your place later."

I wanted to laugh. The girls in my hallway would mess their pants, but I didn't. He touched my shoulder once more before going past me and entering the building. I was thankful this entrance was never used. Emotions I didn't understand and didn't want held me sitting on that step long after Shay was gone.

I stayed and imagined not being able to lift my arms.

# CHAPTER NINE

I was in my room that night when Shay called me. Grateful for Missy's absence, like always, I answered and leaned back in my chair. "What's up, Coleman?"

He paused a beat before laughing under his breath. "Coleman. Okay. I get it. We're like chill buddies? Is that it?"

Was there a better description for us? I shrugged to myself. "We kinda hate each other but still seek each other out. I figured it's time to move on from calling you 'That Guy I Hate' in my head to a name. Last names seem fitting. You can keep calling me Clarke."

"I never know what I'm going to get with you."

I was purposefully keeping it light. I wasn't ready to dive into the deep waters we had been in when I saw him this morning.

Light and surface. That's what I wanted at that moment.

"Guess that's my charm. I'm not like all those other girls whose panties go up in flames when you walk into a room."

I saw a chain email from Gage, and instantly hit reply. "*Stop sending me these stupid things.*"

"What?"

Shay was mocking me. I could literally hear the smile in his voice. I breathed a little easier, grateful he was following my lead.

He said, "You mean that burning aroma I smell isn't your thong? And here I was getting cocky when it came to you."

"First, *ew.*" Burning smell? "That's disgusting. If anything, it'd be me having to smoke a cigarette before seeing you. I don't know if you're aware of this, but you're a little stressful to deal with."

He barked out a laugh. "That's called charisma and primal animal sexiness. It oozes out, and you are affected. You're just so messed up you don't even know what it is. Your body is stressed from fighting itself so you don't lunge at me. I know what's good, Clarke." He dropped his tone. "And it's definitely me."

Insert eye roll.

"And two," I kept on as if he hadn't spoken, "we hate each other. Remember? Let's cut to the chase of why you called so we can resume the vow of silence we've taken around each other."

"Holy fuck, woman. Vow of silence? What are you, a nun?"

"Why'd you call?"

I wasn't starting to enjoy this call. There was no point. This guy wasn't funny. He wasn't sexy—his words, not mine—and there was no thawing at my hatred wall for him. Nope. No thawing at all. My body was warming because I had a sweater on, and in this weather, was that really needed?

I think not.

"I've got those notes for you."

Everything went on high alert. I bolted upright. Red alarms were blaring in my eardrums. "Okay."

"I'm downstairs."

"What?" A myriad of curses spewed from me before I realized I was even cursing. I shoved back the chair to stand. "Why are you here? I have a rule!"

"A rule?"

*Fuck, fuck, fuckity fuck!*

The sweater was too constricting all of a sudden. I felt like I was being choked to death. It was too close to my neck. Hitting the speaker button, I flung my phone onto the bed and tugged at my sweater.

"Yes. Guys I know don't come here. Ever."

"Any guy? Are you serious?"

Pulling off the sweater hadn't helped. I still felt like I couldn't breathe. Scrambling around, I grabbed for a tank top. It was see-through. I almost tore it as I pulled it off. "Yes. Any guy. Especially guys like you."

"Me?" His confusion was clear. "What's wrong with guys like me? Because we hate each other?"

I tore through my drawer and grabbed at a black top. It was short-sleeved, but it'd do. I yanked it on, popping my head out. "Hot guys. Guys who make girls drool. Guys who warrant attention and jealousy. And since we're on the topic, if you ever see me in public, act like you don't know me."

"You're a nutcase."

"Just go right past me." I brushed my hands against each other, going the opposite direction. "Like two passing buses in the night."

"The phrase is two passing ships in the night, and no. I'm not a complete asshole. If I see you in public, I reserve my right to come over and piss you off. I'm starting to get enjoyment from this on the daily."

"No." I almost gasped. "Daily?"

"Daily," he drawled. "Now, get that cute ass down here so I can give you these notes."

I groaned but disconnected the call, grabbed my room key, and headed down. I was fine with letting the door slam behind me. It matched my mood, and fuck those two neighbors who hissed at anything that moved in the hallway. We were people. People had to move to exist.

Their door opened and one appeared, her face already scrunched in annoyance.

I gave her the middle finger, gliding right past. "Save it. I'm in a hurry."

She huffed but retreated back into her room. Their door closed with a soft click.

I rolled my eyes, hurrying down the stairs. Swinging around the last doorway that separated the living area and the lobby, I stopped in confusion.

There was no Shay.

I expected him to be leaning against the desk, four or five girls hanging on his every word, but nothing. Only two girls talking in the waiting lobby and Sabrina, who laughed when she saw me and pointed out the door. "He's at the back door."

"Oh." I brightened. That was much better. "Thanks." I went back inside and down the first floor. It was the quickest way to that door. I was almost grinning from delight as I shoved open the back door. If I hit him, hey, all was fair in the war we were fighting of who could piss each other off the best.

It didn't.

He was leaning against the wall, the back of his head resting on the brick, and he looked over to smirk at me. "I want to see your room."

I thrust my hand out. "I'll take those notes."

That smirk just widened. He patted his bag and pushed off from the wall. "They're in my email. I need to get on a computer." He patted my arm and moved past me, heading inside. "I can use yours."

"Hey!" I followed him in.

He was looking up the stairs. "Sabrina said you were on the fourth floor. You saw my place. I want to see yours. It's only fair."

He wasn't waiting for my go-ahead. He was already up and rounding second floor to third. He'd be at my floor before I could get there. "Stop! I am not okay with this."

He was at the third-floor door. He glanced down with that same goddamn smirk. "Better tell me which room or I'm going to hang out in the hallway."

"Why are you always smirking? Is it permanently attached to your face?"

"What room, Clarke?" He was at my hallway door.

Fucking hell. I gritted my teeth. "Wait. Just wait. My door automatically locks."

He'd opened the door but let it shut. Waiting as I covered the last set of stairs, I refused to let him see me panting. I stood there, purposely holding my breath until he narrowed his eyes and cocked his head to the side. "Breathe, Clarke. You're going to pass out."

I almost burped out the small pocket of air I'd been holding. "I hate you so much."

"Yeah, yeah." He waved that off. "We get it. Eternal damnation in hell, the whole shebang. Whatever." He nodded to the door. "Stop stalling. I want to see your room."

I was picturing pitchforks and fire. Maybe that was the burning smell he mentioned. It was hell, and all the fire in there. I yanked the door, glaring as I did. "Was this Sabrina's idea?"

"Nope. All mine." He was right behind me. I could feel his breathing. "She refused to tell me your room number, said I had to call."

My eyes widened at the thought of him coming up by himself, strolling down the hallway, and then knocking on my door. Good Lordy gracious. Too many would've seen him at my door. I would've been the talk of the dorm.

I shuddered, unlocked, and entered my room. I gestured around. "Here it is. Not a three-story house with God knows how many other players living there, but it's my little home at college."

He came in, and I shut the door behind him.

He was nodding, taking it all in. "I like it. It's cozy." He pointed to Missy's desk. "Yours?"

"I'm *not* going to be insulted by that." Her desk was covered in stuffed animals, framed pictures, and candy. I nodded toward mine. "Much cleaner, and can I say, a lot more tasteful, too." There were no pictures, no stuffed anything, and the only digestible thing was my coffee. My shelves were covered in my textbooks, notepads, and any office stuff I might need like a calculator and stapler. I had a marker board hung up with my schedule and a list of all the homework I needed to get done for the next few weeks.

He sat and gazed at the board. "You have every week planned out?"

"You don't? It's called using a syllabus."

"Pretty sure my syllabus doesn't look like that."

He was right. I was three weeks ahead. I kept that to myself. "Excuse me." I bent close to him, ignoring the proximity of our bodies and how my hip would touch him if I shifted a half-inch to my left.

I typed in my password so he could get to his email.

The room was getting warm again.

Maybe my thermostat was broken?

I finished and stepped back. "There. Pull up the notes, Coleman."

He chuckled under his breath. "Coleman." His fingers were fast as he typed. "Your email?"

I gave it to him, and it was forwarded in the next second.

I pressed my lips together. "You could've done that anywhere."

"I know." He scooted the chair back and looked around the room again. "But like I said, I was in the area and I wanted to see where you lived." He went over to the television and began looking through the movies. "You have a lot of chick flicks." He pulled out one of mine, one that wasn't a chick flick. "This is a good one."

"It's my roommate's." I folded my arms over my chest. "I only watch romantic sappy movies."

"I doubt that, for some reason." He picked up the other one of mine. "We should watch this."

"*Gladiator*?"

"Yeah." He pulled it out and hit the open button on the DVD player.

"What? Now?" Panic was rising again. It had settled, thinking he'd leave as quick as he came. Nope. It was rising to the red needle as he sat on the loveseat.

"Yeah. Why not?" He looked to my clock on the nightstand. "I've got a couple of hours to kill. If I head home, the guys will want to head to the bar or something."

"Don't you have a game tomorrow?" Shouldn't he have training to do? Or carb training? Or . . . what did football players do before a big game day? I looked bleakly to the screen. The movie was starting. Did they watch *Gladiator*? Was that part of their routine? "You can borrow this if you want. You can take it to your house and watch it *there*."

He patted the seat next to him. "Come on, Clarke. I'm not going to put the moves on you. We don't like each other, remember?"

My scowl was back in place. "You're making fun of me."

"Because you're so easy to mess with. Seriously. Come and sit." He patted the seat once again. "If I put my arm around you, it's because I have to stretch. Can't cramp up. I'm the quarterback." He winked.

"Stop fucking with me."

Missy could come in. She usually did at least once or twice. They'd gone to eat, but she always came in to leave her things. Holly and the cousin walked with her because they couldn't walk an entire hallway alone. Then she'd go back to their room before coming back again to change if they decided to go out to a party or somewhere else.

He couldn't be in my room during that prime time.

He narrowed his eyes. "You're upset, for real?"

"Yes. You don't know what it's like."

They'd see him. They'd look at me differently. They'd want to use me or get angry because he was hanging out with me and not them. Missy thought I was beneath her. So did the others.

He cursed, scooting forward and resting his elbows on his knees. "You want me to leave?"

Yes!

I should've said that word, but I didn't. My mouth didn't move. Why didn't it move? I bit my lip, and what I knew would happen, happened.

I heard Missy's voice in the hallway.

New panic that I'd never felt before stuck in my throat. "Get in the closet. Now!"

"Wha—" He stood, and I shoved him in. "Are you serious?" A hanger poked his cheek. He batted it away, scowling at me now. "You're insane."

"Sorry."

They were at the door.

She used her key to unlock it.

I shut my closet door and stood in front of it, feeling like an idiot. My smile would've won the most awkward prize ever. I even twiddled my thumbs together.

Missy came in, saw me, and stopped. Her eyebrows dipped together. "You look weird."

I stopped twiddling my thumbs. "No, I don't."

Holly was right behind her. "What are you doing?"

"Standing."

"We can see that."

I raised one of my feet up behind me. "I mean, I'm practicing my balance. You guys should, too."

Missy snorted, going to her desk. She tossed her keys down and checked her email.

"Your balance?" Holly lifted her left leg up. "An odd way to pass the time, but yeah. I can see the appeal. Do you do yoga, Kennedy?"

I wanted to curse at them. I wanted to rage. I wanted them to go away.

I just smiled. "Maybe I should try."

"Yeah." Her eyes lit up. "We're going to start doing meditation. Missy, we should start tomorrow." She looked back. "We could meet in our room, and if we get too many people, we can use the chapel downstairs. It's a good Zen-like room, has that peaceful feel to it."

That room was creepy, and it would always make me think of Casey. "Sure. You bet."

"Done." Missy shut her computer down and changed into a different shirt. She grabbed her phone, but her hands hovered over her keys. "Are you going to be in here tonight?"

Holly glanced to her, and I knew what she was thinking. *It isn't like she has a life.* My roommate's words hung in the air again, filling the air up with tension.

I wasn't going to do yoga anymore.

I nodded. "I think so." I pointed to her keys. "You can leave them. If I do go somewhere, I'll bring them to Holly's room or leave them with the floor advisor."

"Is she on duty tonight?"

"Yeah. All night." That meant she'd be in her room the whole time.

"Okay." She lifted her mouth in a closed-off smile, though her eyes didn't look it. "See you later."

She moved after Holly as they left. Holly gazed at me a moment, as if she wanted to say something, but she didn't.

As soon as the door closed, Shay reached out.

I started to step aside, but his hand wrapped around my arm and he hauled me inside with him.

"Hey. What are yo—"

My words were swallowed by his mouth.

# CHAPTER TEN

Shay Coleman was kissing me.

That thought barely registered before my blood warmed, a full-body tingle went through me, wracking all the way to my fingers and toes. Holy shit. I couldn't think, and his lips were moving over mine. They were asking for something, and I answered. I didn't know what I was doing, but my mouth opened, and his tongue slid inside. He was kissing me with an extra roughness than I'd felt with guys before, but I was melting.

I lifted my hands to his chest.

What were we doing?

I hated Coleman.

At the reminder, I began to pull away.

He groaned, tightening his hold on my arms. "No, no."

"But wha—"

"Stop. Okay?" He pulled back, just slightly. I could feel him, all of him. His hand fell to my waist, rounded over my hip, and he tugged me closer. I was lined up against him, and I could feel more than just his jeans. "We hate each other. Fine. But not right now." His lips nipped at mine. I felt them smile as he murmured, "I don't hate you right now at all."

But he would. I would.

I was still holding back. What was I doing? Really?

"Sha—"

"Clarke, stop." He dipped his body down, and his other hand touched my other hip. He lifted me and moved between my legs. We were in my closet. He was holding me against the wall, and he was standing there. I was half-straddling him. His lips grazed over mine, softly that time.

That was it. That was all I needed.

The last of my resistance faded, and I wound my arms around his neck, molding my body against him. "Fine." I pressed my lips to his. "But this has new rules. Make-out sessions: first rule, we don't talk."

"Yeah." He growled, his lips covering mine again, drawing a moan from me. "You're damn right. We don't talk." Then he was back to kissing me, and I was right with him.

*Gladiator* played while we made out on my bed.

I locked the door. I'd never been so happy that Missy left her keys. She was locked out, and then the movie was turned up, enough to drown out any vocals that might slip, and I was going to turn the light off, but Shay grabbed me. He lifted me and almost threw me onto the bed, coming with me, and his lips found mine once again. He sank down on top of me, his body resting between my legs, and that was how we spent Friday night.

His hands glided and touched under my shirt, covering my breasts.

I shoved his hand away, but with a wicked grin, he bent down to start kissing my stomach. Whoa. I was a mess, panting, and feeling this flooding sensation all over. His lips were moving over my skin, raising a whole storm of pleasure, and I pawed at his shoulders. He raised up to find my mouth, and I was the one to put his hand on my breast. He didn't undo my bra, but he slipped underneath it, cupping me fully, and his thumb rubbed over my nipple.

I cursed and moaned, tightening my legs around his back right over his waist. He was the one to break away and groan this time. I could feel him, resting so close to my entrance, but we weren't going there.

If these sessions continued, maybe. If not, totally fine with that. And that was a big *if*. I didn't like this guy. Remember?

I paused, pulling my lips away and frowning to myself. Was I trying to remind myself or him?

My head was filled with these dark and swirly feelings. Want. Desire. Lust. I wasn't going to tell him about that. He'd say it was because of his primal animal sexiness, but I whimpered, his mouth capturing mine again. I had to admit there must've been some of that going on. It was infecting me, making me act all wanton, like a girl.

"Stop thinking." He rose so he could whisper the words to my ear, and I melted again. That was a caress, reminding me of all the other times he'd spoken so only I could hear. Goddamn. That was intimate. Then his hands rested on the snap of my jeans, and I woke up. He was about to go to a whole other level of intimacy.

"No." I caught his hand. "I'm not ready."

"Okay." His hand slid back under my shirt. I thought he was going back to my breast, which was a pleasant thought. She was missing him, but he didn't. He lifted my shirt up, and I helped him tug it over my head.

I didn't need that short-sleeved shirt. What a good idea. This was so much better, but no. He had to join me. I raised his shirt, and he lifted, grabbing the fabric and throwing it to the floor. I registered his wicked grin, his heated eyes, and then he was on me once more. Skin to skin. Bare chest to bare chest, except for my bra. He touched the clasp behind me and asked, "Yeah?"

I paused. Should I? Was that too much, too fast?

He waited, and skimmed his thumb over my nipple as he did, and I cursed at him. "That isn't playing fair."

His grin widened. His lips met mine, and he whispered against them, "I don't play fair. Ever. You should know that about me." His other hand began to undo my clasp, but he was going slowly, waiting for my approval, so I nodded. The bra felt like a restriction. It wasn't natural. I was all about being natural at that moment, and then it was off, and the straps were slipped from my arms, and I wound them around his neck once again.

It was gone, and we really were bare chest to bare chest, then. We were exactly how we were supposed to be, and like that, with my jeans on, and his bulging, we made out until way past *Gladiator* was done and the credits had ended.

All the way until the door handle rattled.

"FUCK!"

That was me, but Shay almost levitated off me. He scooted back so he was sitting on the end of the bed.

"Kennedy?" Missy was knocking on the door. "Let me in!"

"Uh—"

My hair was a mess. My boobs felt like they'd been sanded and were incredibly smooth, and I could only gape at Shay. His hair was a mess like mine, but I trickled down his chest. He was so yummy. I bit my lip, and he tipped his head back, a soft groan coming from him. He bent over me, whispering, "That isn't fair."

"Yeah," I whispered back, falling back on the bed. "I don't play fair, either."

"Yeah?" He was smiling, still talking quietly.

"Yeah." I pulled him down. I was losing my mind. We were on a bed, and he didn't have a shirt on, and I only wanted to feel him against me, but . . . was I going to do something?

"Kennedy!" Missy pounded harder on the door. "Let me in. I need to grab my keys."

"Why?"

I stretched on my back, and Shay was on top of me. He fit between my legs, and his lips fell to my shoulder. He murmured, "Get rid of her. I'm not hiding in that damned closet again."

Then his lips began kissing there. He was doing these circle things with his tongue, and I was struggling to remember whose dorm room I was even in.

Missy banged on the door once more. She raised her voice. "Come on. We're going to a party."

I frowned. They had party friends?

"I need my keys." She added, punctuating her impatience with another twist of the doorknob.

I groaned. "Can I just give you your keys? Can you not come in?"

"Why?" Her voice was quieter, as if she took a step backward.

"Because I'm working out, naked."

Shay started laughing, burying his head into my shoulder and neck.

"Naked?" She sounded disgusted. "Are you masturbating?"

His shoulders started shaking.

I was going to take one for the team.

I raised my voice. "Yes. This is a natural thing to do. I am taking control of my body, and that means masturbation. It's healthy."

"That's disgusting." She sighed. "Yeah, just give me the keys. I can get a different shirt from Holly and use her makeup. You owe me, Kennedy."

She wasn't the only one owing someone in this situation. I rolled my eyes and crawled out from under Shay. I tugged on a shirt. I didn't know which one. I just grabbed one. It felt weird walking half-naked in the room even though I knew he'd pull it off as soon as I went back to him. Grabbing her keys, I padded barefoot and opened the door.

"You're so gross."

I shoved her keys out the door and grunted. "So are you." I was going to shut the door hard, but paused. "Thank you." It closed, and I locked it once more. I could hear her walking away as I rested my back against the door.

I took inventory.

I was wearing his shirt. No bra. No socks. No shoes. My jeans were unbuckled, but the zipper was still up. And I still had my underwear on.

Shay sat up, his eyes darkening. "You look good like that."

I raised a hand to my hair. Still a mess. And my lips were swollen and tingly. I touched them, too. "Yeah." He did, too, but I held that in. I stayed there, sober and clear-conscious thinking returning, and the questions were starting to form. What were we doing? What was I doing? With him? I hated him . . . right?

Didn't I?

He rose lithely to his feet and started across the room. "Don't start thinking. Don't. Just—" I was still against the door but straightened to my fullest height and gazed up at him. I could feel his body heat. His chest was right in front of me. One inch away. He dropped his head, his eyes dreamy, and I could feel his breath like a soft whisper on my skin. His finger traced my lip as he added, "We don't talk about it, remember?"

His hand skimmed down my arm, falling to my hand. "No talking."

I added another rule, "No thinking, either."

"Yes." He nodded in approval. "That's the best one yet. No thinking. Just . . ." He bent down, his lips over mine. "Feeling this." He pressed them against mine, and I groaned, grabbing on to his shoulders as he hoisted me into his arms. My legs went around his waist, but instead of the bed, he just held me there and pressed me to the door.

His lips were on mine. His one hand was on my hip, and his other cupped the side of my face. He pulled back, only a fraction of an inch, and said, "This is okay with you?"

I nodded. God, yes. "No talking. No thinking."

"Just feeling."

"Hell yes."

I dragged his mouth to mine. It didn't need to be so far away.

# CHAPTER ELEVEN

It was after midnight when I finally kicked him out.

We maintained our rules. We didn't talk. When I pushed him away, he just nodded, kissed me, pulled his shirt on, and kissed me again. He pulled on his socks and shoes, another kiss. Then grabbed his phone and his own keys. Two more kisses, as I began walking him toward the door.

This wasn't what I did with boyfriends. The few that there'd been, it'd been all business. A grope. A chaste kiss goodbye, and then they were out the door. This was light and fun and sexy and I was forgetting how much I hated the guy.

I pulled away at the door and shook my head. "No more."

I broke the no-talking rule.

His half-smirk reminded me, but he raked a hand through his hair, looked up and down the hallway, and was gone. The door closed with a hard bang, and I jerked back inside so the squawkers didn't know that was me. I heard their door open, and the girl I had flipped off earlier grumbled, "Who was that?" She pulled back into the room. Her voice grew muffled as the door closed.

I went to the window in time to see a shadow dart from the stairway and off to the parking lot. It was then that everything hit me.

I made out with Shay Coleman.

Shay Fucking Coleman.

He wanted to fuck me.

I plopped down on Missy's desk chair since it was closest to the window. Raking a hand through my hair, I was dumbfounded. I was still writhing around on that bed, feeling his hands everywhere, his kisses, feeling *him* on me. Groaning, I buried my head in my hands.

What the hell did I just do?

No. I couldn't go there and let myself be filled with shame. Whatever. I sat back up. So what? So the fucking what? I made out with a guy? Who cares if I couldn't stand him outside the bed? We weren't in a relationship. I wasn't going to date the guy. Hell no. This was physical. And if it happened again—well, I wasn't going to think about that, either.

I stood and actually shrugged it off.

I wasn't going to be filled with remorse, and I wasn't going to feel cheap and dirty. It was kissing. It was healthy, just like I said to Missy. That was healthy, too.

Thirty minutes later, I was dressed for bed and feeling a little better.

My teeth were brushed. Face was washed. I thought about a shower, but I decided to wait till morning. I could feel him still on me through the night, and so what if it was Shay. I hadn't made out with a guy in a while. It actually felt nice, if I just forgot who it was.

I was on my computer when a key fitted into the lock. The door swung open. My roommate came in.

I didn't look over. She could make her belittling comments. I wouldn't care. Gage sent me a second email, asking if I'd go to the football game with him. Why he didn't just text, I had no idea, then the smell of booze tickled my nose. I looked over. She was at her closet, swaying back and forth, and she had pulled her shirt off.

She was alone.

The door was still open, so I shut it and was returning to my desk when I braked. There was a backpack resting on the other side of my desk chair. It wasn't mine. It wasn't Missy's. I was pretty sure it wasn't Holly's or the cousin's.

"Shit," I muttered under my breath.

"Huh?" she barked, her head swinging around to me.

A quick glance confirmed what I already knew. She was drunk.

"Nothing."

She pulled out one of her shirts, but it wasn't her normal pajama top. She was *really* drunk. I picked up Shay's bag and checked the contents to make sure it was his. It was. I saw his planner with his name scrawled at the top, so I zipped that bag and put it in the back of my closet. No one needed to go through it. I didn't think Missy would, but I just never knew.

Dropping into my chair, I picked up my phone to text Shay as Missy fell to the floor. I looked up to watch. I couldn't not see this.

I was tempted to video it, but I was being nice. For once.

As Missy wrestled with her jeans and lifted them over her head to throw into her closet, I texted Shay.

Me: **You left your bag here.**

Missy let out a half-gurgled moan and a cry of frustration at the same time. She didn't stand, instead crawling to the closet. She grabbed another pair of pants.

Those weren't her pajamas, either.

As she pulled them on—or tried since her feet kept eluding the pants' hole—my phone buzzed back.

Coleman: **Can I pick it up in the morning?**

I texted back.

Me: **When?**

Missy got one leg in. Success. I wanted to thrust my fist in the air for her.

My phone buzzed again.

Coleman: **Early. My playbook is in there.**

I groaned.

Me: **When is early? I'm in college, Coleman. Sleeping in is mandatory.**

Coleman: **Nine too early for you? I can come back to get it now.**

Nine was doable.

Me: **Let's do an exchange. You bring me coffee, and I'll meet you at the parking lot curb with your bag.**

Coleman: **Done. Decaf okay?**

I glared at my phone.

Me: **Back to hating you.**

Coleman: **Never stop that. The world's equilibrium will be fucked up. I have to know what's right and wrong. Don't screw with my moral compass, Cute Ass.**

Oh, no! No way.

Me: **Third rule of what we don't talk about. No nicknames unless they reconfirm our mutual dislike for each other. No Cute Ass.**

His response was immediate.

Coleman: **Cunt Ass?**

A second squeak from me.

Me: **NO!**

I could almost hear him laughing.

Coleman: **Relax. I know. Clarke's Ass. That's how you are in my phone.**

The tension left my shoulders.

Me: **See you in the morning. 9 sharp.**

Coleman: **Night.**

I put my phone down, but then it buzzed once again.

Coleman: **Ass.**

I was struggling to wipe this stupid grin off my face. All was right again. I plugged my phone in, pulled my laptop back toward me, and sent a response to Gage's email. *I'll sit with you, but only if we're in the opposing team's section.*

He'd be pissed, but that was the only way. I turned the computer off, and by then Missy was climbing up the ladder in a bright pink silk shirt. The buttons were left buttoned, and her pajama bottoms were a pair of corduroy khakis. I was pretty sure she didn't brush her teeth, but before my head even hit the pillow, she was snoring.

My alarm went off at eight-thirty.

I slept, but the dreams had been filled with kisses, heavy breathing, touching in places all over the body, and a general feeling of being aroused. The whole night.

I was exhausted, but I pulled myself out of bed.

Checking my phone, I knew that Shay would be on time, so I picked up my pace. Dressing, washing, the whole get-go seemed to take longer than normal for some reason. I pulled on jeans, sandals, and a baggy shirt. I didn't need to proclaim any hotness level here.

I wasn't trying to be attractive for Shay Coleman.

Still. I paused after I grabbed my keys, phone, and his bag. I reached for some lip-gloss because my lips looked chapped.

Looked. Didn't feel it, but it never hurt to be proactive.

I was on the curb, his bag next to me, and waiting for five minutes before his black Jeep Wrangler pulled up. He parked in a slot behind me.

I picked up his bag and crossed over the sidewalk and smallest amount of grass. He turned the engine off but didn't move to get out. I walked to his side and lifted his bag. He pulled the bag through his open window, but he nodded to his passenger side. "Want to get in for a second? I got your coffee."

Surprised, I shrugged and went around.

No one would see. If they were walking home, they'd be hungover. No one would pay attention to one Jeep Wrangler in the parking lot.

I opened the door and climbed in.

Shay picked up my coffee, his own in his hand. "Here," he murmured, his voice drowsy.

I shut the door. "Didn't sleep?"

His head was resting against his seat, but he opened one eye and didn't look too happy. "I had the biggest hard-on all night. The fucker wouldn't go away, even after I did its business. Thanks for that."

"Aw!" I smacked his arm. "No talking about it. That's the first rule."

He grumbled but said, "You're all sorts of messed up. You know that, right?"

I shrugged. It wasn't an insult if it was true. "I have reason. This makes my life easier."

He shook his head, sipping some of his coffee. "You going to my game today?" That smirk came back, an extra layer of cockiness added to it. "I *am* the star quarterback, you know."

Football. Good. I relaxed. We could talk about that. "I hate football."

"Oh, my— Are you serious?" he burst out.

"What? I do."

His eyes narrowed. "You never answered." He continued to stare at me, long and hard, then his lips lifted again. "That means you're going, doesn't it?"

No answer from me.

He laughed, going back to sipping his coffee. "I'm starting to be able to read you."

I wrinkled my nose. "That isn't good."

"Who are you going with?"

"This guy I made out with last night."

"I'm playing."

"Who said it was you?" I couldn't help myself.

"You made out with someone before me last night?" He pretended to scowl, but his lip twitched in a half-grin. "And you broke the rule again."

No talking about it. Fuck. I gave in, saying, "I'm going with my brother."

"Yeah?" Interest sparked in his gaze. "What happened to your rule about being seen in public with a guy? Or does he not count because he's your brother?"

I snorted. "No way. He's included in that. He's the main reason I have the rule. Do you know what girls are like when they find out I'm related to Blake or Gage Clarke?" A shiver went down my spine. "They're either too nice or they're not nice at all. All the girls Gage sleeps with and discards? Guess who they're a bitch to?" I stopped a second shiver. "I'm going, but we're sitting in the other team's stands."

He sighed. "I'm not even going to ask if you're being serious. I know you are."

"Completely." I saw his bewilderment, which was mixed with a bit of frustration, and only shook my head. "Girls can be mean. You have no idea."

"Yeah." He raised his coffee. "Maybe I don't. Guys aren't that bad. There was bullying in high school, but that doesn't really happen in college." He amended, dipping his head low, "Unless they're drunk and just assholes. Then it can get a whole different level of scary." He squinted at me over the top of his coffee. "Something tells me you'd reduce them to sniveling cowards."

I grinned. That made me feel better.

Spying a girl I knew from one of my other classes, I reached for the door. "Thank you for the coffee."

He didn't say anything, just watched me. This was when he would've thanked me for bringing his bag out, but he didn't. I got out and glanced back to see him watching me intently. "Well." I felt weird for some reason. "Good luck today."

I walked away.

The coffee was good.

He had put in some cream and sugar.

# CHAPTER TWELVE

I was pissing my pants.

Actually pissing as in full bladder leakage and the whole warm feeling you get at first, followed by embarrassment with shame, and then it's just wet, sticky, and smelly. Okay, that might've been an exaggeration. I checked. My pants were fine, so no real pissing happened, but I wouldn't have been surprised if some got out.

I was standing outside the concession stands. Gage was making me wait while he went into the bathroom, and not only were my roommate and her gang of two others ten feet away but also Becs and Aby from poli-sci were standing a few feet from them.

I was huddled behind a post and had a huge thing of popcorn and a big cup of soda clutched against my chest. I tried to raise them so if anyone came closer, I could shield my face.

"Clarke?"

I jumped. The air flooded with popcorn, and I didn't have to imagine the feel of peeing my pants. I was experiencing it now, with soda. My face and shirt were drenched, and there was no warmth. There was coldness. I gritted my teeth. Too much coldness.

Casey was frowning at me. She was wearing a baggy Dulane University hoodie and tight jeans, and her auburn hair was pulled into two French braids. She was tugging on one, her head tilted to the side as she continued to assess me.

She pointed. "You spilled."

I saw some napkins in her hand and grabbed them, using them to dab at myself. "No, shit, Sherlock."

She only laughed. "What are you doing over here? You look like a creeping psycho."

I almost smiled. "That's the point. I want people to feel weird and look away."

"You're the only person I have ever met who *wants* to look like a creeping psycho." Her hand dropped from her braid to her hip. She glanced around. "For real, what are you doing here?" Her eyes landed on the men's restroom. The women's was on the other side of the concession stands. "Ah. Let me guess. You're waiting for . . ." She raked me over again, chewing the inside of her lip. "No. You're not the type to wait for some secret hot boy. You're waiting for your brother, right?"

"Ding, ding, ding. We have a winner, Vanna."

"Ha!" But she was laughing until the color faded from her face, along with her smile. "Wait. Your brother knows about me, doesn't he?"

I nodded, saying softly, "He's the one who called me about it." I tossed the last of the soda and juggled what was left of the popcorn to the side. I touched her arm, but when she jerked, I withdrew. "Sorry. I didn't think."

"No." Her smile was shaky. "It's fine. I—"

She cut off as Gage suddenly showed up. He rounded the post, an irritated scowl on his face. "Where's the pop—" He saw Casey, and the words stopped. "Oh." A transformation came over him. Annoyed Gage disappeared and instead soft Gage—the one who would blow on my cuts so the antibacterial ointment wouldn't sting so badly—showed up. Technically, my injuries weren't ever his fault, but it hadn't mattered. My big brother took care of me. That was the guy standing in front of us. He ran a hand through his hair, saying to Casey, "I didn't see you there." He glanced to me, an unspoken question of what he should do.

Casey stuck her hand out, a determined look on her face.

"It's nice to meet you, in an official capacity." Her eyes flicked to me and back. "I had no clue Kennedy had a brother, or that *you* were her brother."

"Yeah." He put his hand in hers, treating it as if it were made of glass. "That's my sister, proud to be related to me."

I shot him a look.

He ignored me.

Her mouth firmed, and she pumped his hand in one forceful motion. "It feels wrong. We've partied together, and I didn't know the real you." She was forcing a cheerful tone in her voice.

"Yeah." He cleared his throat.

Gage may have sounded uncomfortable, but he wasn't. His eyes had softened, a tenderness leaked from his voice, and if he could've floated forward on a magic carpet and taken her in his arms, he'd already be singing "A Whole New World."

Casey tucked some invisible strands of her hair behind her ear. They weren't loose. Her two braids were tight, but she was still making sure they were nice and secure. Her cheeks were blossoming with a nice, soft shade of pink, and I was about to vomit.

It was love behind the football post, not love at first sight.

"You two are obviously interested in each other."

Gage shot me a look, hissing, "Kenz!"

Casey laughed, glancing to the ground for a second. "It's fine." Another impish smile tugged at her lips. "I mean, you know. Obviously. Duh. That's why I'm even talking to Kennedy."

"Thanks."

She touched my hand, as if to say she was sorry, but her eyes were all for Gage. I was clueing back to the realization that this was how most girls looked at my brother.

Gage was puffing his chest out, as if he were a goddamn knight in shining armor.

I lifted the half-empty popcorn container. "Whoa. Look at that." My acting skills sucked, but I was committed. "I have *no clue* how that happened. I'll be going to refill this. And, um—"

"Okay. Yeah." Gage touched my arm and nudged me out of the way. He stepped closer to Casey, and they were gone after that.

I could've done jumping jacks naked and gotten arrested, and I didn't think they'd notice.

I went back to the concession stands, but I asked a guy if he wanted the rest of my popcorn. His eyes lit up, and it was another rendition of love at first sight, with him and the popcorn. "Hell yes." He grabbed it before I could change my mind, and I only bought a new soda.

I was returning with it, but there was no sign of Gage or Casey. I spotted them sitting in a corner on our team's section. Kristina, Sarah, and Laura were on the row in front of them.

I'd been rejected.

By my own brother.

"Loser."

Wha—

No way.

I rounded, my neck stiff as Becs and Aby approached. They were dressed similar to Casey, in full Dulane University gear. The only differences were that instead of sweatshirts, they were wearing tight, long-sleeved shirts, their hair was up in high ponytails instead of braids, and they both had lots of glitter on their faces.

I asked, "Did you actually just call me that?"

They stopped and shared a confused look. "What?" Becs asked. "Shay told us to greet you like that. We thought it was an inside joke."

"Shay did?"

She nodded.

Aby, too.

Becs frowned. "It wasn't this whole thing where we were supposed to call you that, and you'd know immediately it was from Shay, then dissolve in laughter? It wasn't that sort of thing?"

"No." But goddamn. It was a good prank. "What do you want?"

Becs barked out, "You've grown some more teeth since the abortion discussion."

"No." I shook my head. "I had teeth then, too." I pointed to my mouth, baring them. "See. Razor sharp. Took a bite out of both of you, if I remember correctly."

Becs said, "Uh. No."

"Well." Aby lifted her hand before letting it drop just as quick. "Kinda. Yeah."

"Whatever." Becs rolled her eyes. "You weren't in class on Friday. Shay said he'd tell you, but since you're here and I'm sure Shay had more important things to deal with, I thought I'd mention it."

"What?"

"We got assigned our presentation on Friday. We have to do a whole paper and present it later, but I saw Linde last night, and he mentioned maybe starting the research tomorrow."

"What's our topic?"

"Social media and how it has affected politics."

"Oh." I was surprised. "That actually sounds fun."

She gave me the once-over. "Yeah. Fun. Sure."

"We're starting tomorrow?"

She nodded. "The guys said they have your contact info, but yeah. We'll meet in the library sometime in the afternoon or evening. I have a ton of other homework to do, too."

"Okay." My Sunday was now planned. Sunday Funday.

Someone called out the name Becca, and she waved at them. She said to me, pointing over her shoulder, "My friends are calling. See you tomorrow."

Aby waved, and I was left with another discovery.

I half-whispered to myself, "Her name isn't actually Becs?" That made a whole lot more sense.

I started for the opposing team's section, but realized I wasn't sitting with Gage anymore. I could sit on my own team's side, and with that, I rotated swiftly, but stopped again.

Wait.

I came because of Gage.

I didn't have to watch at all, but halftime ended, and the teams returned from their locker rooms. They ran past me, and I saw Shay in the middle of the pack. His head was bent forward, listening to one of the coaches who was running beside him.

I was conflicted.

I might hate his personality, but I couldn't deny how good he looked in his football uniform. The shoulder pads. The tight white pants that ended on his calves. And how dark and sweaty his hair was. It stuck up in all the right spots. The black spots under his eyes were smudged, but in a hot way, and I faltered.

Then Linde jogged past, and seeing me, he flashed a blinding smile. "You better be cheering me on, Kennedy Clarke. You hear me? I want to hear you yelling."

Everyone started to clap as they ran past, and feeling myself smiling, I shifted the soda to the side. I began to clap, and by the time the last of the team was on the field, I was hollering and hooting with the best of them.

I stayed, but only for Linde.

And maybe Shay's backside.

# CHAPTER THIRTEEN

We won seventeen to ten.

The opposing team got a field goal in, hence the last three points, and when that happened, our side acted as if we'd been punched in the balls. Even the girls winced. Sure, the other team's offense was finally picking up, getting some drive into their runs, but it was the end of the game. The clock ran out, and it didn't matter. A cheer went up after that, and a bunch of guys sitting near me proclaimed "GOTTA GET DRUNK NOW!" That warranted its own set of cheers.

I was walking down the path toward the parking lot. A lot of others, like parents and little children, were heading out at the same time. Some other students, the quieter, more reserved and sane ones, were in my mix as well. I spotted Kristina lingering on the edge of Casey, Laura, Sarah, and now my brother's group. They formed a circle, and some of the other guys were joining them. There was a whole ton of students staying back, no doubt making plans for the after-game drinking. That was what Gage usually did. Aby and Becs (now Becca) were standing with their own clique, too, and some guys.

"Clarke." A sweaty and heavy arm came down around my shoulders.

I tensed, but it was Linde. "Congrats on the big win." I punched his shoulder in a manly and macho way.

He laughed, and his arm fell back to his side. I looked around. We were getting a few looks, but it was Linde. I was okay being known as his friend. I asked, "We're doing the library tomorrow?"

"That's what I was going to tell you. Shay was supposed to mention it, but he said he forgot." He continued walking beside me, his helmet swinging by his side. "I had another favor to ask of you."

"Sure. What is it?"

"Shay said you might know the girl who was raped." He glanced over his shoulder, back to the football field.

I hadn't been thinking about it, but it hit me then. "That guy's a football player." Casey was here and talking with my brother and looking as normal as ever. Well, not really. She was wearing a baggy sweatshirt. That wasn't normal Casey wardrobe. A tight tank top was, but everything else was normal for her.

"He got suspended. They didn't even let him suit up."

"Really?"

"A bunch of us came forward and told Coach. They don't mess around, especially if there's a court case or media. Listen, the favor I wanted to ask you." He stopped. People began to stream around us. "You know the girl?"

I nodded. "Yeah."

He shifted his helmet to his other hand, then back again. "Um. You heard in class that day, about my sister."

"I remember."

"Do girls know about your friend? I mean, the guys know, but guys don't say that stuff to girls."

"Oh." He was asking about rumors? "Are you asking if it's been spread around, because if you are, you're asking the wrong person. I talk to you, a few others, and that's it. I'm the furthest from 'in the know.'"

"She hasn't said anything?"

"I said something to her, just so she knew I was there if she wanted, but that was it. I haven't pushed her to do anything." I began scratching at the top of my arm, half-covering my body. "She's here. She seems kinda normal, but I don't know the process for that stuff."

"She's not."

"What?"

That word came out clipped and almost harsh. He softened it this time. "She isn't okay. My sister did the same."

"Yeah?"

"She didn't want to accept what happened to her, so she pretended it didn't. But it did, and it ate at her on the inside. Your friend, whether she says something or not, can't lie to herself. If she's here and she's acting normal, she's not."

"What can I do? Besides just be there for her, I mean. I can't make her say anything."

"I know, but just be there for her. Often. Keep a watchful eye out. You know what I mean?"

I thought so. I looked past his shoulder to where their group was starting to venture our way. Gage wasn't with them anymore, and I frowned. I scanned the rest of the crowd, but couldn't see him.

"That's weird."

"What's weird?"

"Nothing." I shook my head.

"What?"

"Oh. Just." I waved it off. It really wasn't a big deal. "It's nothing. My brother was with me today, and he went and sat with her. He knows. He's the one who told me."

"Why would he do that? Why would he sit with her?"

"What?" I was still looking for Gage, but Linde's sharpness caught me off guard. I focused on him again, fully. "My brother just wants to help. He was worried I'd been with her, that I could've been a target, too."

"Some girls don't deal with it the right way. Some girls cling to the nice guy who comes next in line, and they think that's going to wash away the shit they're feeling inside. It never works. Tell him to back off her. She needs good female friends, that's it. Family, too, if they're good to her."

I hadn't thought of that, but it made sense. "Okay. I'll talk to him."

Casey saw us talking, and a small frown tugged at her lips. Her eyes clouded, and she slowed to a snail's pace. Kristina and the others noticed and started glancing back at her, also wearing frowns.

Casey's gaze drifted to Linde and then back to me. A question formed there.

"Go," I said it softly and reached out for Linde. I pushed him, the slightest of touches. "She'll know we're talking about her."

The football team was completely gone. Linde was the last, and he was gaining more attention. I didn't care about me this time, I was worried about how Casey would take it. She knew my brother knew, and she knew someone else knew, but it was starting to sound like the rumor was circulating among the guys. I didn't know the protocol—if guys freely shared when one of their own assaulted someone or if it was even like that. But I knew it wasn't normal for guys to come forward against one of their own, especially a football player. That was good. If I knew anything, I knew that much. If Casey did come out, she'd be believed.

Or I hoped she would.

Kristina and the others were almost to me, and when they started to show signs of slowing to talk, Casey spoke up, "Can you guys give us a minute?"

Kristina frowned, all of them did, but they kept on ahead.

She waited till they were far enough away not to overhear. "Is that the guy?"

My eyes widened. "What?"

"You said a guy knew, not your brother, but someone else."

"Oh." My mind was racing. What was the right play here? "No, he isn't that guy."

"Oh." Air left her, and her shoulders relaxed.

"But he knows."

Those shoulders tightened up. "What?" She visibly swallowed. I saw her throat moving.

"My brother knew. He called me. I called a different frie—someone else."

"Had he heard?" Her eyes were so wide, so frightened. She seemed to shrink before me, looking like a frightened little girl.

Okay. I had to go with complete honesty. That was what I would want. Honest, but kind. "He hadn't when I'd spoken to him."

She closed her eyes, bracing herself.

"But he had by the time I saw him before class Friday morning."

"What class?"

"My poli-sci class."

Her eyes opened, and she was nodding, taking the information in. "And that guy just now, he knows?"

I answered her again, "He and some others on the team went to the coach. The guy who . . . did that to you wasn't allowed to suit up today."

"I know." Her voice was so quiet. "I was so worried. I didn't want to see him, but if I didn't come to the game, the others would know something was wrong. I had to come."

"I don't know who the guy is. Did he come out on the field? Was he on the sidelines?"

She shook her head. "No. Thank God for that, right?" A tear formed in her eyes. She wiped at the corner of them with the back of her hands. "That was really nice of them to do that. That isn't normal, is it?"

"If I were to guess, no."

"Your brother's been really nice."

I frowned.

She explained further, "He told me he's there for me, too. Or you. He said you're all prickly on the outside, but that's to keep others from hurting your soft gooey inside. You're all bark, but no bite."

"Negative. There's bite. A lot of bite. I'm a rabid dog, actually."

She laughed, wiping at her eyes again. "He said you'd say that but that I shouldn't believe you. You might snarl at him, but not me, not if I'm hurting."

I kicked at the ground. Why did I feel like crying?

"Um." She started, but stopped. "I have to know. I mean, not a lot of people are giving me weird looks, but there are some." Her eyes darted to a group of guys coming up behind us. They were loud, obnoxious, and drunk. She moved closer, lowering her head. "It's mainly from guys. I've just been getting the normal bitchy looks from the girls."

I hated being the sponsor-friend. I sucked at this stuff. "The guys know, but it seems like the girls don't."

She didn't talk, not for a moment. Her eyes remained closed, and she sucked in her breath as the group of guys parted, going around us. I saw a few leer at us, their gazes raking Casey up and down.

I narrowed my eyes at one, and he stopped.

He spread his arms out. "What?" He was around five eight, not much taller than I was, but muscular in an athletic way.

He was the kind who gave the word 'cocky' a bad name.

Casey looked, but seemed to wither in front of me.

Not me. I raised my chin. This guy was going to try to intimidate me? I started toward him, knowing my eyes were cool. "You're going to square off against me? Against a girl?"

His friends had stopped. A few started back.

One said, "Come on, man." Another jumped beside him, as if he was going to help him out.

Oh, no.

I dealt with this shit in high school.

This was not going to happen to Casey. Or me. That rabid dog side of me was about to come out, and soon. Damned soon.

I turned my icy gaze at him, my top lip lifted in a sneer. "My, my. What a man you are. Because clearly, your buddy must need help against words." I smiled, but it didn't match what I was feeling. I was pissed. I was seeing red, and right at that moment, I saw a target for the asshole who hurt another girl. No. I saw two targets now. "Your friend must be *really* dumb." I swung my gaze to Asshole One. "Are you dumb? Your friend thinks you are."

Both bristled, puffing up their chests before sharing a confused look.

"See." I pointed between them. "Look at that. You're not even sure what happened here. A girl started your way, but you guys must only be used to being hit on, right?"

They shared another look, small grins starting on their faces.

"Because that *must* be the only reason a girl would come up to you. It isn't like they'd find you disgusting or reprehensible or a small hick coward and then have the balls to tell you." I whispered, leaning forward, "Do the girls you know not tell you the truth? Are they scared of you?" I raised my voice to normal levels again. "You can tell me. Do they only tell you if you were 'good'?" I winked at Asshole One. "Or maybe you guys are only used to chicks if they're in either two categories. If they're ripping their clothes off for you, begging for it." I glanced down at the front of his jeans, grimaced, and then looked back up. "Or they're pissed because, well, you guys must've not satisfied them. Right? It's either of those two? But no. Wait. It's the *girl's* fault. Right? It's never your fault. It isn't like you'd never 'not perform.' Right?"

Asshole Two shook his head, spreading his hands out. "What the fuck are you talking about?"

"Exactly." Acid dripped from my voice. I clapped my hands together, holding them in front of me. "Here's the thing. I'm insulting you. I am being sarcastic, and I'm mocking you guys to your face, and you don't even know it. And as I'm doing it, you have no idea how to deal with me because I'm smiling and I'm talking like I'm going to bake you fucking cookies. The truth is that if I ever did that, I'd put rat poison in them."

I finished, but with a bright cheery smile, and then I waited.

I didn't wait long.

Asshole One charged me.

Casey screamed.

There were other shouts around me.

I didn't pay attention to Asshole Two. He didn't seem to have the abusive balls, but Asshole One did, and I grabbed 'em. Literally.

He ran for me, and I caught his dick in my hand. He jerked to a stop, a choke gurgling from him, and then I squeezed.

"AH!" He started screaming, trying to dislodge my hand.

"Holy fuck," someone said behind us.

Fun time was over. I wasn't nice anymore. I wasn't being sarcastic any longer. I squeezed again, and his entire body shuddered under my hold.

I clipped out, "You're going to fucking swing at me? You're going to hit me? You're going to shove me to the ground? What were you going to do? Huh?" My voice rose until I was outright yelling.

He couldn't talk. His face was turning blue.

"Look at that." I pointed to his face with my free hand. "Blue face, instead of blue balls. But assholes like you don't even get how funny that is because a chick gives you blue balls, too. And here I am, going above and beyond. I'm probably the best you've had, right? I gave you blue face. It's a new thing. No one's experienced this before." Okay. The sarcasm was back, but it was definitely still dripping with anger.

"Hey."

I didn't know who said that, and I didn't care. I was focused on this asshole as I dropped my voice into a hissing whisper only he could hear. "You must be wondering what kind of deranged chick has your dick in her hand? I must be crazy, right?" Fuck. Maybe I was. "You know what makes me crazy? The fact that you've heard what happened to my friend, but instead of looking at how she could've been your sister, your girlfriend, even your mother, you walk past her and look at her like she's a whore." My fingers sank harder around him, and I was enjoying his curdling screams. "She isn't a whore. She's a victim, and you victimized her a second time. So how does it feel? Because I grabbed you against your will. Are you enjoying it?"

His screams answered me. I still wasn't done. "And want to know what the most fun part of this whole thing is? I have a defense. You. Rushed. Me. First. You came at me like you were going to hit me, a girl, someone you'll never be able to call a whore. Aren't you so glad you ran into me? Aren't you?"

I bit out the last part, and I seriously wanted to rip his dick off. If I could've, and if I could've not gone to jail for it, it would've been moved to my highest priority of the day. Rip a cowardly asshole's dick off. I'd love to be able to cross that off my list. Done deal. But I couldn't, because I had to be a better person than him, though I couldn't think why at that moment.

I was still squeezing.

I wasn't sure if I could let go, until an arm wrapped around my waist and I was lifted away.

"Hey!" I yelled.

The person ignored me, dropping me back on my feet. I started forward, but they clamped their hand on my arms, holding me back in an ironclad grasp.

Asshole One fell onto his knees, moaning, and his forehead rested on the ground. His friends didn't move. They looked shocked at everything that just happened. Even Asshole Two didn't go to his friend's side. His hands were cupped over his junk, and he edged back, glancing at me as if I were going to come for him next.

Shit. Maybe I should.

I started forward, but the person yanked me back. He was holding me to his cement-like chest, and I looked up. My protest died in my throat. Shay wasn't even looking at me. He was watching Asshole One, who was still writhing around on the ground crying.

He sounded like a feral animal who'd been mortally wounded.

*Good.*

"Let me go," I said it quietly, and his eyes flicked down to mine. I was back in control. I let him see that.

He did, and I walked forward.

I passed Casey, who was frozen in place.

I walked past Asshole One on the ground.

I walked past his asshole friends.

I walked past some blonde girl who was watching me with wide owl-like eyes. They weren't blinking.

I walked past everyone else who stopped to watch us.

I didn't stop walking until I got to my dorm room, and even there, I walked right past Missy and sat at my desk.

And I stared ahead, still only seeing red.

# CHAPTER FOURTEEN

My phone began ringing. I ignored it. I didn't move, staring at nothing.

The room's phone began ringing next, and Missy answered. Her greeting was muffled, a rush of blood in my ears was deafening, but then she tapped my shoulder. She jerked back when I looked at her, pointing to the phone. "You have a phone call. Some guy."

It could be Gage. I should find out where he went.

I nodded, asking, "Can I have some privacy?"

"Sure. Yeah." She grabbed her coffee mug, the one she never actually used for coffee. "I was just grabbing this anyway. We're partying in Holly's room and might head out to some parties tonight if you want to come along?"

"Are you going to be gone all night?"

I wanted to be alone. Too many people in my life, it was becoming a mess. I just shattered my first two rules in the last twenty-four hours. I needed to go back to how prepared and organized I was in my isolation.

"I can be."

"I just need a few hours."

"Okay. I get that. Um, I'll call you from Holly's room if I come down."

"Thanks." I crossed to her desk and sat down in her chair. The landline was there, and because everyone used cell phones, the college started returning to the phones that had cords. It wasn't a cordless phone. As soon as Missy offered an awkward wave, slipping from the room, I lifted the receiver to my ear. "Hello?"

"You okay?"

Shay, not Gage.

"Yeah. Why wouldn't I be?" It wasn't him. For once, I knew the real culprits were Asshole One, the guy who raped Casey, and all the other assholes who thought they could treat women like that. I knew my rage had ascended DEFCON level, but my voice was ice cold, and I was a shell of a person.

The rage was banked inside. My outside looked completely calm.

Even I got the chills from me.

"Come on, Clarke."

"Look." Okay. I relaxed a tiny bit. Some emotion seeped back into my voice, I was becoming normal again. It wasn't his fault that emotion was frustration. "I'm fine. Thank you for pulling me off before I did any permanent damage and the weasel could've sued me."

"This is how you're going to play it? You went psycho on that guy. I'm not saying he didn't deserve it, but your reaction was . . ."

I laughed. It sounded dull even to my ears. "You're choosing your words now? Is this a new part of our fucked-up hatred for each other? You never held back before," I bit out. "Why now?"

"Because I don't want you to rip my dick off next time."

"Don't!" I clasped my eyes closed, holding the phone so tight against my ear. "First rule is we don't talk about it."

"I came out there because there's a video of what you did. It got sent in an email to a bunch of guys, and Linde showed it to me. He said he'd been talking to you a few minutes earlier, and you were fine, but when I got out there, you were unhinged." He softened his tone. "Look, I get it."

No. He didn't. He was a guy. He wouldn't get it.

He kept on. "I'm calling to make sure you're okay, okay? I'm trying to be a fucking decent human right now."

He made it too easy. A bitter smile formed, and I looked at my reflection. Missy kept a mirror by her computer, and I saw why he was concerned. I was still looking the rageful robot chick, but that girl didn't want kindness right now.

I said, "Don't. We're not friends. There's no reason you need to call me. We're classmates. We're working on a project together, and we made out once. It won't happen again. Don't mistake a few heavy moans for a newfound liking of you. I hated you on the first day of class, and trust me, that never thawed."

I hung up and expelled a ragged breath.

He was being a fucking decent human? Fuck him. I didn't need his kindness or his concern. I didn't need the moments when he'd show up to mess with me, or bring me coffee and ask me to sit in his Jeep with him. Those moments might've messed with another girl's head, but not me.

He was another Parker. I'd just forgotten for a brief second.

I wouldn't again.

# CHAPTER FIFTEEN

Gage should've called by now, but I wasn't in the mood to sit and twiddle my thumbs.

Not wanting to get up and grab my cell, I dialed his number from the landline.

He answered, and I didn't hold back. "You ditched me at the football game, then sat with my friends, and where'd you disappear to afterward? If you're all about Casey, do you realize the looks she was getting? It was like Assholes Abound, Come on Board." My voice went up. I was close to hysteria here. "And if you want to know what happened, there's a video of it going around."

"I just saw it."

He didn't sound like he cared. I barked out a laugh. "Right. I get that you might not care what I did, but I'd think you would've cared about what Casey went through."

"Spare me the lecture."

"Yeah. Okay. Consider it spared." I started to hang up, but he spoke again, stopping me.

"I'm standing outside your dorm, wondering if I should chance your wrath to come and check on you, or just leave you alone. I never have any clue which way to go with you, and I get it. You got a bad hand, more than a few because of Blake and me, but fuck, Kenz. You looked mental in that video."

The second person to say that within a few minutes. I held my tongue. He had some valid points.

"Others aren't going to see your rage, but I did. I—" He sighed into the phone, "It took me back. Okay? I didn't realize how much Parker screwed you over."

"That wasn't about Parker."

"Yes, it was. And it was about all the shit you had to deal with in high school. I get it. I get why you don't want people to know about Blake or me, or that you're friends with Raymond Linde or even that you know Shay Coleman. It was a logical response. That's what I told myself. I thought about it rationally, but it wasn't until that video that I understood it. It was a punch to my junk."

I winced. "Did you have to use that metaphor?"

He laughed. "Yeah. Well. It fit. Look, I'm outside your dorm. I'd like to come inside and hang out with my sister, but it's your choice. I'm currently hiding in the trees, looking like a creep, but I'll do whatever you want."

"What about Casey?"

"I went to the bathroom. I meant to walk out with them, but I ran into some guys I knew and I wanted to find out the plans for tonight. The stands were empty by the time I finished talking, and I just assumed everyone left. I ducked out through a different fence because it was closer to my truck."

"I meant, aren't you worried about Casey?"

"I'm more worried about my sister. You're my first priority over a girl I barely know."

The first thawing shall commence. "Thanks." It felt good to hear that. "Sorry I was a bitch just now."

"Yeah. Yeah. I don't care. Your bitchiness comes in handy. It makes you a fighter, and you've fought for me before. But can I come in? What's the verdict here?"

"Uh." The room suddenly felt too small. "I'll come out. We can get food or something."

"Sounds good."

We made plans for me to meet at his truck, and I stared at the phone after I hung up. I owed Shay an apology. I should call him, tell him I was sorry. I didn't. I sat there, and I couldn't make myself reach out and pick up that phone again. I sat there for a full ten minutes, trying to will myself to do it until I knew it wasn't going to happen.

That was one stone I couldn't put back, but I'd see him tomorrow. I'd be nice-r then. I'd try to make it up, but actually apologizing and saying the words, I don't know why they wouldn't form for me.

I was heading down the stairs through the back door when Casey entered from the second floor. I was a few steps away and paused. My hand was on the handrail, but I put it in my shirt's pocket.

"Hi." She blinked a few times. She was undoing one of her braids, but her hands fell away. She looked down.

"I'm sorry."

"Huh?" She looked back up.

"I went psycho on that guy, and it wasn't all about you." I glanced sideways. "Most of it wasn't about you." Nope. Still wrong. "Pretty sure none of it was about you."

She snorted, grinning. "Well, whatever. It was awesome."

Linde's words about my brother stuck with me. I hadn't known what I was going to do—if I was going to say something to Gage or Casey, but she was here.

This was about to get awkward real fast.

She asked, "You heading out?"

"Yeah. About that—"

"Sorry. I just—did you see who pulled you off that guy?" Her eagerness bubbled out. "Shay Coleman. Shay Coleman, Kennedy!" She grabbed my sleeves, pulled my hands out from my pockets, and shook them up and down. "I can't believe Shay Fucking Coleman came to my rescue. I'm dying. Dying!" She let go and pretended to fan herself.

Right. Her rescue.

"It's nice to see some of the old Casey still in there."

"For Shay Coleman?" Her head tipped back. "Hell yes," she moaned before looking back. "Okay, not really. I'm not ready for any guy. The idea makes me want to curl up in a ball and vomit, but it was Shay Coleman. Even a nun would've swooned at him today. And he told those guys to get lost when you left." She was back to fanning herself. "They didn't say anything or argue with him. They didn't do anything. They picked their friend up and carried him to the parking lot, and then he walked me back. AH! That was the best part. He was all nice and gentlemanly. Swooning here. Just swooning."

I was getting that. Maybe the Gage stuff could wait. "That's good to hear." I looked toward the exit door.

"Are you leaving? I was coming up to get you. We're heading to the Dulane Café to get some food. Did you want to come?"

Twenty-four hours ago, I would've been the one to swoon. Casey Winchem coming to my door? Knocking? Inviting me to eat with her and the girls? And not where I was the backup option for a ride? I would've felt like I had been accepted into the group, but that would've been twenty-four hours ago. Before my brother ditched me, before he sat next to my friends, and before I had a rageful dick-in-the-hands moment.

Because of all that, I shook my head. "No. I should get going. I'm going to grab some food with my brother."

Her eyes lit up. "Invite him with us. The girls know he's your brother. I told them when he sat with us at the football game. Laura thought I was moving in on your guy. She saw you guys and thought I was violating the code. I had to tell her. I hope that's alright?"

Whaaaaaaaaat?

My smile stuck in my cheeks. "Sure. No problem."

Fuuuuuuck.

My phone started buzzing. I only needed one guess to figure out who it was. No doubt Gage got impatient. "I should get going."

"Yeah. Okay." She moved aside so I could go past her. "Talk tonight? Maybe do something later? Laura and Sarah will go drinking, but I was thinking movies?"

Cue my swooning. She was inviting me for a movie night. "Yeah. I'll stop by when I'm done."

That was an evening I could get behind.

# CHAPTER SIXTEEN

Gage asked to go to the campus café, but I snorted as I threw that out. Instead, he took me to a small pub a block from his house. I asked once we got out, "Are you sure I'll be let in?" He'd just turned twenty-one, but I wasn't.

"For sure." He threw his arm around me, flashing that crooked grin so many girls fell for. "I'll just tell 'em you're my girl."

I shrugged his arm off. "That's gross."

"It'll keep guys from hitting on you."

"And when you end up sleeping with someone you know from here, and she finds out I'm your sister?" I gave him a look. "She's going to think we're weird."

He laughed, his hands sliding into his pockets. "True, but be prepared. I have friends here. It isn't like high school. They're going to go out of their way to hit on you."

I waved that off. Rageful dick-in-the-hand moment here. I could handle 'em.

I was wrong. I was so wrong.

Gage just shook his head and laughed. He warned me, and he was right. His friends came over. Some went to Dulane; some didn't. Some were older, and a few girls were my age. It was close enough to the dinner hours, so they were allowed in because the pub served food. One girl explained that was how they got around the age limit. They just stayed, even hiding in the bathroom stalls if needed. I didn't understand the rule protocol, but I followed Gage's lead. If he said we needed to go, that was what we would do.

We got a booth in the back corner so he could drink beer, play pool, throw some darts, and still snack on our food when it arrived. I played a game against him, and that was when the guys really started coming over. They weren't hitting on me, not really, but I hadn't been prepared for the open curiosity about who I was, why hadn't Gage brought me around before, and how old I was. The age was asked the most, and the second question—why I'd stayed hidden for so long. Gage just laughed at my expression. I was forced to explain how I banned Gage from my life, which made me seem like a crazy person.

Some of the girls understood. Most the guys didn't care.

One guy asked, "What if I see you on campus? Can I say hi?"

"If I'm alone."

He started laughing as if he thought I was kidding, but then he realized I wasn't. "Oh. You're serious."

I was taking it a bit far, but whatever. Gage was one thing. Shay, too, but I was friends with Linde. There was nothing there where people could use me to get to him. Same thing with these guys. And the girls who had come over so far, they were already on good terms with Gage. Most were friendly when they met me as the sister, expressed how it made sense because of the whole twin look-a-like, and that was it. No one lingered to become my best friend.

I was starting to wonder if I should rethink the whole philosophy about Gage. Shay, fuck no. People would go batshit crazy if they knew I knew him, even the fact that he'd called me a couple times would make my friends pass out. No, but with Gage, maybe. I watched him after we ate as he was chatting with a bunch of girls.

It hit me then. They didn't need to use me to get to him. He was open, very open to all the girls. I didn't know his status as a manwhore. I knew when he had girlfriends. He talked to me about them, but not his one-night stands. I knew too much about that part of his life in high school because I couldn't get away from the girls. They were in the same classes, but college was different. He could've been taking a new girl home every night, and the chances I didn't know them were good. Really good. Exceedingly good. And I was becoming happier as the night wore on.

I lost track of time, and I lost track of Gage.

Some of his friends sat in the booth with me, and the pitchers started coming after that. I wasn't a big drinker, never had been, but that night I became one. Maybe it was the dick-in-the-hands moment, or that once the video started circulating, Gage's friends recognized me and began shielding me themselves when people came over to talk about the video. Halfway through my third beer, I was nicknamed the Dick Crusher. That would've had me going for the door if I'd been sober. I stayed and I laughed, and I thought Dick Crusher was hilarious.

I was drunk.

I wasn't paying attention to my bladder until it demanded to be released. I was the farthest inside the booth, so I tapped on the girl next to me. She and the guy on the edge scooted out.

Time was of the essence.

I dashed for the nearest bathroom, praying for an empty stall. The smallest one was, and I ran for it. I was washing my hands afterward, trying to smooth down my hair when two shrieking girls entered the bathroom.

Goddamn. My hair was a mess.

"Kennedy Clarke?"

I knew that voice. I'd spoken to it earlier today.

I looked in the mirror. Yep, Becs (now Becca) and another girl came in. Unlike me, who was dressed for a football game since I never changed, they were not. More makeup, a fresh coat of glitter on their faces and chests, and both wore slinky dresses. Her dress was cut short on her legs, but she had the one-sleeve thing going, along with a necklace that dipped low into her cleavage. Her long hair was shiny and hanging free. Her friend's dress was gold-colored and sleeveless.

I forgot my annoyance for a second.

Lowering my hands, I turned around. "Wow. You look nice."

She was holding a beer but glanced down. "Thank you." I think she forgot the mutual dislike as well.

"Who's this?" Her friend wanted to know.

We both remembered.

I snarled.

She wrinkled her nose. "This is the girl I was telling you about that's in my poli-sci class."

"Her?"

The disdain was taught. Her friend had it mastered.

"Where's Aby?" I asked.

Becca motioned behind her with the beer. "Out there somewhere." She began laughing. "We should start researching tonight. The whole gang's here."

I went still. "What?"

"Yeah." Becca moved aside as her friend jerked into my emptied stall. "Linde's up by the bar, and Shay just came in." She snorted, moving to the sink beside me and reaching up to smooth some of her own hair. One imaginary strand might've not been in place. The perfection would've been marred. Wait. She moved the one strand, and whew. I felt the relief flooding out of me.

Perfect, once again.

That'd been close.

"I hear you're a celebrity."

"Huh?"

"The video." She sipped her drink, waiting for her friend to come out. The other stall was occupied. The person had been in there when I came in and still was. "Where you grabbed a guy's dick and not in the porno way."

"Oh, yeah. Dick Crusher."

"What?"

"Nothing." I frowned. "Linde and Shay are here?"

She nodded, raking me up and down as she took another sip. "Speaking of the rest of the upperclassmen, what are you doing here? How'd you get in?"

To incriminate my brother or not? I was feeling light and tipsy. Incriminate, it was. "My brother brought me here to eat." I shrugged. "We stayed."

Her eyes sharpened. "Your brother?"

"Gage." I wasn't going to spell it out. The girl had to think a little. If she figured it out, oh, well. If not, kudos for me.

I couldn't remember if I washed my hands. I better do them again.

Becca was quiet. I could feel her watching me, but her friend shoved open the bathroom stall. She came out, swaying as she zipped up her pants. "Your brother is Gage Clarke?"

"Ew, Lia. Flush the toilet."

"Oh." She did and came back. The same excitement hadn't waned. Her eyes were bright and her face flushed. "Gage Clarke. Right?"

Becca didn't move into the stall. She stood by her friend as both stared at me.

I shrugged. "Aren't you going to wash your hands?"

"Gage Clarke is your brother?"

Neither moved.

I answered Becca, "I just told you that."

"Why didn't you say something in the beginning?"

"Why would I?"

Her mouth opened and hung there.

Her friend translated, "Because Gage Clarke is hot!"

"Oh." I rolled my eyes, wishing I had brought my own drink. "See. This. You. You're why I don't say anything, because now you're going to be all nice to me, and I know it's fake."

"It's fake?"

"You're being fake. My brother will either sleep with you or he won't." I pounded my chest and fell backward into the sink. "I have no bearing on that. At all." I almost fell the other way, but caught myself. I pointed to Becca's beer. "Are you going to drink that? Have you backwashed into it?"

"What?"

The friend snagged it from her and handed it over. "My name is Lia. When you talk to him, tell him how nice I am." She pointed to Becca. "She's a bitch, but not me. I was nice. Tell him."

"I'm not going to remember your name." I already forgot.

"Lia."

"What?"

"LIA!"

"I'm not going to remember." I leaned away from the sink to look at Becca, even though I could see her fine from where I was standing. "Your friend has a thing for my brother?"

She snorted, going into the stall. Finally. "Half the campus has a thing for your brother." She grabbed ahold of the stall door on the top and pulled it shut with a firm and decisive click. The friend leaned forward, beaming at me. "Lia. My name's Lia."

I didn't care. I'd take the bitch title here. Bitch and Dick Crusher. There should be T-shirts made.

I turned to leave.

The friend said something again to me, and Becca yelled something out, but I wasn't listening to them. I lifted a hand over my shoulder, dismissing both, and left.

I took a few steps, but I felt it almost right away.

The air in the bar had changed.

People were more on edge. I frowned. I couldn't place it. Maybe they were more . . . there was an eagerness mixed with a slight edge of hysteria at the same time. I was intoxicated. If I could sense this when I was blasted, it must've been really bad.

I marched over to my booth. Gage's friends were still there, and a new guy had squished in to where I'd been sitting.

"Hey!" A cheer rose from them. "It's Dick Crusher."

I teetered on my feet, holding on to the table. "What's going on?"

Two of them started to stand, saying, "You can take my spot."

"No, no." I waved them back. I needed to sober up. That meant not sitting and drinking more. "I'm good. Stay comfortable. I meant around the bar." I motioned around. "I can feel something's weird."

"Oh." One girl understood. "Shay Coleman came in."

That was right. It all made sense now.

I swung my head around. "Where's he at?"

This was as good of a time as any to apologize. I could do it in the bar, and I could slip away. It'd be a drive-by apology. He'd never know what hit him, and tomorrow, I could go back to being normal. I wouldn't have to be nice.

"What?"

"Coleman. Where's he at?" I was squinting to see the rest of the bar. I couldn't. Our corner was packed, and there was a whole other section by the door. I knew that area was standing room only. This might be more work than I realized.

"You know Coleman?"

"She doesn't know Coleman."

I didn't know who was talking so I asked again, "Where at?"

"He's probably where the football guys always sit."

I looked at the guy who said that. "I've never been here in my life. I have no idea where that is."

One girl stood and took my hand. "I'll show you."

"Wait." The guy waved us back. He leaned forward, shouting so we could hear him better. "What are you doing? Are you going to talk to him or something?"

The girl started laughing. "She doesn't know Coleman. She probably wants to meet him or something."

I nodded. Her words weren't really clicking with me.

I said, "I need to apologize to him. I was a bitch before."

I had a fleeting thought that I just violated something. Wait. My rules. Why did I have those rules again? I was forgetting everything. I added, "And I have to tell him Lael says hello."

"You know Shay Coleman?" the guy asked, sounding doubtful.

The girl was still laughing. She had no clue what was going on.

"I'm in a class with him. It's all good. I'm not like a stalker or anything." I shuddered at that thought, and as the girl pulled me forward and into a large crowd in the bar, I couldn't help but think about the control a stalker had. They chose when to say something. They chose when to approach, when to look, when to retreat. They had all the control.

That was creepy as fuck.

I never wanted to be a stalker. Why was I thinking about that?

The girl was still leading the way. We'd moved into the area that was literally standing room only and had to wait for people to move before we could go farther in. We got halfway before she said over her shoulder, "Do you want to see your brother?" She nodded to the right. "He's in the corner with some people."

I shook my head. I was drunk. There was a high chance he was drunk. I leaned closer and yelled, "He probably forgot I'm here. I'm good. Onward to the football star."

She laughed before inching forward. Then she saw something and veered to where my brother was.

I pulled on her hand. "No. I don't want to see my brother."

Too late.

She almost shoved her way into some guys, and voilà, the waves parted for me. Or, a couple people moved aside, and I got a glimpse of a table in the corner. Gage and one of his other friends were there talking to Shay. I recognized another guy from our political science class, but I searched for Linde. I couldn't find him. Becs said he was also there. I wanted to talk to him, too.

But enough was enough. Apology time had to happen.

The girl who led me started to point, but I nodded. I edged ahead of her.

"Wha—" She tried to grab me, to pull me back.

I evaded her, pushing forward until I was at the table.

Gage had his finger up. His mouth was open. He was in mid-speech, and I recognized all the signs of a big story. He froze, seeing me, and his mouth fell open a few more inches. He swore, turning to face me completely. "I forgot you were here."

I snorted and grabbed the finger he had in the air. I tried to twist it, but he yanked it away. I said, "That's a no-brainer." I sidled up between him and Shay. There was some space there. Gage was standing at the edge of the table, and Shay was leaning against the wall. Someone else could've been standing between them, but the space was empty. It was like a protected area, considering how squashed everyone else was. This space was special, private.

It was Shay's space. No one was going to invade it.

Except me. I had no problem doing that.

I stood in that spot and slapped my brother's shoulder. "You win the best brother award of all time." I laughed. "Just kidding. Blake would have your ass in a sling if he were here."

Gage was speechless.

I turned around to Shay, who seemed just as speechless. His eyes were wide and glued to me.

I moved forward, pressing my hands against his chest, and I grinned up at him. "And you. I have to apologize. I was a bitch, and I'm sorry. I'm always a bitch to you, and I'm not sure why. You're nice to me, or—" I pursed my lips, thinking about it. "Sometimes you're nice to me. You can be a dick sometimes."

He jerked out of his spell. He glanced around the bar, wrapped an arm around my waist, and pulled me close. He bent to whisper-yell into my ear, "You're drunk?"

I nodded. "I sure am."

His lips didn't move from my ear. "Your brother brought you here?"

"He sure did."

"Who the fuck have you been drinking with then?" He leaned back, his eyes drilling into mine. He clenched his jaw. "Your brother's been talking to *me*. Where have *you* been?"

My head felt heavy, but I frowned and moved back so I could see him better.

He looked pissed. He looked *more* than pissed. A vein popped out from his neck.

I swung my head to my brother. "Why is he mad? I just apologized."

Gage's mouth was still open. Some suspicion filtered in his gaze as his eyes jumped from me to Shay and back again. He shook his head. "I don't know, Kenz." Skimming an eye around the table, he drew closer and almost shielded us. Shay was leaning against the wall, the table on his right. I was facing him, the table on my left and my brother came over to box us in.

He ducked his head.

Shay grilled him. "Where's your sister been while you were here? Who's she been drinking with?" His hand tightened on my hip.

A buzzing filled my head, rising over the noise in my ears. Something was off. Something wasn't right. I wasn't remembering to do something.

I suddenly got tired, and my eyelids started to droop. I shook my head to clear that away. I didn't want to sleep, not yet.

"Kenz." Gage pressed in closer.

I glanced around. There'd been a small cocoon, but that diminished. People were closer. There were hungry looks on people's faces. Some seemed shocked. Some seemed pissed. I caught sight of Linde. He was moving toward us, his mouth pressed in a firm line. The girl who brought me over seemed rooted to her spot, her mouth slightly open.

This was what was wrong. That buzzing feeling intensified. It was me. I violated something, but I couldn't quite remember what it was.

"Kenz." Gage was saying again, trying to get my attention.

"What?"

"Who were you with just now?"

"Your friends, in the booth where we ate."

He cursed, hanging his head a moment.

Shay asked, his jaw still clenching, "Who were your friends?"

Gage shook his head. "I don't even remember. She needs to go home."

"No shit." Shay narrowed his eyes at him. "You're wasted, too."

I wasn't sure what was going on. "No. I don't want to go home." I was having fun, finally.

Shay turned those heated eyes on me. "You're underage and drunk. You're not staying."

I started to lean back, but his hand tightened. Who did he think he was? He clipped his head from side to side. "No. I'm not arguing with you. This is not up for debate. You *are* going home." He caught movement at our side and lifted his head. "I'm taking her home."

Linde shoved his way in, reaching for me. "Clarke?"

He just touched my arm. I didn't understand why everyone was so mad. I looked between all of them. "I'm good. I'm having fun. I don't get the problem."

Gage groaned. "I fucked up."

Shay ignored him, saying to Linde, "You sober?"

Linde shook his head, his hand falling back to his side. "No. You?"

"I just downed too much. It's going to hit me." He tugged me closer to him, leaning back to my ear. "I'm going to call for a cab. I'll ride with you to your dorm."

I turned my head so my lips were a few inches from him. He pulled back a little so he could see me, but that just meant our lips were even closer together. There was a small amount of space between our bodies. I wasn't fully leaning on him, but I was beginning to wonder why not. We were so close, and I was getting heated. I was forgetting what I was going to say.

"You don't want me here?"

His eyes darkened. "That isn't it." His hand lifted to the side of my face, but he cursed and let it fall again. He straightened, pulled away, and raised his voice. "If you get caught here, you'll be in a ton of trouble. All of us would since we know you're here. You have to go."

I felt a pang in my chest. That made sense. I turned to Gage and Linde. "I don't want you guys to get in trouble for me. I'm sorry."

Linde started to shake his head, but Gage turned to Shay. "You stay. She's my sister. I'll take her home."

Shay ignored him, asking Linde, "Can you call a cab?"

Linde nodded, pulling his phone out. He pointed to the side door where we stood. "It might be awhile. Tonight's busy. I'll have it pull up out there. You guys can just slip out."

Shay nodded. His arm fell away from around my waist, but he kept one hand on my hip. It anchored me in place, and his hand flexed, clamping down a little harder. It just pulled me toward him again. That same buzzing sensation was building in me, taking over. I shook my head, trying to clear some of the fog that being around Shay formed.

I couldn't fall into him and pull those lips down to mine. There was a reason, but I was fast forgetting it. I was in a bar. There were people around us, and he was so warm. He was so protective. He was dangerous. I felt a slice of awareness. This was the guy who commanded his football team against the opponents. He ran the show, and he hadn't let me see this side of him, but I wasn't worried. That danger wasn't directed at me. It was out, because of me, because he was going to take care of me.

I started to throb, wanting him, almost needing him. But, no. My brother was there. People were there. I held myself back, and I glanced up and felt captured immediately. The same stark hunger was there, and I almost groaned, my tongue darting out to lick my lips. His eyes caught the movement, and I swear that I heard an answering groan from him. His hand took on a different hold. He was keeping me in place and himself back.

We just stood there, waiting, trying not to jump at each other.

Apparently the pub was still serving food because a pizza arrived to the table. I wasn't going to eat any, but Shay's eyes flashed at me. "You need to eat. You need to sober up."

Well, when you put it that way. And my mouth was watering again. Why did everything taste so much better after booze?

I finished my second piece when I felt a soft touch on my arm. Gage flashed me a sad smile. He leaned close. "I didn't know this was going on."

I looked at Shay. He turned his head away. I wasn't sure if he heard or not. The music was drowning everything out, but he was close. He could've heard. Either way, he was acting as if he hadn't. He was giving my brother and me some privacy.

I said back to Gage, "There's nothing going on."

Gage cocked his head to the side, his lips forming a frown. "Are you serious?"

I was beginning to remember the problem. I'd outed myself. People now knew who I knew. The realization flooded in, along with an increasing panic, but I couldn't stop it. It was already done. I was standing in a very small and sheltered circle of these guys whom I didn't want people to know were in my life.

Even knowing the problems this could cause, I had no desire to pull away from Shay's hand. That one touch, one hold, was tantalizing to me. I began to thirst for more, and I looked at his face, at his lips.

They were perfect, especially when they were on me.

Sensing my attention, Shay's lip twitched into a smirk.

Hunger, desire, and a primal need overwhelmed me. I started to sway toward him, but his hand flexed again. He held me back, and he wasn't letting me move any farther away.

Linde leaned in to my brother, said something, and then flashed his phone at Shay.

Gage turned to me. "Your cab is here. I'll talk to you tomorrow."

I already knew I didn't want that, though I nodded.

Shay turned me around, pushing away from the wall. His hands found both sides of my waist, and he started to propel me forward and around the table. We moved through the crowd. There weren't a lot of people between us and the door, but there were enough that it still took a few minutes. I waved to Linde over my shoulder, and he dipped his head in another one of those nods. He turned, his hand going around the waist of the girl who led me to their table. She was saying something to him, and his head bent down to better hear her. Gage waved, too, but his eyes were sad.

I sighed.

Shay reached around me and opened the door.

I stepped out, his hands still on me, and made sure the door shut right behind us. He ushered me behind a truck, stepping around so we were hidden. As soon as we did, the door opened again. I saw a security guard look out. He searched up and down both sides of the sidewalk, frowned, and retreated back inside.

Shay was so close behind me that I could feel his body heat. "No one's supposed to use that door. It's for emergencies. They think someone tried to sneak in."

That made sense. I was trying to tell him that, but my throat stopped working. Everything stopped working, even my brain. I turned around, my back against the truck, and I gazed at Shay. His eyes were almost black, and I knew he was feeling the same need as me. I could feel him on my hip. I reached down and brushed over the bulge in his jeans.

He expelled a ragged breath, closing his eyes. "You're drunk."

My hand curved around him, applying pressure. I murmured, my voice husky, "I'm not that drunk." I'd been sobering up real fast, and I stepped into him, bringing our bodies in line together. I looked up, my thumb rubbing over him through his jeans. "Let's go to your house instead."

He groaned, his eyes lidded and heavy as he watched me, but then there was a flash of lights and a car pulled up by the side door we had just snuck out from. He cursed, taking my hand. "It's the cab. Come on."

# CHAPTER SEVENTEEN

We got into the cab, and Shay told him his address.

He sank back next to me, our hands intertwined, and I didn't know what I was doing. My heart was racing. My entire body was inflamed. Our hips were touching, and he turned so it looked like he was looking out my door, but he wasn't. His lips were at my forehead, and our hands moved to my lap. They pressed down on my leg. The back of his hand was lightly touching where I was throbbing the most.

I wanted to shift, pull his hand farther down, but I didn't dare. I was bold that night, but not that bold. Not yet, anyway.

Grinning slightly, I looked up.

His eyes were there, as if he was waiting for me, and just as soon as I realized that, his lips were on mine. Or maybe mine were on his. Either way, it was exactly what I needed. He picked me up, lifting me to straddle him, and we made out the entire ride home. Shay didn't touch me anywhere inappropriate. No clothing left our bodies, though I ran my hands up under his shirt, making him shudder. I broke off the kiss to catch my breath, but dear God, his chest was amazing. Then he tugged me back, and we were kissing again.

I sensed him pausing a few times. I wasn't sure why, until at one point I looked and saw he was watching the driver. He'd go back to kissing me a second later until we pulled up outside Shay's house. He paid for the cab, taking my hand and pulling me around to the back of the house.

"Some of the guys didn't go out." He pointed to the living room windows where I could see a lit-up television screen. The rest of the house seemed quiet and dark. We crossed the back patio, but instead of heading for the door that we'd used the last time I was there, Shay went to a far left door.

He used his key to unlock it, and I was surprised to see another stairway going up. It was sectioned off from the rest of the house as if it were its own unit. A door led off to our right, which I assumed would've taken us to the kitchen and the main house.

Shay flipped on some lights so I could see and then stepped back to let me go first. He took his shoes off by the door, locked it, and then his hands went back to my hips.

On our way up the stairs, I stopped, just once, and leaned back against him. His lips skimmed up my neck, lingering on my chin before I turned my head halfway to him and our lips caught and held again. I groaned softly. I could stay just like that. In fact, I turned toward him.

I felt him grinning against my lips. "What are you doing?"

I wound my arms around him and lifted myself up, hooking my legs behind his back. "I have no idea." Then I was kissing him again, and it was true. I really didn't. My mind didn't like Shay, but my body did, and right now, I was only listening to my body. I was doing whatever it wanted, and holding on to him, crawling up him, kissing him, raking my hands through his hair—that was what I was going to do.

"Fuck it," he half-growled and hoisted me farther up him, his hands clamping under my ass. He carried me the rest of the way, going into a back bedroom and then tumbling down onto a bed.

He pulled away once to close the door and lock it. Then he was back, and I lay on that bed, staring up at him. The moonlight lit up his face, and I gulped.

He was the most masterful thing I'd seen.

"Come here," I said, my voice hoarse again.

"Are you sure?"

I nodded. I was so beyond being sure.

He fell onto the bed, catching himself so he was braced above me on his hands. Long minutes passed as he took his time to look me up and down. That only made me hotter. I began writhing, just wanting him, needing him to fulfill a throb between my legs.

He paused, his eyes finding mine, and he shifted on his weight so he was resting on his side. He propped himself up, his hand tracing down the side of my face tenderly. His thumb rested on my lips, and he asked so softly. "Are you for sure about this? Really?"

"Yeah." I turned my head so I was facing him directly. Our lips were inches apart. "Why?"

"You hate me."

I shook my head. "I don't right now."

"You will tomorrow."

I touched the side of his face and shook my head. "I might hate you if you don't touch me."

He groaned, his eyes smoldering. "Then God help us." And his lips were on mine again, where I'd been aching for them since they left.

He was demanding. He was commanding. He was consuming. I answered every call of his. I was panting as he skimmed his hand down my front, smoothed over my stomach, and pushed up under my shirt. I was breathing heavy as it was lifted up, and I wound my arms back around his neck, feeling him fall back down slowly until his weight was on top of me.

Goddamn. That felt right, so right.

We were kissing, our lips fused together, and his tongue moved inside. I answered it with mine, and there was a whole other battle ensuing there as he unclasped my bra and then caught one breast in his hand. He encircled it, his thumb rubbing over my nipple, making me shiver. I ran a hand down his back, down his side, and delighted as he trembled under my touch. Returning the favor, I pulled his shirt up, forcing him to break the kiss long enough to free him of the fabric.

Then he was back on me, skin to skin, lips to lips, and I could've lain like that for hours. We did the other night, but this had a different feel to it. There was more. I needed more. He wanted more. We were giving more.

"Fucking hell," he moaned, pulling away but only to start kissing down my throat, my chest, then he found one of my nipples.

I gasped, grabbing on to him as if he were my anchor.

He chuckled, his breath another sensual caress, and his tongue laved over my nipple. Then he moved to the other one, and he began the same. He tasted it. He ran his tongue over it, and he enjoyed how I was gasping at each swirl, each lick, each nip, and every time he touched me. He was worshipping my body, moving down my stomach, lingering there as his hands paused over my jeans. He found the button, and he glanced up. He was waiting. Biting my lip, I nodded my assent, and his fingers popped the button before slowly sliding the zipper down.

His hand slid inside my underwear, finding my center, and then he slid a finger in.

I arched my back, wanting him to go deeper. I wasn't even joking. I croaked out, "Move that finger, or I'm going to go crazy."

He laughed, dipping his head down to press a kiss on my stomach, and then he started moving in and out. His hand kept going. I began moving with him, only answering whatever his hand wanted of me, and after a bit, he slipped a second finger, then a third. He kept going deeper with each thrust until I swore I could feel him in my stomach. He'd pull them out and start all over again.

The pleasure was almost blinding.

I kept gasping and moving with him, but he didn't pick up the pace. He went at his own, content to watch me go nuts. At one point, he looked up, a tenderness in his eyes that I'd never seen before, and he grinned. The smile was slow, and it broke me.

I went over the edge, and I was gasping as my climax slammed into me.

I didn't understand that look. It was something deep, and it moved something in me, something that I'd never felt touched before. I wasn't talking about my body or physical caresses. I didn't understand it, but when he pulled his hand out and moved farther up my body, I reached and guided his lips to mine.

This kiss was different.

It was slow. It was tender. It was special.

It made my toes curl, and it felt like the most natural thing in the world for him to reach for a condom. He grabbed one and then helped me tug the rest of my clothes off. His found the floor next to mine, and Shay rose above me. He waited at my center. I'd just had his fingers there. I was more than ready for the rest of him, and with another kiss, he dipped his mouth down to my shoulder and edged inside.

He felt right.

He stretched my insides and waited for me to acclimate to him before he began thrusting. In and out. He was moving in me, and I was moving with him. It was what I'd been wanting, and it felt so right.

I grasped his shoulders, my nails curving into his skin, and as he thrust inside me, I raked those nails down him.

I felt a scream building, and I muffled it in my throat, but I wanted to yell out.

My mouth was open as he kept moving, in and out, deeper and deeper. The rhythm was steady, the waves were riding over me, and he began going faster.

"Shay," I whimpered, needing something I couldn't articulate.

His lips found mine, and he paused, grinding into me. Good God, that felt good. He raised himself, pulling out, only to slide back in once more. He went as deep as he had gone with his fingers, and I could feel him coming close. My body was beginning to twitch. The pressure was building, but he pulled out and turned me over. He bent over my back, sliding back inside, and I moved my head. Our lips caught and held.

He began pounding into me.

I gasped, arching my chest out.

Shay leaned up, his hands finding my hips, and he went harder and harder.

I hurtled over the edge, falling down onto the bed. I caught myself, as his hand skimmed my back. He kissed me tenderly, and then he finished.

We stayed in place. I was bent over. He was holding himself upright, his hand resting on my ass, and then he bent over me. His lips grazed my shoulder, and he pulled out, falling to the bed beside me.

I was panting for breath.

He was, too, and he curled an arm around my waist, spooning me from the back. He fit alongside me, molding his body to mine as his arms wrapped tightly around me. I lie there, riding out the tremors of my climax as he peppered my bare shoulder with slow, lazy kisses.

After a moment, once our breathing had returned to normal, he slipped his leg between mine and buried his head into my shoulder.

"So." He kissed my neck softly. "We did that."

I laughed, patting his hand tucked under my breast. "Is that what we did?"

He chuckled into me, and I closed my eyes, enjoying the feel of him. "Something like that." He rested on his back, loosening his hold on me, and I turned over so I was lying on my side, facing him. I rested a hand on his chest, and his eyes watched mine until his hand found my own.

I murmured, "I don't regret that."

He hooked his finger around mine. "Really?"

I nodded. I couldn't, not anymore. Not after we made out in my closet, then my bed, and after I was practically begging him for it at the bar.

I croaked, "I touched your bulge."

He started laughing, curving more into me. "You did."

"It was the most momentous and memorable part of the night."

I was grinning.

He lifted his head. "Really?"

He wasn't.

I nodded. "For sure. I became the definition of a wanton hussy."

He started laughing again.

I kept going, "I can imagine all the stories that start with, 'The day she touched my bulge', or 'The day I touched his bulge,' 'The moment my hand felt his jeans, and his dick swelled underneath', or even . . ." I was laughing now, "'I laid my hands on him, right over his jeans, and he rose up. He answered my call. I called out, Come forth, hard penis, and answer milady's beckoning. My hips call upon your touch. You must heed and give forth plentiful of your pleasure.'"

He continued laughing, wrapping his arms around me, and somehow he had curled his entire body around mine again. I was lying on my back once more, and he stopped, lifting his head from my neck. He gazed down at me, shifting to rise up on his elbow. He caught some hairs and tucked them behind my ear, letting his hand linger there, holding me gently.

He grew serious. "I want to keep doing this."

I rested my hand over his on my face. "Fucking me from behind?"

He grinned and then sobered. "No. This, whatever it is. We don't need to put words to it, if you don't want to."

I groaned. "Please, don't. I tend to get bitchy when words are applied to situations." I sobered a bit and let the joking slide. "I won't date you."

His eyes sharpened.

I added, "But I'm okay with this." Good gracious, my body was already going through withdrawals. A renewed need was rising, but I pushed it off. "Maybe we can talk about it, as in we're making plans to do more of this, but no real talking otherwise."

He shook his head, grinning. "You're like a guy's wet dream. Do you realize that?"

I smiled, shrugging. "I like to think I'm my own wet dream."

He groaned, his lips finding mine again. He pulled back a moment later. "Are you sure about this?"

Moment of truth? I said, "No." His eyes held mine, and I clarified, "But I don't care right now." I grabbed his head, found his lips with mine, and it wasn't long before we were both groaning again.

# CHAPTER EIGHTEEN

The stairs creaked under my weight, and I paused for the thirtieth time that morning.

"What are you doing?"

I sucked in my breath and looked up. Shay was at the top of the stairs, shirtless, and his sweats rested deliciously low on his hips. I managed a smile. "Experiencing a new term called 'stairway of shame.'" I cracked a grin. "I'm going to call a cab to avoid that one."

He groaned, scratching his chest idly. "Get your cute ass up here. I'll change. We'll get breakfast. I'll give you a ride home."

"You have your Jeep here?"

He nodded, yawning. "I got a ride to the bar last night." He motioned for me to follow him. "Come on. I could use a shower, too."

I followed him and somehow found myself in the shower with him, grabbing on to the showerhead as Shay was thrusting inside me ten minutes later.

I gasped, and he adjusted his hands, holding me upright as I tightened my legs around his waist.

After we both climaxed—which was another whole holy-fuck-shit-mother-of-God moment—my legs were definitely weaker, I fell to his bed and rolled onto my back. "Your dick is out of me, and I swear that I'm feeling withdrawals."

He barked out a laugh, reaching into his closet. He pulled out another pair of sweats and a couple of shirts. He tossed a sweatshirt my way, along with a smaller pair of black pants. I asked, "What's this?"

"I'm taking you to breakfast. Figured you wouldn't want to wear the same clothes from yesterday."

He had a point. Mine had smells I didn't want to identify. I pushed onto my elbows so I could watch him as he began pulling on his sweats and sweatshirt.

I groaned, falling back down. "You're going to ruin me. I just know it."

He laughed, tossing my bra and underwear at me. "Do you want those?"

I grabbed them and wrinkled my nose. They were filled with smoke from the bar, but they'd have to do. I wasn't willing to be completely willy-nilly. Sitting up, I started to dress.

My entire body was satiated. I hadn't felt like this since a really hard workout, and I'm talking my senior year. I was feeling the same effects, even some of the same sore spots, but this one had been so worth it.

A few minutes later, we headed down the stairs as Shay explained that a few other football players lived on the same floor with him. The house was divided so each floor was like its own apartment, but the biggest kitchen and living room were on the main floor. While some might use the second floor or third floor's living room, the main floor was the main hub of the house.

I asked, as we went down the stairs, "What floor are you on?"

His hand touched my waist. "We're on the third. The least amount of rooms and the most privacy."

We were nearing the door that attached the stairway to the main floor and the kitchen. I could hear voices, male and female, along with dishes and chairs scraping over the floor. Someone was coming toward us, and as we got to the end, Shay leaned around me and flicked the lock on the door. The knob turned, and we heard, "Who locked this door?"

Shay urged me outside, and we hurried.

Once we got on the driveway and walked to the street, he explained, "I didn't want to deal with a lot of ribbing this morning."

I shrugged. I was okay with that.

He caught my hand and led me the rest of the way to his Jeep Wrangler. Fifteen minutes later, we were heading inside a little diner.

I knew we should have a real talk, but I didn't want to. I knew who this guy was. He was near a celebrity at our school, and he was sleeping with me. It wasn't normal for a guy like him to be with a girl like me, but it was happening. Maybe I hated him at the beginning because I knew this was where we were going, or maybe because I could sense he'd affect me. Or maybe it really was because he reminded me of Parker.

I tilted my head, considering him . . .

Shay looked up from his menu. "What's wrong?"

"Nothing." And that was the answer to my internal question. Nothing. I couldn't find anything in him that was like Parker, except that he was the last guy I had between my legs. Maybe that counted? Maybe that was the reason for my dislike?

As if sensing my thoughts, Shay ordered us both coffee and leaned back after the hostess left. His face grew guarded.

"What's going on with you? Already remembering that you hate me?"

I shook my head, admitting the truth. "I don't hate you." Maybe I never did—well, I wasn't going to go that far. There'd been genuine dislike. I couldn't pull that out of my ass.

He didn't respond, and we stared at each other until the coffee came.

I groaned, reaching to pour myself a cup once the girl left. "My body freaking loves you."

He rolled his eyes, rubbing a hand over his face. "We're doing this again? I thought we established our rules."

We had sex. Nothing else.

I put the carafe back onto the table. "You can't sleep with anyone else."

"What?"

He was mocking me and joking at the same time, and he reached for the coffee. He added, "I can't put my dick in someone else? That's barbaric."

I'd been reaching for the cream, but paused. "Are you joking? You better be joking."

"Of course, I'm joking."

My shoulders relaxed, and I finished putting cream and sugar into my coffee. Gage liked it the same way. He tended to joke he liked it black, and I had to put the "fruity" stuff in. That was what he called cream and sugar, but fuck him. If both of us had to endure a month of black coffee, only one of us would survive. Me. Because I'd drink the shit. He'd have given up and begged for his cream and sugar.

"What are you laughing at?"

I looked up. I'd been grinning, and I shook it off. "Thinking something stupid about my brother."

"Speaking of your brother." Shay leaned forward, dropping his voice. "He and everyone else in the bar last night are going to talk about us. Right?"

I'd fucked up last night. Big time. I broke all of my rules, and it'd been my bidding. Not Shay's. Not my brother's. No one else. I groaned, banging my forehead against the table gently. "I'm so screwed."

"No, you're not."

"I'm not?" How could he say that? "Everyone saw."

"A few people saw. Those people will say something, but if you really want to commit to this where no one knows, it's possible."

"How?" I shook my head. "You can't tease me like that, not if it isn't true."

"It is true. Look." He leaned forward. "We do our own thing. No touching. No secret looks. We don't talk about it. It'll blow over in a few weeks, if that's what you want."

I nodded. Hell yes. "It isn't you or me. It's my roommate. It's my friends. It's girls who get pissed because you like me and not them."

"I get it." He frowned. "Kind of. Not really, but whatever you want."

I held up my finger. "And there are no strings, but if you do start sleeping with someone else, you tell me. I'd rather wait till that's done, then have your dick double-dipping somewhere."

He'd been reaching for more coffee, but his hands settled on the table for a second. He watched me, and I asked, "What?"

"You're so crude sometimes."

I was. "Say it how I see it."

He shook his head, blinking a few times. "I don't know if that's refreshing or unnerving."

The food came, and I reached for one of my pieces of toast. "You tell me the next time you're bent over my ass. I'm thinking, you'll find me refreshing then."

He groaned, dropping the knife and fork he'd picked up. "Fucking hell, Clarke."

*Clarke.* I grinned. Last names again. I was already feeling more comfortable. I preened at him, waving my toast in the air. "You'll be happy. Just think how jealous I'll be when Becs is flashing her cleavage at you later today. Bet you don't get that from other girls you used to sleep with."

He shook his head again. "You're slightly mental."

I shrugged, taking a big bite out of my toast. I was just being me.

# CHAPTER NINETEEN

I wasn't sure about my game plan for the dorms.

Shay dropped me off, and I decided the best course of action was no course. I hid. Or, to be more accurate, I avoided. Everyone.

It was around eleven in the morning when I walked into my dorm room. Missy was gone, but I was Dick Crusher now. I had little doubt I could sit in there, get comfortable, and expect her not to know about my new nickname. I bolted. To be more exact, I showered, changed, grabbed every textbook I could think of for studying, packed my laptop, and headed for the library. My only stop was the coffee cart, and I'd been on the third floor, in the farthest study room in the corner, all day.

Or I was, until Shay texted and I got a bunch of emails from everyone in our political science group. They were meeting in the large computer lab at six that evening. I had an hour to collect myself and get ready. Once I went down there, all eyes would be on me. The Dick Crusher video and maybe the rumors about Shay and me had already spread, it didn't matter. Just being at the same table as Shay would get the rumor mill going.

One hour.

I did what every normal college student did—I went and ate ice cream (along with other substances, but ice cream was the main priority) and loaded up on caffeine. I purchased two energy drinks from the shop, and in case I didn't want to pull out the energy drinks, I grabbed another large coffee.

I was loaded and primed. I wasn't sure what for, but I was ready. I could be a goddamn doomsday prepper.

I purposely went to the computer lab late. Becca and Aby were divas. They were also going to be late, and I was right. I was late on purpose, and they were just setting their things down when I shouldered past the glass doors.

Shay was sitting with his back to me. Linde was next to him.

This would be lovely.

Aby and Becca took the two seats across from the guys. The only two empty seats were next to Becca or next to Shay. Talk about adding gasoline to a fire. I wasn't even forced into a choice.

I sat by Becca.

Shay looked at me, humor damped down in those gorgeous eyes, and he lifted two fingers in the laziest greeting I'd seen in a long time. Linde narrowed his eyes, looking between the two of us, but just nodded. "What's up? You got home okay last night?" His eyes skirted back to Shay.

I unzipped my bag and dumped my political science textbook onto the table in front of me. "Sure did. Nice and rested, and no hangover today."

Becca groaned, pulling her books out of her backpack. "Aren't you the most chipper person here?" She rolled her eyes. "Can this day suck any more than it does?" She shoved back her chair and left in a huff.

Aby leaned over. "Her ex called last night. They got together, and he broke back up with her this morning."

Linde started laughing.

Aby shook her head at him. "You wouldn't laugh if you had to spend all day with her. My advice? Plop her down in front of a computer over there and tell her what to research. Keep her away from us, or she's going to draw blood."

"You're joking?"

She said to Linde, "Nope. You'll see for yourself in an hour."

And in an hour, we did. She bitched. She griped. She complained. She bitched again. There was ranting, raving, a full-blown vent session about someone I had no clue about, and she started to cycle back around to the bitching portion of the evening.

"Okay." Shay took one of the worksheets and slapped it in front of her. "Research all of this shit." He pointed to the farthest empty computer. "Over there."

"You're just trying to get rid of me." Her lips puckered out in a pout.

Aby's eyes widened, but she didn't say anything. She slid down an inch in her seat, lifting her book so it completely covered her face.

"Yes," Shay clipped out. "Will it work?"

She growled. It was soft, but it was an actual growl. She snatched up the paper. "Yes, but only because it's you asking." She softened her tone. A sweet and adoring smile was the cherry on top. "Because you're so gorgeous, Shay."

She left for the computer, and I twisted around. "Oh, look at that." Her hips had an extra sway to them. "Even her ass looks like a bitch."

She braked, rotating swiftly to glare at me.

I glared back. "I'll let you know if your ex calls again."

She sucked in her breath but went to the computer.

When I sat straight again, everyone was watching me. "What?"

Aby said, "That was mean, even for you."

I shrugged, ignoring Linde and Shay and flipping to a new page in my book. "Why do people assume I have no backbone or that I'm only nice? Seriously. People need to stop underestimating me. It's annoying when my normal, real-human side comes out."

"Uh." Aby frowned. "I don't think we assume that. Any of that."

A group of books landed on the table in front of me with a *thud.* I jumped, cursing, and then Gage dropped to the seat. He had his bag in front of him, and he nodded to everyone at the table. "Hey-a!"

He paused on Aby, pointing his phone at her. "Did we sleep together sometime?"

I expected a no.

I got a, "Freshman year, second semester. My boyfriend and I were on a break."

He snapped his fingers in triumph. "Ah-ha! I knew it." He tapped the side of his head. "I forget faces all the time, but not yours and especially not anymore." He checked her out, sliding his eyes up and down.

I remarked, "They're back together."

"Ah." He nodded to Linde and to Shay, his eyes narrowing slightly at Shay before focusing back on me. He propped his elbows on the table, nudging my arm with one of them. "Hey, sis. I figured I can talk to you now that you went public last night. How's your day? What are you up to?"

Aby muttered under her breath, "Being a bitch."

Gage shrugged. "She does that." He leaned down and dropped his voice, whispering so everyone could still hear, "You haven't answered my texts or called me back. Are you mad at me?"

"What for?"

He straightened, his voice going back to normal. "For last night? I forgot you were at the bar." He glanced to Shay. "Right?" When no one responded right away, Gage's frown deepened. "Or was I really, really, really drunk last night? I could've sworn I had dinner with you."

Linde started laughing. Shay was grinning.

Gage took their cue, his eyes widening. "It *did* happen then? I'm not losing my mind?"

Aby cut in, "It's too cute to lose. I didn't see her, but I heard she was there."

I couldn't. I looked at her. "My brother's brain is too cute to lose? Have you seen a brain in real life? Or even a picture? *That's* your pick-up line? You have a boyfriend."

"Man." She edged her seat over an inch. "Maybe the bitch vibe stayed here." She shot me a meaningful look.

I rolled my eyes. I had more retorts to spew, but swallowed them. Every single one. I didn't know why I was irritated with Aby or even Becca. They weren't my favorite people in the world, but they weren't my enemies.

"Oh, no. This is total Kennedy. Don't piss her off, because you'll see a whole other level."

Aby snorted. "I think we all know. Matt Carruthers found that out for us."

I asked, "Who's Matt Carruthers?"

"The guy whose dick you crushed," Gage told me.

"Got it." Asshole One was Matt Carruthers in real life. I hoped I'd never have to deal with him again. "Could I get arrested for that?"

"You know what?" Shay grinned at me, a sharpness in his eyes. "You can look that up yourself in your textbook." He pointed to my book. There was an extra tone in his voice, and I frowned long enough to figure out he was telling me to shut up.

I nodded. The video would open up a whole conversation I probably wanted to avoid. Like why I was so mad, what I did afterward, and eventually round to the bar and what happened after the bar.

I was happy to shut up.

But first, I grabbed Gage's arm and pulled him with me. I headed out of the lab, past a blonde girl standing in the doorway, past the front desk clerk, through the metal detectors, even past the coffee cart until we were outside. It was the best place for privacy. There were a few people there, so I kept walking until we hit a private alcove of trees.

"What are you doing here?"

"I've been calling you all day. Do you not check your phone?"

"You called my cell or my room phone?" I asked as I was pulling my phone out of my pocket. I lit the screen up and saw a few missed calls, along with some text messages.

"Both."

I waved my phone in the air before putting it back in my pocket. "I didn't check it today." Shay's one text lit the screen up so I hadn't needed to see all the rest. "I'm sorry if you were worried."

"I wasn't worried about you getting home last night. I was worried how pissed you were at me today, and," he lowered his voice, "I can't help but be worried about whatever you have going on with Shay Coleman."

I narrowed my eyes. "Nothing's going on with Shay."

"Right."

He didn't believe me.

"If there were, I wouldn't be stupid about it."

He studied me before nodding. "I guess that's all I can hope for as a big brother. You're not mad at me for forgetting about you last night?"

"I'm not mad at you for last night."

He released a deep breath he'd been holding. "Good." His hand patted his chest. "I was worried about that. I even went around your dorm."

"Wait. What?"

"Your dorm."

"I haven't been there all day."

"Yeah, I know." He held his hands up. "Don't worry. I followed your rules. I went to see Casey, technically, and she went up and talked to your roommate. Your roommate has no clue."

He saw Casey.

He probably saw Kristina and the others.

My only semblance of normality was my roommate now. I was fucked.

I groaned. "You can't come around my dorm."

"Casey and her friends already know. She said she didn't say anything to your roommate."

It didn't matter. Everyone knew. I didn't care about my roommate. Well, I did, but in the grand scheme of things, she was an ant. "Gage," I moaned. "You're making things so difficult for me." That wasn't totally true. I was doing plenty myself.

"Me?" He pointed to the library. "What about you and whatever you have going on with the starting quarterback of the university's football team? You want to stay low-key? Don't sleep with a guy like that. Date down, Kenz. Don't shoot for the top tier, because Shay Coleman *is* the top tier. He's the whole tier at the very fucking top."

"I know," I started.

He kept going.

I shouted to shut him up, "I know!"

He stopped.

"Okay? I know. And it isn't as if this was planned. We just, he just—I just . . ." No. No. No. I wasn't explaining how I ended up in Shay's bed last night. I pressed my hands to my forehead. A headache was forming, and I began to rub there, hoping to smooth it away.

It wasn't working. I knew it wouldn't work. I gave up.

Gage was looking at the ground. He stuffed his hands into his pockets. "You never said you weren't in his bed. You would've jumped on that instantly if it wasn't true." He let his sentence hang, and I couldn't refute it. He was right. I would've. I wasn't pre-law anymore, but I still had that fighting spirit in me. I would've been all over that.

"No one knows."

"Do you even know?"

My eyes flicked to his. "What do you mean?"

"Do you know what you're doing? With him. I know what Parker did to you, and I wouldn't wan—"

"Shay is not Parker. He's the farthest thing from Parker." I hoped.

My inside voice, the one I kept in the back of my mind, piped up, *That isn't true.* I shut it down. Parker was popular. Parker was charismatic, and he had the whole school eating out of his hands. Parker was gorgeous, but that was it. The similarities ended there.

Parker was not Shay—no. Shay was not Parker.

I shook my head. What was I thinking there?

I laughed. "I'm good. It isn't emotional. It's just physical. I mean, we have rules."

"I don't need to hear them. Seriously. Please. No."

"I get that."

"I *am* sorry about last night. I felt horrible, and then I saw how furious Coleman was, and that made me feel even worse. Look, I don't want to get involved with whatever you have going on, but he cares. I saw that last night. Linde cares, too. Whatever you have going on, those two guys are good friends right now."

Right now.

I knew why my brother said that, because friendships end. Friendships fade. Friendships crash and burn sometimes. I nodded. "I know." And since he mentioned Linde, I started, "Hey. Um. I have to talk to you about Casey."

He'd started to head back but faced me again. "Sure. What?"

I had no other way to say this, so— "Don't date her."

"What?" He laughed this time, a hitch of nerves in there. "What are you talking about?"

"Linde's sister was raped."

"What does that have to do with Casey and me?"

I gave him a look. "Come on." I didn't wait for him to acknowledge what I knew was going on. The way his voice just sounded verified it for me. "Linde said that after his sister was raped, she used another guy to try to erase what the rapist did to her. She thought he could, I don't know, replace what she was feeling on the inside."

Gage had gone so still. He asked so quietly, "Did it work?"

I shook my head.

Another confirmation. My brother was already involved. He had feelings.

I murmured, "No. She pushed him away. Gage, did you—"

He shoved through the trees' opening and went back to the library. I followed at a slower pace, but he was packing up his stuff when I got there. Shay and Linde were both watching. Aby was gone.

I stood behind my seat. "Gage, I—"

"Stop." He was dead serious. "I think it's really fucking stupid what you're doing, so don't tell me what I should do."

"It isn't the same thing." I would not look at Shay.

Gage did. His eyes glanced to him before finding mine again. "Isn't it? One guy destroyed you . . ." He didn't finish his sentence. He let the insinuation linger, and I flushed.

Gage zipped his bag closed and left.

Fuck.

I sank down onto my chair.

Linde cleared his throat. "Do we even want to know what that was about?"

I shook my head. "No." I didn't look at him. I still didn't look at Shay, and when Aby and Becca returned to the table, I didn't look at them. I went back to the old Kennedy, the one who kept quiet, kept under the radar, and yearned for the sanctity of her planner and isolation.

# CHAPTER TWENTY

"Clarke!"

I'd just left the library. We researched for a few more hours, but I was tired and that headache never left. It only got worse, and Shay was coming after me now. He called again, "Kennedy!"

I stopped and turned around. My bag fell off my shoulder, catching on my elbow with a *thump* before it could fall to the ground. "I'm tired, Shay. I just want to go back to my dorm."

He slowed his pace, sliding his hands into his pockets as he drew near. "You were quiet after your brother left."

"You don't have to do this." I didn't want this. "We're not dating."

His eyes narrowed, and he tilted his head to the side. "This is called human decency. I still did stuff like this when we weren't sleeping together, remember?"

"See." I pointed to my face. "This idiot here is being bitchy to the wrong person." I rubbed a hand down my face. "I've had an eventful weekend. This loner is salivating at the thought of hanging out in her room alone for the rest of the night."

"Okay, but I still wanted to check on you. If I hadn't come, Linde would've."

"Ah." I liked Linde. We were pals, but I could be honest in a different way with Shay. I was now relieved it'd been him. "Thank you. Again." I waved and started back down the sidewalk.

I got a couple feet before he called my name again in a low voice. "If you can't sleep, just give me a call. I can pick you up."

I stared at him. For a moment, just a moment, I considered it. Going back to his house, sleeping in his bed, in his arms, sounded like a sheltered seclusion away from whatever my roommate would say to me about the video, with Casey and worrying about her or how she was going to hurt my brother, and even the loneliness that came along with being a loner. Shay was warm. Shay was nice, and in that moment, as I stared at him, I forgot why I ever hated him in the beginning.

But that would bring other problems. Maybe not right away, but eventually. Bad shit always came along. A person couldn't hide from it, and I shook my head. "I'm going to be the responsible freshman."

"My phone will be on. I'm just saying."

"Okay."

He held his hand up before heading back for the library.

I walked the rest of the way alone.

Missy was leaving the room in a pair of sweats and some slippers. She had a bag of Twizzlers and chips in hand, her blanket thrown over her arm. "Hey." She stopped in the hallway, popping a Twizzler into her mouth. She spoke around it, "Where'd you sleep last night? I didn't hear you come in at all."

"I got in late and left early." I indicated my backpack. "Long day at the library."

"Oh." Her eyebrows pinched together. She pointed down the hall with her Twizzler. "We're watching movies in Holly's room if you want to come. Did you go to the game yesterday?"

Had she not seen the Dick Crusher video? "Uh." I itched behind my ear. "Yeah. I was there."

"That's weird. I didn't see you."

"I was."

"Oh." She took another chomp. "Come watch a movie with us. We're all bringing snacks."

"I don't have any."

"Order a pizza. You'd be the hit of the room." She grinned.

I refueled with food only once today, and it was after ten. My stomach growled to remind me. Maybe a pizza was a good idea, but I shook my head. "I kinda just want to curl up and watch a movie in our room tonight."

"Okay." She waved with a new Twizzler. "See ya later. I don't have my morning class tomorrow, so I'm staying up later."

I breathed a thank you prayer under my breath as I headed for the room, and she went the opposite way. Not only could I relax but I'd also be able to sleep and not get woken up from six to seven, all the way until I had to finally crawl out of bed.

I checked my email, typed up some leftover notes from our research project, and ordered a pizza.

I put a movie on, pulled out the fluffy robe, and the pizza arrived. It was all for me.

Best. Night. Ever.

I was sleeping when Missy came in, rocking the bunk beds as she climbed to her mattress. She was snoring five minutes later. She snored her way through my alarm and as I got ready for class. I was a little later than normal because I went slow so as not to wake her up, but I wasn't missing my coffee. I *needed* my coffee, so I made a quick detour through the library first. When I got to my classroom's building, I bypassed the main door everyone used and headed down the barren sidewalk Shay and I had been standing when we had talked about Casey on Friday.

I was able to slip into the building, up the stairs, and I came from the north hallway. There was no line like there was heading up from the stairs. I headed in, and immediately a cheer rose from the room.

"It's Dick Crusher!" a guy I didn't know led the crowd. He waved his hands in a worshipping motion. "All hail the DC."

Some girls laughed. Some guys echoed him, making the same motions, and I rolled my eyes. The back row was still empty, and I marched right there. I'd seek shelter with friends. Screw my rules. I had a feeling I'd need the support, and I plopped down in the far right seat. It was the only one the guys didn't sit in.

The guy who led the cheer sat up and turned around. "I know Carruthers. How'd it feel to hold his dick? Did you get a little turned on? You can be honest. This is just between you and me."

More snickers sounded.

One guy started to add to it, but Shay walked into the room with Linde and the rest of their friends following.

Shay said, "Only you would go dirty from that video." He skewered the guy with a look, walking down the aisle. He let his bag fall from his shoulder, catching it before it hit the floor. "Tell the truth, James. Do you have your girlfriend grab your nutsack like that? You like it a little kinky?"

He stood in the aisle and waited.

The guy sat back down. "I was just joking, Coleman."

"Yeah, you were." Shay shook his head, dropping into the seat next to me. Linde didn't miss a beat. He sat in the third chair, right on the aisle. The other four guys paused, but moved into the other seats.

Shay asked under his breath, "You okay?"

The girl who usually sat beside me looked over her shoulder to us. Her eyes slid from Shay to me, then back again before she turned to the front.

I nodded, feeling the back of my neck warming.

Linde leaned forward to see me. "Say the word, Clarke. That James guy likes to work out with us in the afternoons. I can have some guys spot him and give him some uncomfortable time under those weights if you want." He winked. "Just say the word."

"Thanks, Linde." I said before turning to Shay, "I'm fine. I'll be fine."

Shay nodded, leaning back in his seat and pulling out his notebook. "I'm pretty sure I was doing him a favor. If he provoked you enough, he'd be in the hospital bed right alongside Carruthers."

Linde snorted. "You haven't had a problem with him or his buddies, have you?"

"No." I hadn't even considered that. Besides Parker, no one messed with me in high school, not like that. The girl shit happened, but this wasn't the same. Guys found out who Blake and Gage were and backed off. Usually. I never had an altercation like I had on Saturday. That was new for me. "Are they the type to do that?"

Linde didn't say anything. He just sat back in his seat, as if he were slinking away.

Shay shook his head. "I'm sure you'll be fine. I wouldn't worry about it."

He looked like he was going to say something else, but the professor came in, and we spent the next hour learning about the political dynamics in the United Kingdom.

Once we were dismissed, Shay asked, "Have you already done the reading for Wednesday?"

I nodded. "I'm caught up through next week, but it isn't really sticking in my head. Everything he said today was all new stuff. I should go over the book again."

"You want to do that together?"

Linde and the other football players already left.

A couple girls stayed behind, sneaking glances at us. Or no. They were watching Shay.

He was standing in the aisle, and I hadn't yet cleared the desk where Linde sat. A few of the other students lingered, as well, mostly to talk to the professor, but I caught a few other curious looks our way.

I lowered my voice. "Like in the library with our group?"

He didn't even know the girls were there. "Like in my room, or in the living room if you're uncomfortable." His eyes darkened as they held mine.

He wasn't just talking about studying, though I was sure we'd also do that. "I—" Fuck. I was going to decline, but I didn't want to. I wanted to spend time with him, or maybe it was that whole hiding away factor. I'd been hiding before, but in a different way. I hid who I knew, who I was related to, and that seemed to be getting out more and more. But that feeling to hide again was there, and going to Shay's house was the perfect place.

I felt flutters in my chest.

I couldn't lie to myself. There were other reasons I wanted to go to his place, but studying and hiding were at the top of that list. I nodded. "Yeah. I'd be game for that."

His lips lifted in a half-grin. "You have a couple classes still, don't you?"

"One. I'm done by two-thirty Monday, Wednesday, and Friday."

"You want a ride?"

"Uh . . ." I considered it. "I should drive my own car. You know, since we're not—"

"We're classmates, Clarke." He led the way down the aisle and out the door. He bypassed the girls completely. "You're always bringing up the dating thing. Maybe you're the one who wants to be dating."

He started down the stairs. I was following behind him, and I didn't answer. It was too difficult. People were going the opposite direction for their classes, and still others trickled in behind us from the floors above. When we pushed through the bottom doors, it was like a dam and the students were spilling free. I glanced over my shoulder and spotted Kristina walking out.

"Hey." I stopped to wave.

She looked up, a grin spreading over her face. She'd been frowning down at her planner, but put it away as she drew near. Her eyes flicked to Shay. "We meet again."

"Kristina."

She nodded. "And everyone knows who you are." She asked me, "Where have you been all weekend? Oh, my God. You've missed a ton."

"What are you talking about?" I assumed she would've seen the dick-in-the-hands video.

Her eyes widened dramatically. "Laura, Sarah, and Casey had a massive fight last night. Massive. I must share the details."

Shay began edging backward. His eyes found mine. "That's my exit. I'll see you later." He held a hand out toward Kristina. "It was nice seeing you again."

"You, too."

Kristina sighed as he left. "I know I have a boyfriend, but damn, girl. He's gorgeous. I can't believe you're still holding out telling the girls about him."

I groaned. "Are you kidding me? They know about Gage. I'm already stress-eating that situation. I got home from the library and ordered a pizza last night."

"Did you eat it all?"

"My stomach made me stop after three slices. Don't judge me. I was hungry."

"No judgment here. And talking of no judgment," she whacked my arm, "you didn't tell me about your video this weekend. I think it went viral yesterday."

Kristina grabbed the door leading into the food court, and I went ahead. "I was hoping you hadn't viewed it."

"Are you kidding me? Casey was there. She had front-row tickets."

Yeah. Casey. She'd become a different sort of problem. I cleared my throat as we got into the line for the cafeteria. "You said the girls got into a fight last night? Are they eating with us?"

She snorted, pulling out her ID. "I doubt it. Casey took off. I have no idea where she went, and Laura and Sarah have been at the guys' building all day. I saw them in the dorm bathroom this morning, but Sarah said they needed a mental day."

The amount of stress that just left my body was comedic. I tipped my head back. "Thank God."

She handed her card over to run through the machine. Mine was next, and our conversation was paused. It was food time, which meant ice cream first for me. If the other girls weren't eating with us, I snagged a table in the far corner. Kristina found me. She'd gone the healthy route today with a salad, an orange, and a carton of milk.

I looked at mine. I had pizza last night. My tray consisted of ice cream, a piece of cake, two chicken strips, and a small bowl of yogurt.

I said, "You're not holding up your end of the Freshman Fifteen Agenda. I can't eat your end for you."

She picked up her milk and pointed at me. "You're doing quite fine, Miss I Have the Longest Legs Ever, But Act Like They're Short and Chubby. Kennedy, you can eat like this and still be drop-dead gorgeous. Not me."

I pointed to the Double Ds. "You have your own blessings. Don't cut yourself short." Not to mention, she was gorgeous.

"Yeah. Those." She gazed down. "If anyone tells you big breasts are the way to go, they're an idiot. I want to do a reduction."

"Really?"

"Casey thinks I'm nuts, but she doesn't understand. She's tiny and compact. Guys love her body."

I frowned. "If you didn't have a serious boyfriend, you'd find out how many guys love your body. Trust me." Since she brought up the C word, I prompted, "Tell me about the fight."

"The fight." She let out a breath of air and then started.

Casey had been withdrawing a little more each day. Sarah and Laura hadn't been happy about it all week. Kristina wasn't sure what started it, but Casey said something. Laura and Sarah weren't having it. They said something back. It was Casey's turn. Then theirs. They were going back and forth, and as Kristina was curled up on their couch with her social work textbook on her lap, an entire fight ensued.

Laura and Sarah wanted to know what was up with Casey.

She refused to say.

This enraged them further. It was time to double down, so they bluffed. She had to tell them or they weren't going to drink together at Rugger's (another name I didn't know). Casey got so mad she stormed out of the room, but came back in, grabbed her backpack, purse, and her phone. Her second storming out was the real deal. Kristina hasn't heard from her all night, except one text to let her know that Casey was sleeping somewhere else, and that'd been it.

Laura and Sarah went to their room, and Kristina only saw them in the bathroom.

She was saying, "I mean, I can kind of see Laura and Sarah's point. Casey has been different. She doesn't pick up after herself, and she's been snappy. She's herself sometimes, but other times, it's like she pulls into herself and puts up a wall. Have you noticed anything?"

A chicken strip caught in my throat. I gulped it down, wincing at the pain. "What?"

"You've been hanging out with her more lately. Have you noticed anything?"

"She wore a sweatshirt to the football game. That isn't normal."

"Yeah. See. Things like that. They just don't add up. It's almost like she's becoming a new person." She finished her milk and stabbed at some lettuce with her fork. "Can I talk to you about something else?"

Her tone went serious. The hairs on the back of my neck stood up. I thought the fight had been the sobering topic. I was wrong. "Sure. What is it?"

Shay . . .

Where I slept last night . . .

How I'd been "off" lately . . .

Those three things and so many others flashed in my head, but she said, "I think Casey likes your brother."

Another floodgate of relief.

I waved my hand in the air. "I know."

Her mouth opened slightly. "You know?"

"Uh." I grabbed the last chicken strip but began pulling it apart into little pieces instead of eating it. "Gage asked me about Casey a while back. I'm not really surprised."

"You're not joking?"

"No. Why?"

Her eyebrows dipped together. "I can't tell. Sometimes you're sarcastic. For real, though? You knew?"

"I guessed. I saw him sitting with you guys at the game."

"Is that why you didn't come over?"

Kristina had been my first friend at Dulane, but she didn't know my rules. I nodded.

"I wondered why you didn't sit with us. I mean, we saw you at the game, but I was kind of hurt. I thought you didn't like us anymore."

My eyes shot to hers, and the second chicken strip dropped from my hands. "Are you serious?"

"Yeah." She stabbed at more of her lettuce. "I mean, you avoid us sometimes. I know you're comfortable being alone, but I don't know.

Sometimes I wonder, you know? Like, did we do something, or are you upset with us, or something like that." Her eyes glanced away.

She thought she was the reason I stayed away.

She thought she was the one who wasn't good enough.

I was an asshole.

I shook my head and reached over to squeeze her hand. "I have trust issues, and I let them have too much power over me. I'm sorry. You've never done anything. It's the opposite. I don't feel good enough to be your friend."

A sheen of tears rested on the underside of her eyelids. "No. No. Never. Why would you ever think that?"

I shrugged, pulling my hand back and tucking it on my lap. "Because some really bitchy and catty girls made me think that my senior year of high school."

"They were jealous."

Those words came out so strong. She was so sure of it. Hope rose in me, just a little bit, but I held it in check. Maybe. Maybe not. Those girls really did hate me. I had a hard time believing it was all because of jealousy.

She was waiting for me to respond, and I gave her a half-hearted grin. "Maybe." My throat was swelling. Topic change, please. "Let's talk about how we can get Sarah, Laura, and Casey to make up."

That was what we did for the rest of our lunch, but when we left and I headed for my second class, I felt a heaviness on my shoulders. It settled there once she started talking about Casey, and it only intensified when we realized both of us thought we weren't good enough for the other. I thought it would've lifted once the conversation switched, but it didn't. It grew lighter, but it was still there.

Or maybe it was Carruthers, because as we walked out of the cafeteria, a bunch of guys began chanting, "Dick Crusher." Some students were confused but others started laughing. I saw a few heated expressions and felt a similar experience as James from class.

I went a little faster.

If I heard comments like that, I'd have to engage, and I was suddenly so tired. I didn't want to constantly battle every day, every hour, but the video made me a target.

I walked into my second class's building, and more guys were heading out. They whipped around, recognizing me.

"Hey!" one shouted at me.

Veering through a group of short hallways, I took different turns until I lost them. Whatever he had to say wasn't going to be congratulatory. I could sense it.

Once I was sure they left, I stopped around a corner and let out a shaky breath. I clutched my bag to my chest.

This was going to be harder than I thought.

There were ten minutes until my next class. I liked to get there early and go over the day's notes. Sarah and Laura's mental day excuse was sounding like a good idea.

I was still weighing the idea. To skip or not? To fight other assholes in my class, if they were in there or . . . I felt my phone in my pocket. I could go to Shay's right now. Even if he wasn't there, he'd probably let me hide in his room.

I snorted.

I used to hate the guy, and somehow he'd become my refuge.

No. I stepped back into the hall. No matter where I'd go, or how long I hid, they'd be there. I'd have to deal with them at some point.

I went to class.

# CHAPTER TWENTY-ONE

Shay met me at the back door.

I texted him when I was walking up the driveway, and I'd taken one step onto the patio before the door opened. He stood there, wearing those same sweatpants that rode sinfully low on his hips. He had a shirt on, barring the view that I knew was there, and ran a hand through his hair. He gave me a crooked grin. "Have you had dinner yet?"

He moved back, and I stepped inside.

We were close, and he brushed against me, reaching around to close the door. I started to shake my head, but as he touched me, other sensations were already overriding the tightness in my stomach. That second class had been okay, but there were two assholes with smart comments. I sniped back, but I hadn't shut them up. I only pushed off another verbal attack that would probably come Wednesday. And because I knew Shay would be able to pick up something was wrong, I lingered in my dorm room a couple hours before coming over. He had practice anyway.

"Kennedy?"

"What?" He asked me something. What was it? "Oh! Um. No."

His hand touched my hip, and I almost closed my eyes. Right there, that small touch gave me some extra strength. When had this happened? Where I needed him outside the bedroom, too? It was an unnerving thought, and I shook it off like I did when things got to be too much.

"I could make you something in the kitchen."

He was studying me as he made the suggestion, and seeing the small panic I felt at the thought of seeing his roommates, seeing Linde, he added, "Or we can order in." That'd be better. I relaxed, and then he had one last suggestion. "Or we can study a while and head out for a bite as a study break."

I tapped his chest, enjoying his firm muscles there. "That sounds like a winner."

"The last?"

I nodded.

The close proximity, his hand on my waist, how he was gazing down at me—my ability to breathe was suffering. My finger was still touching his chest, and I flattened my palm there. A soft chuckle came from him, reverberating against my hand. "Or we can do something else before studying?"

A short laugh caught in my throat. We both knew where this was going. It was part of the reason I came over. I just didn't think it'd be the first thing that happened, though it made sense. Get it out of the way so we could clear our heads and be productive afterward.

Neither of us wasted words.

Shay took my hand, led the way up to his room, and once that door was closed, we were on each other. He tugged me against him, his mouth on mine, and we stood like that, kissing. Slowly, he dragged his lips from me, but he pressed me back against the door. He lifted his head. "We're not going to get much studying done."

"Yes, we will." I wrapped my arms around his neck and pulled him back down. "Just not right now."

"We're getting this out of the way." He nipped my lips with his.

I nodded and gasped. "You read my mind."

He groaned, opening his mouth even more over mine. His tongue swept in, exploring me, and there were no more words. I grabbed ahold of his neck and began to lift up. He bent, caught me under my legs, and lifted me the rest of the way. He held me, suspended in the air, and pressed me back against the door. We continued to kiss. I don't think I'd ever get tired of his kisses.

His lips. His mouth. How he used his tongue.

I melted even more, and he shifted me closer against him, stepping back from the door. His hand left my leg for a second. The sound of a lock barely registered in the back of my head, and then we were on his bed.

My shirt came off first.

His shirt was next.

My bra.

I unsnapped his jeans.

Mine.

Then his hand moved between my legs, and he pushed a finger inside. I stopped kissing, just a moment, and arched my back. I bared my neck to him, and he groaned, his mouth falling there and tasting me.

A second finger moved in.

He paused. One second, then he began moving in and out. He was building up a rhythm. I could only hold on as he assaulted me there, and then my neck with his mouth, my chest, my breast, my other breast. He moved all the way down my stomach, still working his fingers, and I was riding them. I was clenching, my head thrown back on his bed, and I was trying not to scream.

He lowered his lips, resting right over where his fingers were thrusting.

"Kennedy." A soft beckon from him.

I looked down, saw the wicked grin, and widened my eyes. What was—he pulled his fingers out and kissed me there. His tongue slid inside, and my entire body clenched over the sensations. God. His tongue was moving in and out. He was circling me, sliding back in, and he continued.

My lungs were being constricted. I wanted to reach down, grab his head, and move against him. The need was so powerful, I grabbed fistfuls of his blanket.

I held on, forcibly holding myself back.

"Shay." I was panting.

The pressure was building. I was nearing a climax, and I didn't know if I could handle it. He was making me hurl over it before I was ready. He wouldn't slow down. His tongue kept working, and then he began rubbing at my nub, and that was it. It was like my body crashed over the edge, and the tremors took over, wracking my body.

Shay lifted his head, but his fingers went back in me. They were slow and tender. He was helping ease the shaking, and I reached down, grasped his wrist, but I didn't stop him. Our eyes caught and held, our faces were so close.

I never had a guy do that to me, and it made me feel as if I were stripped and bare to him. I never felt naked to him, even when my clothes were off, but I felt raw right now.

His eyebrows dipped together briefly. "You okay?"

My air was still stuck in my throat, so I nodded. "Yeah." I swallowed. "I've never had someone do that before."

A tenderness came over him again, and his grin softened. "You haven't?" His fingers slid out of me, and a warm glow spread over my body. It washed down my spine, through every arm and leg, even down to my toes and fingers. I was tingling, like an out-of-body experience just happened.

I laughed at that thought. Talk about an ego-booster.

"What are you laughing about?" He stretched back up over me, gazing down.

"Nothing." I framed both sides of his face. "Ready to study?"

He barked out a laugh. "Give me a second, then I'm coming back and working you up all over again."

He stood from the bed, and I rolled over. His ass, I was almost drooling. It was so tight, but his front side was just as much of a masterpiece. He padded back to the bed, a condom in hand, and then he lay over me once again. He rested between my legs, his mouth finding mine in the sweetest kiss I'd ever had, and it wasn't long before I was longing for him to be inside me. This time, when he eased inside, his mouth remained on mine, and it was slow, it was tender, and it was drawn out.

Shay took his time, worshipping my body all over again, until I exploded around him. Then he began thrusting harder and harder. He picked up his pace, and I wound my legs around his waist as he was pounding into me for his own release.

I raked my fingers through his hair as he moved to rest on his side. I moved with him, sliding my leg between his, and I tugged his face back to mine. One last kiss. It was tender, like so much else from him today. It was exactly what I needed.

He pulled back, then nipped me once more. "What was that for?"

"The whole thing?"

He rested his head on the bed, looking at me. "The kiss." He touched my lips for a moment before falling to lie on his stomach. "It was nice."

"The whole thing was nice."

"Yeah. It was."

If we were boyfriend and girlfriend, I would tell him my feelings from the day. I'd talk about the assholes in the food court, the assholes I ran from, the two in my class who would continue to be a problem. I'd tell him how the world seemed so heavy today, until I came here and he kissed so sweetly and touched me so gently, as if he knew that was exactly what I needed to push the heaviness away. I didn't, because we weren't. This was just sex, but a budding actual friendship was starting, too. I couldn't lie to myself any longer about that, and I gazed back at him. I reached for his hand on my stomach and laced our fingers together.

He lifted his head, as if he was waiting for me to say something.

I couldn't. I couldn't share the last of what I had. I'd be too exposed, too vulnerable. I squeezed his hand one last time, then rolled to sit up on the side of the bed. I reached for my clothes. "We should probably study."

He sat up behind me. I thought he'd go around me and start dressing. He didn't. He slid in behind me, his legs coming around, and he draped himself over me. He tugged me back so I was resting against his chest, and he rested his chin on my shoulder. "What's wrong?"

I tensed, but flashed him a grin. "Nothing." I kept my tone light, though I knew he knew I was lying. "We really should dress, or we won't get any studying done tonight."

"Kennedy—"

I pulled away from him, standing with my clothes in hand. "Mind if I take a quick shower?" I didn't wait. I hurried in, shut the door, and was under that water like my life depended on it. I took a pause then. What was going on with me? I'd dealt with assholes before. Why were they still with me? Still under my skin? And why was I running from Shay? I wouldn't be sleeping with him if I thought he wanted to hurt me. I didn't need to hold things back, but . . . no. I just needed a moment. The wall was down. That was what it was.

I was feeling everything.

I wasn't protected.

One wrong word, one wrong look, and he had the power to hurt me. I was completely vulnerable.

I lingered in the shower, taking my time drying and dressing before I went back into the bedroom. The wall was back up and in place. I felt in control again.

Shay was at his desk, dressed in those sweats and shirt he'd worn when he opened the door downstairs. He lowered his pen. "Better?"

I nodded, feeling my throat swell. "Much."

He wasn't asking for specifics, but he knew I'd been affected. He just didn't know from what. I sat on his bed and grabbed for my backpack.

He nodded, going back to his textbook.

I unzipped my bag. "It isn't you."

He looked back up. "What is it?"

"I . . ." I glanced down to my bag, though I wasn't seeing it. "I, um, I don't really know, but it isn't you."

"If you want to talk about it, I'll listen."

I looked back to him, saw the lack of judgment, the lack of expectation, the lack of impatience. He was there for me if I needed him, and that was it. It was the epitome of what every friendship should be. No demands. No pressure. Just there.

The bag fell from my hands, and I rose, going over to him.

He moved his chair back, and I lifted my leg, coming down on his lap to straddle him.

Maybe this was venturing too far into the territory of feelings, and being more than friends with benefits, but I didn't care at that moment.

Shay's hands went to my legs, and I dipped down to find his lips with mine. I sighed into them. We sat like that, kissing, him holding me, me just needing this touch from him until a long time later when he carried me back to the bed. Then he was back inside me, but a part of me could've spent the entire night like that, just kissing him.

# CHAPTER TWENTY-TWO

A few hours later and my stomach was growling.

I was stretched out on the bed, fully clothed. Shay was at his desk again, and we hadn't talked in the last hour. It felt wonderful. It was one of those silences where nothing needed to be spoken—just like being at home.

He looked up now. "Want to go out for something to eat?"

I checked my phone. It was around ten. "What's open at this time of night?"

He named a local diner that was open twenty-four hours, and because of that, it was a popular studying hangout. I rolled to my side so I could see him better. "You sure you want to go there?"

He tapped his computer. "We're classmates, and we have a project due. There's nothing wrong with that."

I shrugged. I'd hidden enough for the day. It was time to face the world, even if it was a local diner. I brought my feet around and sat up. "Okay. Let's do this."

It didn't take either of us long. I toed on my shoes and had my stuff in my bag and then waited while he went to the bathroom. He put his stuff in his bag, grabbing his keys on the way out. I went first, his hand on the small of my back, until we got to the top of the stairs. His floor was relatively quiet, had been the other time, too, but I could hear male voices in the kitchen on the main floor.

"What's wrong?"

"Do they know about me?" I didn't know if his phone was off, but no one had bothered us all evening. I had a hard time imagining

Shay could go a couple hours without someone emailing, calling, or knocking on his door.

"They knew I had a girl up there, but not that it's you. Linde would be confused."

That was what I was worried about.

Shay studied my face. "You still don't want him to know?"

"I—" I hesitated, biting my lip. "I'm worried he'll look at me differently."

"I'd hope he would."

"What do you mean?"

He moved around me. "Come on. Let's continue this conversation in my Jeep." So, we did. I tiptoed down the stairs behind Shay. When he noticed, he started laughing. "They're not going to open the door. They're respecting my privacy. They're good friends like that."

I still remained quiet, waiting on the last step with my heart in my throat, and a hand on his back as he pulled on his shoes. When he was done, he grabbed my hand again, and led the way outside, down the driveway, and to his Jeep. I'd parked behind it, but even as I thought about just driving behind him, he said, "Don't even think it. Get in the vehicle, Clarke."

Hearing my last name unwound the last of the knots in my stomach. For some reason, I loosened, and it stayed that way on the drive to the diner.

We didn't pick up the same conversation until we got a back booth and ordered. Once the server left, our water and coffee already filled, I asked, "What did you mean about Linde looking at me differently?"

Shay angled his head to see behind me before focusing on me again. "I didn't see anyone I knew in the other section."

I hadn't either. "Shay."

He hunched forward, picking up his coffee. "Linde likes you. I'm sleeping with you. Yeah, call me selfish, but I'd be okay with him looking at you differently."

I sat there. Stunned.

He noticed my look. "You didn't know?"

I shook my head. "Are you sure?"

"Yes." There was no question on his face. "I don't think he has it bad for you, but yeah. He's interested."

"I thought we were friends."

"And he thought that since you didn't hate him, you had the hots for him." He shook his head, sipping his coffee again. "You might want to deal with that before it gets awkward."

"You guys are good friends."

"Look." His mug was lowered to the table, and he leaned close. "I didn't poach, if that's what you're thinking. He didn't lay claim to you, and the shit that went down between us, that was happening long before I realized he was interested in you."

I widened my eyes. "I didn't say you did. There was no judgment there."

He frowned. "Maybe I do feel some guilt, but I shouldn't." His jaw clenched, and his eyes grew hooded. "If you do end up going on a date with him, you and I are no longer doing what we're doing. I'm not going to sleep with a chick my friend is dating."

I sat there and could only blink a few times. Those words were so fast and had such bite to them.

He was jealous. Right?

I frowned. "Are you pissed at me because your friend is interested in me? I'm not going to date Linde. I had no idea how he felt until *you* told me. I thought he was my friend, only my friend."

"But now that you know, does that change your feelings?"

"For him?"

"Yes." He rolled his eyes. "Who else do you think I was talking about?"

Him, but that'd be ridiculous. There was a rule. We didn't talk about us, though that was all we'd been doing since we got to the diner. Or, well, kind of. We were, but we weren't. We were definitely avoiding talking about one aspect of us, the emotional stuff.

*Because there is nothing there,* I had to remind myself. Sex and now friendship. That was it. And he was my classmate.

"Clarke."

"What? No. No. I don't want to date Linde. I wouldn't have wanted to date him even if you and I weren't doing what we're doing."

"Good." And that was all he could say because the server returned to take our order.

I hadn't looked at the menu yet.

Shay said, "I already know what I want."

The girl looked annoyed. She had a glazed-over expression in her eyes, and she began tapping on her order pad.

I said to Shay, "You order, and I'll look."

He took his time, stalling for me, and once he was done, I just ordered a muffin and some fruit.

"That's it?" he asked once the server left.

"I ate shitty last night and at lunch."

"You want to keep talking about Linde?"

"No." I waved my hands between us. "Time out on the Linde talk. I don't want to date him. I won't be dating him, and there was never any intention of me dating him."

"As long as we're clear." His smirk was back in place, and goddamn, a part of me settled just seeing it. It'd been a long-lost friend at this point. I laughed under my breath at that, pulling my laptop out of my bag.

"What?"

I looked up. "What?"

"You laughed at something."

"It's nothing. You have this smirk you get when you're being cocky. You know you're being kind of a jackass, but you think you're so irresistible."

His eyebrows went up. "That's what my smirk says to you?"

"It doesn't? You don't think that when you're smirking?"

"No." He shook his head. "I'm just usually laughing at something stupid in my head. I don't even know I'm smirking half the time."

"Well." I had to laugh at *that*. "Whatever you're thinking, it works."

I was beginning to have a weakness when it came to his smirks.

I pointed to his textbook. "Our studying was drastically cut short. We need to do more of that, less of this." I pointed between the two of us.

"What is this?" He repeated the same motion. "What are we doing?"

"We're flirting." I gave him a look. "You know that as well as I do, and it's just going to end with us not studying and going back to your room."

His eyes warmed. "Would that be so bad?"

"Yes. If my grade average is affected by what we do, we're going cold turkey until my grades go back up."

He snapped to attention. The smirk dropped. The flirting banter ended, and he coughed. "Incumbents and oversight, huh? Let's talk about those."

That was more like it.

We ate our food and studied for another two hours. It was around midnight when we left. Once we parked on the street outside his house, he looked over. "What'd you mean earlier?"

"What?"

"You said you didn't want Linde to look at you differently. We talked about what I meant, but not you. What'd you mean by that?"

"Oh." I shifted in my seat, tugging down my shirt and smoothing it out. "It's stupid."

"What is it?"

The lights were on in his house, and a few people were leaving through the front door. I thought I recognized them, but I wasn't sure. "It's—I don't know how to explain slut shaming to a guy."

His mouth lifted in a half-grin. "You don't think a guy knows what that is?"

"Do you?"

"Guys are every bit as observant and intelligent as girls. There are some stupid guys, but there are stupid girls, too. Same thing with being smart. Some of us do exist. Yes, I know what slut shaming is. You think that's what he'd do to you?"

"I think he would look at me like I'm a whore. We're having sex and we're not dating. A lot of people would call me a whore, but call you a player."

That was why the Dick Crusher movement weighed on me so heavily, because those guys weren't mad at Carruthers. They were mad at me. I didn't have a right to talk back to him, to defend a friend, or defend myself when he came at me. He could do those things, but not me. *That* was the culture I lived in.

I held those words in and only said quietly, "Rules are different for girls."

"You're not a whore, and you're not a slut, and I know Linde wouldn't think of you that way."

"You'd be surprised at who would think of me that way. You don't know what people really believe deep down until you do something you're not "supposed" to do because it's 'not your right.' Like being raped. Girls aren't supposed to say no, right?"

He drew in his breath, his eyes hard on mine. "You really think that?"

"No, but I know some who think that way. It's all those assholes who were coming at me today. Carruthers, the guys from the food court, the guys I ran from before my second class, they're not saying anything about how Carruthers would've physically attacked me. They're mad that I humiliated him."

He was quiet a moment.

I said too much. I was already regretting it, and then I heard from him, "What guys who you ran from?"

The hairs on the back of my neck stood on end. The dangerous side of Shay was staring back at me. He was heated, but he was keeping it restrained. Barely. I sensed the danger under his surface. A shiver went down my spine.

My mouth felt dry. "Just some idiots. I ditched them."

"What guys at the food court? Did you have problems in your second class?"

"Shay—" I started but stopped. What could I say? "What are you going to do? Hunt them down and beat 'em up? Do you realize how many guys you'd be doing that to? You'd get kicked off the team. Every one you hit down, two more pop up. It's endless. You can't beat up everyone."

He cursed, his jaw clenching as he sat back in his seat and raked a hand over his face. "I don't want them messing with you."

"Yeah, but—"

"Not you."

I fell silent, sitting with him for a minute. "It's always different when it's someone you know."

He frowned, saying so soft that I almost didn't hear, "Yeah."

# CHAPTER TWENTY-THREE

I was walking through my hallway's back door when the door to my room opened.

Missy stood in there. She saw me and bit down on her lip. She was clutching her phone to her chest.

I frowned. "What is it?"

Shay invited me to his room again, but I thought it'd be better to head home. I could go up there. We both knew what we'd do, and I could even spend the night. A part of me wanted to. It was the part that enjoyed being around Shay, the part that enjoyed his touch, but there was another part of me that didn't want to come back to my dorm. I didn't know why that was, and I ignored it for the night. Besides, things just started with Shay and me. Spending the night was too much, too fast. It would have been too hard to ignore the friendship budding into something more if I did that.

But now, seeing the strained lines around Missy's mouth and the bags under her eyes, I wished I had stayed. I'd be wrapped up in bed, not feeling the pit of my stomach drop to the ground.

"I've been calling you. Don't you check your phone?"

Shit. My phone had been buzzing on and off all night, but seeing they were only alerts for my social media, I turned it off. "I'm here now. What is it?"

"Your friends from second floor, one of them is in the hospital."

"What?"

"You're supposed to call Kristina."

Icy panic lined my veins as I dug through my bag, turning and heading downstairs at the same time. I was rounding to their floor when the line connected to Kristina's phone. It began ringing, and I was through the door and onto their floor. I was racing for their room. If they weren't here, maybe there'd be a note on their door board, or maybe someone else knew.

A second ring.

I was at their door, searching. I couldn't find anything but the normal scribblings from Casey's friends.

The phone rang a third time.

A door opened farther down the hallway, and Sarah appeared. Her wide eyes filled with tears, and she sniffled, pressing a Kleenex to her reddened nose. "It's Casey."

"What happened?" I asked as Kristina answered, "Kennedy?"

"Kristina!" I exclaimed. My heart was pumping so fast. "What's going on? Did something happen to Casey?"

She got quiet. "She drank too much. They had to pump her stomach."

Sarah stepped closer to me, asking under her breath, "What's she saying?"

I frowned. She didn't know, but I asked Kristina, "Is she okay?"

"Yeah, but she wants you to come here. She said she's going to make a statement and you'd know what it was about."

The rape.

The entire bottom lining of my stomach opened up. It all fell out.

I could only say, "Okay."

Kristina sounded strained. "I don't know what's going on, but can you get here as soon as possible?"

"Of course." I was turning for the back door again.

"Hey." Sarah hurried behind me, her hand stretched out. She was chewing the inside of her cheek. "Is she okay? Can we come?"

"Uh."

I relayed the questions, and Kristina's response was as subdued. "Casey doesn't want to see them. That's all she'll say."

"That's ridiculous."

"I know, but those are her wishes."

"Okay. I'm leaving right now. I'll be there in a few minutes. Text me what hospital and room number."

I hung up, and Sarah edged even closer. Both her hands were pressed against her chest, holding on to that flimsy Kleenex. She was waiting.

I hated this. "She doesn't want to see you, but she doesn't have a say who sits in the hospital lobby."

"Are you saying to come?"

"It's up to you."

I headed right back out to my car. The texts came through a moment later, and I knew which hospital that was and where. It took ten minutes with barely any traffic, and I didn't have to get lost or drive around searching for the parking lot. Gage came to this same hospital and emergency room a year ago with a broken leg, so I was familiar with the layout.

I went inside, emptied my pockets for the security guard, and did the same for the nurse manning the last emergency room entrance.

Kristina was outside Casey's room, her arms hugging herself and her head bent down. My heart ached seeing her like that. Casey was just changing to her. She didn't know why, but she'd be hurting just as much once she found out the reason.

"Hey."

Kristina's head came up, and she opened her arms. I walked right into them. I ran a hand down her arm. "How are you?"

She shook her head, stepping back. "Confused. Concerned. And a whole ton of other emotions."

I nodded to the door. "She's awake?"

"Yeah." She turned around. "She was at some party. Laura and Sarah didn't recognize the guys' names who were throwing it. I guess that's where she stayed last night."

"I thought she went to my brother's."

"Me, too, but I guess not."

Kristina looked so torn, and I made a decision. I took her hand. "Come with me."

"What? No. Casey doesn't want me in there. She said only you."

"Trust me. Okay?"

With wide and fearful eyes, she did, and I led the way inside. Casey saw me first, and I could see the exhaustion sweep over her. She seemed to fold into the bed, and she was so pale she almost blended in with the white sheets. I'd never seen someone so sick. Her lips were cracked and rimmed with a black charcoal substance, and her hair was matted into knots.

Then she saw Kristina, and she surged back upright.

"No," she started to say.

"Listen to me." My insides were tense and twisting into pretzel knots, but my voice was calm. I knew my face looked it, as well. I was channeling a Zen goddess, and I brought Kristina deeper into the room. "Casey, I can't pretend to have any understanding what you're going through, but I *can* attempt to imagine what I would want in your situation. I would want the closest people to me to be around me. I would want to gain strength from them. It's their hand I would want to hold, and I get it. I do. I know what happened, but I'm not in your inner circle. We've shared meals, a few movies, but that's it. I'm not your roommate, your best friend, or even your mother. You have to tell *them*."

She began crying as I spoke, and by the time I was finished, fat tears freely cascaded down her face. She wasn't trying to stop them. When she spoke, it was the little six-year-old girl inside her. "It's real if they know."

"I know." I covered her hand with mine. "I know, but it's real anyway. It's time to let them know."

"Can you still stay? I asked the nurse to call the cops."

"Of course."

She nodded, hiccupping on the tears before grabbing for Kristina's hand.

I sat in the corner, but it was no longer my place. I was there for support. I was there to give Kristina what answers I knew, but she was the closest person to Casey. It was her time to replace me, and she did.

Casey folded into her arms, and it wasn't long before she asked for Laura and Sarah.

I moved out of the room when they came in.

I remained outside the room, waiting for a little bit. Kristina came out a few minutes later, hugged me, and thanked me, but she didn't need to. I hadn't done much. It was my final cue that I could leave, and as I was walking back down that hallway, two female cops were going the opposite direction. I paused once to watch them knock on Casey's door, and I heard one say, "Miss Winchem?"

*Good.* I nodded to myself.

She sounded good. She sounded nice, patient. She wasn't going to walk into that room and treat Casey like she was a joke or she asked for it. I didn't hear that condescension.

After I left the hospital, I didn't drive to the dorm. If Missy were up, she'd have questions, and when I would give her a vague brush-off, there'd be the looks. It was always the looks.

I drove to Shay's, and after texting him, I walked up his driveway, past all of his roommates' vehicles, and stepped onto the patio. I waited outside the back door, and a minute later, he opened it from inside.

It felt good to walk past him, good to feel his hand on the small of my back, and good to feel his arms around me.

I knew something was happening.

I was feeling something.

He was feeling something.

And maybe I should care, but not that night.

That night, sleeping in his arms, felt like the most right thing in the world.

# CHAPTER TWENTY-FOUR

Shay was moving around the room. It was still dark, and I felt the morning chill in the room. I could hear the swish of his clothes as he came closer to the bed, and I asked around a yawn, "You get up this early?"

He chuckled softly and then turned on a lamp. "Yeah. Sorry." He was dressed in Dulane sports clothes—a Dulane lightweight jacket and Dulane lightweight sweats. "Some of us go running in the morning."

He looked damned good, but I groaned. "You're not human. You have classes all day, then practice, and we didn't sleep much last night."

His mouth curved up.

I gestured to him, even my arm and hand felt too tired to be awake. "Now you're going running?"

"If I don't go, the guys will want to know what's going on." He sat on the bed next to me, his hand rubbing my back. "How are you doing? You didn't say much last night."

I shook my head. Those were serious thoughts and a serious conversation. It was too early for that, too. "I'll tell you later."

"But you're okay?"

I nodded. "Yes, I am." I groaned again. "My roommate's probably freaking out. I guess she was calling me last night and I never answered."

"About what?"

I waved that off, another yawn. "That's for later, too."

A soft knock sounded on his door.

His hand ran down my back. "Okay. I'll be back in an hour."

"You run for an entire hour?" I curled up, pulling the blankets tight around me. "You're insane. I'm sleeping with a crazy man."

He chuckled. A look passed in his eyes, but it was gone in a flash and he stood, crossing the room. He grabbed for his phone and opened the door. I heard a soft and muffled, "I'm ready."

Then the other person asked, "I wasn't sure if you were coming. Thought you'd skip because of . . ." His voice trailed off.

I tensed, recognizing Linde's voice.

Shay just laughed. "Nah. I'm ready to go."

"I'm sure you are."

I fought against rolling my eyes, holding my breath, but Shay kept himself as a barrier. Linde couldn't see me, not as long as Shay was in the doorway. A second later, he stepped out and pulled the door closed. I listened, but could barely hear them descending the stairs and leaving.

I reached for my phone, checking for messages before I went back to sleep.

Deleting all of Missy's texts asking where I was, I lingered on the one sent after I would've already left for the hospital.

Missy: **Not sure what's going on, but I'm here if you need me.**

That was nice of her. I thumbed off a response, knowing she didn't turn her phone on until she was leaving for her morning classes.

Me: **I'm good. Slept at a friend's. Be back later. Have a good day.**

I didn't expect a response, and I rolled over, tossing my phone on the floor.

It buzzed a second later, and I grabbed for it, surprised.

Missy: **Good. Up half the night. I was worried. If you're okay, then I'm going back to bed.**

I cringed, muttering to myself, "And the award for the Most Insensitive Roommate goes to . . ."

Me: **Sorry. I thought you'd go to sleep, but I'm fine. Sorry again.**

Missy: **No problem. Good night/good morning!**

I grinned, dropped my phone back to the floor, and curled back over. I was asleep within seconds.

A bang woke me up the second time, and I assessed my surroundings. Shay was still gone. The bathroom door was open so he wasn't in there. I looked for his running clothes, but didn't see them dropped in a pile. Reaching for my phone, I'd slept an hour. They were probably still going, but hearing a second bang, I realized it was from the kitchen.

The guys were up.

That meant I probably wasn't getting any more sleep, so with too much effort this early in the morning, I got up, used the bathroom, got dressed, and grabbed my things. I was sneaking down the stairs when a roar of laughter came from the kitchen. I jerked, flattening against the wall for a second, but no one opened the door.

I slipped outside, feeling like a criminal. I was at my car when I heard a light pounding of feet. I looked over, the group of guys were heading back to the house, but two broke off and came my way.

Shay was in front, and Linde was slightly beside and behind him at the same time. Both slowed when they got to my car. Shay stopped a few feet from me, but Linde looked almost dumbstruck. His eyes were opened wider than normal, and a shadow formed in them seconds before his lips pressed back together.

Shay was looking between the two of us, just waiting.

"So." Linde rested a hand on the top of my car's trunk. Sweat glistened from his face, rolling down to plop on his clothes and on the cement by his shoes. His headphones were hanging around his neck, the cords leading to his shirt's pocket. "This is going on."

Shay was sweating, too, but no headphones. He straightened, both his hands going in his pockets. His shoulders were slightly hunched. He didn't say anything.

I tried for a smile. "Uh, yeah. We're not dating or anything." Let the shame kick in, and I shared a look with Shay. He shook his head, the slightest of twitches, and I knew he was telling me not to worry about that.

Linde was one of my first friends. I would.

Linde pulled his gaze between us slowly. "You're just fucking? Is that it?"

Shay opened his mouth, but then Linde held his hands up. "Look. It's none of my business. Though, if this joker hurts you, let me know. I'll rough him up in practice one day. Maybe clip him extra hard so he has to miss a game."

Shay swore, though he was grinning.

Linde was smiling back, but it seemed forced. That shadow still lingered in his eyes.

He held a hand up in a goodbye, heading back to the sidewalk and toward the house where the others had gone.

Shay waited until he'd gone farther up the driveway before pointing to my car. "Taking off?"

I glanced around. Besides us, the entire street was empty. The houses were cookie-cutter types. Bright, green, and crisp lawns. No one's porches had fading paint or chipped walls. The roofs were even shiny, like they'd just been built. Brightly potted flowers in the landscapes, and there was a fresh dew smell in the air.

I murmured, "I can see why you run at this time. It's peaceful."

"It's a good start to the day. Coach depends on us doing this extra conditioning. We run drills and go over plays for practices. And lift weights. Lots of lifting weights."

He stood there, sweat darkening the front of his shirt, sweat glinted from his forehead, and he ran a hand through his hair, shaking out the excess sweat. With those high cheekbones, perfect and kissable lips, and his ice-blue eyes, I was reminded who stood in front of me. Shay Coleman, from the top tier of Dulane University. He *was* the top, how Gage described him.

And I was sleeping with him.

I laughed to myself. "I think I hated you from the first day because you were so smug."

"Okay. We're going there." He nodded, sighing. "I was smug?"

"You know you were."

"I thought you were funny." His lip twitched.

"And cocky."

"Yes. That smirk of mine. I can smirk more, if you want. You must miss him."

I swatted him, my grin deepening, but I didn't mean it. I leaned back against my car, and Shay stepped in, his hand resting by my shoulder. He was half-leaning over me, half just watching me with his head cocked back, like he wasn't sure what was coming his way.

"I'm trying to say that if I thought we would be here when you first walked into class, I would've laughed my ass off."

"Not your ass. I like your ass. It's delectable."

I ignored his flirting. "I'm just being introspective. I started college with the plan of befriending one, maybe two people, and I was going to study. I was going places. There would be no boys, no gossiping, no cattiness. I wasn't going to get involved in any drama, and fast-forward a few weeks, and I'm sleeping with the star quarterback, friends with a starting offensive lineman, and I came over last night because I left the hospital where a girl who I thought had it all, decided to report her rape."

The smirk disappeared, and his eyes grew serious. I felt the joking slip away, like sunlight chasing away the darkness. Slow, gradual, but inevitable.

I let out a deep sigh. "I was standing up for Casey with Matt Carruthers, and I hid from it yesterday. I can't hide anymore."

His hand moved closer to my shoulder. His thumb began rubbing there, back and forth in a comforting motion. "You mentioned the guys before. I still want to know who they are."

"I know you do."

He waited for me to continue. When I didn't, he said, "You shouldn't have to deal with them alone."

"You'd think, right?" I tried to smile, but I wasn't feeling it. That heaviness returned, and it wasn't on my shoulders anymore. It was pressing smack down on my chest. "Casey reported the rape. That's a big step."

"You have any experience with that?"

"What?"

He lifted up a shoulder, his head bobbing toward it. "You know, being assaulted. Sexually."

I expected him to start tugging at his collar or shifting on his feet, but he didn't. He asked the question, and he waited, holding out for me to give him the answer.

A small thread of pride bloomed in my chest, pushing some of that pressure aside. "Not sexually, but the girls were not nice my senior year of high school. They came at me hard and brutal. I don't know if you know this, but I kinda have issues with trust and emotions."

"No." He pretended to be surprised, his mouth gaping open. "Really? I never would've guessed."

I laughed and swatted at him again, but this time, he caught my hand and held it against his chest, angling closer until his side touched mine. For a second, he gazed down into my eyes, and then he softly said, "I get the trust issues, but I like you despite them. I might even like you because of them."

My breath was caught in my throat. I tipped my head back, and he drew in, his lips were a hair's width away. I murmured, "You like me? Like, like me, like me?"

That smirk showed again, almost taunting me.

I said, "You should watch it, Coleman. I think you might be moving too fast."

The ends of his mouth dipped down, and he eased back a step. "What?"

"I mean, if we're doing the feelings talk. That's all I'm saying. It's been four days."

"I said I liked you, not that I'm in love with you." He moved even farther back, his jaw clenching. "Fuck's sake, Clarke. I screwed you the last two nights and had a hard-on for the entire first night. You think I'd do all that for a chick I didn't like? Like, not love, and no. I quite agree. This is not a 'dating' talk, how you keep throwing that word around." Anger tightened his features, thinning his lips, and pulling his eyebrows together. "You might want to consider the thought that you're the one who wants to date, not me. Maybe I'm a normal guy, not turning down sex?"

I was gut-punched by that one. Air left my lungs, and I didn't have anything to shoot back. Not at first, then a whole torrent bubbled up. I straightened from my car. "Are you kidding me?"

"No, but I'm not going to take this bullshit, either. You can't talk down to me, Clarke. I like you, as in the you who's so goddamn feisty, the one who makes me laugh because it's so obvious she has trust issues, the one who must've been crushed by some asshole so hard that she hides how fucking beautiful she is from everyone, even from herself. I don't know who that guy is, or what he did to you, but I am not that guy. I can be a dick sometimes. I'll admit that, but I'm not the guy you can walk over. It's normal for me to say I might like you. That's a normal thing to do."

My mind was amok. I had no idea what was up or down. "What are you talking about?"

"Nothing." He held his hands up, surrendering, and backed away. "I'm not saying anything. We're not dating. I guess we're not even friends, but hey, if you want to get fucked so hard you see stars, I guess I'm the guy for that." He shook his head, and turning, he left.

I drove back to school, but it wasn't until I parked and was walking up to my dorm that I realized I didn't even remember the drive. I was physically there, but nothing else had left Shay's street.

I was still wondering what the hell just happened.

# CHAPTER TWENTY-FIVE

When I went to my first class, then my next, then lunch, and finally my last before heading home, a weird déjà vu hit me.

Everything was back to normal.

No guys called out to me. It was like the Dick Crusher video hadn't happened. Missy was back to being her condescending, yet passively friendly self. Holly and the cousin stopped by afterward before the three of them went to supper together. I had no phone calls. No Gage hiding out or sending my friends to find me or calling me. Even Sabrina, Shay's gorgeous friend, was busy studying at the desk. She didn't look up to say hello. No Linde. No Shay. No political science group meetings.

The only difference was that there was also no Kristina, and that meant no Casey, Laura, or Sarah.

I understood that part.

They would've had an eventful night. If they were around, I had no doubt they were sleeping. Emotional hangovers were a thing, and after Missy and her crew left, I was alone. Like really alone, like pre-Shay alone.

It felt glorious.

Well, maybe not. I didn't feel right about Shay, but I'd see him in a day. We could sort out whatever happened on his street. Till then, I studied to my heart's content. I made trips to my dorm's computer lab, and I even got naughty. I stole some of the computer's printing papers, stuffing them down the front of my shirt. My inner dork was coming out full-force. It was like I'd been around "cool" people too much for my system. It was rebelling. It needed an outlet, and I indulged. All of the colored highlighters came out. Not just the primary colors, all of them. I used pink for one textbook, and added purple on the next.

All caution was thrown to the wind. It was only eight, but I went to the library.

I really let my freak out.

An energy drink. Coffee from the cart. My own Twizzlers this time. Even a bag of chocolate candies. I was going nuts on the caffeine and sugar, and then I found an empty study room on the top and most isolated floor in the library.

I stayed until midnight.

It was some of the best studying I've had. Ever. Mind-blowing.

I was caught up and refreshed for the midterms coming up.

I was almost drooling as I headed back to the dorm.

I was in a nerd high, not thinking about Shay and all the confusion in my life. The day made sense. Everything was back in order. I was studying and being prepared.

I left the library and turned down a sidewalk that cut to my dorm.

I didn't know they were hiding in the same set of trees where Gage and I talked about Casey. Or that as I went past them, they looked to make sure no one else was around. It was Monday night, and it was when the library closed. Everyone left around ten, then more trickled out until eleven-thirty. Only the most determined or the most desperate stayed till actual closing time, and I was one of those. I was determined.

So were they.

They came up behind me.

Two shadows fell on top of mine. The shadows were cast ahead of me since the biggest light was by the library behind us. I glanced down, a half second, and saw them.

The hair on the back of my neck stood.

Another half of a second.

Something long and thick fell from one of the guy's hands.

Another half of a second.

It was a bat.

Another half of a second.

Fear pooled in my gut, and they were lifting the bat.

Another half of a second.

They were going to attack me.

I turned, a scream ripping from my depths, and the bat hit me clear across the face. It stopped the scream, paralyzed the inside me, and then one more half second. I was falling down.

I looked, my face burning, and I saw the bottom of their shoes before everything went black.

Three seconds.

That was all it took.

The smell woke me up.

It was foul and metallic, but then the sounds were next. Like an ambulance's siren. It was looping around and around, and it was so loud. It was becoming louder. I wanted to cover my ears. It hurt. I wanted the ambulance to go past me, but it never did. It kept coming. It kept getting louder and louder, shrieking incessantly, and then I heard the voices.

A male and a female.

I felt two fingers pressing into my wrist.

That hurt, too. I wanted to tell them to stop, but I couldn't.

I wanted to wake up and move, but I couldn't do anything. I was trapped.

"BP is—"

More beeps and alarms sounded. I couldn't hear what the female was saying. The guy asked, "Pulse?"

She said something again.

I could open my eyes. I looked up—the ceiling was white. I shook. No, I was in a vehicle, and *that* shook. I couldn't move. My neck felt like it was on fire, and it was constricted. My arms, hands, legs. I was strapped to a bed, a stretcher.

I was in an ambulance.

"Miss." The female bent over me. "Miss, we called your family. Your brother is meeting us at the hospital."

But . . .

I tried to speak. My mouth couldn't move. What was going on?

Then my eyelids were growing heavy again, really heavy, and I fell asleep wondering one thing: Why was I going to the hospital?

A low and steady beeping woke me first.

The pain really woke me next. I opened my eyes, and it was a different ceiling. This one was bare. There were silver creases. I followed one and saw some curtains hanging from it attached by wheels. This time I could open my mouth. I could turn my head. I wasn't strapped down anymore, and I looked over, my entire body screaming for me not to move.

I did anyway.

Gage sat in the chair beside me, his head propped up by his hand. His chest rose and a deep breath came out. I didn't say anything, not at first. My mouth hurt, but Gage didn't look okay. He was pale, there were purple smudges under his eyes, and strained wrinkles around his mouth. Those showed whenever he was under stress.

"You're awake?"

I looked the other way. Slowly. God, it hurt.

A nurse approached the bed, a clipboard in hand, whispering, "There's been quite some activity around here because of you."

I glanced again to see if Gage woke, but he hadn't.

The nurse touched the inside of my wrist, watching her clock.

I asked, my voice so hoarse, "I'm in a hospital?"

She nodded, counting under breath, "Ten . . . nine . . . eight . . ." Once she finished, she wrote a number on her clipboard. "Yeah. Do you know what happened?"

There was pain. Fog. An image of a silhouette, then something big by it.

I winced as I tried to remember. "No."

"Are you in pain?"

I nodded. "Yes." Another croak from me.

She reached for an IV and pressed some buttons on a little box hanging from it. "Your morphine must be low. I started another dose." She reached for a black arm cuff. "I need to take your blood pressure. Are you okay with that?"

I lifted my arm as much as I could, and she applied it. She pressed a button above me, and the cuff tightened until it felt as if it would cut off my whole arm.

She murmured, watching the numbers, "What do you remember?"

I told her as a machine beeped, and those numbers were written down, too. She stared at me a moment. I was waiting for her to fill in the gaps, to explain everything to me, but she didn't.

"Wh— Hey!"

Gage woke, surging upright. His hand reached for me, and he half-rose out of his seat. "You're okay?" He searched my face.

"Yeah."

"Her vitals are all normal." The nurse gave us both a cheerful grin. "I'm going to let the doctor know you're awake. He'll want to talk to you."

"You're in pain?" Gage asked once she pulled the door shut behind her.

"She started morphine or something." I frowned. The headache was still there, and I could not wait for it to go away. "Gage, what happened?"

"What do you remember?"

I told him the same, and like the nurse, there was a bated moment of silence.

"What?" The silhouette, the dark thing by it. Why was it flashing in my memory? "Gage. Tell me. Please." Fear started to bloom under my ribs, spreading all over.

He just stared at me before squeezing his eyes shut. He let out a pocket of air, and his shoulders dropped dramatically. He nodded. "Okay." His hand went to the bedrail by me, and his fingers curled around it. "You were attacked—"

As he spoke, the silhouette became one.

"—Matt Carruthers and another guy waited for you to leave the library—"

It was dark. After midnight. There was no one else around.

"—The other guy hit you with a bat—"

The bat swung, and I jerked in the bed as if it hit me once again. I could feel it.

"—then Carruthers kicked you—"

In the face.

I looked up, and a foot was lifted.

I couldn't move. I was reliving the entire thing. A droplet landed on my hand, and I glanced down. I was crying. I had no idea.

Gage paused, but I gutted out, "Tell me the rest."

"There isn't much after that."

"What?"

He lifted a shoulder. "One of the librarians was leaving and saw the whole thing. She yelled and called 9-1-1 right away. They took off, but campus cameras caught them. They know it was them. I talked to the security officer, but since Dulane doesn't have its own campus police, the city police is going to be charging them. The one detective stopped by this morning. He said they probably had enough evidence so you wouldn't have to testify, plus the whole video from before clearly shows Carruthers advancing on you first. It was self-defense, though the cop said you went a little far with it." A half-grin cracked the heavy mask of exhaustion. He raked a hand over his face. "Shit, Kenz. I was so worried about you. Everyone was."

I sat there. The whole thing was unbelievable, but I remembered it.

The fear was still there, and I waited. I wasn't one to be afraid. The anger would be coming, but after another minute's wait, I frowned. It wasn't there. It was just fear.

"Kenz?"

Gage was watching me. He tilted his head to the side, his fingers uncurling from around the rail so he could reach toward me. "What's going on in there?"

I shook my head.

A lump was in my throat.

I didn't want to be scared.

I didn't want to be anything.

I shoved it down.

Maybe it was the morphine. Maybe it was me, but I didn't feel. I was numb, and I smiled at my brother. "I'm fine."

"You're lying." We heard voices nearing the door, and Gage glanced to it. He leaned forward again, dropping his voice. "We can talk about it later, but you *have* to talk about it. Okay? You have to. You can't keep that stuff bottled inside."

The door opened, and a doctor came in behind the nurse. I was poked, prodded, and questioned over the next thirty minutes. They told me I suffered a concussion, and half of my face looked like a giant red onion. Other than that, the doctor said I was lucky that librarian was there.

I suppressed a shiver.

Before they left, after taking another round of vitals, the doctor said I could go home in the morning. He asked Gage, "Are you going to fill her in on everything that's happened since her attack?"

"I hadn't gotten to it yet. I will."

He nodded his approval, saying to me, "I'll be back in the morning for another set of rounds, so I'll be seeing you one more time before you can go home. It's nice to have met you. I have to say it's been an honor and an adventure all at the same time."

The nurse laughed softly, following him out.

I asked Gage, "What was that about?"

He sighed. "Shay."

# CHAPTER TWENTY-SIX

*Shay.*

His name was an echo in me, resonating like a bouncing ball.

"What about him?"

Gage's chest rose and held, before lowering again. He sat up straighter, his hands on his lap, and he started. "Okay. Here goes. You don't know this, but if you were to leave this room, there are two policemen outside your door."

"What?"

"Carruthers and the other guy are in the hospital. Those police are out there for your safety, since Carruthers already tried to attack you one time. They figure he might retaliate again, but I don't see that happening."

"Did I hit them back or something? Are they here as patients?"

"No." A quick laughter slipped out. "They're in here because Shay beat the shit out of them."

The ball dropped.

"What?"

"The librarian told someone in administration about you, and they called your roommate. Your roommate is an idiot. She told your floor's RA that you had one friend, Kristina. She knew about me, so at the same time she was calling me, so was Mom."

"Mom." I groaned. This would get interesting.

"I wasn't totally thinking clearly. Mom was on one line, going nuts. I could hear Blake in the background yelling."

I groaned again.

"I do have to give it to your friend. She was calm. I mean, I could hear how scared she was, but she was calm at the same time. I hung up with her, and I talked to Mom."

"How did Shay find out?"

He held up a finger, his Adam's apple moving up and down in a swallowing motion. "That's why I'm explaining that I wasn't thinking clearly. I blurted out that she needed to call and let Shay know. After that, I can only assume her phone call to him wasn't good. The next thing I know, I'm parking outside the hospital. Mom and Blake are on their way, and Casey calls."

*Casey?*

Gage continues, "Word spread fast who attacked you, and before the cops could get to Carruther's apartment . . ." He let me do the rest.

"Shay did."

"Exactly." He nodded. "He beat the shit out of him, and he was still there, pounding him when the cops arrived. They were all arrested and brought here to get checked out. Shay knocked Carruther's friend out cold at the apartment, and the guy woke up here. He said something smart to Shay, and they didn't have enough cops in the room. Shay went at them one more time. He didn't make contact, but he tried. He almost did. A nurse stood in the way and stopped him. He would've had to hit her if he wanted to hit them, and before he could get around her, the cops were on him by then. They were all separated after that and handcuffed to their beds."

"No!" My mind was racing. They could charge Shay. They could do worse than that. He could go to prison.

"There's talk that they'll throw out Shay's attack if they throw out Carruthers's first attack on you, when he lunged at you after the football game."

"Really?" It worked like that?

"They had legal jargon. I talked to a lawyer, but Shay's a big fucking deal. The football coaches got involved. I wouldn't be surprised if the college Dean did, too. Carruthers agreed. He's only going to be charged on the attack outside the library if Shay can walk."

"He went for that?" I wasn't thinking about Shay going Terminator on me. I'd process that later.

Gage shook his head, shrugging his shoulders. "My guess is that they threw some big intimidation his way for him to do that. I don't get it, either, but Shay isn't going to be charged."

"That's unbelievable."

"Yeah, but it means that Shay's banned from the hospital. He can't see you until you leave."

Shay did all of that for me.

I couldn't—I still couldn't process it all.

A different thought came to me. "Where is everyone? Mom, Blake, Kristina?"

"Your merry band of friends were here all day, but they went back to the dorm. Same thing for Mom and Blake. They were here during the day. They drove all day and night to get here, but they went to a hotel to get some sleep. It's my shift. I was gone for classes today, and I wanted to hear what was being said on campus about the whole thing."

A different feeling of dread slithered around me. I didn't want to hear that, either, not yet. "What day is it?"

"It's Wednesday morning." He turned the television on, and I saw the time.

Two in the morning.

I was attacked Monday after midnight, so early Tuesday.

I lost an entire day.

All that happened over a twenty-four hour period.

I was going to pass out again.

Gage softened his voice. "It's all over campus that Shay went after Carruthers. The rumors were rampant, and those were the ones people were telling me. I can't imagine what people are saying that I haven't heard."

"Oh, my God."

I could. My last year at high school flashed before my eyes, but Shay defended me. That was...

I felt the walls closing in. The room shrank in size.

What was going on?

Was the oxygen cut off, too? There wasn't any left.

"Kenz." Gage stood up, leaning over me. His eyes filled with concern. "Hey. What's happening?"

I couldn't talk. Why couldn't I...

The room was tipping over now.

I heard muffled voices.

Then it was all black again.

I fainted.

In the grand scheme of things, it was embarrassing, but survivable.

My mom swooped in when she got to my room later that afternoon. Her arms opened wide and an afghan draped around her back and arms. She pulled me in for a hug, rocking me gently.

"Oh, honey," she crooned, smoothing a hand down my hair like I was a pet. "You scared me so much. I didn't know what happened. I didn't know if you were alive, if it was just you, if Gage got attacked, too. An uninformed mother's mind is not a good place." She pulled back, sticking out her bottom lip in a pout as she continued to smooth down my hair. "You're just as beautiful to me as you were the day you were born. The whole moldy pickle look is in."

"Mom!" My face looked like a moldy pickle?

A low chuckle sounded behind her, and then my older brother stepped to the side. He looked normal, an inch taller than Gage and myself. His head was still shaved, and he looked like he'd been lifting weights a bit more. But the normal part was his clothes. He was dressed in a sweatshirt and jeans, and he had a Styrofoam cup in his hand.

I could smell the coffee, and my mouth was instantly watering. "Is that what I think it is?"

He laughed, setting it on the table stand beside me. "I wasn't sure if you could have it yet. Thought I might check with the nurse first." He moved in to hug me, and it felt good to fold into his arms.

Gage was my brother in the real sense of the word.

We fought, wrestled, yelled at each other, but we're also friends. Blake was four years older than me, and he'd been the father figure since ours died from cancer when we were little. He was dark coloring, dark hair, and dark eyes, like Gage and myself, but he had a slightly rounder face. He was bigger in build, too. More muscular, a bit gruffer, and slightly rougher around the edges, Blake had a temperament to match.

He was exactly what I needed.

He held me a second longer, and I brushed away a tear. "Hi. You guys drove here?"

His eyes were so sad. He smoothed some of my hair from my forehead. "You know Mom. She hates flying. Family emergency."

He grimaced, his eyes lingering over the side of my face. "I heard your boy packed quite a punch back at those assholes."

*My boy.*

"Oh." I ducked my head, feeling my hands grow clammy. "Yes. That's what I heard, too."

He stepped back, and I focused on our mother again. The afghan was still there, half covering a pair of blue scrubs and fur-lined clogs. Her dark hair was pulled up into a high bun, and she even had a pair of glasses hanging from a beaded string around her neck. Red lipstick, yellow eye shadow, and an extra amount of blush was spread on her cheeks.

"What are you doing? You're not a nurse." I pointed at her clothes.

"I know." She looked down, so pleased with herself. "Isn't it fabulous? I dressed like this for two reasons." She migrated closer, taking my hand, and including Blake in the conversation. He drifted over to where Gage had slept, but hoisted himself up so he was sitting on the windowsill, his feet resting on Gage's chair.

He shook his head. "Don't talk to me. You look crazy. I don't want to be included."

She batted her eyelashes at me. "It's a fashion-forward trend. No one's thought of this before. I brought everything so I'm prepared. I'm blending in. I'm dressing the part. I'm going to take care of you, so what better outfit to wear than someone who does it for a profession? Isn't this fabulous? And I'm comfortable. Nurses are so comfortable. It's like going to work in your pajamas. I'm kind of jealous. Maybe I should be a nurse?"

Blake had pulled his phone out, but he waved a hand toward me. "Tell her the other reason. The real reason you're dressed like that."

"Oh." Her hand splayed out on her chest. "Yes. If I need to sneak anywhere, I have a better chance looking like I belong. You know? They have all sorts of weird rooms in hospitals. You never know where you might have to go and where you're not supposed to be."

I agreed with Blake. "You're a lunatic."

She laughed, waving her hand in the air. "My children are so funny." She turned around as she spoke, and a nurse was entering the room. She stopped, frowning at our mother before shaking her head and approaching the bed.

She explained what I already knew—I was being discharged. The doctor had come through earlier, and I was given a clean bill of health. I wasn't supposed to drive for the next two weeks, and I had to "keep it easy" for the same time period because that was how long it would take for the concussion to go away.

Until then, foggy thoughts, slurred speech, feeling nauseous, dizzy, off-balance, and a whole list of other criteria were to be expected. I shouldn't be alarmed if I couldn't do simple math anymore. That'd go away, but I had to be careful so I didn't reinjure my head. That happened, apparently.

When I left, Blake was the one to wheel me out in the wheelchair, and I had no clue what Mom was doing. She was talking to everyone as we went down a hallway, acting as if we were in a parade. I wouldn't have been surprised if she'd been doing the elbow, elbow, wrist, wrist, wrist wave to them. She was laughing, telling everyone how blessed we were, how scared she'd been as a mother, and I had enough by the time we got to the front door.

I was supposed to stay in the wheelchair until the car, but I couldn't handle it. Irritation and general tension (though I didn't know why) sat like two boulders in the bottom of my gut. They wouldn't go away, no matter what I thought to myself. I had a prescription for painkillers, but I wished I'd upped the morphine dose, just to get me to the car.

"The minivan, huh?" I remarked as Blake wheeled me up to the side door.

We could still hear Mom chattering to someone behind us. "Yeah, not the car. She wasn't sure how long we'd stay, so she insisted. She brought half the house with us. More room with this one."

He opened the door and held my hand as I stood and got in. My legs were a little unsteady, but nothing major. The nerves were from leaving, nothing else.

I'd been attacked, but I wasn't thinking about that.

I wasn't thinking about Shay, Missy, or Kristina, or what anyone was saying on campus.

And I wasn't lying to myself, either.

"How are you doing? Really?"

Blake paused by the door, waiting for my answer.

"Okay! Sounds amazing. I'll be DMing it. It's all about Instagram, or wait. Do you have a Snipchat?"

We both looked back.

My mom meant well. She worked as a hotel manager, but her hobby and life's passion was an actress. So far, she only got starring roles in our local community plays, but she was dedicated. We all gave her grief, but if our mother ended up on the big screen somewhere, I wouldn't be surprised.

She was playing the "cool mother" at this moment. Or trying.

I nodded to Blake. "Just tired, is all."

He nodded back, though he didn't look convinced, and shut the door. Mom piled into the passenger door, turning around to me, and Blake got behind the steering wheel.

"We got a hotel room. Did Gage tell you that? He has that apartment, but he has roommates, and you have that dorm. Blake can't be there past hours, right? I talked to your roommate. She explained everything." She took a breath. "So, honey, where would you like to go?"

There was one place, but I said instead, "Your hotel is fine."

"Splendid!" She beamed at me.

# CHAPTER TWENTY-SEVEN

I had enough.

It was hour five at the hotel. Blake left for the hotel's gym, and I grabbed my phone and snuck out into thc hallway. I called Gage and hissed once he answered, "Mom is driving me crazy."

He laughed, and I could hear people in his background. He said, "She just wants to make sure you're okay, but not be too overbearing. She does that by doing weird stuff. You know that."

"She's acting like she's a real nurse. She called the front desk and asked if they had an IV pole. When they didn't, she asked for anything that stood high, upright, and was skinny. She told the room service guy she'd need something for the morphine drip. I don't have a morphine drip. I have pills, and she's counted all of them and put them into a dispenser that's broken up into the days of the week. I swear, Gage, if she asks me one more time to sit so she can practice her manual blood pressure skills, I'll throw them in her face."

He smothered some laughter. "You know what she's like. She's scared and worried. Your attack was traumatic to us all. I thought for a second you were gone. I'm sure Mom did, too. Heck, I know she did. She was screaming when she called me."

I heard her calling me inside the hotel and glanced back. I sighed.

I wasn't upset with her. I wasn't upset with anyone.

There were two truths ringing in me, and I only wanted to acknowledge one. I wanted to see Shay. And pulling my big girl panties on, I asked, "Have you talked to Shay today?"

"Yeah." I could almost hear him grinning through the phone. "I was wondering when you were going to ask."

I swore at him.

He laughed. "He said he can't miss football practice, but asked if he could see you tonight."

I groaned into the phone. "Mom is going to be so embarrassing."

"She already was. She fawned all over him. He was still in the hospital when she and Blake arrived. She went gaga over him, touching him all over, hugging him, crying. If she could date him, I think she would. She wouldn't care if you already were or not."

"You're not helping."

"Not trying to, but yes, he's asked. I told him you were in Witness Protection, i.e., our mother."

I grinned. The label had some merit. "Would you be pissed if I snuck out to see him?"

"No, but Mom would."

"Really?"

"Well." He thought about it. "Maybe not, but she'd be jealous, and she'd ask you all the details I don't want to hear as your brother."

I cringed, imagining her asking if he "pounded" or "made sweet, sweet love." The nausea was coming back. "Let's tell her after I'm gone."

He barked out a laugh. "Okay. I'll tell him you're game."

"I don't want him to come here."

"You want to go to his house?"

"Yeah." I was breathless just thinking about it.

"I'll give you a ride. After what he did to Carruthers and that other asshole, he's a solid guy. He cares about you, genuinely."

That had that lump back in my throat, swelling again. I blinked back a few tears. "Thank you, Gage."

"Don't thank me. Do you realize how popular I am in school the last two days? People are using me to get to you. I feel like a damn celebrity." His tone sobered. "Love ya, Kenz. There's a bunch here who do. We're all going to take care of you."

That lump swelled up so that I couldn't talk. I choked out, "Thank you." Then hung up because the tears weren't waiting. They fell free, and I was still in the hallway when my mom opened the door. She took one look at me, saw the tears, and opened her arms wide. “Oh, honey.” She wasn’t pretending to be an actress. This wasn’t a show. I heard the love, and I walked into them.

I might’ve needed Blake’s hug before, but this time, I needed my mom’s.

# CHAPTER TWENTY-EIGHT

I was back in that hallway, hugging myself and listening in on my mom and Gage talking. "I don't understand why he can't come here," she said.

Because I wanted privacy.

Because I wanted to be somewhere I could think.

The door was open an inch, but every word said was like a blow to my chest.

When we stood to leave, Mom started with the questions. Where were we going? How long would I be gone? I was going to see a boy? And that last question, it was her third time asking. She did again, "I just don't get it. We don't live here, so this is her home away from home. Doesn't a daughter need her mother?"

"Mom, she's only going for a few hours. She'll be back tonight. I'll pick her up."

"But—"

The door creaked. Blake stood there, leaning against the doorframe. He rested his head against the paneling, using one finger to open the door a little wider. He took me in, one sweep of his gaze, and gave me a pitying smile. Then he turned and said, "Nothing's going to happen to her, Mom. She'll be safe. Gage vouches for this guy, and we already know he went after her two attackers."

I jerked, hearing those last two words. But he was right. I had been attacked. That was me. I was the girl who was attacked.

*Victim.*

That word felt like a blow in itself.

I had become a victim.

"But—"

"Mom." Blake pushed off from the doorframe, crossing the room. "She'll be fine there."

"That's a whole house of boys. Right? And he's on the football team. There must be other players there. What if they're not like this guy? And we don't really know him. He attacked the two boys. What if he's violent, too?"

"He's not," Gage said, frustrated. "I would've done the exact same thing if I'd known who they were at first. I just wouldn't have gotten away with it like he did."

"See. Right there. He got away with it. He could get away with other things, with—"

I had enough. I pushed the door the rest of the way and stood, still hugging myself. "I'm alive. I'm safe. Nothing will happen to me there. I will be back in a few hours."

Her face was wet from tears, and she was hugging herself. That damned afghan was draped over her again, and she sniffled, using the corner to wipe her face. That was why she wore it. It wasn't to keep her warm. It wasn't for decoration. It was for the tears.

I let out a sigh. "I'll be fine, Mom. I promise."

Blake was on her left. Gage on her right. Both sons reached out a hand, comforting her. She managed a smile and bobbed her head in an awkward nod. "Okay. I'm just being a mother, you know. I worry."

"I know." I moved in for a hug, and once she let me go, Gage and I almost sprinted for the door.

He moved around me, holding the door to the stairs open for me. "She might change her mind."

"You don't have to tell me." I swept past him, not pausing a beat as I went down the stairs. Two flights later, we were outside and in Gage's truck.

He chuckled under his breath as he pulled out of the parking lot. "I can't believe I'm giving you a ride to see Shay Coleman."

"I'm not supposed to be insulted you said that?"

"No! No." He lifted a shoulder. "You have to agree with me, though. Shay Coleman? Man. When I realized something was going on between you two at the bar, I almost shit my pants. I talked to him about you at that party, but I never suspected he was interested in you. He acted like you were an annoying little sister."

"Stop. I don't want to hear that."

"He was putting on a front. I'm trying to say that he's cool. He's a cool guy."

"I know." I frowned. He was being weird. This conversation was weird. "Are you trying to say something without saying it?"

"No. I—" He rolled his eyes. "I'm impressed, I guess." His lip lifted up again. "You kinda have a type. You date older guys. You date up."

Parker was a year younger than Blake, so he was three years older than I was.

I flushed. "Let's not talk about him. Please." Remembering my last conversation with Shay, I said, "And I'm not technically dating Shay." I didn't think.

"What?"

"It was never official between us."

He snorted. "It's official now. No guy would beat the shit out of another guy and try again even when cops were in the room for a side chick. He cares, Kenz."

That lump was back, but it was resting on top of my throat. "It was me, Gage. I didn't want anyone to know."

I could feel him glancing at me, but I kept staring straight ahead. Tears blurred my vision, so I looked down to my lap. "He told me he liked me the last time I saw him, and I told him he was moving too fast."

"Are you serious?"

"I went to him after Casey reported her rape. I didn't think. It just felt right to go there. I got scared afterwards."

He turned down Shay's street. "You might want to stop bullshitting yourself."

"Yeah."

He parked in the driveway, and I took my cell. I'd barely used it once I got it back.

When I checked earlier that day, the voice mail was full. Hundred plus text messages. It became too overwhelming. Everyone wanted to know what happened. There were just as many people wishing me well. There were a few who said the opposite. I saw the first one and handed the phone over to Gage. There was nothing on there I was embarrassed about, and he went through the messages one by one. The ones who wished me harm were turned over to the cops. The well-wishers got a reply back saying it was Gage texting on my behalf, and a polite and general thank you greeting. Once they thought Gage was in charge of my phone, those texts stopped coming. Word must've gotten out they couldn't get in touch with me that way.

Still, I made sure to send a few personal texts to Missy and Kristina. They wanted to make sure I was okay. I was, or I was better. I asked Kristina about Casey, who replied that she was doing better. Linde texted, too, and I thanked him, as well. But the person whose texts I read over and over again, yet still hadn't replied to, were Shay's.

I don't know why I couldn't reply.

I read over them again, from the first that he sent me that night.

*12:38 am*

Coleman: **Heard something. Call me!**

*12:48 am*

Coleman: **For real. I'm hearing more, and I'm going nuts. If it isn't true, I need to know or I'm going to do something.**

*2:48 am*

Coleman: **Gage said you're in the hospital. So am I. I lost it, but I'd do it again. Text me when you can.**

*4:18 am*

Coleman: **Did something again. Thinking of you.**

*4:38 am*

Coleman: **I tried to see you, but got kicked out of the hospital. I can't come in. Your mom's interesting. I like your brothers. Good guys.**

*9:15 am*

Coleman: **Just left a meeting with coaches and some detectives. Lawyers, too. I'm not going to be charged, thank the fuck, right? Okay. You're getting a pile of texts from me. Gage said you're not doing calls or messages. Call when you can, if you want to.**

*11:17 pm*

Coleman: **I blew your cover. Word's out. You're going to be pissed, but I don't even care. I told people you're my girlfriend. It shut most of the rumors up, but figured I should text and let you know. I'm sure your brothers told you already. So. Yeah. Get pissed and call me, if you want. I'll take the yelling. I'll enjoy it, even.**

*4:23 pm*

Coleman: **Gage called. I told him, but texting you again. Yes. You can come to me any time, any day, any minute. I'm here. Or I'll come to you.**

It was a little under forty-eight hours later, and I texted him for the first time.

Me: **We're outside.**

His reply was immediate.

Coleman: **I'm here.**

I looked up. He was gazing back at me from the driveway.

A sudden wave of nerves rose inside me. I'd avoided looking in the mirror so far, but I needed to see the damage. Taking a deep breath, I flipped down the visor. My mom wasn't joking about the moldy pickle. The entire right side of my face was swollen with a Monet of black, blue, green, and yellow bruises. I had a fat lip.

I was a mess. There wasn't another way to say it, and I was going to see Shay like this?

"I'm hideous."

"What?"

"Nothing." I grabbed the hooded sweatshirt in the back of his car and pulled it on. Sunglasses were on his dashboard, and I took those, too.

"Hey!"

I got out, yanked the hood up and over my face, and put the glasses on. "I'll call you later to pick me up?"

"That, or he can drop you off."

"Got it."

I hunched forward, my hands in the sweatshirt's pockets, and I didn't look at Shay as I went right past him. He turned to follow. "Hello?"

"Can we do this upstairs?" I was reaching for the door, and I opened it as Shay got behind me. We weren't the only ones at the intersection. Linde was in the stairway, leaving the main floor. He was pulling the door closed behind him and automatically issued a, "Oh, excuse me . . ." The word died in his throat when he looked from me, to Shay, then back, and his eyes narrowed, lingering on me.

A soft, "Clarke?" came from him. He had a bowl of oatmeal in his hands, and it almost dropped. He tightened his hold quick, cleared his throat, and stepped all the way into the stairs. The door shut with a click behind him. He looked from me to Shay again. "Uh . . ." He blinked a few times before coughing once again. "I . . . sorry. I'm at a loss. That is you, Clarke, right?"

"Yeah." My throat got stomped on. The husky sound that came out hadn't bothered me until that moment. I cringed. "Can we not, uh, do this here?"

Linde moved aside, and I hurried up the stairs.

Turning down the hallway, both were following me, but I didn't want to do this with Linde. Not right then. I wanted to talk to Shay and then regroup. I'd feel more centered if that was done and out of the way first.

Stopping outside Shay's room, I said over my shoulder, "Can I talk to Shay first? I . . . can we do this another day, Linde? I'm sorry. I . . . just—"

"No. No." He went to a different door. "Talk. It's good to see you up and walking." He cracked a grin, tapping the side of his head. "The mind does weird tricks on a person. You never know." He indicated me with the bowl. "It's real good to see you. Miss you in class."

I was reaching for the doorknob but paused at those words.

I looked back up. "Thank yo—" He was in his room already.

Had I been a bitch there? Was that wrong to do?

I was rooted in place, but Shay moved me and opened the door. He ran a hand down my side, curved it around my waist, and rested it on the small of my back. For a second, one second, I didn't move. He opened the door, but neither of us moved. Feeling his heat, his strength, I closed my eyes and rested my forehead to his chest.

He remained like that, and after another second, I felt him rest his head against the top of mine, but with the barest of touches. No. Those were his lips. He grazed a soft kiss there, and feeling the tears falling, I went inside.

We didn't move far.

Shay shut the door, and I whirled around. He didn't even move, I just pressed myself against him, and his arms wrapped around me. My hood was still in place. Gage's sunglasses on. He held me, and I soaked it up. He ran his hand up and down my arm and dipped his head to rest his chin on my good shoulder. He kissed my cheek before lying his own cheek next to it. He let out a deep breath, and it was as if he were breathing for both of us.

So much of the tension, anxiety, and fear left me. There was so much else still in there, but my chest was considerably lighter.

I stepped back after another few minutes and murmured hoarsely, "Thank you."

His hand came to the glasses. He started to touch them. "Can I?"

No! Fear slammed back in me, but I forced myself to nod. Then I waited. My heart against my chest cavity.

He pulled them off. There was no change in his eyes. He took them, folded them, and put them on his dresser. Slowly, so agonizingly slowly, he reached back up and gently pushed the hood back from my head. When I felt completely bare, he gazed at me.

I couldn't look, not at first. I focused on his chest, but when he didn't make a motion, or a sound, I looked up.

So much warmth was there that my lungs were empty for a moment.

He murmured, "You're still as beautiful as you were the first day in class."

Oh, God.

Another teardrop formed and hung off my eyelid. "You're lying."

"I'm not." He reached up, another tender touch, and he raised his thumbs to clear the tears from my eyes. Wiping them away, he caught a tendril of my hair and tucked it behind my ear. His hand lingered there, and he stared at the bruising.

I choked up. "Maybe I shouldn't have come."

I made a movement toward the door, but his hand touched my wrist, gentle, but still firm. "No." He stepped in front, blocking the door fully. "I just got you."

Those words—I laughed, shaking my head. "Smooth operator."

"Or a truthful one."

I went to the bed but didn't sit. Hugging myself, I turned back around, raising a hand so I could bite at my nail. My mother would've been yelling at me, but I didn't care. My anxiety was back and off the charts. It was, but it wasn't. This was a different form of anxiety. This wasn't the kind where I felt the walls closing in on me. This was the kind where I was worried the guy who used to laugh with me, poke at me until he got a reaction, or made me gasp in bed wouldn't want to do any of those anymore. It was *that* kind of anxiety.

Maybe it was the tears welling up. They never stopped anymore, or maybe because I was half through my nail, but whatever he saw, he came forward. He cupped the good side of my face and sighed. "Everything will be okay."

"You don't know that."

"Carruthers will never hurt you again."

It wasn't about Carruthers. It wasn't about his friend. "Casey was raped. I was attacked. There'll be others."

Agony flared in his eyes. "Not for you. I won't let it."

"You can't know."

"I do. This time, I do." He raised his head up in a challenge. "No one will hurt you again."

I whispered, my voice cracking, “I want to believe you.”

He whispered back, inching closer until we were touching. His other hand was on my neck, and I was literally in the palm of his hands. He was gazing down. I was looking up, and he said again, “You can.”

He touched his lips to mine, a tender whisper of a touch, and I did.

# CHAPTER TWENTY-NINE

I called my mom, telling her I was staying with Shay. She tried to get me to change my mind, but all I wanted to do was lie in bed with Shay that night, so I did. We held hands. I was in his arms, and he rubbed my back as I told him everything.

The day felt weird.

I was confused after I left him, but enjoyed being a nobody again.

The library.

How I embraced my inner geekdom.

The sidewalk afterward.

The two shadows.

The bat.

When I was hit.

The ambulance.

Waking up in the hospital room.

The medical staff, and how great they were.

How crazy my mother was.

How great my brothers were, and how I enjoyed having Blake here.

My mother's tearful worry before I went to his place.

When I was done, he continued to stroke my back. "But how are you doing?"

I shook my head. "I can't answer that." I lifted my head to peer at him. I didn't want to lie, so I didn't. "I'm broken now."

His eyes clouded over, and he shook his head. They were brimming with fierce emotion, but everything about him was gentle. So were his words. "You're not. It's like a sports injury. It can bench you, or you can rest, go to rehab, and do everything in your power to heal it."

"Being attacked isn't like a sports injury."

He shifted to sit up, but he pulled me back against his chest. He ran a hand down my hair instead, circling around my arm and raising to repeat. "Maybe like cancer. You can't deny it. You deal with it, and if you get the right treatment, maybe you'll come out in one piece. I believe in that, Kennedy." He stopped his hand and held me. I felt his head resting against mine and a quiet, "I have to," left him.

We kissed a few times that night, nothing heavy. But he held me, and it was what I needed.

The next morning I was going to stay in the room until Blake could pick me up since Gage had classes. But Shay said everyone knew I was there, and the word was that I was his girlfriend. I went down with him after he got back from his morning run and we ate breakfast before getting ready for classes.

The guys were respectful.

A few stared at my face, but no one acted like my being at the table was weird.

Shay was on one side, and Linde was on the other. He asked for a hug, and I murmured before he pulled away, "Thank you for being a good friend."

He was wiping at his eyes and excused himself afterward.

He came back after a few minutes, his smile reinforced, and as the guys left for campus, Shay took me to the hotel. He sat back in his seat, the engine idling. "Do you want me to come up with you?"

I laughed. "Are you kidding? My mom won't let you leave."

"I can stop by tonight."

"Or, you can pick me up, and we'll repeat last night." Unless he had plans? Unless he didn't want to? Unless . . . my mind wouldn't stop. "If you want, I mean."

"Of course, I do." His eyebrows dipped close before smoothing back out. Those ice-blue eyes were questioning, but genuine. The concern rested on the bottom, lining it with a smidge shadow of darkness. "Is that okay with you? I mean, you're the one who was adamant we weren't dating." The side of his mouth lifted in a half-grin, but I saw how serious those eyes were. He wasn't joking.

"I said all that so I wouldn't get hurt."

"You're saying it now?"

I tried to smile. "I'm beyond hurt now. A little heartache on top of this is nothing." I failed.

His eyes darkened, and he leaned over the seat for me. His lips were on mine before he cursed and pulled back. "Did that hurt?"

I shook my head. "Only when you stopped. They hit my head, not my vagina."

He grimaced, scratching behind his ear. "I don't want to hurt you."

"I know, but I just wanted to remind you." I pointed to my face. "They hurt this." My hand went between my legs. "Not this. They didn't hurt this. They didn't touch this."

His eyes darkened again, anger flaring. He growled, "If they had, I'd probably be in jail."

I reached for his hand, hooking my finger around his and letting it rest on the console between us. "I know I'm going to be messed up by this attack, but I don't want them to take all the normal stuff from my life. I know we can't, not yet, but I want to have sex with you. I want to feel like a normal girl again, like a," I hesitated, "normal girl being with her boyfriend."

Some of that anger faded, and he smiled. "I was wondering if you were going to bring that up."

"Yeah."

I wanted to go back to picking at my nail.

"Do you want to be? Or do you want me to tell everyone we're not dating?"

I let out a laugh. "How'd that make me look?"

"Fuck how you look. Fuck everyone else. What do you want?" He nodded to me with his chin. "If you haven't noticed, I'm in. I beat up two guys for you. I think that says enough. I'm all in, Kenz."

My heart swelled. It was the first time he used my nickname.

I was blinking back more tears as I was smiling widely. "I'm all in, too."

"Thank God," he said under his breath, leaning over for another kiss. He was still gentle.

I could've stayed there forever, but the doorman began pacing back and forth. I saw him from the corner of my eye once, and I pulled back. "You have class."

"I do."

"Later tonight?"

"Later tonight," he agreed.

That became the routine for a while.

I'd spend the days with my family, and nights with Shay.

After a week, Blake flew home. He couldn't take any more time off from work, but my mom stayed. The hotel became too expensive, so she moved into the spare room that Gage and his roommates created for her. Two of the guys agreed to share a room, and she was elated. Gage offered to have one of the guys move in with him. They lived in a four-bedroom apartment, but the two who shared said it made sense. One had night classes, and the other had day classes, along with a day job. It was like they still had their own room, and my mother unofficially adopted Gage and his three roommates.

It was another two weeks before I met Kristina for coffee.

Missy packed some of my stuff up and helped my mom grab anything I needed. She was being sweet and helpful. So was everyone. Casey. Laura. Sarah. Everyone.

As for college, the administration said I could take time off.

I was seeing a counselor, and she said the same thing, but I hadn't wanted to do that. We reached an agreement. I would keep with my studies, but off-campus. The professors had someone tape their courses, and those were put online for me. It was a project already in the works. They sped their timetable up for me. I went to campus one time, but it was into one of the higher administration buildings so not many saw me, and I was put into a small office where I took all my midterms.

I was able to do my papers at home, emailing them in. The only thing I couldn't partake in was the group presentations, but I still participated. I sent in the work that the groups needed for my two other classes. I didn't have to do a presentation for my third class, and I fully participated with the political science one.

Aby and Becca came to Shay and Linde's house, and I was there for that segment, but I wouldn't be when they stood in front of the class. All of them agreed I shouldn't be penalized for that, but I still helped with everything else.

Aby and Becca weren't catty when I saw them for researching.

The bruises had long ago faded, and I was back to my old physical self. What was different was my relationship with Shay. It was out in the open, and while we weren't a public display of affection couple, there was the random back rub or hand graze, or how I just liked to stand by him and lean into his side.

I forgot how noticeable those were until the two girls openly stared.

I grew more aware afterward, but neither sniped at me. Both were quiet, and each even gave me a hug the last time our group met.

My mom, Gage, Kristina, and the rest of the other girls helped to pack up all my stuff. I was going to move into a new room with Kristina and Casey. I explained to the committee that I'd feel safer with them. My roommate was barely in her room, except for when she slept, and I was closer to Kristina and Casey anyway.

After finals, I met Casey, Laura, and Sarah out for dinner.

Kristina came, too, but she was a few minutes late. Everything was almost normal. Almost. I enjoyed listening to them gossip and using last names of people I didn't know. But then the conversation changed. The feeling grew more somber.

I didn't know why until Casey said, "I'd cry." She snapped her fingers. "At the drop of a hat, or if someone wanted to watch something I didn't. I never knew what would set it off, but man, they'd just flow. It was annoying."

She glanced over to meet my gaze.

We both were knocked down. We were both standing.

Or I was still trying to.

Hiding was holding me back, and I knew it. A shared look passed between us. I knew Casey knew it, too. I had to step out of the shadows, but my first semester was done except for one more event.

Shay's last football game.

He said he didn't care if I came, but I was girlfriend status now. I had to go. There was no reason not to go, and yes, he was a junior. He'd have one more year to play, and I would go to every single game, but I knew this one was important. It was their last. They hadn't won enough to continue on to nationals, so it was their last whether they won or not.

I wanted to go. I was terrified—but I wanted to go.

"You sure about this?" Casey asked, standing in front of me that day.

I was in a Dulane sweatshirt, and I wanted to pull that hood up. I wanted to hide again.

I didn't do that, but I did nod. "I'm sure."

"People are going to stare." Kristina stood behind her.

There wasn't anything to stare at. There were no scars. No more fat lip. No bruises. My hair was good, even. I looked better than I had before, if I was going to toot my own horn. My skin had a glow to it. I lost a few pounds, and I'd started working out with Shay. I didn't do the runs, but they had a makeshift gym in their basement. I joined Linde and Shay when they lifted weights. I was a little more toned.

I remarked now, "Let them stare."

Sarah added, "They're going to talk."

"Bring it on." I raised my chin.

Laura said, "Half are going to feel sorry for you, and half are going to hate you."

I pressed my lips together. "Fuck the haters."

Every single one of them tried to hold back their grins. Every single one failed.

Kristina moved forward, separating one of my curls from the others. Once it looked how she wanted, she stepped back. She waved her hands in the air. "Perfect."

I was doing this.
I had to do this.
I was ready to go.

# CHAPTER THIRTY

I was returning to the original scene of the crime.

Not the real crime, but what jump-started it all. A large crowd of people was moving toward the bleachers with us. Casey and I shared a look when we walked over to where the Dick Crushing event happened. She leaned over, a faint trace of a smile showing. "You were very fierce that day."

"The fucker had to come at me from behind the next time. Imagine if he hadn't? Forget Dick Crusher. It could've been a Dick Rip-Off Event."

She smothered her laughter into her sleeve.

Kristina glanced back. "What are you guys talking about?"

"I'll tell you later," Casey said.

Sarah and Laura were farther ahead, weaving through the crowds and leading us. We got to the bleachers, and it was then that it happened.

A small hush settled over the seats closest to us. I didn't look, but felt Kristina and Casey close ranks around me. I focused on the field. The team was already out there, warming up, and as I looked, Shay dropped back from a huddle. His arm went back, football in hand, and he threw. It was a perfect arch, soaring all the way into the end zone. A second ball was hiked to him, and he repeated.

I focused on him.

One of the girls took my hand in hers, and they led me past the rest of the bleachers. As we went, more and more conversations stopped until everyone started to notice. They looked to see what had everyone's attention, and the whispers rose in volume.

I overheard one girl ask, "Who's that?"

Her friend hissed back, “Shay Coleman’s girlfriend.”

“Oh! Dick Crusher?”

“Shhhh!” a third friend shushed them.

Casey started laughing. She squeezed my hand. “You should embrace the name. A guy started selling T-shirts.”

“I should get a cut.”

“Hey! Up here.”

Sarah and Laura had gone down an aisle. We went too far.

Casey said as we backtracked, “They’re hyped for the parties tonight.”

I was halfway to them since they were in the middle when the first person stood. She said to me, reaching out, “I’m sorry about what happened to you.”

I swung around, reacting to her hand. I wasn’t expecting it and jumped back. Then her words filtered through, and I felt another sucker punch, but a good one. This was an emotional one, and I grew misty-eyed.

She saw, and a sheen of tears formed in her eyes. She brushed at them. “My daughter was raped when she was fourteen. You weren’t raped, but you were attacked. What happened to you shouldn’t have. I just wanted to say I’m sorry, that I understand.”

Casey gasped silently.

The rumor mill had been silent about her assault, as far as I knew. The guys who knew hadn’t spread it around. Her hand curved into mine again. I squeezed it back, nodding to the woman. “Thank you for that.”

I came onto these bleachers with my head turned away and eyes only on Shay. When I wasn’t looking at him, my head was down. It was up now, and I was looking at this woman.

I didn’t know what I expected, but it wasn’t this.

Casey and Kristina were dabbing at their eyes when we got to the row where Laura and Sarah were sitting. Two guys were at the end, and there was an empty space between them. It’d be a tight fit for three of us, but the two guys stood.

They stepped into the aisle. "You can have our seats."

"No, that's oka—" Kristina started to say.

The guy cut her off, gently but firmly, "No. I was one of the guys mad about what you did to Carruthers."

I tensed, meeting his gaze.

I saw only remorse there. "Giving up my seat so you can sit comfortably is a small price to pay, believe me." He dipped his head in a nod. "I'm sorry for what happened to you."

Casey's eyes were wide, matching the storm inside me.

I hadn't expected any of this. "Thank you."

He and his friend moved farther up in the bleachers, and we sat down. It was just the small area where we were, but I saw a few others dabbing at their eyes. They had been watching the woman, and then the two guys.

The announcers started talking soon after.

The cheerleaders ran out and began cheering, and slowly, one by one, people began looking away.

I didn't move. I didn't talk. I sat like a statue until some normalcy returned around us, and I was just another student again.

I let out my breath, which felt like I'd been holding it forever.

"Uh, Kennedy." Casey pulled at her hand.

I had it in a cement-like hold, pressed on top of my leg. "Oh!" I released it. "Sorry." I hadn't realized.

Her hand was completely white. She laughed, rubbing at it to get the blood flowing again. "Trust me, I understand."

I glanced around, dipping my head low as I did. "That was nice of them."

"Could you imagine any other reception with Shay Coleman as your boyfriend? I mean, that helps."

"I know."

"There's Gage." She stood and waved for him.

He was coming down the front aisle, two containers of popcorn in hand and snacks sticking out of his pockets. His roommates followed behind, one of them holding two sodas. There was a space behind us, and the four of them scooted in. Gage was right behind me, and he leaned down. "How you doing?"

Oh, yeah. Evading that question. I pointed to his popcorn. "Is that for me?"

"What? No! Get your own."

Casey turned around, too, her eyes wide, her lips puckered in a pout. She was giving him the puppy-dog look, and he groaned, throwing his head back. "You two suck. Here." He gave us the smaller container of popcorn. Then he reached over to his roommate. "We gotta share. The girls sucker-punched me with guilt."

The roommate laughed, handing over one of the sodas. "That's fine with me. Give me one of the candies."

Gage growled again, but tossed him one of the bags. After he settled, his soda in one hand and his popcorn situated beside him, he leaned down once more. "For real, how are you?"

I waved him off. "I don't want to talk about it."

Casey did. "A woman was really nice and two guys gave us their seats. It was a good reception."

"Cool." He eyed me. "You're okay, though?"

I nodded. A big knot formed when we first came to the game, and some of it had loosened by the time we sat, but I was feeling emotions I didn't understand. I didn't want to dwell on them. I just wanted to watch the game.

Once it started, no one paid me attention.

It became all about Shay and the team. He threw three touchdowns, running a fourth in himself, and Linde helped smash his way through for that last one. My voice was hoarse by the time the game ended, and there was a bittersweet feeling that swept over the crowd. Some were drunk and cheering like mad, while others were clapping with a somber expression on their features. They stood at the end for the team. They were done. Their last game was complete.

There wasn't a huge celebratory feel to the atmosphere, but I knew there'd be lots of partying going on that night.

Gage asked, "What are you and Shay doing tonight?"

I shook my head. "We haven't talked about it."

"Mom went home this morning."

"Yeah."

"She took the van. I figured we could take your car back or my car tomorrow."

We began following Casey out. Kristina was behind me, and Sarah and Laura were already off talking to other people. I doubted they'd go back to the girls' dorm rooms with us, opting to go straight for a party instead.

I said to my brother, "Maybe we should all go out for breakfast tomorrow, too. One last hurrah before heading home for break."

Casey glanced back at me. "Were you able to finish all your exams and finals?"

"Yeah. I took a little hit on one presentation, but it wasn't much."

"You're feeling okay? Being around everyone?"

The truth was, there was a cold trickle of sweat going down my back, but that was it. Gage was walking behind me, Casey and Kristina on either side of me, and I knew it was all purposeful. They were shielding me.

*They* came up from behind before.

Someone could slip through. I'd never see them coming, but I could walk forward and still breathe at the same time in this formation. I looked back, my eyes meeting my brother's. A knowing look passed between us, and I answered Kristina, "I'm better than I expected."

He dipped his chin down to me.

I mouthed "thank you" to him.

"Kennedy?"

All of us paused. I froze, but felt relief flood me when it was only Missy. Holly and the cousin were with her, along with another girl.

"Hey!" Missy wore a warm smile as she came toward us. "I didn't know you were coming to the game."

My things had been packed away in the minivan already. They'd be brought back in a month when I'd move into a triple room with Casey and Kristina. The room change had been approved, but I thought she had left this past week.

"You, too. I thought you went home yesterday."

"Oh." She shook her head, gesturing to Holly. "We're sticking around for the weekend, going back on Sunday." She saw Gage and paused, frowning. Her eyebrows pinched together. "You're . . ."

"Oh!" My one secret that remained a secret. "This is my brother."

Holly noted, her eyes wide in awe, "You're Gage Clarke."

Gage nodded, his arm coming around my shoulders. "I am. I'm famous. I'm Kennedy's brother."

"You were in my stats class."

Gage nodded like he already knew this. I knew he didn't. He said, "Hopc you did better than I did. Mr. Trellyps was not a fan of mine."

"Yeah . . ."

This was why I kept it a secret all semester, or tried. This look of shock, awe, and something else darker in Holly's gaze.

Missy said, "Your brother is Gage Clarke, and I'm kicking myself now for not putting the two together."

Holly's cheeks reddened, and she glanced away.

Missy added, "And you're dating Shay Coleman." She shook her head, her eyes narrowing at me. "You're like a stranger. I thought I knew who you were."

Kristina shifted closer to me, but it was Casey who spoke up. "Ever thought maybe she did that for a reason?" She gestured to Holly. "Both of your reactions proved why she doesn't. You're already looking at her differently. When I stopped up there once, I got the distinct impression you couldn't believe she was friends with me. Imagine how you would've been when you realized Shay Coleman was in your room."

The closet!

I forgot, and started laughing.

When they looked at me, I waved a hand in front of my face. "Nothing. Sorry. Uh, yeah. I'm private for good reason."

Missy shot back at Casey, "You obviously knew. Is that why you're friends with her?"

A death look came over Casey's face. "I became friends with her when she supported me through my rape."

Holly's head snapped back up.

Missy's face drained of color. "O-o-h. I'm sorry. I didn't know."

"Exactly."

Casey turned her back on them, her nostrils flaring.

Feeling a twinge of sympathy, I nodded to Missy, indicating we should step to the side to talk. She hesitated, but in the end, she came with me. I felt the others watching, but to some extent, this was none of their business.

She stuffed her hands into her jacket, kicking at a rock on the ground. "This is it, huh?"

"I don't want you to think I kept things from you on purpose. It was never personal."

Her foot paused, but she didn't look.

"You were attacked, and you didn't reach out to me." She lifted her head, her bottom lip trembling. "How's that not personal?"

"You treated me like I was beneath you."

"When?"

"In looks. In things you said. You were surprised I had *a* friend when Kristina came up to the room, and you fell over when Casey did. You can't tell me you would've looked at me differently if Gage came knocking on the door, or if you knew about the one time Shay was in the room."

She went still. "He really was in our room?"

"Our closet. I made him hide, but he refused the second time you came to the room."

She cocked her head to the side, her forehead wrinkling then clearing as her eyes rounded. "That night I thought you were masturbating? I was so grossed out by you."

"Yeah." I itched behind my ear.

She expelled a breath of air, shifting back on her feet. Her shoulders relaxed. "Do you know what it was like when I heard about your attack? Then I heard what Shay Coleman did because of you? And that you were dating? I almost fell to the ground. I thought it was a lie, but the front desk girl said it wasn't."

"Sabrina." I nodded. "She knows Shay. She knew we knew each other."

"I just don't get why you didn't tell me."

I shook my head. "I have reasons."

Missy brushed some of her coarse black hair back, readjusting the hood on her coat. I had to think about how I would react if I found out she knew another football player, or maybe the other team captain. I wouldn't have. No, that wasn't true. I would've felt a little relief because if I saw her in the house, I could say hello or we could talk freely about things. I wouldn't have felt hurt. Then again, I was only coming from my point of view.

I tried to imagine from hers.

She knew Holly and Holly's cousin. Holly knew guys. She was the one in the group who had a different crush every week. I couldn't remember hearing Missy talking about guys or anyone else. It was always Holly or the cousin.

Those were the only two people I saw her with. Ever.

She looked at me. I felt compelled to apologize, but I didn't. I'd been hurt by her in the beginning, and I didn't keep quiet to hurt her personally.

"Oh, hey." She tugged at her coat's collar. "Some girl stopped by the room and asked about you."

"What? Who?"

She shook her head. "I've never seen her in my life. I don't know. She didn't leave a name or number, or anything. I just thought I should mention it."

A girl? Someone she didn't know, too. Maybe it'd been Aby or Becca looking for me before they knew to find me at Shay's house?

Maybe.

"What'd she look like?"

Another shrug from Missy. "Blonde hair. That's all I remember."

Becca had blonde hair.

Then I was distracted when Missy asked, "I suppose you're going to some big parties tonight?"

I shrugged. "I haven't talked about it." I caught sight of Sarah and Laura. They were heading out in a different group of people. "They are, but I don't know what we're doing."

"You and Shay . . ."

"Yeah . . ." I trailed off, too. This was becoming awkward. I cleared my throat. "Thank you for being nice to my mom and helping with my stuff."

A smile cracked her rigid exterior. "Your mom is funny. She dressed up as a college student when she came to get your things. I think she missed a few decades. She had a Trapper Keeper with her."

I groaned. "Of course, she would."

I didn't know what else to say after that. Missy must not have either because we both fell silent. She went back to kicking that rock around.

"I guess I'll see you next semester?"

I nodded. "Looks like it."

"I'll see you then."

She lifted a hand in a small wave, returning to her group, and it felt like a chapter closing. Kristina came over, rested an arm around my shoulders, and sighed. "How'd that go?"

"Was I wrong in not telling her about Gage and Shay?"

"No one should ever make you feel guilty for not opening up about yourself. You'll *want* to open up to the right ones."

That was true. "Thank you. I needed to hear that."

"Come on." She patted my arm. "Your man's probably waiting by now."

I sagged closer to her. I liked hearing those words.

My man.

# CHAPTER THIRTY-ONE

Shay parked on the street outside his house. Every light on the main floor was on, as well as the lights in the basement, a few more on the second floor, and one from thc third floor.

Shay grunted. "I do believe we're having a party." He looked at me. "What do you want to do?"

"What do you mean?"

"We can go somewhere else."

I frowned.

Kristina and Casey asked about our evening plans, but I hadn't known what we were doing. I knew now. Reaching over, I laced our fingers together, resting our hands on his leg. "I think I should call Kristina and Casey, and we should all go to the party."

Surprise flitted over his features. "You sure? We can just hang out in the room, if you want?"

I shook my head. "No way. You were the MVP. That party is for you. I'm not going to be the girlfriend who pulls you away."

"You sure?" He was grinning.

"Yes. I'll be with my friends, and what are you smiling about?"

"Nothing." He leaned over, his lips finding mine for a quick second. "It's just nice to hear you call yourself my girlfriend."

I knew what he meant, and I felt like I was glowing as we headed inside the house. We were hand in hand, but instead of going through the back door, I led Shay to the front. It was his moment. After that first step inside, I knew I was right. The place was filled with people. His teammates, girls, and other friends all cheered for Shay. He was grabbed up by the guys, being literally pulled away. He flashed an apologetic smile my way, but I waved it off.

I was pulling my phone out when Linde appeared next to me. He handed me a cup. "Here."

"What is it?" But I took it, sniffing it. The alcohol was strong enough to kill a fly in the general proximity. "Holy shit, Linde. That's strong."

He laughed. "Last party before we all head home tomorrow. I figured what the hell, right?" He draped his arm around my shoulders, nodding to where Shay had been taken. A group formed at the bar, and he was being challenged in a shot-drinking contest. "Thinking it's going to be a rough morning for both of you tomorrow."

"Here." I wasn't listening. I gave him the cup back. "I need to text my friends."

Thirty minutes later, Kristina and Casey both walked in. Their eyes were huge. The music had gotten louder, and I had to shout into Kristina's ear. "Thanks for coming!" I nodded in Casey's direction. She was glancing around the room. The edges of her mouth turned white. I asked Kristina, "Is this going to be okay for her?"

Kristina put her mouth next to my ear. "We talked about it before coming, but she's okay. She isn't going to drink, and she'll stay with you or me the whole time, but she trusts these guys. That asshole wasn't partying with other football players when it happened. He was at a fraternity."

"Okay." I reached over to tap Casey on the arm. She moved closer, leaning forward to better hear me. I asked her anyway, "Are you okay being here?"

She nodded, giving me two thumbs up. She yelled back, "I won't drink, and I'll leave if I get uncomfortable."

"Me, too!" Kristina joined in, then we heard a nearby shriek and someone launched themselves at us. Two skinny arms wrapped around us, followed by another pair of equally thin arms. Sarah and Laura bounced up and down, both beaming and both looking flushed in the faces. "You guys are here! We weren't sure. We're all partying together."

They were so excited, but the shared look between Kristina and Casey told me they weren't. Both were cautious and wary.

"Yeah." Casey untangled their arms. "Should be fun."

"Shots, shots, shots!" Laura began clapping, turning, and looking around. Then, "Kreigerson! Get over here. Look who's here!" She looped an elbow through Casey's.

A guy ventured over, holding a drink in each hand. His dark hair was slicked back, and he had a baby face with round cheeks, smooth complexion, and dark eyes to match his hair. He was good-looking, and I saw the lurking arrogance. He knew it, too. "Hey! Winchem! It's been forever." He handed her one of the drinks. "Fuck yeah."

She shook her head. "No, thank you."

"Ah. Come on."

"No. Really. No, thank you."

Sarah was the closest to me, and she'd stopped jumping up and down. The flushed coloring was fading, and she was no longer smiling. She leaned to me. "It was his party where it happened." She shook her head. "What is Laura thinking?"

But she didn't wait for my response. She waded in and took the drink that he was offering Casey. Firmly situating herself between the two, she held it up to his face. "Are you kidding me? You know what happened to her, and it was a drink *you* gave her."

"Hey—" His persuasive smile fell away, and he drew back to his fullest height. "If you're saying I drugged her—"

"No, but he gave you the cup and you gave it to her. It could've been Laura or me. It could've been any girl and you're giving her another one?"

"I said—" he started to bark back.

She flung the liquid in his face.

"HEY!" he roared, swiping the alcohol out of his eyes. "What the fuck, Sarah?"

She crossed her arms over her chest and lowered her chin in place. She wasn't moving. "Get out of here, Kreigerson. We're done partying with you."

"I—" His hand was in the air. I didn't know what he was going to do, but I was back there.

It was dark out.

Night.

The library closed.

I was on that sidewalk.

"Hey!" a new voice rushed in, and there was movement. I was grabbed and pulled away, but I didn't know what was going on. I was on that sidewalk again. Those two shadows were looming over me, growing larger and larger.

They were raising the bat.

I screamed and tried to cover my face.

"Hey, hey, hey."

I was caught and held against a chest. I was frozen, the impending attack was coming, but I recognized Shay in the back of my mind. I was safe. I wasn't. I was in his arms. No, I was going to get hit. I was going to fall to the ground, and I was shuddering.

"It's okay, Kenz. It's okay."

My head was being cradled against a chest, a strong chest that I knew intimately. I looked up and saw Shay's loving eyes. The flashback left, but I was drained. I sucked in some breath and pressed my forehead to him again. "I was back there."

"You're safe. I'm here." He twisted around and shouted, "Get him the fuck out of here! NOW!"

"Hey, man. I didn't know—"

A growl cut him off, and I recognized Linde's voice. "You know now, and it's time you left."

"No." I looked up, but Shay was holding me against the wall. His back was protecting me, shielding me, and I tried to step out of his arms.

"No." He tightened them. "What are you doing?"

I shook free from his hold. "I'm fine."

I walked forward.

Linde and another guy had Kreigerson's arms twisted and behind him. They were beginning to walk him out when I hurried forward. "No."

Linde looked over, his eyebrows pulling together. "What are you doing, Clar—"

I balled up my fist and swung.

It wasn't this insensitive asshole I was lashing out at. It was Carruthers. It was the other guy. It was Casey's rapist. It was all of the assholes who thought they could attack a girl and get away with it, but this was really about me.

My fist hit him across the face, and the pain blasted me. I didn't think I could smile any wider.

"What the fuck?" His head jerked to the side and then he looked back at me.

I said to him, "You helped hurt her."

Casey stood right there, and her eyes filled with tears. She clasped her hands together and looked down to the floor.

"You helped hurt me."

"What? No, I didn't. I didn't even—"

"If you hurt one and don't change from it, you'll hurt another." I flexed my hand out. I wasn't making sense, but I didn't care. He'd understand when he had a daughter one day. I turned my back on him, giving Linde the nod to kick him out.

*Then* the pain started.

I whimpered, "Ice bag, please. Or morphine. Whichever is closest."

Shay already had an ice bag in his hand. "Here. Let's go upstairs."

I put the ice on my knuckles as I looked over my shoulder. Kristina, Casey, and both the other girls all had dazed looks on their faces.

I said, "I'll be back in a bit."

"Yeah." Kristina blinked a few times. "Take your time."

We went through the kitchen, through the door, and up the stairs to Shay's bedroom. It was half mine now. I had a nice pile of clothes in the corner and grabbed one of my T-shirts to wrap around the ice bag.

I sank down on his bed and fell back, groaning softly. "Why did I do that?"

Shay went to his closet and pulled his shirt off.

My mouth watered at the sight. He was beautiful, and my eyes dipped down to that V. It dipped under his pants. And suddenly, I wasn't feeling my hand pain at all. He crossed to sit next to me, the bed dipping under his weight. He lifted the ice bag to inspect my hand and grimaced. "How bad does it hurt?"

"Less and less." I was focused on his lips, licking my own.

He looked up and laughed softly. "Oh, yeah?"

"Yeah." He smoothed some hair back from my forehead and I closed my eyes, savoring the small touch. I reached up, sliding my fingers through his own. "You know, you had a pretty great game today."

"You're the one with the hurt hand."

"Which was my choice. I knew it'd hurt when I hit him." A different thought came to me. "You think I could get in trouble for that?"

"I highly doubt anyone would corroborate his side." His gaze dropped to my lips and stayed. He murmured, huskily, "He can try to bring a case against a girl who was recently attacked on campus, especially with his participation in your friend's rape."

That reassured me. I grinned. "Oh, yeah. I forgot about that."

He stood, ducking into the bathroom. I heard him rummaging through the cabinets and he came back. He handed me a pill before grabbing a water bottle from his desk. He opened it, handing that over, too. "That's a painkiller. You should take it now or your hand is going to be killing you later."

I swallowed it and then handed him the bottle, which he set on the dresser for me.

Instead of coming back to join me on the bed, he stood and looked at me. The hunger was full force in his eyes. It was growing the more he gazed at me. I felt an answering ache forming between my legs. Biting down on my lip, I said, "We seem to have a situation here."

"Yeah?"

"Yeah."

His head cocked to the side, watching me, and that hunger was positively emanating from him, but he didn't move to me. He stayed there, even crossing his arms over his chest. I let out a small groan. Good God, he looked good.

I felt like I should point out, "You have an entire party going on down there, and they're mainly here for you."

"But?"

"But we're up here, and I'm starting not to want to return to the party."

He moved closer. "How's that hand of yours?"

"Getting better." I tipped my head back, gazing up at him as he loomed over me. I almost groaned. "Getting better and better."

His hand touched the bed beside me, a knowing smirk in his eyes. "Yeah?"

I started to repeat what I said earlier, but his hand slid under my leg and I stopped on a gasp. The feel of him sent shivers through me, blasting my insides, and I bit down on my lip, groaning. His fingers tightened their hold, and his other hand slid under me. He moved me farther up in the bed, following behind and kneeling over me.

I let out a soft sigh. Hunger licked my insides, fanning the flame that only leapt for him. Running a hand down his chest, my fingers felt and lingered over every dip between his muscles. He really was so gorgeous.

It wasn't that I forgot.

It was that he became better looking to me every day. It was startling some days, and when others reacted to him, I remembered it wasn't just me. But he was mine, and I started grinning, thinking about how that came about.

"What are you laughing at?" His lips were almost on mine.

I curled a hand around his neck, falling down to the pillow and pulling him with me. His body came down, half-resting on me, and his lips instead moved to my shoulder. He grazed a kiss there, his hand sliding under my shirt and pushing it up as he sought out my breast. I almost groaned again when he cupped one of them, moving the bra out of his way, and his thumb began to rub over my nipple.

"I'm laughing at how much I hated you in the beginning."

He sat up, his mouth moving over my shoulder to my neck. He trailed kisses down to my throat.

I raked my fingers through his hair, half-holding him there, and half-wanting to pull him up to my lips. I waited, my breaths becoming increasingly shallower and shallower.

"I don't even know why I hated you."

He stopped, lifting his head. He was so close, a whisper away, and I wanted to touch my lips to his so badly it was almost a physical pain. I still didn't. I still held off.

"I think you hated me because—"

He cut himself off, and my eyes almost bulged out. I caught the sides of his face in my hands. "You can't stop there. Finish what you were going to say."

He shook his head, raising himself up again so he was almost towering over me. "It's nothing." He bent and his lips caught mine.

Oh—hmmm!

"No. I want to know."

He didn't answer, just opening his mouth and his kisses grew more demanding. His tongue slid inside, and as he began to take over, I was barely conscious of him pulling my shirt up until he paused. I moved back so he could pull it the rest of the way and over my head, then he was back. His lips fused with mine, and he worked at my bra. He slowed down, letting the bra straps slide down my arms and acting as a caress.

It worked.

Sensations trailed behind them until he tossed it to the floor, as well. His mouth moved from my lips—licking, tasting, nipping down my throat and between my breasts until he caught one of them in his mouth.

A deep groan ripped from me.

I was holding on to every touch and taste from him. His tongue swirled around my nipple.

I almost lost it, wanting to grab his hair again.

"Hmmm, no." He sensed my thoughts and caught my hands. He pinned them down by my head, kissing and lavishing over my breast. "You don't get to distract me."

I laughed, the sound weak even to my ears. "You're killing me."

"Goddamn, not enough." A low growl emitted from him, and I felt his teeth scrape over my nipple.

My back surged up, arching and pressing against him. He chuckled, but moved back down with me when I rested on the bed again. "Shay." A half-growl from me. I began moving against him, locking my legs around his waist. We both had our jeans on, but I was wondering why. I ground against him, trying to evoke a response where he'd put us both out of our misery.

He laughed, his breath coating my breast. "You can keep it up, Princess. I'm still going to worship you."

Princess.

I groaned. I wasn't one for cute nicknames, but that one worked, and my ache just took on a whole other level.

I was growing more and more desperate. I could feel him. He was rock-hard and pressing against me. Lower his jeans, move aside his boxer briefs, pull my jeans and underwear down, and I could get him to sink into me. He was straining there, pressing right where I wanted him, but it was as if he wasn't aware of his own needs. He moved to my other breast, catching it in his mouth, and his tongue and teeth assaulted me all over again.

"Shay." I groaned, arching my neck up. A whimper left me.

A guttural scream was building in my throat. I felt it coming. It was going to tear free, and everyone downstairs would know what we were doing.

"Shay!"

He laughed, finally releasing my hand as his fingers stroked over my stomach. I trembled there, right under his palm, and he moved, so agonizingly slow, slipping one finger under my jeans. Then the other. A third finger. He moved them back and forth, tracing circles. It was torture, pure and simple.

"If you don't do something with those fingers, I'm going to—" I was panting, lifting my head to look him in the eye.

He was smirking. He was so damned cocky, but I saw a wildness in there, too. It was laying on the outside edges, as if he was holding that back. I couldn't endure this much longer. The need to touch him back was growing in me, threatening to overcome any control I might've still had.

I slipped my hands from his, pushing up against him.

We rolled, and I was on top this time. I straddled him, gazing down at his perfect features. My legs were snug against his, but I sank farther down, feeling him rising up into me. He wanted inside me as much as I did, and my fingers went to his jeans. I toyed with the button and zipper.

His ice-blue eyes were nearly black as he watched me. "You're going to play with me now?"

"Maybe." I bit down on my lip to keep my own cocky smile from showing. I got it. I did. The control, the power . . . they were addicting. I could ride him how I wanted. I could play with him how I wanted. I could exact my own torture, and I started by undoing his jeans and reaching inside for him. My hand wrapped around him, and I tightened my hold just a bit, enough to give him a slight vise-like hold, then slowly, I began to move up and down.

His nostrils flared. He let out a hissing breath. It was the control again. He was losing his as I gained mine.

"Fucking hell, Kenned—"

I dipped down, my lips catching his in a kiss.

This kiss was different. He opened up beneath me, but he was taking over the kiss. Another whimper left me, and I was helpless from pulling away from him. As I continued moving my hand over him, going slow, his kiss grew rougher. I paused, dipped my thumb over his tip, and he caught me under the arms. A savage growl erupted from him, lifting me in the air.

He flipped me over, coming down, and he didn't pause.

My jeans were ripped away. His were flung off, and he was in me.

I had a second's notice, and he was in there. I gasped from the force, but I was trembling. I was shaking. I was needing more. He didn't wait for me to get used to him. He began thrusting. He went hard and deep and rough, and I was coming apart in his arms.

I clung to him. Our mouths never separated, not once as we breathed for each other. I raked my nails down his side as he kept plunging inside of me.

Over and over.

He didn't slow down.

I stretched, my hips working as hard as his, and he caught my breast in one of his hands. He used the other like an anchor on my hip, and his fingers sank down over my skin, he began to quicken his pace.

God.

He was fucking me.

Ripping his mouth from me, he caught my breast in it instead, sucking there. He was bent over, still diving in and out of me.

I gasped for breath, my chest and lungs heaving as he was pounding into me. Then he pulled out, and he began to turn me over. No. I sat up and pushed him over. It was my turn. He fell to his back, and I was over him.

"Wait." His hands flexed into my hips. He caught me, holding me in place. He nodded to the nightstand. "Condom."

I groaned from frustration, but reached, my body resting over him as I grabbed one from the drawer. He nipped my shoulder and ran his hand down my side, cupping my ass, then moving around to push up into my vagina. I hissed, air leaving me from the force, and I glared once at him. "Not fair."

He was grinning wickedly. "I don't care."

A second finger went in me, thrusting in and out. I was struggling to focus from the sensations. He wasn't waiting for me to sink down on him. He was intoxicating me, demanding a release, but I held off. I was biting down so hard on my lip, trying to hold it back, because dammit, I wanted him to explode with me.

"Shay."

I was becoming blind with pleasure, but as his fingers were still plunging into me, I reached down and grasped him again. He stopped, an answering groan coming from him, and I took advantage. I ripped the wrapper, rolled the condom over him, then rose up, moved over him, pulled his fingers out, and was on him. I sank down and we both paused for a second, just a second.

He grabbed for my waist, and I braced one hand on his chest. I began moving my hips.

I rode him this time.

I went slow at first, gradually quickening my pace. He sat up so he could catch my nipple as I leaned back. He wrapped an arm around my back, holding me upright, as I was going up and down over him. We went together. He caught my waist, moving into me with an unrelenting force before he couldn't hold out any longer.

I felt his release, his entire body convulsing.

His fingers went to my nub, and I exploded at the first touch.

My body was quivering. He held me gently in his arms as we both rode out the tremors.

"Babe," he whispered, kissing me and then my shoulder. He lifted me, pulling out.

"Wha—"

He rolled me over to my back and then slid right back in. My legs wound around him again, and he grunted, "I wanted you to come first." He tucked his head into the crook of my neck and shoulders until he exploded once again. He had started to release before, but stopped himself. He held off like I had for him earlier.

He lay on top of me, both of us sweaty, and grazed a hand down my naked body. "Holy fuck." He pressed a kiss to my throat before pushing up to meet my mouth with his. "I'll never get used to that. Ever."

I shivered, feeling it all the way through my body, and I agreed. Each time we were together, each mind-blowing orgasm, pushed me deeper into my addiction to him.

The thought terrified me.

# CHAPTER THIRTY-TWO

He was curled around me, his breathing deep and even on the back of my neck.

We could hear the music downstairs and the sounds of people. They were walking around. The doors were opening and shutting. There were voices outside, then more voices inside. Car doors were shutting. More people arrived. Others were leaving. It was a free-for-all below.

And I didn't want to move one bit.

Shay and I were in a protective bubble. He turned his lights off, flipping the switch on a lighted Mason jar so it lit up the room in a soft glow. I had trouble sleeping a few nights after the attack, so he bought it to help soothe me at night.

We were huddled under the blankets, his hand inching closer and closer to my breast.

I was waiting for when he'd start playing with it, but a new light shone up from the floor. I heard the accompanying buzzing and groaned.

"Is that yours or mine?"

"Mine." I recognized the colors the screen was lighting up the ceiling. Red and green. "It's Gage."

I felt Shay's lips brush my back. "Thirty bucks he's downstairs."

"Nope. I'm not betting you." I scooted to the edge of the bed and snagged my phone from the floor. I was stretched at an angle so my hips hadn't moved away from him, just the rest of me, and I felt his hands falling from under my breast to my hips. He held them, and as I keyed in my code and read my brother's text message, Shay started to grind behind me. I looked over my shoulder. "Are you kidding? Again?"

He shrugged, that wicked grin appearing. He shoved up against my ass, and leaned down to nip at my arm. "Why not? I'm a young stud, Clarke. Thought you knew this by now."

He brushed against me a few more times, and I was feeling that ache begin all over again.

I shook my head and returned to my phone.

Gage: **Casey texted. Said she was at your party, but you're not here. Come down here. I'm not going up there.**

I showed Shay the phone, rolling onto my back as I did, and he moved over me once again. He took the phone, reaching for me absent-mindedly, and as he read it, he was right at my entrance.

He replied something before turning it off and tossing the phone back to the floor.

"What'd you say?"

He was hard again, and I ran a hand down his chest as he reached for another condom. He put it on, kissing my stomach as he murmured, "We'd be down in an hour."

He lined up again, and looking up to meet my gaze, he slid back inside.

I groaned, closing my eyes. My hands fell to his, and our fingers laced as he began rolling his hips into me.

This wasn't like last time. It was hot and rough before. This time was easy-going, like sex was something we could do any day we wanted and any time we wanted, and today was just one of those days. It wasn't a habit, but an activity we could enjoy because neither of us was going anywhere. We were becoming that couple, and I tasted that same fear I had before. Maybe that was how it was for me, as I watched him under lidded eyes, as he was thrusting in and out of me. It gave me a dark thrill. This was my man, and he was bowing under my touch. He was mine for the taking, and I knew he felt the same for me.

A ripple of power sliced through me.

It was exhilarating.

All those girls downstairs, or most of them, would've traded places with me. He was mine. This was my place in his bed. Hell, it was half my bed by now.

He looked back up, his eyes dark and hungry. "Are you with me?" he rasped out.

I nodded. I was moving with him, but I sat up again, and he readjusted. My legs went over his and I was riding him, my breasts brushing up and down against his chest. He reached up, caught one in his hand, the other flexing into my hip, and his lips were on mine again. We rode each other until we both climaxed together.

"Fuck," he grunted into my ear, holding me clasped to him. He pressed a kiss to my naked shoulder, then stood, still holding me.

I squeaked, but he carried me to the bathroom and stepped into the shower after waiting for the water to warm. Once both of us were wet, he let me slide down him so I was on my own feet, but we still pressed against each other. We cleaned the other, our hands sliding over the other's body, and more stolen kisses. He leaned over me, shielding me completely from the shower spray for a moment, and his eyes found mine. "Am I ever going to get used to this?" He was asking himself, his eyes roaming all over me, and he didn't wait for an answer. He caught my lips in his again before standing away. He gave me a half-grin. "If I keep touching you, we're never getting downstairs."

I finished rinsing off, ducking around him and out of the shower. I reached for a towel, then handed him one as he was right behind me.

I said, "They're going to know what we did up here."

He ran his towel through his hair a few times before looping it and tossing it around me. He held both ends in his hands and reined me in, his lips finding mine again before he said, "Good. Because if they don't know by now, you're mine."

Those words stayed with me. I must've been glowing. I was feeling it. There wasn't a part of my body Shay hadn't worshipped. I was sated, all of me. When we headed down, I trailed behind him. I liked to let him lead the way into the party. I kept my hand tucked in the back of his jeans until he opened that door. The music was suddenly louder. The people were everywhere, huddled in every corner of the room, most holding their drinks in hand. Two guys let out another cheer when Shay entered the room, and he was torn from me. He glanced back to make sure I was okay as one guy threw his arm around his shoulders.

I nodded, evading another guy as he was dead set on heading right to Shay's side. I stepped back, and he passed right in front of me. I gave Shay a reassuring smile, trying to let him know I'd be fine, then I headed through the house in search of my friends.

They were standing in the corner by the kitchen. A card game was being played on the kitchen table and they seemed to be watching. Gage had his arm wrapped around Casey. He was whispering something into her ear, making her laugh. Kristina was watching next to them and listening to Sarah. I glanced around for Laura, but couldn't—nope. She was in the kitchen, a guy's arm around her, making her laugh, too. I started for them, but felt someone tap my arm.

Missy was there, and the other three girls behind her. They were looking around with wide eyes.

"Hey." I frowned slightly, moving closer so Missy could hear me. "What are you doing here?"

She flushed. "I hope it's okay we came. We heard about the party and told the guys in the front we knew you."

I stared at her. What was she talking about? "Guys in the front?"

She pointed over her shoulder. "Yeah. There are guys out front. They're not letting everyone inside. You haven't seen the front yard?"

I shook my head.

"It's full of people waiting to get in."

"Are you serious?"

She nodded.

Holly edged in closer to join the conversation. She half-yelled, half-spoke over the music, "Can we be here?"

"Yeah. Yeah!" I waved my hand inside, even though they were already in the house. I leaned closer to Missy and said to her, tucking some of my wet hair behind my ear, "It isn't even really my party. I didn't know it was happening till we got here."

Missy's smile had been strained, but a few of those lines disappeared. Her grin became easier and she grasped my arm, yelling into my ear, "I know it's probably the beer I've had, but I wanted to tell you that I'm going to miss you next semester. I'm glad you were my roommate, if only for a semester."

I nodded, giving a smile.

I didn't want to start divulging my secrets with her because she was a little inebriated, and I had moved out. No matter how things seemed, the truth was that Missy treated me like I was beneath her since the beginning. Little comments added up, and a part of me wondered if she really did care or if some of this was because of whom I was dating.

I was tempted to ask, just to see her reaction, but someone put a hand on my shoulder, saying, "Excuse me."

Missy's and Holly's eyes grew in size.

It was Linde.

He wasn't looking our way, but trying to get past us into the kitchen.

I hit his arm, and he frowned, lifting his head to see who hit him. Recognition flooded his face when he saw me.

"Oh!" He wrapped an arm around me instead. "It's Clarke." He swung his head to Missy and frowned a little.

I gestured to her. "This was my roommate this past semester."

His arm came around her shoulder, too, holding his cup so it didn't spill. He laughed. "You must've enjoyed having a single room."

"Hey." I poked him in the chest.

He gave me a grin, his eyes twinkling. He was a little faded, but not that much. "You know what I mean. You've slept here every night for the last month and a half."

He was right. I ducked my head down, feeling a small bit of heat coming to my cheeks.

Missy's eyes were still so wide, as if she couldn't believe who was talking to her. Her gaze kept going from Linde's face to his hand on her shoulder and back to me, then him, and repeating the cycle.

Holly straightened, her chin rising, and she shuffled to close out our circle. She wanted to be a part of the conversation.

Linde gestured to her with his glass. "Who are you?"

"I'm a friend of Clarke's."

He frowned to me, and I explained, "She's high school best friends with her." I nodded toward Missy before pointing to the cousin and their fourth friend. Both were still on the outskirts of our little bubble. "This is her posse."

Linde tipped his head back, a hearty laugh coming out. He lifted his arm from around Missy and bobbed his head up and down. "I get it. My girl's got some hooks in her."

"Your girl?"

"You know what I mean." He shrugged, still grinning. "My friend, but Shay's girl." He leaned closer to me, standing so his back was toward the others. "Watch out how many hooks sink in you, okay? It's never good to get ripped apart."

He was telling me? He was football royalty.

I nodded, standing on my tiptoes as he lowered his head for me. "I learned from high school."

He nodded, more solemn, and held up a fist to me. I met it with mine, and he nodded toward the kitchen. "Going to refill my drink and head out back to hang with your boy." He noticed my empty hands. "You want a drink?" He pointed to the others. "Drinks? Anyone?"

Missy looked to me, questioning.

I nodded for her. "Yes. You need help carrying?"

He smirked at me. "Are you kidding? It's like you don't know me." He started to leave, waving to the girls as he did.

Missy stepped in closer, pointing to him.

I answered before she could say something, "He's bringing drinks."

"That's Raymond Linde." Holly took his place. Her cousin took her spot. Their fourth friend was still on the outskirts. "I can't believe Raymond Linde is getting me a drink right now."

That was my cue to escape. I began to edge away from them. "I see someone I have to talk to. I'll see you guys later on."

All of them nodded, even the fourth girl waved to me.

I felt bad for her. From what I'd seen so far, she was on the bottom of their hierarchy.

As for me, I was heading toward mine.

Kristina was doubled over in laughter. Sarah was giggling. Casey was shaking her head at something Gage said, and he was laughing right along with Kristina. His arm was still around Casey, but he was half-leaning around her to talk to Kristina.

"Clarke." I glanced over, seeing one of Gage's roommates lifting his beer up in a salute. I nodded back, closing the distance. I had to move around the kitchen table to come up behind my brother. Kristina saw me first, pointing in earnest. Casey and Gage looked, and then I was swept up in a big hug from my brother.

He lifted me off my feet. "My little sister!" He set me back down and pretended to scold me, "Took you long enough."

I pointed to where I'd just come from. "My old roommate stopped me."

Linde was starting back with the drinks, and I yelled over to him. He was on the other side of the table, but saw me. "Hey!"

"I'm here. They're still over there."

He nodded and tapped a guy on the shoulder who was seated at the table. He handed him a cup and pointed to me. The guy said something to someone across the table and the drink was passed over. I took it, thanking the guy, and raising it like a toast to Linde. "Thank you!"

He nodded, shouldering his way through the crowd and back to Missy and the girls.

I sipped my drink, watching. He handed the drinks to them, said a few more words, then turned to me and pointed to the back hallway. He mouthed, "Outside."

I nodded, giving him a thumbs-up sign.

"We're supposed to go outside?" Gage had been watching, too.

I shrugged. "Shay's out there."

"Well, let's go."

I led the way.

Some people said hello to me. I saw Becca and Aby from poli-sci in a corner, both looking dressed as if they should be in a nightclub. They turned, but I snuck behind a group of guys to hide from their eyesight. It hit me then—this was what I'd been putting off from the beginning. Becca and Aby would've been nice to me, just like my roommate and her friends were doing right now. Kristina always was, and the same for Casey. Even Sarah was the same. She rarely talked to me pre-attack, and it was like that now.

I didn't begrudge her. She wasn't being fake. I appreciated that.

Once we got outside, I asked Kristina, "Who was the guy Laura was talking to?"

Sarah overheard, answering with a snort, "A guy she met last weekend. He's an asshole to everyone *but* her." She shook her head, going off to follow Casey and Gage, who had taken the lead. Shay, Linde, and a bunch of others were sitting on the far side of the patio around a picnic table. They looked to just be talking.

Kristina shook her head at me. "There was a fight. Casey and Sarah think he's bad news, but Laura isn't listening. I don't have a good feeling about this."

Gage threw his hand out to the table. "Hey! What's up?"

Linde barked out a laugh. "It's Clarke's brother."

Gage drew up short, rolling his eyes. "Nice one, Linde."

Linde laughed, pounding the table. He looked less sober than when I saw him a minute earlier. "Sit down, Clarke's brother, who is awesome and the best guy to play darts against." He raised his drink, pointing to a different guy across the table. "You want a new darts guy? This is the guy. Clarke beat the shit out of the whole house the other night."

The guy looked over to assess my brother and held his hand out for Gage to shake. "Cameron—"

Gage shook the guy's hand, sitting beside Linde at the same time. "I know. Cameron Brewski. You're the quarterback for the team we stomped all over today."

"Hey." A low warning.

Gage laughed. "I'm just kidding. I had nothing to do with that beatdown."

The whole table started laughing.

Cameron had to take it. He only shook his head, pointing his finger at my brother.

"Gage Clarke. You like to play darts?"

The two began to talk.

Casey sat down next to my brother. Sarah beside her, and Kristina started to sit last.

The Cameron guy stopped her, holding his hand out over the table. "No, no, no. You girls can sit over here by us."

Kristina looked to me, her eyebrows raised in question.

Sarah raised her hand. "I'm saving you the time. She's got a serious boyfriend."

He laughed, sounding sincere. "Only gentlemanly intentions here. I promise." He dropped his voice an octave, indicating me, "How about you?"

A hush fell over the table.

Cameron's eyebrows pulled together as he glanced around.

I felt Shay watching me. I'd felt him since stepping outside, and I looked over, seeing his hooded gaze intent on me. I gestured to him. "I have a seat—"

Shay finished for me, "She's taken."

I crossed to him, and he scooted back for me. His hand came to my hip, and he helped guide me down. He'd been straddling the bench, turned toward the rest of the table, and I was smack in front of him. I leaned back against his chest.

"Well. Then." Cameron grew quiet, his gaze thoughtful. "I heard rumors, but didn't know that was confirmed."

I sipped my drink as Shay's arms encircled me, falling to my lap. He spoke from behind my ear, "I don't know what you're smoking. I know Sabrina told you about us."

The Cameron guy didn't respond, his eyes falling on me.

I grew uneasy, not knowing why.

Shay was tense, and then Linde said something and Cameron's gaze was pulled from us. It felt like a weight had lifted, and I could breathe easier.

I looked back to Shay over my shoulder, making sure no one else could hear me as I asked, "Why'd that guy give me the creeps?"

He shook his head, bending down and placing his lips to my ear. "I'll explain later."

We hung out there the entire night, laughing and drinking with friends. Everyone started to leave around five in the morning, and we both collapsed in bed. By that time, the guy was pushed so far down in my mind, that I barely registered anything Shay was saying.

I just wanted his mouth and his body.

And giving up trying to tell me whatever he was supposed to, Shay kissed me back and moved over me in bed.

No one and nothing else mattered.

I was right where I wanted to be.

# CHAPTER THIRTY-THREE

The holiday break was agonizingly slow and way too fast at the same time.

Gage drove my car the next day for home, and we left after a late breakfast with Kristina, Casey, Sarah, Shay, and Linde. I asked where Laura was, but Sarah just pressed her lips together and slumped down in a chair on the other side of Casey.

Kristina winced. "That's a sore subject right now."

I never did find out what happened, but I got an earful about Cameron Brewski. It was mentioned the night before that he was the opposing team's quarterback, and I learned that he had also been Shay's rival for a long time. They'd gone to the same high school, went to different colleges, and dated the same girl.

"Same girl?"

Linde added that last bit, watching Shay with a teasing glint in his eyes.

Shay swore under his breath. "You're such an asshole."

Linde laughed. "I have no problem spilling the beans."

"I'm aware." Shay rolled his eyes, tapping his fingers over the table before making a decision. He turned to me. "Sabrina."

"Huh?"

"Sabrina?" Casey frowned. "That front desk girl?"

Shay said to me, "I dated her."

"What?" My mouth dropped. I specifically asked her, too. "She said you were friends. That was it. Why is this the first time I'm hearing you dated?"

His grin morphed into a smirk. "Because we usually don't talk when we're alone."

"Ah!" Gage dropped his toast back onto his plate. He stood, threw his hands in the air, and backed away from the table. "I do not want to hear about my sister's sex life." He picked the piece of bread up again and motioned to a different booth. "I know some of those people and I'm going to finish my breakfast *there*."

Shay raked a hand through his hair before letting it fall to grasp the back of my chair. "I thought I told you that."

"You didn't say shit to me."

And thinking about it, he rarely did. He knew my stuff: my problems, my trauma, my family, my friends. I started to scowl. What did I know about him? Besides the obvious, that he was damn good in bed and—I felt flutters in my stomach—there was a whole lot of good I knew about him.

The smirk lessened, going back to a grin. "To be honest, there isn't much to say. I dated her last year for a few months. We broke up and she came back to school this year dating Brewski."

Linde laughed. "I love that his last name is Brewski. I feel like I'm ordering a beer every time I hear it."

I ignored our pal. "If it was nothing, you could've mentioned it."

"Like you, I'm private. You didn't go around proclaiming our relationship. I tend to do the same thing about girls I date, even girls I used to date. There's nothing there, not really. We're just friends, and we hardly talk anyway."

"Then why didn't you mention it to me?"

He reached for my coffee, lifting it to take a sip. He said, right before, "Because there's nothing to say. And we had our own drama to handle. Sabrina was and is a non-factor to us."

"You're breaking Brewski's heart, and you know it."

Shay cursed, throwing a glare in Linde's direction. "You're not helping."

"Every guy knows that eventually there's an ex-conversation. You tell each other about the exes, especially ones the girl you're dating might know." Linde pointed to me. "She told you about hers."

I gritted my teeth.

Shay's grin became triumphant. "Actually, she hasn't really." He was watching me, saying to him, "She's just mentioned him."

Gage chose that time to return, taking his seat. "What'd I miss?"

Casey said, "Your sister's ex."

"Fucking hell." Gage shoved his chair out again. He grabbed his entire plate this time. "Just let me know when it's time to go home." He backtracked and took the coffee carafe with him.

That conversation was one of the reasons holiday break took forever.

Shay didn't say much on the topic, and every time we talked on the phone, he evaded the conversation as a whole. I was beyond frustrated. I wanted to yell and throw a tantrum, but I couldn't because we were talking over a phone, I couldn't look him in the eyes (not really even though we were FaceTiming), and I couldn't straddle him and work some magic so he had to tell me.

We were having one of those conversations again and I was in my bedroom, lying on my bed. He hovered above me, but on my phone's screen. I asked, "Why won't you talk about Sabrina? You said she didn't matter, but you're acting like she did."

*Or does . . .*

His permanent grin faded. "It isn't her I don't want to talk about. I don't have feelings for Sabrina, honestly. It's *him* I don't enjoy talking about."

"How did you break up?"

"Me and Cameron?"

"Shay." A low warning from me.

He let out a long and surrendering sigh. "Sabrina and I broke up because of me, not her. I didn't want to say anything because I don't want you thinking the same thing."

A knot formed in my stomach. I hadn't had one of those in a while. I almost missed them.

I scowled. "What happened?"

"Another girl kissed me one night at a party, and that kinda spun into a whole story where I cheated on her."

"You're a cheater?" It was worse than I thought.

"No! No. That's the thing. I'm not. A girl kissed me. I didn't kiss her back, but the rumor spread to Sabrina before I could give her a heads-up, and well, I don't know. I might've let her think the worst of me."

I frowned. "Why?"

"Because I was over the relationship." He readjusted on his end, and I could tell he was lying down on his bed. He added, "I didn't cheat on her. I don't want you to think I'm a cheater, but I didn't push the girl away as quick as I should have." He raised his voice. "But I didn't kiss her back. That's important here."

I grew quiet. We got together in secret. I'd been the one not wanting to go further in any official capacity until my attack. Everything changed then, but now, a storm was picking up inside me, swirling around.

I hadn't considered the thought that he might lose interest in me.

He could get tired of me, like he had with her.

I gulped, feeling that knot move to my throat. "Hey, hey." He leaned closer, his voice dropping low to a soothing murmur. "That was me and her. That isn't *you* and *me*. Sabrina is beautiful inside and out, but she isn't a match for me. We didn't fit. That's all. Even she would tell you the same thing. I think we both used the kissing rumor to save face."

"So, she still has feelings for you?"

She'd been nice to me, and what if I saw her on campus next semester? That'd be awkward. Wouldn't it?

"No. She's in love with Cameron. She's told me before, and they're here, even. They're in town. I ran into them at the grocery store. She said she's meeting his parents and spending the holiday here. That says something. They're serious, not how she and I were. I was never serious with her before. I've never been serious about any girl before. Before yo—"

I was hanging on to his every word. He stopped and I abruptly rolled off the bed. "Oomph!"

"What happened?" I could hear him from my phone, which was on the floor beside me. "Kenz?"

I sat up, ran a hand through my hair, and reached for the phone. My door opened, and Gage popped his head inside. "You okay?"

I twisted around. "I'm fine. Just fell off the bed." I showed him my phone. "Talking to Shay."

Shay called out, "Hey, Gage."

Gage nodded back, frowning next. "I don't want to know why talking to your boyfriend would make you fall off the bed. Hey, man. See you in a few days."

"You, too."

Gage left, shutting the door behind him, but I could hear my mom asking if I was okay. I looked back to Shay, wishing again we lived three hours away from each other and not three states. "My mom is asking Gage if I'm okay. She isn't going to believe him, and"—her footsteps were in the hallway; I was narrating it—"and she's going to open that door to make sure I'm okay in three, two—" The footsteps stopped, and she opened my door.

"Honey?"

"I'm talking to Shay."

"Oh!" A smile spread over her face. She was dressed in a blue and white dress. A frilly apron rested over the dress, and her hair was pulled into a French twist. The only thing missing from her outfit was a vacuum and duster. "Hi, Shay. How are you?"

"I'm good, Ms. Clarke."

She said to me, "The cookies are ready to be rolled. You promised."

I sighed. I had.

I was an idiot.

"Yeah. Okay. I'll be down in a few minutes."

She lifted a hand and wiggled her fingers. "Talk to you later, Shay. It was so nice to see you again."

She left, and Shay had a perplexed look on his face. "What was your mom wearing?"

I winced. "She's convinced our society is returning to the fifties so she's practicing. She's dressed up like an old housewife. I promised to help her make cookies." I cursed under my breath, standing up. "Can we reschedule this move-in thing a couple days earlier? Can I see you in two days instead of four?"

He couldn't answer. I could only see him shaking his head and his shaking shoulders. When he looked back up, I heard his laughter. "I'm sorry." He tried to calm down. He couldn't. A new batch of laughter spilled out. "My mom's a lawyer with political aspirations. It should be interesting when they meet."

His mom . . .

I let those words soak in. He was talking about them meeting. That was a good sign, a really good sign. I tried to calm my irrational happiness by laughing with him. "Yeah, well, you don't live with her. She was a soccer mom last week when she had to take our neighbor's kids to their soccer game. Everyone was very confused, especially the referee. She came as him for the second game."

He was still laughing. "Okay." He wiped a hand over his face, trying to stop. "Oh, man. Okay. I'll talk to you later. I lo—"

The screen went black.

No.

I couldn't.

I lo what? I love? I look forward? I lo . . . I racked my brain thinking of other 'l-o' words. No, no. I couldn't go where my heart already was. The 'lo' was short for 'look.' He looked forward to seeing me in four days, or he looked forward to talking later?

I left my phone on my nightstand and went to the door. I got as far as reaching for the doorknob, before turning back and diving over the bed. I grabbed the phone and texted him.

Me: **You look forward? Is that what you said?**

It was the longest wait ever.

I willed my phone to buzz back. It didn't.

I rolled to my back, letting my phone rest on my chest.

*Text back. Text back.*

Then it did, buzzing close to the breasts that had been missing him.

Coleman: **I'm looking forward to fucking your brains out. ;)**

I groaned, tossed the phone back onto the stand, and muttered under my breath, "Tease." But I still had a ridiculous smile on my face when I went to the kitchen.

It was fitting that my mom put on "Hound Dog" by Elvis in the background.

# CHAPTER THIRTY-FOUR

Kristina and Casey had to change rooms since I was moving in. That meant having to wait and move everything once that triple room was open. My stuff had been taken home, but I didn't have much to take back. I didn't bring any furniture in the first place. That'd been Missy's love seat and everything else. I offered a television and microwave, but she said her stuff was already packed. She didn't want to unpack, so we used her things all semester.

This new semester was different.

I was back on campus, and we came up a day early to get into the room. Shay showed up, along with half the football team. Gage and his roommates were there, as well, and the move took an hour. That was it.

A few other girls came back to campus early, their mouths were half-open as the guys walked past them. Our new room was at the end of a hallway, so we were close to an entrance and exit, and it was on the first floor. It was a double win to me. I could sneak out through the window if I really needed to.

Then the floor's advisor showed up, a clipboard in hand, and a scowl permanently etched on her face. Or she was trying to scowl. Shay introduced himself, and the team followed suit. She was fumbling for words by the end and just handed us a sheet of the rules, saying, "Read that. Follow it to the letter. I'm strict." She looked back to Shay, blushed, and left the room. The back of her neck was red.

Linde laughed, clapping Shay on the shoulder. "Still got that magic."

Shay grunted. "I should. One more year of football glory and we're all adults."

Gage shuddered, traipsing past him with his roommates in tow. "Dude. You don't say it. We all don't need to be depressed."

"That's right." One of his roommates clapped him on the shoulders. "We got tonight to be the epitome of immaturity still. Where's the party?"

Gage stopped right before disappearing back into the hallway. He pointed to me. "You good?"

I nodded. I was putting away my clothes. It was the only thing I brought up that had to be put away.

That wasn't completely true.

We were using Casey and Kristina's couch, their microwave, but they had a small television before. I insisted on bringing mine, which was already set up.

Once Gage left with his roommates, the team began to trickle out.

Shay came over. "I can help put some of this away." He held up a bra, a twinkle in his eyes as he stuffed it in the drawer. He only touched the bras, underwear, and sexy shirts. He gave me a few of them as a Christmas present. Once my clothes were put away, the only things left were my books. They were left in a pile on my desk, but Shay had other things on his mind.

He wrapped his arms around me from behind. "Can we take a break?"

I leaned back, looking up at him. I felt a matching grin coming to my face. We both knew what he wanted to do for his break. "It's my first night with my roommates."

"And we're going to Shay's," Casey said, coming into the main room from the solitary bedroom it was attached to. Our dorm consisted of two rooms. One with some closets, all of the desks, and the main living area. The second room held the rest of our closets and the beds. Casey and Kristina had been in there helping the guys get the beds all put together. I wasn't sure which was mine, but it didn't really matter. I'd sleep wherever.

I asked, "Shay's?"

Shay's hand moved to my waist, but he was still pressed up against me.

"Yeah." She picked up one of her books and put it on the shelf above her desk. "They're having people over for beer and pizza. He didn't tell you?" She nodded to the boyfriend behind me.

"No."

Shay barked out a laugh, his fingers flexing against my skin. "I didn't know myself, but the guys might've talked about it and I might not have been listening." He kissed my neck and murmured into my ear, "We can leave early."

I suppressed one of those addictive shivers. "You guys are heading there soon?"

Kristina was still in the bedroom, but Casey waved at me. "Go. Make sweet, sweet love to your man. I have a car up here now, so we'll be over in an hour or two."

Shay didn't waste time. He caught my hand and led the way out. A few girls were coming in through the back door, and one gasped at the sight of Shay. Her eyes went wide, and her hand jumped to cover her mouth. Two of her friends paused, and one asked as we passed and headed out, "Who was that?"

"That was Sha—"

The door closed behind us.

Shay glanced to me, but I just shook my head. He was sporting a smirk. I didn't need to let his head grow any bigger than it was. "Keep walking, Hard-On."

He barked out a laugh and tightened his hold on me.

We went to his house, but Linde and a group of people I didn't know were on the back patio. They all wanted to say hello to Shay. He went round the table, fisting those who held their closed fists up, saying hello to some of the others, and hugging a few girls. The girls initiated the hug, not Shay, but I knew he couldn't reject them. I understood. This was part of his life. He was already popular when I met him. Nothing changed over the year, except us. He was still the big man on campus, and it wasn't because he threw his weight around. He just was.

And moments like this, where I was pretty sure even he didn't know who some of these people were, he never let them know. They knew him, so he returned the greeting, and when he caught my hand and said our goodbyes, I saw the residue he left. It was a good kind of residue, where they felt warm and important, like they mattered.

That was Shay being himself, polite and considerate.

I had another come-to-Jesus moment. Shay wasn't anything like I first thought. He was almost the opposite.

"What?" he asked, frowning as he opened his bedroom door.

"Nothing."

"No." He put his keys on his dresser and stood there as I sat on the edge of his bed. He started to reach for his shirt to pull it off, but paused. He gave me a thoughtful look, cocking his head to the side and narrowing his eyes. "What is it? You definitely thought something there."

He whisked his shirt off, disappearing into the closet and pulling a new one out. He pulled it on, his hands going to his pants. He paused, looked down, as if he forgot what he'd been doing, and shrugged. He left them on, crossing to pull his desk chair out and he sat, right in front of me. Catching my hands between his, he leaned forward. His elbows rested on his knees, and his legs rested on the outside of mine, trapping me in place. "Tell me what's up."

I watched as he toyed with one of my hands, tracing it with his fingers. "I was just really wrong about you in the beginning." I shrugged. "That's all."

"Wrong?" He lifted his head. "You know, we never really did talk about the beginning when you hated me."

My throat stopped working. "You want me to tell you why I hated you?"

He nodded solemnly. "Why not?"

My throat was full for some reason. I coughed, clearing it, and started again. "I think I assumed you were like my ex."

"The Parker guy?"

I raked my fingers through his hair. He ducked his head, a small rakish grin showing, and I felt flutters in my stomach. I sighed. "He looked like you."

"He did?" Shay grimaced, continuing to trace his fingers over my palms.

"He wasn't as good-looking as you. You beat him in spades in that area."

He stopped tracing my palm and held my hands between his. "Thank goodness for that, huh?"

I gazed at our hands, my mind in memories. "He was arrogant, but I didn't notice. Not at first."

He asked me for coffee. I thought how mature he must've thought I was. But no. He knew exactly the effect of his charm. A mere freshman being asked out by a senior.

I had swooned.

"We went on a few dates before anything happened. I thought maybe he was scared to make a move, since most guys were. You know, because of Gage." I could only shake my head. "That was so far from the truth. He was biding his time. He wanted me to fall completely in love with him." A bitter laugh slipped out. "I found out later that he had a timetable. He wanted to make sure I was under his thumb by the time Christmas came around. Blake had been gone on a work thing. He was coming back then, and he wanted to meet my new boyfriend. Parker told me to keep it as a surprise. He thought Blake would get a kick out of it, so I never said his name. I was vague on the details, too. Blake just knew there was *a* guy."

"He didn't ask Gage?"

"Gage didn't know how much Blake hated Parker. Blake kept everything a secret. We didn't find out what happened until later."

So, I told him.

Parker was a year younger than Blake, but he was still leader of the debate team, Yearbook Jr. Editor, and then Senior Editor later on, and in all sorts of academic events.

He was captain of the swimming and boys tennis team.

Blake was the opposite.

He excelled at partying, football, wrestling, and baseball. They were both popular, but Blake ran with friends who didn't fight with words. They fought with their hands, and one night at a party, the two went at it. It didn't matter that Parker was younger.

Blake humiliated him.

Parker was stripped of his clothes. The guys were laughing at him. There was an incident about running through a field where they chased him like he was a deer.

It wasn't right, and I heard enough to be horrified.

The police charged my brother, and he did a year of probation. He never went to college, instead he stayed home and got a job with a local construction company.

"You didn't know it was Parker?"

I shook my head. "I knew about the incident, but I never knew it was Parker. I might've heard, but I was four years younger than Blake. I only knew his friends. I didn't know anyone else in his grade. I just knew it had been some guy."

"I'm sorry." Shay squeezed my hands, dropping a soft kiss to them.

I relished that small graze before I kept going. "It was like a bomb went off when Blake did get home. Parker came over for a dinner, a kind of 'meet the parents' thing, but it was Blake he was meeting. My mom was meeting him for the first time, too."

*Yelling.*

*Dishes shattered.*

*My mom yelped in surprise, and that stopped Blake from flinging a chair into the wall. He lowered it and pointed to the door. "Get out! NOW!"*

"Parker left that night. So did I." I met Shay's eyes, saw the sympathy there, and knew I didn't deserve it. "I chose sides that night. I chose Parker's."

"Kenz," Shay murmured, rubbing my hand between his. "You can't blame yourself. You were a kid. He was playing a game with you."

"I lost the game. He slept with my best friend a month later. I walked in on them. He had her bent over the bed, and they dated for the rest of the year." I could see them walking down the hallways, holding hands. "They laughed at me, almost every time they saw me for the rest of the year."

"What an asshole."

It still stung. I felt it in my side. "Yeah."

"Hey." His voice grew husky. He tipped my head up to meet his eyes. "Nothing right will happen for him. You know that, right? If he did that shit back in high school, he'll do worse now. He'll keep going until something bad happens to him. Guys like that get fucked in the end. They always do."

No. They didn't always, but I did feel a bit better. "Thank you for that."

"For what?"

I shrugged. "For making some of the regret go away."

"That?" He waved that off, standing. "That was nothing."

I leaned back.

He started to crawl onto the bed.

I scooted farther back, making room for him, and after I was all the way to the headboard, he paused. He rested his legs over me, but he didn't sit down. He was half-kneeling over me, bending down so we were looking each other in the eyes.

He dropped his voice, almost to a whisper. "We're not really a serious kind of couple. I mean, we can be."

We shared a look, both thinking of my attack.

He kept on, "But you know what I mean. You made me laugh from the beginning." He cupped the side of my face, his thumb brushing over my cheek, lingering by my lips. "The feistier you got, the more I became entranced. I wanted to push your buttons. I wanted to see life flood to your eyes, make your face warm. I wanted to see the sparkle come back. It was like it took over you. It transformed you. Like you were on autopilot until something I said or did pissed you off. It could've been just a look, or hell, if I put my foot on the back of your chair."

I stiffened. "I hated that."

"See." He chuckled, his eyes damn near melting me. "A switch flipped on just now. You're here. You're fine. You're normal, and then you get mad, and it's as if you glow. You light up the room." He rested on the bed beside me, catching me and turning me so I was half-lying on him. He brushed some of my hair back, and I tilted my head to see him better.

I asked, "I'm like a neon light?"

"Exactly."

"Are you kidding me? That's your romantic speech?"

"Romantic speech? We have to do speeches now in this relationship?" He sat up, caught my waist, and lifted me to straddle him.

I gazed down at him, resting my hands on his stomach. He leaned back, folding his hands behind his head. He looked like he was a king and didn't have a care in the world at that moment.

"Maybe we should." I raised my chin up in a challenge. "Maybe you have to tell me five good things about me every da—"

"Sexy. Hot." He was listing them off with his fingers. "Funny. Smart. Spunky." His grin turned smug. "Your turn."

I laughed, finishing, "—ay, and I'll do the same for you."

He sat up again, taking me by surprise, but he only ran his hands down my arms to my waist. They slid up under my shirt, and he angled his head to look me in the eyes. Our lips were only inches apart. "You're supposed to compliment me, Clarke."

"Ha-ha." But I was game. "Fine. You're sexy and hot."

"Think of new words. Don't copy mine."

I changed without missing a beat. "Handsome and drool-worthy gorgeous—"

"Much better." His smile grew.

My body heated as his hand began to explore, moving farther up my back. I added, hitching on a note, "You're smart. Kind. You support me."

"You know what else I'm good at?"

"What?" His hand circled over my ribs and slipped under my bra before cupping my breast. I had a good idea what he was going to say, but I waited.

I loved waiting.

He murmured huskily, "I'm *damned* good in bed."

His lips covered mine, and the past fled from my mind.

Everything fled, clothes included.

# CHAPTER THIRTY-FIVE

I was in my new dorm floor's bathroom, getting ready for bed. It was later that night, around two in the morning, so it was technically the next day. Kristina and Casey came over and watched movies in the living room with Linde and the same group of friends. Shay and I joined after another hour spent in bed, and the whole night had been fun. Beer. Pizza. Movies. And laughter, lots of laughter. Linde's friends, whoever they were, had been nice. A few of the girls gave me a dark look when Shay pulled me onto his lap, but some of their other roommates joined us and the girls were distracted in no time.

Shay drove us back. Casey left her car there since she and Kristina both had a few too many beers. They were in the room now, laughing about something on the computer, but I was actually tired. I grabbed my bathroom caddy and was finishing up when a girl came in.

She went down a few sinks from mine.

I gave her the hello smile when she first came in, but I hadn't spoken. I felt her attention after a few seconds. She kept looking over, until she was done washing her hands. Then, she just stood there. Her face was turned toward me, her hands resting on the sink.

"You're dating Shay Coleman." She added, "You're his girlfriend. You're the one who got attacked last semester."

I hadn't been expecting that, but a feeling that I knew her took root in me.

Maybe?

There was nothing that stood out about her.

She was slender, hair that went past her shoulders, and brown eyes. Her eyes were set a little too far apart and her nose seemed a little too big for her face. She had thin lips.

I tried to remember . . .

"Have we met before?"

"No."

Oh.

"Okay." I swallowed over a lump. "What's your name?"

"What's yours?" She didn't pause a beat. She came right back with that question, and she didn't blink. She was looking at me like we were talking about the weather, but she didn't care if a tornado was coming right at us or not.

Something shifted in my stomach, a gut instinct. I clamped down on it. I didn't need to make enemies on my first night in this dorm.

"I think you know my name."

She narrowed her eyes for a split second before she broke out into a grin. "You're right. I do. You're Gage Clarke's sister, too."

People had been talking about me since my attack. It was known I was with Shay, and I knew people would include who my brother was in the gossip. I shouldn't have been surprised, but this girl was coming at me in a different way.

She was being smug about knowing who I was, while I didn't know her. That didn't sit right with me.

"Well, aren't you the busy bee, knowing all about me." I turned to face her squarely, though I didn't step toward her. I was content with the little bit of space there was between us, and the door was behind me. I'd swing it open and use it to clip her in the head if anything happened.

"What'd you say?"

"You heard me." I folded my arms over my chest, still holding my toothbrush. "I can find out who you are, if that's what you're thinking. All I have to do is ask the floor advisor what girl would know all about me, who came a day earlier like we did. Something tells me she'd know exactly whom I was talking about."

But I knew her. I couldn't shake that feeling. I just didn't know where from.

There was more, too. A feeling in my gut, like I should've been remembering something else.

I couldn't place it.

Her lip curved up, breaking the oddly stone-facial expression into a grin. "I'm Phoebe, Cameron Brewski's sister. I know Shay from high school."

Another sideways punch. Okay. I didn't know her. I would've remembered that tidbit. "Not what I was expecting you to say."

She laughed. "I'm not here to start a fight. I was just letting you know that I know you in case you ever wanted to talk. I'm a few doors down from you and your roommates."

"You've met my roommates?"

"I heard them. You guys were loud tonight."

I flinched. "We woke you up." I noticed her pajama pants and shirt, and how she wasn't carrying a bathroom caddy, because she'd already been in bed. "I'm sorry about that."

She shook her head. "It's fine. I'd tell you to tell Shay hello for me, but that'd be pointless. He never knew who I was in school."

"Uh." I frowned. "I'm sure he did. I'll tell him."

She stood there for another second and then abruptly went into one of the bathroom stalls. I headed out and was walking back to the room when I heard her flush and the stall door open again. I could hear the squeak, but I was going in my room when I heard the bathroom door swing open.

Casey had Kristina in a headlock, both flushed in the face and sweating. They paused, looked at me, and nope. I wasn't going there. I walked right past, put my caddy away, grabbed my phone, and crawled under the covers.

They resumed their wrestling so I put in two earplugs and texted Shay.

Me: **I'm sleeping at your place tomorrow night.**

Coleman: **Okay. Going to sleep now?**

Me: **Yes.**

Coleman: **Wanna do some sexting?**

I grinned.

Me: **No. It'll wake me up.**

Coleman: **You sure? I can take pictures.**

Me: **Don't send me a di–** Before I could finish my text, my phone buzzed, and a picture of a penis was right there. I finished my text, **—ck. Is that yours?**

I could envision him grinning.

Coleman: **You think I have a file of other dick pics to send in an off-chance you'd ever ask for one?**

Me: **Yes.**

Coleman: **You know me so well, but what do you think? Mine's better, right?**

I grinned to myself, feeling the slight tension from meeting the girl fade away. Suddenly, the wrestling sounds weren't as loud, and my bed was becoming comfier. I snuggled down, tucking the cover up over my chin.

Me: **You know it is.**

Coleman: **Still don't want to do some dirty sexting?**

I laughed softly.

Me: **Touch yourself.**

Coleman: **You first.**

Me: **I already am.**

Coleman: **You are? Pic?**

I made a face.

Me: **Gross. No.**

Coleman: **Okay. I have a good memory. I'm remembering right now.**

Me: **Still touching yourself?**

Coleman: **Wishing it were you.**

I groaned, and my fingers moved lower on my stomach.

Me: **Are you really touching yourself?**

Coleman: **Aren't you?**

I couldn't believe I was doing this, but I pushed two fingers into me, between my folds, and bit down on my lip.

Me: **I am now.**

Coleman: **Fuck.**

I widened my eyes. That was all he was going to say?

Me: **That's it? Serious?**

Coleman: **I'm driving to pick you up right now. Get dressed.**

I whelped, throwing back the covers. Lathering some antibacterial gel on, I hurried into some sweats and nabbed a sweatshirt. Socks and sneakers were next, and then I went into the front room. Kristina and Casey were on the couch, a bag of chips between them, and *Fifty Shades of Grey* on the television screen.

"Let me guess." Casey pointed at me, a chip in hand. "Sexy times with your man?"

Kristina's eyes were glazed.

She didn't say anything, just reached for a handful of chips and stuffed them into her mouth.

"Is that okay? I'll be here tomorrow night because of classes the next day, but we still have one day left."

Casey waved me off, popping the chip into her mouth. "You have fun and tell us everything later. We'll live vicariously through you."

"Speak for yourself." Kristina grabbed another handful of chips. "I have a man."

Casey sighed. "You both have men. I hate you."

They each waved as I left. Going to the back door, I texted Shay where I was, but it wasn't long until headlights flashed over the building. His Jeep pulled into our parking lot and turned so the passenger's door was facing me.

I said as I got in, "Hey."

"Hey." He raked me over, his eyes darkened from hunger.

I didn't have a smart comment to make. I was feeling the same hunger he was, but I reached for my seat belt and looked up.

Everything froze for a second.

I gasped, seeing Phoebe at her window. She wore the same blank and almost dead expression, and she was looking right back at me. There was no reason for me to gasp. It was late at night. She'd been up.

It made sense she might be curious about a car's headlights at night, but it was *how* she was standing at the window.

Like she'd been waiting.

Like she knew to watch for me.

It sent a shiver down my spine.

Shay was pulling away from the curb, and he glanced over. "What is it?"

I told him about Phoebe, but he only frowned. "Cameron has a sister? I had no clue. What's she like?"

"She's . . . odd."

He shrugged. "Did you want me to say something to Cameron about her?"

"No. I don't even really know why I said something now." I still felt unsettled, that was why, but I didn't know if I should feel that way?

He nodded, and when we got to his place, and in his room, he turned that wicked grin back on. "Now. About that sexting we were doing . . ."

# CHAPTER THIRTY-SIX

Shay woke me the next morning by trailing kisses up my naked back. He was braced over me, and I looked, my head buried into the pillow. "Morning."

He grinned, dropping one last kiss to the back of my shoulder. "Morning." He jumped over me in one smooth and lithe movement, landing quietly on the floor where he didn't pause as he bent down and scooped up my phone. He tossed it to land on the bed where he just vacated. "Your friends keep calling you. The buzzing woke me up."

"My friends?" I rolled over to grab it, pulling his sheet to cover my breasts. How did he know? But he was right. He went into the bathroom in his naked gloriousness, and I opened the first text from Kristina when I heard the shower turn on.

Kristina: **Hey, girl! Get back here. C, S, L, and I are going to the campus diner for food. Your presence is necessary!**

Another text an hour later.

Kristina: **Okay. We're seriously going. Getting dressed. I'm going to unleash Casey on you. She's about to start calling.**

Casey: **Roommate dinner. Now! Where are you?**

Five minutes after that one.

Casey: **Okay. Correction. S and L are coming, but we're all going to be roommates one day. Get your cute ass here now!**

Then the phone calls started.

I had one every five minutes.

My phone started ringing, and I hit answer, not needing to see who it was first. "Morning, Casey."

"AH! You're awake? You guys stopped having sex?"

I laughed, rolling to my side with my back to the bathroom. The shower had stopped, and I didn't need to get more distracted than I already was. I tucked the phone close to my ear. "Ha-ha. We just woke up."

"It's eleven in the morning."

"And we didn't get to sleep—"

Shay said, coming back into the room, "Does she really have to know that?"

I changed, "—later than when I left."

"Hm-mm." A knowing grunt came from her. "Okay. Listen, we were going to meet the girls there now, but we'll wait another thirty minutes. Can you get here by then? We want you to come today. It was a whole tradition we started last semester, and you're a part of it now."

Warmth spread over me, and I sat up, meeting Shay's gaze. "Yeah. Just go there. I have clothes here. I can change and meet you guys."

Shay frowned, ducking his head to pull a shirt on. He already pulled on some jeans, but he didn't buckle them.

"Okay. We will see you there, then!"

I hung up and said, pulling my knees up against my chest, "They're doing a dinner thing, but I think it's a lunch thing."

He grabbed his socks and shoes and padded over to sit next to me. "In that case, I better leave the room while you're in the shower. I don't trust myself." He leaned over, kissing me, and I sighed. I fell into him, and he growled, picking me up to sit on his lap. I wound my arms around his neck, still kissing, and it wasn't long before he began tugging that sheet away from me.

"No, no." I stood, taking the sheet with me. "You take this off, and we won't be leaving until long after I was supposed to be there." I whisked it around me, grinning over my shoulder. "Don't come into the shower."

He laughed, raking a hand through his wet hair. "Christ. I think I'm addicted to you." He grabbed his own phone and gestured for the door, taking his keys and wallet, too. "I'll be downstairs."

After a quick shower, I decided to let my hair air-dry and pull it into a braid later. I grabbed clean clothes from a drawer I'd been using, dressed, and headed downstairs.

I found Shay sitting on the back patio. He was talking with more people I didn't recognize, and all said bye when we took off.

We had five minutes to get there.

I asked, after we were in his Jeep and heading back, "Who were those people?"

"One of our roommates goes to a different college in town. Those were some of his buddies."

"I thought it was only football players in the house?"

"Nah." He shook his head. "Most of us are football players, but we have two who aren't. One is Linde's cousin. He's the dude who goes to the other college. Those were his friends, but we got another guy I know from high school. That's why Cameron was at the house that night. He's good buddies with the same guy. He stayed to hang out with him."

Cameron.

Who was dating the gorgeous Sabrina.

Whose sister was on my floor.

I was hearing about the high school buddy he and Shay shared *now*?

None of it was sitting right with me. I didn't know why. I mean, Shay and I didn't have a lot of serious talks, like he said earlier, but a girl should maybe know certain things about the guy she's sleeping with.

Right?

Then again, we started dating under extenuating circumstances. Fuck. We started making out and sleeping together under extenuating circumstances. I'd practically been living with him for a month and a half before holiday break.

Some of these conversations should've come up then.

Maybe?

But no. I was attacked. I was dealing with that whole situation. The normal conversations a guy and a girl starting to date have didn't happen. It was like we were playing catch-up. It felt weird to be the one asking the questions. I didn't want to be the girlfriend who'd appear like she was nagging or needling for information.

The whole thing gave me a hot rash.

I needed to think about something else. "I have a counselor appointment at the end of the week."

*Good one, Clarke.* I cringed at myself. That was what I went with? My counselor?

"Yeah? You want a ride there?"

I shook my head. "You have classes, I think. I can drive myself."

"You're not seeing the one on campus?"

Another shake of my head. "I liked the hospital one better, so I'm going back to her."

"That's good." He glanced over to me, pulling into campus now. "That you're continuing with the sessions. I know that was a criteria for school last semester, but you're keeping it up."

"Yeah. Well." I had to talk to someone about it. It never worked its way into my normal daily conversations, with reason. I didn't like talking about it.

"Well?" He took another right, turning into the parking lot by the campus diner.

"What?"

"You said 'well.' What'd you mean by that?"

"Oh." He stopped in front of the diner, and I reached for the door handle.

"Hey." He softened his tone. "Look at me."

I did, holding on to that door handle so tightly my knuckles strained. "Yeah?"

I didn't want to look into his eyes. I didn't want to see the kindness, sympathy, concern, all those emotions and qualities that had me fall for him as fast as I did, despite how I fought against it. But I looked, and I was hooked, like every time he smiled at me, brushed a hand over my face, tucked some hair behind my ear, or kissed me in that so-gentle way he did sometimes. It made my heart speed up, and I was feeling the repercussions all over again.

Fucking A.

I was falling in love.

"You okay?"

I couldn't answer. My throat was momentarily paralyzed.

"Kennedy?" He reached over, brushing the back of his knuckles over my cheek.

I felt a tear forming and cleared my throat. I managed a smile. "I'm fine. Just . . . I don't talk about the attack that much. It still affects me."

He frowned, his hand falling away. "I've noticed. Am I supposed to ask you about it? I don't really know my role regarding that area. Should I just let you talk when you want to? Shit. Maybe I shouldn't even be asking you this right now." He looked so torn, and I took pity on him.

I caught his hand, squeezing it. "You're doing just fine. I don't like to think about it, honestly, but I know I have to, and when I need to talk, I will."

He nodded. "Okay. Well, I'm here. You know that, right?" He gestured between us, a half-grin appearing. "I mean, the sex is fucking fantastic, but I'm here for the serious stuff, too."

I matched his grin. "You always know the right things to say."

His half-grin formed into a full one, and he leaned over. He whispered, his lips meeting mine as I met him halfway, "You know it. That's why you're dating me, because I say the right things."

I barked out a laugh, opening the door and getting out. "Right. Totally PC, too."

"You're damn straight." He winked.

I laughed once more, giving him a small wave. "I'll talk to you later."

"Have fun with your friends. Call me if you want to see me tonight. Otherwise, I'll call later."

I nodded and then headed in as he pulled away. There were people outside the diner who'd recognized Shay and his Jeep, but I ignored the looks as they watched me walk inside. I had a feeling it'd be like that for the rest of my time dating him.

The diner wasn't too crowded when I went inside. Most students were just arriving back that day. It was close to noon, and I had no doubt the place would be packed in the evening. Everyone would want to catch up with their friends.

Kristina and Casey waved from a back booth. Sarah and Laura were there, and they turned to give me welcoming smiles.

Casey pulled out her phone when I got to the table. "You're only two minutes late. Holy shit, woman. I was for sure you and that hot man of yours would try for a quickie." She whistled. "I'm impressed."

"Ha-ha." I nodded hello to everyone, dropping into the seat beside Sarah and across from Kristina.

A large pizza was on the table, and everyone had one or two pieces on their plates. I asked, noting the pizza didn't look touched, "Is this the second pizza you ordered?"

Kristina nodded. "We were hungry."

Casey grunted. "We were hungover. Pizza cures that shit."

Sarah and Laura laughed, grabbing their pieces to nibble on.

"Did you have fun last night?"

Casey choked on her piece. "You're going to have to be more specific. Our girl lives a pretty active life."

Kristina's cheeks pinked, but she rolled her eyes. "Last night, movies at Shay's house. Did you have fun?"

"I did. Did you?"

She nodded. "Linde's a lot of fun. He's a good guy."

Casey asked, "Is he single?"

I frowned. "Why? Are you interested?"

Casey lifted up a shoulder. "Maybe."

I frowned again. "What about my brother?"

"You want the details on your brother's love life?" Sarah laughed as she asked me.

I didn't, but I saw the look in Casey's eyes. I was thinking I was going to find out more than I wanted.

Casey leaned forward, propping her elbows on the table. "I have a thing for your brother. I don't think he has one for me. I haven't talked to him in forever."

"Really?"

I was surprised. I asked Gage to back off, but he hadn't, and then I stopped caring.

I was thinking back over the holiday. "I don't remember him talking about other girls when we were home. Usually, he'll mention one or two. That's why you asked about Linde?" I didn't wait for her answer. I dropped my voice. "He's a great guy."

"I know." Her head lowered. "That's why I'm asking."

I didn't know what to say, and I also didn't see any waitresses around the place. Spotting a few people going to their tables with trays of food, I asked, "Do I need to go up and order?"

Kristina didn't answer. She started to slip out of the booth. "I'll go with you." Once we were out of earshot, she asked, "You okay? Is it weird with the whole Casey/Gage/Linde thing?"

There was a line at the counter to order, and we stood at the end. "I just don't want anyone to get hurt."

"I think *she* doesn't want to get hurt. She's a bit sensitive after, you know."

The rape.

My attack.

The aftereffects would never end, I was realizing.

"Yeah. I get that."

We moved forward with the line. We were three people away, and I began to scan the boards to figure out what I wanted to order.

"You and Shay are doing good?"

I remembered the moment just minutes ago in his Jeep, where I didn't want to talk about my attack, but should, and that I was falling in love with him. My throat burned again. I could relate to Casey not wanting to get hurt. "We have fun together."

"Just fun?"

I nodded. "Fun. Sex. Talking. The whole thing. He was really great after my attack last semester."

I could feel her watching me.

One person away.

Fuck. I needed to find something to order.

"What's going on here? I'm missing something."

I said, "I'm missing what I want to eat. You guys ordered pizza. I could eat that, too, maybe?"

"What's going on with you?"

The last person stepped aside. It was my turn. The guy had a pad of paper ready for my order. Shit, shit, shit. I was under the gun.

"Just a soda."

He wrote it down and then rang it up on the register. "You sure? Nothing else?"

My thoughts were scrambled so I said the first thing I read from the board, "Mozzarella sticks."

"Okay." He gave me the total, and I handed over my cash. After he gave me the empty cup to fill, I moved to stand by the window and wait for them to call my order. I'd forgotten this was how the diner operated, but Kristina waited with me.

I suggested, "You can go back. You don't have to wait with me."

She snorted. "Right, and let you get off the hook? I think not." She nudged me with her shoulder. "Talk to me. What's going on?"

"Nothing." Which was the truth. Kind of. Then I blurted out, "I love him."

"You love Shay?"

"No." I threw her a look. "I love Linde. We have a wild and forbidden passion for each other. Of course, it's Shay. *He's* the guy I'm dating."

"I know." She held her hands up. "You hold your cards close to your chest. I just wanted to make sure."

I felt like an ass right away. "I'm sorry. I—fuck! I'm . . . I don't know. I just realized it, but I should've known long ago." This was why I hated him. This was why I'd been adamant about not befriending him, about not being in a study group with him, about not looking at him, talking to him, anything.

Because I knew, deep inside, that I was going to fall in love with him. I felt a lump forming in my throat again. That hated feeling was back, but it was different. It had a whole twisted side to it because it was me, hating that I loved him.

I was so fucked.

They called my mozzarella sticks. I blindly took them back to the booth.

The girls were happy, descending on them until only one was left for me. Kristina hadn't said anything else, sensing the shitstorm going on inside me, but I felt her watching me the whole time during the meal.

I left the last mozzarella stick.

I never ate any of the pizza.

Even my soda was left untouched. I dumped the whole thing out when we left.

The girls wanted to check their mail, and I trudged behind them, lost in my own thoughts.

Casey persuaded them to come to our room with us afterwards and we were turning down our hallway when Sabrina appeared. The very gorgeous front desk clerk of our old dorm and the very beautiful ex-girlfriend of Shay, was coming toward us.

No.

There was no way I could get hurt.

There was no way Shay would suddenly realize he made a mistake with me and remember that maybe he should be with her instead?

There was no way . . .

# CHAPTER THIRTY-SEVEN

"Hey, guys." She had a friendly smile and wave.

God. She was even more beautiful than I remembered. Why'd Shay have to date such beautiful creatures? And kind. I could tell. She'd always been so nice before, and it was there again. She was so much nicer than I was. I was brash, mean, feisty, and I could be rude at times. I had good qualities, too, but they weren't on the surface like hers.

Suddenly, I felt very small standing next to her.

I forced a smile.

The rest said an easy hello, heading to the room, but I was rooted in place. This girl had once been with Shay. It shouldn't bother me, but it did.

She noticed I wasn't leaving. A soft frown formed. "You okay?"

"Did you love him?"

Her eyes widened a fraction of an inch. "Oh." She blinked a few times. "You know, huh?"

I nodded, my neck feeling like it was made of wood. "Yeah."

She cleared her throat. "We could talk in one of the waiting rooms? It'll be more private."

"Sure." My legs felt like they were made of wood, too, as I followed behind her. The whole twisty effect in my stomach was full-force and on steroids. I didn't know why I was so scared. Shay said he let the relationship go, so what was my damage here? Why was I insecure around her?

"Here." She found a private sitting area and sat in an archaic-looking armchair. It was dusty rose colored, and something you'd find in a Victorian-era home. She folded her hands on her lap, her back so straight, and her shoulders rolled back. She looked so prim and proper, she matched the chair.

"So." She smoothed out the bottom of her shirt, spreading it over her legs. "You know about Shay and me then?"

"I met your boyfriend, too."

"He mentioned that, said you and Shay looked happy together." She swallowed, her slim throat moving with the motion.

She didn't like hearing that. I could tell.

This was what I'd been worried about. It wasn't Shay. It was her. "You still have feelings for him."

She sucked in her breath, but her eyes said everything.

"Yeah," I murmured. "That's what I thought."

"It doesn't matter. He doesn't love me."

"He doesn't love me, either."

Her eyebrows pinched together, and she spoke so softly, "But you're together?"

I shrugged. I'd had my heart ripped out before. I wouldn't put anything past anyone. "He cares."

"Cameron told me that you two fit. Those were his words."

Why did it bother me that she still loved him? It shouldn't. She was the ex-girlfriend. He wasn't going to go back. My insecurity was unfounded.

"You don't fit?" Sabrina had been watching me, confused.

"We do. Ironically."

"Why ironically? That's good, right?"

She hadn't said much, but I had to ask. "Did he break you?"

"Oh." Understanding dawned, and she looked down to her lap. Her bottom lip trembled slightly. "He, uh . . . not completely, but yes. He kind of did."

I remembered his account of why they broke up. "Because he cheated on you?"

She laughed, such a sad twinge to it. "No, because he let me think he did."

My eyes rounded. "You knew the truth?"

She nodded. "Yeah. I knew the other girl. She told me what really happened, that she kissed him, and he didn't push her away immediately. She found me later and told me the truth. He waited a second before stepping away from her. She pursued him after that, and that's when he really put a stop to it. She knew what people were saying and wanted me to know the truth. I respect her for telling me and apologizing, but he let me think it was about the cheating. I knew it was over even before I brought it up to him, just because he didn't care to. He never told me about the girl. He let me find out on my own, and he still didn't say anything. I had to bring it up. I had to ask him about it." She looked down. Her hands were gripping each other so tightly. "He just said he'd be okay if I didn't want to be in the relationship anymore."

There was no fight on his end.

"He just—there was nothing there. I didn't have the heart to admit the truth. I loved him, but he enjoyed my company. That was our relationship." She flicked a tear away. "We could've gone on longer. I don't think he would've broken up with me, but that wasn't fair to me."

She loved him while he enjoyed her presence.

I couldn't get over those words. They were on repeat in my mind.

Shit.

Was that how he and I were?

I loved him. I think I had loved him from the beginning, even from the first day I walked into that class.

I reached over and clasped her hands with mine. "I'm sorry."

She laughed again, sniffling, and squeezed my hands back. "What for? Shay cares about you."

I nodded. He did.

"And I'm with Cameron now. I love him. I really do."

She didn't. I could see that in her eyes, too. She loved him because he cared back, but it wasn't the real gut-wrenching type of love, the kind she felt for Shay.

My chest was so damned tight. I had to change the topic, or lighten it somehow. I was starting not to be able to breathe.

"I met Cameron's sister last night."

"Yeah." She smiled, letting out a deep breath. "That's why I'm here. I was just visiting with her a little bit. Cameron goes to school an hour away, so he comes up every now and then, but he doesn't always see his little sister. The two should connect more. It's always weird with them. I don't get it."

A faraway look came over her before her eyes focused on me again. "I was sorry to hear you moved dorms. I enjoyed our random hellos."

I frowned. "I'm sorry I didn't stop and talk more."

"Oh." She waved that off before going back to smoothing out the bottom of her shirt. "I know what it's like. I was usually studying."

"You had my back with Shay once."

"Yeah." She touched my knee, a soft reassuring touch. "I can see you're worried about something, but you don't have to be. Your relationship with Shay isn't what I had with him. I already know that. If I'd been attacked, Shay would've comforted me. That's it. He would've been there for me to cry on his shoulder, and he would've been the doting and supportive boyfriend, and everyone would've thought how perfect he was being. But he wouldn't have done what he did for you. He really cares about you."

She said cares. Even she couldn't say he loved me.

I forced a smile, feeling a burning sensation in my chest. "You're right. I really care about him, too."

"See." Her smile grew. "I might be seeing you a bit more here than I did in the other dorm. I come over to see Phoebe a lot." She stood, and we made our way back to the main front entrance. Her step was a little lighter, and she spoke a bit more freely. "Now, if she *wants* to see me is a different story. I think she's lonely. I don't want her to feel that way. Sometimes she lets me stay. Sometimes she doesn't."

She waved a goodbye, saying she'd see me later.

I was rooted in place. Again.

She was a good person. She was beautiful on the inside and outside, and it hit me. If Shay hadn't loved someone like her, what chance did I have?

# CHAPTER THIRTY-EIGHT

"What's going on with you?" Shay asked me later that night. We were studying in his room. He was at his desk while I was stretched out on his bed. We were both dressed in lounging clothes. He had on a shirt and sweatpants, but I went the boy-shorts route. They were hidden underneath a large sweater that hung on me like a dress.

After talking to Sabrina, I tried to shake my insecurities off.

Shay wasn't Parker.

I wasn't going to become Sabrina.

Right?

I kept trying to reassure myself, but it was useless. For whatever reason—maybe the fact that I admitted to myself I was falling for him—my irrational sense of doom hung over me like a storm cloud. I couldn't shake it, and seeing the puzzled look on Shay's gorgeous face, I thought, *fuck it*.

I sat up, crossing my legs over each other. I faced him squarely from the bed. "Are you going to hurt me?"

His eyes widened. He'd been holding a pen in his hand, but it dropped to the floor. "What? Where did that come from?"

"You heard me."

I was watching.

I was waiting.

But no reaction, other than his shock. I didn't see any flicker of guilt in his eyes, and I instantly felt stupid. I needed to get a handle on my issues. "Nothing." I dropped back to the bed with a sigh, letting my textbook fall to the side. "I'm being a girl."

"Whoa. What's going on?"

I heard the desk squeak. Shay came into view as he stood over me, frowning down at me. He folded his arms over his chest, and I tried not to gawk at how that defined his already spectacular chest, shoulders, and arm muscles.

I failed.

I was pretty sure I felt a little drool, but I wiped it away and scooted so I was sitting back against the wall facing him. He sat next to me, his hand on my leg.

I looked down at my hands, folded on my lap. "My feelings are stronger than I want them to be. Last time this happened, Parker squashed me like a damned bug." I looked up. "Are you going to squash me?"

"No." He shook his head from side to side, his eyebrows knitting together. "You really think that? Haven't I shown you enough how much I care?"

My mouth went dry.

He had.

But . . . I gave him a small smile. "Could you maybe write it down? Like on flashcards?"

"Flashcards?"

I nodded. "I can pull those out anytime I start getting freaked about us."

"You want me to profess my feelings for you on flashcards?"

"Makes total sense to me."

I didn't bat an eyelash.

That was all he did, raking a hand over his face. "I shouldn't be surprised by anything by now with you."

I nodded. That sounded completely reasonable.

But I was still waiting, and he saw that, too. He stood, going back to his desk. "Okay. Fine. Shay's Flashcards of Love coming right up." He picked up a pen and grabbed a deck of blank cards he'd been using for studying. "Silly me, I thought I would be using them to quiz myself tonight. Nope. They're the new form of emotional reassurance."

I closed my eyes, half-grinning, but half-cringing on the inside.

Whatever.

I'd been nuts since the beginning. It wasn't as if I was starting a new protocol for our relationship. He enjoyed the sex enough. I was banking on that keeping him around if his real feelings started to fade.

"Flashcard one," Shay started.

I could feel his gaze, and I looked up again, meeting it. I felt zapped. There was a fierceness in him, a smoldering emotion that I wasn't sure if I was seeing correctly. I gulped. He wasn't breaking eye contact as he started, "Spontaneous." He scribbled the word down, then flipped to the back. "She's down to have sex almost anytime and anywhere."

I looked back down. The tips of my ears started to burn.

He continued, "She's up for any adventure, too. Antonyms: boring or dull." He coughed and then I heard him pull out a second flashcard. "Funny." He flipped it over. "She can make me laugh just by being herself. She sits, and I think it's cute and funny. She breathes, and I get aroused or I start chuckling. She gets upset about something, and I'm walking around with a hard-on."

I didn't think "funny" described all of that, but I bit down on my lip. I wanted to hear more, and I didn't at the same time.

"Smart." Backside of the card. "She's a freshman, and she held her own with upperclassmen in a class I know she thought was boring as hell. She can challenge me to think beyond myself or my friends. How she acts makes me want to be a better man."

My whole ear was inflamed. It was growing to my cheeks and farther down.

"Sweet." He flipped it. "She had a roommate who treated her like shit at times, but she was so sweet, Kennedy never wanted to hurt her feelings. She could've humiliated her roommate and never did. She didn't want anyone to know about our relationship in the beginning, which leads me to . . ." He pulled out a new card. "Fearful. She's scared of being hurt by me, which is the opposite of annoying, which she thinks I am right now."

I looked up, my hands clasped tightly together. I swallowed over a lump.

He wasn't even writing. He was looking right at me, unflinching and unwavering, "The fact that you're worried I'm going to hurt you is the very reason why I never will. It doesn't make me want to run for the hills or jump on this chance to leave you. Because I could. I'm a guy. Guys know how to screw with a girl's mind and insecurities, but I don't do that. Not with you."

He shoved the cards aside and stood.

He said, his voice eerily soft, "When I see you're hurting, I want to wipe it away. When I see you doubting yourself, I want to give you the best damned pep talk in history. When you cry, I want to make you smile. When you laugh, I want to make you laugh harder. When you moan in my arms, I want to make you dissolve into a puddle. When you're insecure about how I feel about you, I want to replace that with a proclamation that I love you so hard that I never want you to question us again."

He was standing right above the bed, looking down on me, and I could only gape at him.

A moment passed.

A second.

Complete silence.

And a strangled gurgle left me. I was holding on to my sweater to keep myself from either jumping him or running away. I choked out, "You love me?"

"Completely."

"I—"

"Do you love me?"

"I—"

HOLY.

FUCK.

FUCK.

FUCK!

My insides were screaming.

I only gutted out, "What?"

A glimmer of a smile showed, but then it was erased. He stared back at me, hard. "I'm not the nice guy who will say it and not expect a response. I'm not that guy. I'm selfish with you. I want to know. Right here and now. Do you love me back?"

My throat stopped working, but I nodded. I was crying—when'd that happen?

"Ye-yes." I kept lifting my head up and down. "Yes. I love you."

"Yeah?"

The hardness dropped from his eyes, and I saw vulnerability there.

He hadn't been sure. His relief was so clear, and it humbled me. I thought I'd been the only one not sure.

I sat up on my knees, my oversized sweater fell to my legs. "I love you."

We moved at once.

I went to him, and he caught me, his hand cradling the back of my head like that was the only place it was supposed to be.

Our lips met, and he whispered, "I love you," before lifting me in the air and turning to sit on the bed. I was straddling him, my fingers in his hair, and I didn't want to move. Fuck my insecurities. This night would be on repeat in my mind forever.

I didn't think I'd doubt him again. Ever.

He showed me over and over again that night just how much he loved me.

# CHAPTER THIRTY-NINE

Shay dropped me off at the front door instead of the back. It was late, around three in the morning, but I didn't want to sleep at his place for the second night in a row after moving in with my new roommates. And since the last time I left from the back door and got creeped out, I thought maybe going the front way would be better.

I was wrong.

The lights were low when I walked through the front entrance. Only a single lamp was on at the front desk, and the girl there was sleeping, her head cradled by her arms over a textbook. Her snores were quiet as I went past and opened the door to our hall.

Like the last time I left, the hall was dark. There was minimal light from a few places down the hall illuminating the carpet.

I got ready for bed at Shay's, so I only had to go inside my dorm room and slip into bed.

I hadn't gone a few steps before I heard from the darkness, "He doesn't know about me, does he?"

My heart leapt into my chest, fear slamming my throat. I stopped, and then a shadow detached itself from the floor.

Phoebe stood from where she'd been sitting and took a few steps toward me. Her hand was on the wall as if she was a little unsteady. Her eyes were narrowed, and her head cocked to the side, making me think she was deep in thought. I didn't see any malice from her face, but a shiver raised the hairs on the back of my neck anyway.

I swallowed, taking an instinctive step backward before stopping myself.

"You don't have to be scared of me."

A grunt left me before I caught myself. "Not the best comment to lead with."

She stared at me, almost calm, but I couldn't shake the uneasiness growing in my gut. She laughed, half of her face lighting up in a smile. "That's true. I never thought about that." She itched at her ear. "I meant what I said, though. You don't have to be scared of me."

A slightly unhinged laugh slipped out. "A second comment you shouldn't have to say."

Her gaze grew clouded, her forehead wrinkling. "I haven't been able to shake this feeling."

The hairs on my neck were sticking straight up.

That feeling that I already knew her came back, and it was twisting inside me.

How did I know her?

"She still cares about him." She frowned. That dead look in her eyes found me again.

I couldn't stop myself. I took another step backward.

"Phoebe." My voice started to shake. I stopped myself, waiting until I knew my voice would be firm. "I'm not trying to be rude here, but you're starting to scare the shit out of me." Fake the fear. Shake her. Make her feel insecure. Instead of being on the defense, go on the offense. It might jar her, enough where I could get to my room.

"I get that."

Nope. Total failure.

She sounded completely normal, as if I wished her a casual goodnight.

Seriously, how did I know her? I know I did. I couldn't shake it.

I needed a plan B. My gut was telling me to be prepared. Unlike the last time when I didn't get warning, she was taking her sweet time. I had a whole bunch of warning here.

I reached inside my pocket where my phone was and felt over the keys until I hit 9-1-1.

If I hung up, I didn't know if they would come, but I wanted to call Shay. He'd been promoted to speed dial number two. I could do it.

I ended the call and felt around, hitting the right buttons until I felt my phone buzzing from the ringing.

I made a mental note, thanking myself that I silenced my phone before wanting to go into the room. I hadn't wanted to wake Kristina and Casey up.

"I heard about you last semester. All the girls were talking about you. Shay's like a celebrity here." She lifted a shoulder, holding it against her cheek a moment. "I never told anyone I knew him. I mean, I kind of do. I kind of don't. I didn't actually go to the school where Cameron and Shay did. My parents homeschooled me. Said I was different. Special. They found out about my weird habits, and I became something else. Scary. I overheard one of Cameron's girlfriends saying that about me. I don't know why she would care. I mean, it isn't like my brother cared about me or anything. Sabrina's the only one who does. She visits me sometimes."

I coughed. "She told me that."

She nodded, letting her shoulder drop again, and she raised her arms to hug herself tightly. Her eyes didn't track back to mine.

Maybe I didn't need to worry?

Maybe I had overreacted?

I started to wonder, and then Phoebe kept talking. "You see, I normally wouldn't care. I don't care about a lot of people, but I like Sabrina. She's the glue that makes Cameron still like me sometimes." Her head whipped back to mine.

I sucked in my breath, startled by how piercing her gaze was.

It was so clear, like she knew exactly what she was saying, what she was doing.

She asked, "Your brother loves you. I can tell from the things I've heard. That's nice. You've never had to feel like a burden to your family. I did. That's how Cameron looked at me. Me and Shay. Cameron used to be so jealous of Shay. He liked him, but he hated him, too." A soft laugh slipped from her.

It sent another wave of chills down my spine.

"I felt this camaraderie with Shay. He was all my brother thought about. He had to get the girls Shay got. He had to break the records Shay made. He had to get better grades than Shay. All these things." Her head hung low. She was still hugging herself tightly. "It made it all confusing in my head. Things go round and round. You stop noticing what's up or down, where the ground is. You just focus on what's ahead of you." She paused, lost in thought.

I edged backward, pressing against the closed door. I could run this way if I had to. Sprint for it.

"I came here because of Shay. I wanted to keep an eye on him for Cameron. If he did well, I wanted my brother to know. He could break Shay's record at his school. That was the plan. Shay doesn't know me, but I know him. I know him better than anybody."

Her eyes found me again.

I felt sick to my stomach.

"I do know you, don't I?"

She ignored my question. "I probably know him better than even you."

My mouth was parched. I tried to talk, but nothing came out. A whisper then, "You're a freshman?"

"Sophomore. I'm here because I couldn't get a single in a regular sophomore dorm. No one wanted to room with me. The girl they assigned to me refused, so they put me back here. The RA knows about me, about my special circumstances."

Her special circumstances?

That she was a psycho?

I tried again, my voice a little louder now, "What circumstances?"

"That I'm crazy."

She said it as if it made total sense and I was the idiot for not acknowledging it.

My eyes shot to hers. "What?"

She rolled hers. "I'm angry at him because he's only allowed my brother to be number two all his life. Cameron deserves to be number one. Then Sabrina entered the picture. Shay dated her, and I didn't care. She didn't know my brother. That changed one day." Her eyes narrowed. Her face tilted to the side again, still watching me with the unnerving resolve. "It was the end of classes, and I begged my parents to make Cameron pick me up. He did, and Sabrina was there. We lived on the same dorm floor last year. She was walking out as he was walking in, and he did a double take. I think he fell in love that day with her." Her gaze darkened, and her top lip curled up. "I knew it was my job to watch over them, and they were doing great . . . until she met you." Her head lowered, but she never looked away from me. "She wants another chance with Shay, and as long as you're here, as long as she keeps running into you, I know she can't help herself. You'll remind her what she didn't have with him, and she'll always yearn for a second shot."

She snarled.

It hit me then. The library.

My eyes bulged out. "You were there, at the library."

She pulled back, her eyes narrowing.

"Yes!" It came back then. "You were standing by the doors watching Shay. I saw you, and you saw me, and then you started reading like you hadn't been watching him."

I hadn't cared, or noticed. I was avoiding Shay then. It was so long ago, but Shay found me. He walked right past her like she hadn't been there at all and dragged me out to study for a quiz. I hadn't looked for her again.

No—there was more.

I started remembering—the football game. She was there, too.

"You were there. The Dick Crushing moment."

Missy's words came to me. *"Some girl stopped by the room and asked about you."*

"That was you. You went to my old dorm room, asking about me."

Phoebe paused, her head tilting. Her eyes were so flat.

A chill went down my spine.

"You might not understand it, but you being here is a problem. You'll bring him into her life again, and she'll end up leaving my brother.

Then my relationship with him will end, too. He'll stop coming to see me. I can't let that happen."

I saw the two shadows again.

They'd been behind me before. They were in front of me this time.

They were coming, coming, getting bigger and bigger.

I couldn't look away from her.

I barely glimpsed them before.

She became those two shadows.

And then hearing her last words, it was like seeing the bat appear for the first time again.

She said, "I've been racking my brain about how to handle you, and then I remembered that you were attacked."

She started forward.

She said, "I need to finish what they started. That's why you were brought here."

She started for me—

# CHAPTER FORTY

No.

I knew what she was going to do in the back of my mind, but time turned off for me. It slowed. She was starting for me.

It didn't matter.

An eerie calm came over me.

This was my make-up time. I was getting a second chance.

I wouldn't be a victim this time. She was giving me that opportunity. She didn't sneak up behind me. She was coming at me from the front.

I could fight back this time.

I *would* fight back. I felt the need to do this rising up in me.

"Hey!"

I stopped.

Time snapped back to reality.

That was Casey's voice.

Phoebe stopped also, turning around. Both of my roommates were running toward us. They were in their pajamas. Kristina had grabbed a robe, but it flopped open, flying behind her like a cape.

Casey had a perpetual scowl on her face. She pointed at us. "What's going on? That's my roommate."

Phoebe was a deer in headlights. She was right in front of me, a dumbstruck look on her face, and she gaped between us.

This whole thing was surreal.

Kristina was right next to Casey, our room phone in her hand. She was holding it up toward me. "Shay called. He said something was wrong."

Phoebe was trapped.

I was standing in the only opened door. The other one was locked in place, and my roommates boxed her in. Her only way out was through us, or if the dorm room opened behind her. I doubted she could crawl through the window, and for what?

I said, "Just give it up."

Beads of sweat formed on her forehead. She looked between my roommates and me.

Then, one by one, the doors all along the hallway started opening until the RA came out and the lights were switched on.

Our little triangle of four that had formed now doubled.

The resident advisor saw Phoebe, then me, and stopped in her tracks. She let out a sigh. "Oh, boy."

Casey reeled to her. "Oh, boy? What does that mean?"

She ignored Casey, looking at me. "What happened?"

"Call security. She threatened me. She's psycho because of Shay."

"Me?" I could hear from the phone in Kristina's hand.

She handed it over. "He's on the phone. He said your phone cut out, and when he couldn't get ahold of you, he called us. We called the cops."

"Yeah." Casey waved her cell around. "They're coming."

"No." Two uniformed police opened the door from behind me with a security guard beside them. "We're here," one of the cops spoke, raking over the group. His eyes fell to me and then Phoebe. "We received a 9-1-1 call that hung up. It was traced back here. Took a bit to coordinate with campus security what dorm until," he nodded at Casey, "your call. Thank you, ma'am."

"Ma'am." She fought against grinning. "He called me ma'am. I don't know if that's insulting or flattering."

"Kennedy!" Shay barked from the phone, and I took it, saying into it, "Cops are here."

"Good, but why?"

The first officer took out his notepad. "Someone needs to start talking."

The resident advisor ran a hand through her hair. “Uh . . .” Her eyes found mine again. “Go with Kennedy.”

Casey shot her hand up again, cell phone still in it. “We came out to the hallway, and swear to God, we saw this bitch”—she pointed at Phoebe—“starting to chase our roommate.”

“That true?”

The cop was waiting, and I nodded, hearing Shay’s voice from the phone. “Yeah. I don’t know what she was going to do, but she was going to do something.”

“That true?” The same question, directed at Phoebe.

She only swallowed, her mouth closed, and she raised her chin.

“You’re not talking?” The second cop moved forward, taking her by the arm. He asked the RA, “You know both of these girls?”

“I know Phoebe, but not Kennedy that well. She and her roommates just moved in this semester.”

“She’s Shay Coleman’s girlfriend.”

Both cops and the guard looked at one of the girls who spoke. She had on a robe like Kristina, but hers was tied at the waist. “And Phoebe’s obsessed with Shay Coleman.”

The resident advisor winced.

Kristina and Casey both gaped at Phoebe before turning their wide eyes to me. “Is that true?”

I nodded. “From what she was saying, yes.”

“I’m not obsessed with Shay.”

“No. She’s obsessed with her brother, who’s obsessed with Shay.”

“Who?”

My heart leapt at the same time I did. Shay appeared behind the cop, just on the other side of the opened door, his phone in hand and Linde following close behind.

Shay found me. “You okay?”

I started to nod but hurled myself into his arms instead.

As soon as I hit his strong chest and his arms folded around me, I could breathe easier. Phoebe might not have been the same as my first attack, but it didn’t matter. It’d been the second time something almost happened, with the first actually putting me in the hospital. I'd been more in shock until Shay was there. Standing in his shelter, the fear started coming down on me.

I was trembling soon, and he gathered me close, tucking his head down beside mine. He whispered so no one could hear, "You're okay."

He ran a hand down my hair and back.

"You're Shay Coleman? The football guy?" Both cops shared a look.

The security guard nodded, hitching up his pants. "Yep. That's Shay Coleman."

The cops turned to the guard, shared a brief look, and turned back to Shay.

"Yeah." Shay nodded.

They looked at Linde, asking, "And you are?"

"That's Raymond Linde. He's an offensive lineman for our team, too." The security guard's keys jingled as he gestured to Linde. He sounded all authoritative, clearing his throat. "We never usually have trouble with those two."

"Uh, yeah. He's a roommate of mine." Shay frowned at the guard before asking me, "What exactly happened?"

"We'll take both girls down to the station and ask 'em some questions, but it looks like nothing happened."

"This time."

Both stilled, looking at Shay.

He repeated, his jaw clenching as he raked over Phoebe, "My girlfriend was attacked before. She didn't walk from the scene the last time."

The first cop pointed to Phoebe. "By her?"

"No." I cleared my throat, tucking my shaking hands into my sweatshirt. "By two guys."

"They obsessed with your boyfriend, too?"

I shook my head. Both cops thought this was funny. I could hear the amusement in one and saw the glint of laughter in the other before he coughed, covering it up. But this wasn't funny. It was so far from funny.

I looked right at Phoebe. "I'm going to get a restraining order."

Her eyes narrowed, but she looked back down to the floor. The resident advisor was right next to her and said to the second cop, "I'll go with you guys. I can answer some of your questions about Phoebe."

The humor fled as both seemed to assess the RA for a second time, raking her up and down. It was as if they realized something more was going on. The first one clipped his head in a nod, reaching for his radio. "Sounds good." He pressed the button, speaking quickly into it. He looked at us. "You want a ride in the squad car or follow behind us?"

We moved as one.

I moved back into Shay at the same time he moved forward, folding me behind him. "We'll meet you there."

"I'm coming with you guys." Casey's shoulders were rolled back and set in a determined line. Kristina was next to her, and Casey clipped her head to the right. "Her, too. We're Kennedy's roommates."

"Sounds good to me." The first cop led the way. "See you all at the station."

The second cop trailed behind, holding on to Phoebe's arm with our resident advisor behind them.

"Are they arresting that girl?"

Casey snorted. "They should."

"Come on." Shay nodded to Linde, guiding me forward with his hand behind my back. "I'll drop you off—"

"He can ride with us."

Casey spoke again, and Linde stopped to appraise her. She looked at him. "If you want."

He narrowed his eyes and then nodded slowly. "Okay. I'll ride with them."

Kristina stepped forward, leaning close to me. "Are you okay?"

She genuinely wanted to know, and it was enough.

The tears burst free.

Shay pulled me back into his arms. "Come on. I have you."

# CHAPTER FORTY-ONE

*I have you.*

I clung to those words and Shay's hand through the rest of the morning.

After I recounted the entire story to the police officer, we were led into a room. A detective came for a few questions to wrap everything up. It was then that we learned they were aware of Phoebe.

Phoebe had stalked two girls and a guy in high school. All were connected to her brother so a protocol was put in place when she was accepted to Dulane University. She was supposed to have been checked in on twice a day, once by the RA and once by another staff member. If they noticed any changes in behavior, they were to notify her parents.

Phoebe had been fine, but they hadn't known about her connection to Shay Coleman.

The more I heard, the further my stomach dropped.

I could only shake my head at the end. "I don't get how she can go to school and live across the hall from me. I mean, it sounds like she's dangerous."

"She can be if she isn't on the right meds." The detective brought the advisor into our room, and she was answering our questions. She was choosing her words carefully. "She never hurt the other victims, and it'd been a few years since the last incident. I really and truly had no idea her connection to Shay." She looked at him. "I'm so sorry. If I'd known, I never would've let Kennedy move to our floor. You have to believe me. I feel awful that something could've happened."

He glanced to me, worry lines forming around his mouth and bags under his eyes. "Just move into the house. For now, anyway."

I shared a look with him, but that wasn't going to be a problem.

"I'm so sorry again, Kennedy." My RA extended a hand toward me, laying it on the desk.

I ignored it. "Is she going to stay there? Or is she going to get kicked out?"

"Uh . . ." She glanced to Shay before clearing her throat and pulling her hand back to her lap. "She will be removed from campus. Her parents are already on the way. She will be suspended for at least a semester."

"A semester?" I'd have to see her again?

"I can't speak for what the administration will do, but—"

Shay added, "Her parents are wealthy."

A flicker of anger surged in me. I schooled it down, locking away all of my emotions. "What do you mean?" I looked from her to the RA. "They'll fight it?"

She nodded, a flash of apology in her eyes. "My guess is that they will. They've gone to extraordinary lengths to have her attend college as a normal student. I doubt they'll stop, even with this incident."

"What if we can prove she came here under false pretenses?"

She and the detective both frowned at him. The detective leaned forward. "What are you talking about?"

He held up his cell. It wasn't the one he'd been holding in his hand before. "Kennedy did call me, and the call does go in and out, but I recorded it. I heard it. She admitted that she came to this college under the pretense of watching me."

"How'd you call the other phone?"

"My roommate's phone. I kept this one on." He looked to me. "There was no way I was leaving her alone, even on that line."

The detective took the phone. "That's helpful. We'll take this, then?"

He nodded.

She said further, "That recording, as long as it says what you say it says, will come in handy. We'll see how much weight we can put behind the university expelling her."

She stood, and it was an unspoken message to the rest of us. We followed behind her toward the front lobby.

Casey, Kristina, and Linde were all waiting.

They weren't alone.

Sabrina was also there, pale and haggard.

She stood and started to cross to me. "Oh, my gosh, Kennedy—"

I stepped back from her. "Get away."

Her hands had lifted for a hug, but she jerked to a stop. Her body swayed forward from the abrupt motion, and I watched, waiting. Guilt filled her eyes, darkening them before her hands crossed back in front of her.

"Kennedy." Her voice was so soft. "I didn't know."

"Bullshit." She had to have. "You should've warned me." I shook my head, feeling . . . I didn't even know anymore. I turned it all off, but it was still there. Still pressing into my chest, my stomach, flipping all around and reminding me too much of worse memories. "I thought you were so nice, Sabrina. I felt bad for you, and I thought—" I stopped, feeling the tears in my throat. I shoved them down. "I thought if Shay didn't love you, then what chance did I have with him?"

"Kennedy." It was just my name, but I still heard the plea from her.

I shook my head again, stepping farther away from her. "No matter what you say, you knew deep down. You might not have known the extent of her crazy, but you knew she was dangerous."

"I didn't—"

"You knew in your gut."

As I said those words, I saw the truth. She did, and she was admitting it to herself. I didn't care if it was the first time or the last time. She knew, and she stood by and let it happen. As far as I was concerned, that was worse in some ways.

"Maybe."

"You knew."

I let my disdain drip from those two words before I left. At this point, I didn't care who walked behind me.

I was fed up with being attacked. I was fed up with being scared. I was fed up with being a target.

Shay followed behind, calling my name.

I ignored him, walking to his Jeep in a fast clip. I waited, my hand on the handle, and he paused behind me. He stood there, watching me, but I kept staring forward. I saw his gaze in the window. After a second, he went to his side and unlocked the doors.

I opened mine, but looked back.

Kristina, Casey, and Linde were leaving the station, too.

"You okay?" Kristina asked.

I wasn't. "I'll be fine." I forced a smile.

Kristina narrowed her eyes. "You sure?"

Casey snorted. "Well, fuck that. I'm not okay. Can we all stay at the house?"

Linde grinned. "Hell yeah. We're not going to kick out two chicks, especially hot ones like you ladies."

Kristina smiled her thanks but edged closer to me.

Casey turned to give him crap, and the two were soon engaged in whatever they were doing. Flirting. Sparring. Tic-tac-toe. I didn't know, and I didn't care at that moment.

"You sure you're okay?"

Kristina wasn't one to be fooled easily, but I lied through my fucking teeth. "I'll be fine. I just need to get away for a bit. That's all."

"Okay." She looked past my shoulders to Shay. Her smile faded a bit before she stepped back.

Shay called out, "Linde, you're okay?"

"Yep!" His roommate looked over, saluting him. "See you guys in a few." His gaze fell to me, and the joking surface faded a bit. He sobered and nodded. I knew what he was saying. He had stayed in the background, but he cared. Same with Casey. She might've been flirting with Linde at the moment, but she came to protect me.

She'd been in my shoes.

"Ready?"

I got in, closed the door, and leaned back.

One giant breath of air left me, and along with it, my last semblance of control.

# CHAPTER FORTY-TWO

"Hey."

Shay's hand came down on my back. He meant it in a comforting manner, but I knocked it away. I flared up. "You didn't know? You had no idea?"

I couldn't believe that.

She was there for him.

She came for him.

She was watching him!

"How can you have a stalker and have no clue? She's been here a year and a half." Then again, a bitter laugh left me. There was so much about Shay I didn't know.

"I had no clue."

"Yeah," I bit out. "That's apparent. No clue. You have all these friends and had no idea. This"—I motioned between us—"has been going on for a full semester, and I still don't feel like I know you. You know me. You know I was attacked. You know my brothers. You know my mom is weird. You know my friends. You know almost everything there is to know about me, but I have no clue about you!"

"You know my friends," he started.

I shook my head. "I don't. I actually don't. I had no clue about Cameron. He scared me when I met him, and I met him on your back porch! Are you not getting how screwed up this all is? I don't know you. You said your mom is a lawyer. You live in a house with other football players. I know you're friends with Linde. You're sleeping with me. That's all I know! And surprise, you've had a stalker you had no clue about for a full fucking year and a half. I am still racking my brain. How is that possible?"

His mouth dropped. Pain flitted over his features. "I'm a guy. Girls like me. Guys want to be my friend. I . . . I don't know. I don't have any big skeletons in my closet, if that's what you're thinking."

"You never talk about yourself. Why is that?"

"I—" He was shaking his head, perplexed. "I just don't think about it. I'm focused on you when we're together. We have sex, a lot of it. That takes up my attention."

"No." I shook my head. "No." The second one was quieter. A pit was starting in my chest, and it was getting bigger and bigger. "That isn't fair. You can't say that. We have sex, but there are nights you just hold me. You know all about me."

"But do I?"

I sucked in a breath. "What do you mean?"

"I'm not asking that to be a dick, but do I really know you? We went backward with this whole thing. You didn't like me, then suddenly we're making out, and that went to sex real quick. We've never stopped to look back. You were living with me, even. I mean, we are not normal. The whole getting to know each other, we skipped over that part."

"You know about me. I told you about me." I was remembering seeing strangers at his house. Cameron. Finding out about Sabrina. The last piece—Phoebe. "I feel blindsided, and I'm playing catch-up. These hurdles are coming at me, and I can't see them until I'm already knocked out by them. That's what it's like dating you."

He drew in his own breath now. "That isn't fair. That was a low blow."

Was it? Yeah, maybe. "I'm sorry." I was hurting. I wanted to hurt him, too. "I can't date you and not know you."

His head whipped back to mine. "What are you saying?"

"I—" I had no clue, just that . . . "I have to know who you are."

"I'm Shay Coleman. I'm thinking about going to law school, but I'm into the second semester of my junior year, and I'm still not sure.

I'm taking all these different courses trying to figure out what I want to do."

"Okay." He was going this way. Fine. Forget the secret stalker. First date questions—I could do that. "What does your dad do?"

"A lawyer like my mom. They got divorced my freshman year of high school." He didn't let me ask another. He plowed through, "My mom has a new husband. I have two stepsisters, who are both in high school. They're total brats, but I love them anyway. I have a little brother who lives with my dad. I went with my mom. Nathan went with my dad, and he hates being called by any nicknames. You have to call him Nathan or he won't talk to you. He's in eighth grade. They live in New Orleans, so I don't get to see him or my dad that often. My dad is newly remarried. They got married last summer, and I've only met her that one time, but she seems like a nice lady. My stepfather is a partner where my mom works. I have no idea what my stepmom does, and I should, but I don't care. My little brother plays soccer. My two stepsisters are cheerleaders, and I'm pretty sure they're on a dance team. I don't go home that often because every weekend is a sparkle and glitter party. My stepsisters have their friends over, a lot." He stopped, still staring at me. A hard glint formed in his eyes. "Anything else?"

"Any past trials, tribulations, or trauma?"

His nostrils flared. "Is that a joke?"

No. Yes.

I hung my head. "I don't know." I shrugged. "Maybe?"

"I got my girlfriend pregnant when we were freshmen. It was during the time of my parents' divorce, and she got an abortion. She told me afterward."

I felt punched by that statement. I could only stare at him. "Shay—"

"I'm pretty sure one of my stepsisters has an eating disorder. I told my mom, but she doesn't want to deal with it, or has no clue how to, so she ignores it. I think my little brother is gay, and I worry about him. If he is, he hasn't told anyone and I want to support him and protect him when and *if* he comes out. Anything else?"

He would've had a kid . . .

He hadn't known . . .

I asked, feeling so small now, "You found out she was pregnant after the abortion?"

"Yeah," he clipped out. His jaw clenched. "I've never told anyone, so you're the first."

What had I done? He was hurting.

"I'm sorry," I said.

He looked away, straightening in his seat. A moment passed. A second one. Total silence. Then he hit the steering wheel. "Shit!" His head went down, and I looked over. His eyes were closed. Another moment later, his voice was so soft, "I've never talked about that." He looked up, his eyes in agony. "It wasn't meant to keep you out. I don't talk about that with anyone. My closest friend is Linde, or *was* Linde. It's you now. I'm not really close to people. It isn't that I purposely keep secrets. I, just, don't talk. To anyone."

He was loved by so many.

He was wanted by so many.

He confided in no one.

He was alone.

I reached over and took his hand. "I'm sorry."

He squeezed it. "You already said that."

"I mean it. I was being a bitch. I was hurting, and—"

He shook his head. "You're fine. I need to talk, and I don't. I never have. That girlfriend, when she told me about the abortion, she shattered me. Then my parents got divorced and started building their new families. I don't want to be all 'woe is me, feel sorry for me.' It was never like that. I've always had friends. I've dated, but no one got in." His gaze fell to my lips, then back to my eyes. "Until you. You got in. And I still don't quite know how it happened, but you're in, and I thought I was dying when I heard you were in trouble tonight. I couldn't drive here fast enough. I wanted to hurt whoever was hurting you, and then I saw it was Phoebe, and I still have no clue who she is."

"Cameron's sister."

He laughed. "I know." He began playing with my hand. "I heard that much, and to be honest, I wasn't even fully aware of Cameron. I knew he wasn't a good guy. I'd always been cautious around him, but I never really questioned it. I just had these instincts, and I followed them. Now, hearing about his sister, how they kept her away because of her problems makes me wonder how the hell I hadn't known. But there really was nothing." He shook his head again, sounding so dumbfounded. "Cameron never acted like he was jealous of me. I knew we competed for things, but I had no clue it bothered him. He never showed me. He never acted as if he didn't like me. He never acted jealous, or whatever. There was no indication. Though, now that I'm thinking about it, he did date a lot of my girlfriends."

I began to laugh.

"How could I have not paid attention?"

Because he didn't care.

Because he had enough going on at home.

Because his attention was directed elsewhere.

Because . . . he was just being himself.

"A lot of people love you." In not good ways, too. It must've been the same in high school. "I get it. Kind of."

He nodded, frowning. "Yeah. I'm just being myself, but I don't let any of the attention get to me. I can't. If I do that, I'll lose myself. Does that make sense?"

It made perfect sense. "You can let me in."

"You're in. You're so far in that I don't know what I'd do if I lost you."

"Then I'm in, and you're in, too."

The corner of his mouth started to lift, and I shook my head. "Don't make that dirty. We're having a serious moment here."

"Right." The corner flattened again, and his eyes grew somber. "I meant what I said last night." His eyes held mine captive. Everything about me was captive right now. "I love you, Kennedy."

All the pain was swept away.

"I love you, too, Shay."

# CHAPTER FORTY-THREE

Professional movers came the next week to move Phoebe's stuff out of her room.

Sarah came over, and she sat in the hallway with Casey. They decided to watch the movers taking everything out, and somehow it turned into a drinking game.

The RA told Kristina that Phoebe never came back to her room. She was whisked away to a hotel with her parents, so the movers had to literally pack everything. It took four hours, but half that time was spent lingering in the hallway and flirting with Sarah. Casey was a little more reserved, but I didn't know what was going on with her and Linde.

I knew things had fizzled out between her and Gage. He was off being a manwhore again. I asked him once what happened and he said he hadn't been ready for a serious relationship. Casey deserved a guy who was head over heels for her, and he couldn't give her that.

I was rooting for her and Linde.

I'd been trying to study, but hearing another shout of laughter, I decided to admit defeat.

My new sociology class was not going to be understood that day.

I closed my book, and glanced over my shoulder. Kristina's desk was behind me, facing the wall. "I'm giving up."

It was already close to eight at night.

She sighed, pushing back from her computer. "Me, too."

"Oh!" Casey shouted from the hallway. "Another box. Drink."

Kristina gestured toward the opened door. "They're already drunk out there."

It was obvious. Sarah had been slurring her words for the last hour.

"I'm surprised the RA hasn't said anything."

Kristina rolled her eyes. "She won't. She feels so bad about Phoebe and not telling you, that I think one of us could have an orgy in the hallway and she'd look the other way."

"True." I winced as I remembered the times she tried to apologize in the bathroom, when I left the bathroom, anytime I walked past her room to the bathroom. I started going up the stairs and using the second floor's bathroom.

I hadn't paid attention to her name when we moved in, and I refused to learn it now. It was out of spite. She would only be the RA to me. Kristina knew, but Kristina was the only one of us who let her talk whenever she approached us. I always walked away, but Casey went on the attack. The RA didn't realize who was in the stall next to her one day and asked for some toilet paper. She got it, but not after Casey launched into a lecture about sisterhood and moral ethics, and how she sucked at them. I heard one of the girls taped it, and Casey had made the RA stay there for thirty minutes before she finally got toilet paper from someone else who took pity on her.

I walked into the bathroom at one point, heard Casey, and walked out.

The whole thing was raw with me still.

The plan had been to stay with Shay for the rest of the semester, but when I heard Phoebe was for sure gone, I wanted to try to resume regular dorm living. If I spent too much time with him, I thought I would miss out on some of those normal college living memories. Plus, Kristina and Casey moved an entire dorm for me. They left their other two friends. I felt like I owed them.

Suddenly, a bunch of whistles and cheers sounded.

Casey yelled, "Everyone clear a path. The football gods have descended upon us!"

"Yeah!" Sarah burped. "En the werr hodt do!"

"And they're hot, too?" Casey translated. "Girl, you've had enough."

"NOoo."

Kristina and I looked at the doorway.

Sarah fell over, her head and shoulders showing. She raised her arm slightly over her head, holding her drink away from someone.

"Come on." Casey groaned, and she appeared, too. She stood, bending to grab Sarah's water bottle. "You're cut off, or someone will tattle to the dorm advisor. We'll for sure get written up. Amy will have to do something, then."

Amy.

That was the RA's name.

I made a face, grimacing.

Casey noticed my look, cocked her head to the side. Then she got it. "Oh. Sorry."

"Traitor." But I didn't mean it. I flashed her a small grin to make sure. "I'm still only calling her RA in my head."

I gestured to the hallway. "Who's out there?"

"Not for you, Princess. It's the two guys who are dating the twins at the end."

Another cringe.

Shay called me that one night at his house in front of others. He hadn't realized it until everyone started hooting and hollering, which sounded a lot like the commotion in our dorm right now.

Casey added, "The movers are leaving. They got everything, but if they didn't, we're hoping to scope it out before the RA has to lock it up." Casey wiggled her eyebrows. "If we can get an extra key, that means an extra room for us. Studying, or," she dropped her tone, "other stuff, if you know what I mean."

I didn't want to know what she meant.

Kristina must've thought the same because she asked, "Anyone hungry? We didn't get dinner before."

Casey held up her water bottle that was not filled with water. "Yeah. We went straight to booze."

Sarah was struggling to her feet. She tried to stand up, but toppled back to the floor so she crawled into the room. Scurrying right past us, her eyes were glazed, and I didn't think she remembered we were even there. She went right to the couch, pulled herself up, and hugged one of the pillows to her chest.

She was snoring in two seconds.

Casey belched, slapping her chest. "Sorry. That was disgusting." She wavered in the doorway, looking back out. We could hear voices still out there, guys and girls, but I didn't want to look myself.

Kristina asked me, "Have you talked to Shay today?"

I shook my head. I slept here the night before and then had classes all day. I knew he did, too, but I was expecting a phone call or a surprise visit any minute.

Casey looked back in. "Let's go there. The guys are always up for grilling."

Kristina added, "And drinking."

The two shared a grin because it was true. Since they were no longer playing or training, the house had become a booze fest. It was more common to walk through the place and see the guys drinking than to find them not. That didn't mean they got drunk. They built up a tolerance, but I know at least a few would get a good buzz by the end of the night. Since the Phoebe fiasco, which was last weekend, I'd only been at Shay's place and heard someone intoxicated twice. Okay, so maybe it was more.

I still wasn't that nervous. They were decent guys. They might've been rougher around the edges if Shay and Linde weren't there, but I didn't think anything would happen to me or my friends.

"Call 'em up, Kenz." Casey nodded at me. "I'd rather spend the evening with the guys than here with some girls."

And as if on cue, two of our neighbors appeared in the doorway.

Casey was still standing there so they couldn't knock on the door, but they were laughing. Their red cheeks told me they'd participated in the drinking game. They both had coffee mugs in hand.

"What are you guys doing tonight?" one asked. I thought her name was Melissa. Again, Kristina would know.

Her friend tucked some of her hair behind her ears. "We were thinking of ordering a pizza, maybe watch some of *The Last Kingdom*. Uhtred is fucking hot."

Casey's eyes got big.

She'd been turned on to the Netflix series, and had been raving about the Dane for the last three days.

"Oh, my gosh!" Her eyes suddenly got smaller, and her shoulders slumped a bit. "We can't. We're going to the Football House tonight."

"Well." Kristina held her hand out. "No. We don't know. We haven't called yet."

All four of them looked at me.

I reached for my phone. "And that's my hint."

I sent a text to Shay, and when he didn't respond right away, I texted Linde, too.

Linde: **Guys are always up for grilling and drinking. Need a ride over?**

Me: **Can you drive?**

Linde: **I can right now. Might not be able to in an hour. I don't have classes in the morning.**

I still hadn't gotten a reply from Shay so I typed out another text.

Me: **Is Shay there? You know where he is?**

Linde: **I thought the library?**

I frowned.

Me: **The library?**

Linde: **He said he was going there, then to your place. I figured you guys had plans.**

Not that I knew, but only sent back:

Me: **We can drive over. We'll take Casey's car. If she sleeps there, she'll want to drive it back in the morning.**

Linde: **Will do. I'll let the guys know. We'll have the grill going when you get here.**

Instead of sending another text to Shay, I called him, but his voicemail came on right away. There was no ring.

"What's the plan, Stan?" Casey was leaning against the doorway, keeping herself upright.

On second thought, I asked Kristina, "I told Linde you would drive over in Casey's car. Should I text him back to come and get you guys?"

Kristina's forehead wrinkled as her eyebrows pinched together. "You're not going?"

"You think you can drive?" I skipped over the question.

She chewed on her lip. I was asking if she wanted to drink when she was there. I knew Casey always wanted her car available, but sometimes it was a hassle if they drank there and still wanted to sleep in their own beds. If they couldn't find someone sober to drive them, they would take an Uber, and Casey would have to get another ride back to pick up her car. It was all in Kristina's hands, because Casey might've been sounding normal, but she wasn't. She had a better tolerance level than Sarah, but she was still buzzed where rational thinking wasn't a given.

Kristina sighed. "Between all of us, and you, we can always get her car back in the morning if we leave it there."

Which meant Kristina didn't want to sleep there. Casey never cared. She'd been curling up in Linde's bed the last week.

I nodded. "That's the plan, then."

"You're not coming with us?"

I shook my head. "Linde said Shay was at the library, so I'm going to go and scope it out. See if he's there."

"You want us to go with you? We can just swing by the library. If he isn't there, come with us to the house."

Casey was nodding. She kept going, not stopping.

"If you don't stop, you're going to get sick."

She stopped, laughing. "I feel a little dizzy. You're right."

I asked Kristina, "Can you handle her?"

She stared at Casey a moment before turning to Sarah, who was still snoring. She looked at the other two girls next. "What are you two going to do?"

Their eyes got big and Melissa cleared her throat. "Um. I mean . . . can we come with or . . ." Her eyes jetted to me, and her cheeks pinked a little more. I got it. I did. The Football House was infamous not only for who lived there but also for their parties.

I shrugged. "I doubt they would care."

Both girls were my neighbors. It wasn't a bad idea to get to know them, which was something I had to keep reminding myself.

Kristina's hand came over my arm, as if she understood my hesitancy. She patted me in comfort and said to the girls, "If you're ready to go like that, let's leave in ten minutes."

The girls took off. They didn't need to be told twice.

"Ten minutes?" Casey lifted some of her hair so she could inspect it. "I need more than ten minutes to get myself together."

"You now have nine minutes."

"Shit." Casey sped out of the room, grabbing her makeup container and shower caddy to the bathroom.

"You sure you're okay?"

It had been almost a full week since Phoebe tried to attack me. Almost a week where I had to force myself to stay in my own dorm room because I didn't want another person to take that away from me.

I dipped my head in a firm nod. "I'm good."

"I'm here if you need to talk. You know that, right?"

My smile was genuine. "I do. Thank you."

Kristina and Casey had become two of my best friends here. I never would've imagined it from the first day of college. I was thankful.

Casey returned a few minutes later out of breath and in a rush. She was flying around the room getting ready, and it was fifteen minutes later when the other two girls came back.

"Okay." Casey appeared from the bedroom, her chest heaving. She spread her arms out and did a circle. "How do I look?"

Skin-tight jeans, a low-cut tank top, and a small, sequined purse hung from her arm. Her hair looked flawless, but this was typical Casey.

Kristina and I shared a look.

"Man." I shook my head. "Are you sure you want to leave like that? I mean, does Linde like messy hair in the back?"

"What?" Her eyes got wide, and her hand clamped on to the back of her hair. "No, no, no . . ." Her eyes narrowed at me, then at Kristina who was trying not to laugh, and she dropped her hand. "You fuckers! You can't mess with me like that."

She surged to me and hit my arm.

I backed away, laughing. "You make it so easy. You always look amazing."

One of the other girls nodded. "You could wear a Santa Claus suit and make it look sexy."

"See." I jerked a thumb toward the girl. "You have nothing to worry about, and if you're dressing up for Linde, he doesn't care about that stuff."

"I know." She dipped her head down, adjusting her purse. "This year's been hard. You know. Your brother rejected me, and Linde seems nice, but you never know."

I frowned. "My brother's a shithead."

Sarah's snores rose to a new volume.

Kristina said to me, "Should we leave her?"

"Nope. Hold on."

Casey went into motion. She grabbed towels, putting one under Sarah's head, then another that hung down from the couch to the floor. She positioned Sarah so she was on her side, her mouth hanging open and pulled to the edge. A garbage bin was placed underneath her with a fresh new bag inside. A glass of water was placed a few inches away from the bin. Two painkillers were next to that.

A note was left under Sarah's phone, telling her where we were and a list of numbers to call if she needed something.

I thought we were ready to go, but Casey held up one finger. "One more minute."

She zipped out to the hallway and was back in a few minutes. "Okay." She grabbed her keys and phone. Her purse was still hanging from her shoulder. "I'm ready to go."

"You sure?" Kristina asked, but the other two girls were already in the hallway.

I grabbed my backpack, and a hair tie to pull my hair up.

"Yep." Casey backed up, saying, "The RA will check on Sarah. She knows she's in there. Sarah's sick." Casey winked at us.

Kristina locked the door and then looked at me. "You sure you don't want a ride to the library?"

I had been considering it. "Nah. It isn't far. Plus, if Shay is walking here, I'll intercept him then."

“Okay. Call if you need anything.” Kristina waved, so did Casey. The other two did as well, but they had an extra bounce to their step. I knew they were more excited to hang out at the Football House.

They left through the back door, and I headed in the opposite direction.

# CHAPTER FORTY-FOUR

There was something about walking alone at night.

The campus dorms were lit up, and there were people hanging out in the entryways. As I left my dorm and passed a few others on the way toward the library, I heard their laughter, their conversation, and I felt how peaceful they seemed.

It plays a trick on the mind sometimes.

When you thought you were safe, when you thought you could walk among buildings at night, and you thought you're alone. There was a beauty around you when a person did that, but it could be shattered at any moment. The bubble I used to have where I thought I was safe, where I never even considered that I could be attacked—that was gone.

I knew there was bad in people.

I came to college assuming the worst. I wanted a few loyal friends. That'd been the rule and my goal. The other rule had been no drama. The third was a new me. I'd been so bound and determined to fulfill all of those.

This year destroyed every single rule.

Shay broke them, and just thinking of him brought a wistful smile to my lips. Anyone who was watching me probably thought I was high, but it wasn't that.

All the shit that happened to me, I came out stronger.

I thought I'd been strong in the beginning, but I wasn't. It was nothing compared to how I felt now.

I was almost attacked a second time, and in a place that was considered close to my home. My dorm was supposed to be home. It happened in the hallway just outside of it, but I had been safe. Phoebe hadn't been like the first time where they gave me no warning. Two guys and they had to strike from the back. She came at me from the front. She gave me warning. She told me why she was going to hurt me.

I shivered, wondering what her ultimate goal had been.

But it didn't matter, because it hadn't happened.

She was away.

I would do everything possible to keep her away, too.

But I wasn't going to let her take away my joy of being a college student.

I would live in my dorm. I would sleep in my bed. I would be with my boyfriend, and not constantly look over my shoulder. I would walk on this damn campus and my fear would not rule me. It would not dictate what I wanted to do, and if I goddamn wanted to walk to the library at eight-thirty at night, I goddamn would.

I cut through the food court building and where the post office boxes were. I was just leaving that, with the library being the next building, when I heard the two beeps signifying someone was just locking their car.

There was a parking lot tucked in the corner between the two buildings. It was there for workers, and some students got special permits to park there, too. Mainly off-campus students who wanted the closest parking lot to the library. I knew Shay had a permit there, and I was already turning my head to see if his Jeep was there.

That was when I saw him, and a bolt of panic jolted me.

I stopped in my tracks, my little pep talk and the short-term benefits I'd felt shriveled up. They fell at my feet. I could almost imagine them there, and I could kick them away because that's how I felt.

My knees locked.

It was Cameron.

He was walking toward me, his head down. His broad shoulders were slouched down, but they were tense. He had on a button-down shirt, the ends pulled out from his khaki pants. His hair was mussed, as if he'd come from a long day at the office or an event.

I couldn't move.

Someone was screaming at me to move in the back of my mind, but she wasn't loud enough for my body to take action.

The fear was back. It was pooling in the bottom of my gut.

I was an unwilling participant to watching this train wreck happen. I was even watching myself, and in slow motion, his head came up. There were bags under his eyes. He held keys in his hands, and he threw them up, his hand absent-mindedly snatching out of the air before tossing them again.

His eyes were straight ahead. They weren't focused on anyone or anything, but then he caught me in the corner of his eye.

He paused, slowing down, and his head turned.

His eyes locked on mine, and I saw his emotions play out as if they were on screen.

Surprise.

Confusion.

Then anger.

The last one burned bright in his gaze, and he faltered to a stop.

We were seven feet apart. If I had hidden in the doorway, he would've gone straight past me. This confrontation could've been avoided, but I still couldn't do a thing. I tried to get myself to talk.

My throat wasn't working.

He stared at me, his jaw clenching. His eyes narrowed. I watched as his shoulders straightened and then rolled back. He looked ready to fight me.

But he still didn't talk for a second.

I had just walked past three buildings that had people in front of them, hanging out for the evening, but I was in the heart of the campus, and there was no one.

I half-expected a tumbleweed to roll between us.

"Seriously?" He grunted, stuffing his hands in his khaki pockets. His shoulders lowered a fraction. "You're just going to stand there like a deaf mute?"

I flushed.

For whatever reason, that worked.

I could suddenly talk again.

"You don't have to insult the deaf mute."

He snorted. More of the fight left him, but the anger was still there. I felt it under the surface, simmering. My insides were still in knots, waiting for it to be unleashed.

"I don't know what that means." His eyes flicked to the side before jerking back. "What's your problem?" He looked at me closer, trailing down then back up. "What? Are you scared of me?"

*Okay, Kennedy.*

I started to give myself another pep talk. This one was going to be for the win. I needed it.

*He isn't going to strike you down. He isn't his sister. He isn't Carruthers or his dickless friend. He isn't the assholes who chased after you, or jeered you in the classroom. He isn't here to scare you, to harm you, to break you.*

*Because. You. Won't. Let. Him.*

*You got that, Kennedy?*

*You got that?*

I was shaking my hands in triumph. I was cheering myself on. I was making all sorts of rallying cries inside my own head.

Because the truth was that I was too damned scared to say anything more.

He cocked his head to the side. "What's wrong with you? You had more fight the last I saw you."

A gargled laugh ripped from me.

"Really?" I laughed again. "I had more fight the last time you saw me?"

He didn't respond, and his shoulders slumped another inch down.

I took a step toward him. It felt like I was walking through wet cement, but I moved it ahead. "You want to know what happened to me? You motherfucker."

One corner of his mouth turned down. "You don't have to insult me."

"You called me a deaf mute."

"That isn't an insult if it's true."

Fuck's sake. He was an asshole. My nostrils flared. "You didn't throw it at me like a term of endearment. You shouldn't even think that phrase. It shouldn't be a part of your vocabulary, because the truth is that you have no idea what it would be like to be someone who can't hear, who can't talk, who can't walk, who can't do the simplest things that you take for granted."

I breathed in relief.

I could talk again.

That fight he wanted, it was coming. I felt it sparking, fueling me.

I raised my head higher. "You're so pissed off. I can see it, and you want to know what happened to me? Your sister happened. Assholes like Carruthers happened to me. Assholes like his friends who thought they could bag on me, push me down because I dared to stand up against one of their own. Girls like my roommate who thought she was better than me, because she felt strong with her posse and thought she could tear me down because I was a loner. You're the last person I'm seeing right now, and you're the last one I'm going to let hurt me."

Right.

I pumped up my fist—and it almost hit me.

I moved it over an inch, and raised it higher. I puffed up my chest.

I sneered at him. How was that, dickbag? Huh?

He only raised an eyebrow. "You drunk right now?"

He was unmoved, and I felt a needle taken to my pep talk balloon. My chest sank back in so it was normal.

I rolled my eyes. "What are you doing here? This isn't your campus."

He pulled out the keys and dangled them in the air. "My sister's things were moved out today. I had to drop her keys off. We're heading out of town tomorrow."

Oh.

I felt like an ass. "I thought you were here to hurt me."

His eyebrows lifted again. I saw the surprise there. "No way. I don't want anything to do with you or Shay again. I'm done with everyone at Dulane."

"What do you mean? What about Sabrina?"

He glanced down for a moment. "She broke up with me. Apparently, she was with me for the wrong reasons." He rolled his eyes again and hissed out, "She's still in love with Coleman, so head's up, Clarke. She might be after your man."

That rolled off my back. It didn't even make a dent, and I threw back, "Sure she doesn't want to be associated with your stalking-obsessed sister?"

His eyes formed to slits. He grew unnaturally still. "Watch it, Clarke. That's my blood you're talking about."

"Who is obsessed with you. Who is obsessed with my boyfriend. Who was starting to become obsessed with me. Your blood is messed up."

"Yeah, well." The hand with the keys went back in his khaki pocket and his other rubbed the back of his neck. "Every family is fucked in some way. We got ours, and despite what you think, Phoebe's just sick. That's all. She isn't the bad guy here."

"Really?" My tone was dry. "So, who is?"

"No one. There are no bad guys. Everyone's bad. Everyone's good. Everyone changes and the whole situation can be flipped tomorrow. Sabrina dumped me because you laid into her. I could be pissed at you and blame you, but I don't."

Another, "Really?"

"Yeah." For the first time, pain flashed in his eyes. "I mean, the dipshit in me wants to and maybe a part of me does, but I shouldn't. You didn't make Sabrina dump me. She did that on her own. She did that because she didn't want to be a part of the whole thing with my sis and me. And for the record, I don't hate your boyfriend."

"What is it, then?"

Neither of us noticed, but Shay was there. He'd been coming from the library and had stopped at the end of the sidewalk where it would've merged with the one Cameron was standing on. All three of us on different sections of pavement, but all merged at one point. All three of us remained in our end, forming a triangle.

"Oh." Cameron visibly seemed shaken. He stepped back, his shoulders falling as he raked both his hands through his hair. "Coleman. I didn't see you there."

Shay was cold. His face was impassive, but his eyes flicked to mine briefly. He was furious. I saw it there, far more controlled and pushed down than the anger Cameron let simmer to his surface.

I felt a ripple of violence in the air, like any moment Shay was ready to go.

I felt those knots start to tighten again, but it wasn't fear for me this time.

If Shay was going to do anything, so would I. I wouldn't let him get hurt, either.

Shay jerked forward a step, his head rising in challenge. "What is the fucking deal, then, Cameron? I'd really like to know, because your whole sister thing came out of left field. I didn't even know I should be watching for a stalker, much less worrying she'd try to beat the shit out of my girlfriend."

There was the quarterback who led his team on the field, the reason he was the 'big guy' on campus. Shay stood alone, but if his entire team were behind him, they would've been at the ready to do what he commanded.

He didn't need them, though.

He looked ready to tear into Cameron by himself and that he would thrive on it.

This was the Shay who beat the shit out of Carruthers and his friend and then attacked them a second time in full view of a police officer.

Cameron seemed to sense it, too, and he held up his hands. "I'm not here to do any harm. I'm supposed to drop off my sister's keys and then go home. I don't have any plans to come back here. Trust me." He paused a second before turning to me. "Look. I get that my sister wanted to hurt you. I do. Honestly. And a part of me hates that. I don't like knowing that she was going psycho, but you gotta understand—there are no bad guys here. My sister is sick, and my parents are the bad guys in her situation. They're not getting her the help she needs. They just want to push her off and keep going on all their stupid trips.

"And I'm the bad guy, too, because if they're not going to deal with her, then I should. And I didn't. Because I'm selfish, and I'm an asshole, and yeah, a part of me just wanted to be a normal guy partying in college and having a good time before I grow up. So, I'm the bad guy in her situation. She's the bad guy in your situation, and you never know." He gestured to me. "You might be the bad guy in someone else's situation, and you might not even know it. Like I said before, we're all bad, and we're all good, and we're all human, but if you're standing there thinking that I'm going to be the villain, and I'm going to attack you or something—it ain't going to happen. Right now, I'm hurting because the girl I hoped to be my wife one day dumped me. And I'm ashamed because I have to drop off keys for my sister, and I don't even know where her dorm is. I've never been to her room. In a year and a half, I didn't have the time. I came here a lot. One of my best friends lives with Shay. My girlfriend visited my sister, but I can't even remember the last time I really visited with Phoebe. Maybe she met me at a fast food joint for breakfast before I left to go back to my college."

He sucked in a breath, letting it out.

His head hung low. "I saw you just now, and I was so pissed at you because I *wanted* to blame this all on you. And then I saw how scared you were, and you have no idea the shame and anger that ripped me inside because I know that I made my sister feel the same level of fear you just did. But it wasn't fear, it was hurt. I hurt her, and just my presence hurt you now." He stopped, his throat moving up and down rapidly.

His chest rose, then paused, and settled down again.

"And I guess I'm sorry for that." He looked at Shay. "And I'm sorry for being jealous of you in high school. You were the golden boy and you didn't seem to care. It all happened so naturally for you. I hated you at times. I wanted to be your best friend at times. And I respected you at times. And now I'm just embarrassed to be around you because of my fuck-ups."

Shay glanced to me.

I knew what happened to him in high school. The golden boy image wasn't one he donned on purpose. He just didn't let people know the other side of him.

He coughed. The threat of violence was no longer in the air.

"Look."

Cameron didn't seem capable of looking him in the eye, so Shay turned to me. He spoke to Cameron, though, "I'm sorry to hear about Sabrina."

Cameron lifted his head at that.

Shay looked at him. "I do know how much you loved her. I can only imagine the pain I'd feel if I lost Kennedy."

I felt a flutter in my chest.

Shay cleared his throat again. "And I hope your sister gets the help she needs."

Cameron looked away, and his eyes closed tight. He held still a moment before wiping a hand over his face and coughing a few times. "Yeah, man." He blinked a few times and held his hand out. Shay shook it, and Cameron nodded. "That means a lot." He stepped back, glancing to me. "I really am sorry for what my sister did."

I felt his apology and nodded, my chest feeling a little lighter.

I held out my hand. "I can take the keys for you. I'll give them to Amy."

Shay's lip tweaked at her name, and I rolled my eyes. If Cameron got a pass, I could start using the RA's actual name. Little steps, right?

Cameron ducked his head one last time and held his hand up in a wave.

After he was gone, I could only look at Shay.

"Why do I feel suddenly exhausted and like I shed thirty pounds at the same time?"

His eyes softened as he came toward me. He held his arms open, and I moved into them, my head going to his chest. He cupped the back of it, and cradled me, murmuring by my ear, "Because life can be fucking exhausting, and I think we're going to be fine now."

I wound my arms around him, and held him back.

I hoped so.

We ended up going to his place, and after we hung out with our friends, and then went to his bedroom, I started to feel the same thing.

I burrowed into his arms and closed my eyes as his hand smoothed down my back. He murmured, "What happened to you sleeping at your dorm every night this week?"

I laughed, lifting my head. "Maybe Sunday through Thursday nights?"

"It is Thursday for another hour."

"Maybe I'll start that on Sunday." I rose, finding his lips with mine. "Thank you."

He drew back, frowning slightly. His hand skimmed down my arm. "For what?"

For loving me.

I didn't say that. Instead, "For being the guy I needed to fall in love with." We'd been through hell already, and no matter what else was going to come at us, we could handle anything.

Raw emotion moved in his eyes, and he was letting me see inside.

I loved him even more for it.

I kissed him again, and like he said, I knew everything was going to be okay.

And it was.

THE END

For more stories, go to:
www.tijansbooks.com

CPSIA information can be obtained
at www.ICGtesting.com
Printed in the USA
LVHW051200010321
680178LV00005B/47